Gregg
P9-DCJ-240

Dear Readers,

Charles Dickens once said, "Make them laugh, make them cry, and make them *wait.*" For a romance writer, this means that if you're doing a series, save the most irresistible hero for last! I've loved writing about all of my Fallen Angels, and here, finally, is the passionate, adventurous story of Michael, the darkest and most dangerous of them all.

Lord Michael Kenyon is full of contradictions: a warrior who values peace, a man of honor who cannot forgive himself for a horrendous breach of his own code, someone with a great capacity for love who has loved unwisely in the past.

In Catherine Melbourne, he finds the warmth and compassion he has always craved. But when they first meet, the time is not right for loving. And when they meet again, Catherine's secrets stand between them. Only after the fiercest tests of love and loyalty and courage will the two of them find the happiness they so richly deserve.

So is this the end of the Fallen Angels series? Well, yes and no. Michael is the last of the four friends who are the official Fallen Angels, but as I suspected, he has a friend whom you will meet in *Shattered Rainbows.* Expect that story in late summer of 1996. And there may be one more book beyond that.

After all, good men are hard to find—it wouldn't do to waste one!

Happy reading,
Mary Jo Putney

PRAISE FOR MARY JO PUTNEY,
HAILED BY *ROMANTIC TIMES*
AS "A DREAMSPINNER
OF THE HIGHEST ORDER."

The Fallen Angels series:

"A quintessential teller of tales, in *Angel Rogue* the superlative Mary Jo Putney pens a love story of superior merit, blending exquisite perception and elegant sensitivity. A sumptuous reading experience."

—*Romantic Times*

"I loved *Angel Rogue*. It was a great story—the perfect 'rainy afternoon' book."

—A. M., California

"Wonderfully readable, subtle and intriguing, exciting and humorous—a Mary Jo Putney novel is not to be missed."

—Jo Beverley, author of *Dangerous Joy*

"I loved *Dancing on the Wind.* You had me completely hooked. There was a marvelous balance of light and dark. I had a wonderful time with this story—so much to think about, so many different elements holding me fascinated, and so beautifully constructed."

—Loretta Chase, author of *Lord of Scoundrels*

"If you read but one book this year, I would recommend [*Dancing on the Wind*]—I loved every page of it."

—*Rendezvous*

"I truly loved *Petals in the Storm.* Rafe was HOT! All of your books are real "keepers," fun each time I read them."

—T. G., Texas

"*Petals in the Storm* is a stunning tour-de-force; a moving testament to the resiliency of the human spirit and its ability to emerge from the fires of hell stronger and wiser than before. The protagonists are riveting characters with a tempestuous relationship played out against a mesmerizing backdrop of intrigue. Congratulations to Mary Jo Putney for another winner." —*Affaire de Coeur*

"Once in a great while comes a love story so special that it literally leaps off the bookshelf and into your heart. Both sublimely romantic and scorchingly sensual, *Thunder and Roses* is an extraordinary romance from an extraordinary author."

—*Romantic Times*

Other titles:

"I have just read *Silk and Shadows*. 'Read' is perhaps the wrong word—'devoured' might be better. What a fabulous, fabulous book. Bravo!"

—Mary Balogh, author of *Longing*

"*Veil of Silk* is terrific. Haunting! Wonderful characterization and a true sense that something is really at stake. First-rate work!"

—Susan Elizabeth Phillips, author of *Kiss an Angel*

"*Silk and Secrets* was wonderful and a welcome change; romance is glutted with brooding males in need of distemper shots, so a gentleman like Ross is certainly a delight. Your attention to the hero's feelings as well as the heroine's has always made your books special."

—S. O., Bookseller, Hawaii

"I just finished reading *Uncommon Vows* and wanted to let you know how much I enjoyed it. What a bold, brave story you have written! Your characterization was outstanding. Congratulations on a superb book."

—Susan Wiggs, author of *Vows Made in Wine*

"In *Dearly Beloved,* Ms. Putney raises historical romance to new standards of excellence with her articulate and perceptive characterizations. . . . One of the best books of this or any other year." —*Romantic Times*

DAZZLING ROMANCES BY MARY JO PUTNEY

☐ **ANGEL ROGUE** A master spy, Lord Robert Andreville, returns to his home after a dozen harrowing years spying against Napoleon. Half-Mohawk and all-American, Maxima Collins is a wary stranger in a strange land, but she will let nothing halt her journey to London to learn the truth about her father's death. Together they travel across England, evading pursuers and circling each other in a dance of desire. (405986—$5.99)

☐ **PETALS IN THE STORM** Highborn, and wild, Rafe Whitbourne, Duke of Candover, earned his reputation as a rake in the silken boudoirs of England's aristocracy, never giving away his heart—or his secrets. Until the sensual "Countess Magda Janos" lifts her gaze to meet his grey eyes as cold as the devil's himself. Despite her skill at deception, she cannot hide her real identity from Rafe. (404459—$4.99)

☐ **THUNDER AND ROSES** Paying a price for his aid, Clare Morgan agrees to live with the Demon Earl for three months, letting the world think the worst. As allies, they fight to save her community. As adversaries, they explore the terrains of power and sensuality. And as lovers, they surrender to a passion that threatens the very foundation of their lives. (403673—$4.99)

☐ **DANCING ON THE WIND** Lord Strathmore is known for his unearthly good looks and diabolical cleverness. A tragic past has driven him to use his formidable talents to protect his country from secret enemies, and it is a job he does superlatively well—until he meets a mysterious woman whose skill at deception is the equal of his own. (404866—$4.99)

*Prices slightly higher in Canada

Shattered Rainbows

by

Mary Jo Putney

A TOPAZ BOOK

TOPAZ
Published by the Penguin Group
Penguin Books USA Inc., 375 Hudson Street,
New York, New York 10014, U.S.A.
Penguin Books Ltd, 27 Wrights Lane,
London W8 5TZ, England
Penguin Books Australia Ltd, Ringwood,
Victoria, Australia
Penguin Books Canada Ltd, 10 Alcorn Avenue,
Toronto, Ontario, Canada M4V 3B2
Penguin Books (N.Z.) Ltd, 182–190 Wairau Road,
Auckland 10, New Zealand

Penguin Books Ltd, Registered Offices:
Harmondsworth, Middlesex, England

First published by Topaz, an imprint of Dutton Signet,
a division of Penguin Books USA Inc.

First Printing, February, 1996
10 9 8 7 6 5 4 3 2 1

Cover art by Gregg Gulbronson

Printed in the United States of America

In honor of the healing power of friendship—
and therefore to
Alice, Suzl, Merril, and Bobby

Prologue

London
June 1816

She needed a husband, and she needed one fast.

Choking back a hysterical laugh, Catherine Melbourne glanced over her shoulder at the building she had just left. The sight of the solicitor's office instantly sobered her.

This was not a dream. In the last half hour, she had acquired a grandfather she'd never heard of, and the chance for a legacy that would make all the difference in the world. Instead of having to seek employment that would barely support her and Amy, there would be enough money to live in comfort. There was also an ancient home, an island, a heritage. Her daughter would have the future she deserved. There would be responsibilities as well, but that was all right. Catherine had been bearing heavy responsibilities all her life.

There was only one problem. She must convince her newfound grandfather that she and her husband were worthy of being the next Lord and Lady of Skoal. She felt hysteria rising again, this time without laughter. *What could she do?*

Her mouth tightened. It was perfectly obvious that she was going to lie. The time to admit that Colin had recently died had been in Mr. Harwell's office. But the solicitor had said bluntly that her grandfather would not consider Catherine as his sole heir. Torquil Penrose, the twenty-seventh Laird of Skoal, did not believe a woman worthy of ruling his island. She would have to find a man to play the role of her husband, and do the job well enough to persuade her dying grandfather to designate her as his heir. But who could she ask?

The answer came immediately: Lord Michael Kenyon.

He had been a good friend, with the vital qualification that he had never fancied himself in love with her. At their last meeting, he had also given her carte blanche to call on him if she ever needed help.

She knew exactly where to find him. As the son of a duke and a war hero, he was mentioned regularly in the society news. *Lord M— K— is in town for the Season as a guest of the Earl and Countess of S—. Lord M— K— was seen riding in the park with Miss F—. Lord M— K— escorted the lovely Lady A— to the opera.* Catherine had read the notices compulsively.

If Michael was willing to help, she would have to spend considerable time with him, which meant rigidly controlling her feelings. But she had managed that the previous spring in Brussels. She could do it again.

Far worse was the fact that she would have to lie to him. Michael felt that he owed her a great debt. If he learned that she was a widow in dire financial straits, it was possible, even probable, that he would think the best assistance he could offer was marriage. The thought gave her a peculiar fluttering sensation somewhere under her ribs.

But Michael would never accept the kind of marriage she had had with Colin. No normal man would. Nor could she reveal her horrible failing; the mere thought made her stomach knot. It would be simplest, and safest, to let him think Colin was still alive.

It was a long walk to Mayfair. By the time she got there, she would have her lies ready.

After a day full of wretched shocks, Michael Kenyon walked into Strathmore House and was given a card by the butler. "There is a lady waiting to see you, my lord."

Michael's immediate reaction was unprintable. Then he glanced at the card. Mrs. Colin Melbourne.

Good God, Catherine. It only needed that. Yet the thought that she was here, under this roof, made him so impatient that he barely took time to ask where she was waiting. As soon as the butler replied, Michael strode to the small salon and swung the door open. "Catherine?"

She was gazing out the window, but she turned as he entered. The simple style of her dark hair and her modest gray gown only emphasized her beauty.

When they had parted, he had uttered a silent prayer that they would never meet again. He had spent considerable time and energy in the last year trying to forget her. Yet now that she was here, he didn't give a damn how much it would cost him later; seeing her was like a breath of fresh air in a coal mine.

She said uncertainly, "I'm sorry to bother you, Lord Michael."

He spent a moment mastering himself, then crossed the room. "Are we on such formal terms, Catherine?" he said easily. "It's good to see you. You're as lovely as ever."

He caught her hands, and for a precarious instant he feared he would do something unforgivable. The moment passed and he gave her a light kiss on the cheek. The kiss of a friend.

Releasing her hands, he withdrew to a safe distance. "How is Amy?" Deliberately he forced himself to add, "And Colin?"

Catherine smiled. "Amy is wonderful. You'd scarcely know her. I swear she's grown three inches since last spring. Colin—" she hesitated briefly, "is still in France."

Her tone was neutral, as it always was when she referred to her husband. Michael admired her quiet dignity. "I'm forgetting my manners," he said. "Please, sit down. I'll ring for tea."

She looked down at her clasped hands. Her profile had the sweet clarity of a Renaissance saint. "I'd better state my piece first. I need some rather unusual aid. You—you may want to throw me out when you hear what it is."

"Never," he said quietly. "I owe you my life, Catherine. You can ask anything of me."

"You give me more credit than I deserve." She looked up, her amazing aqua eyes piercing in their frame of dark lashes. "I'm afraid that . . . that I need a husband. A temporary husband."

BOOK I

The Road to Hell

Chapter 1

Salamanca, Spain
June 1812

The white-haired surgeon wiped his forehead wearily, leaving a smear of blood, as he studied the man on the crude operating table. "You certainly made a mess of yourself, Captain," the surgeon said with a distinct Scottish burr. "Didn't anyone ever tell you not to block a charge of grapeshot with your chest?"

" 'Fraid not," Lord Michael Kenyon said in a strained whisper. "At Oxford, they teach the classics rather than practical matters. Maybe I should have gone to the new military college."

"It will be a real challenge to see if I can pick all the bits out," the surgeon said with macabre cheer. "Have some brandy. Then I'll get to work."

An orderly held a bottle to Michael's lips. He forced himself to consume as much of the fiery liquid as possible. A pity there wasn't time or brandy enough to get seriously drunk.

When Michael finished drinking, the surgeon slashed away the remnants of his patient's jacket and shirt. "You were amazingly lucky, Captain. If the French gunners had loaded the powder right, there wouldn't be enough pieces of you left to identify."

There was an ugly sound of metal scraping on metal. Then the surgeon wrenched a ball from Michael's shoulder. The resultant blaze of agony made the whole world darken. Michael bit his lip until it bled. Before the surgeon could strike again, he asked haltingly, "The battle—is it won?"

"I believe so. They say the French are haring away at full speed. Your lads have done it again." The surgeon began digging at the next buried fragment.

It was a relief to surrender to the blackness.

Michael returned to awareness imperfectly, floating in a sea of agony that numbed his senses and hazed his vision. Every breath sent stiletto-sharp pains stabbing through his chest and lungs. He was lying on a straw pallet in the corner of a barn that had been commandeered for a field hospital. It was dark, and fretful pigeons cooed from the rafters, complaining about the invasion of their home.

Judging by the mingled groans and labored breathing, the earthen floor must be covered almost elbow to elbow with wounded men. The scorching Spanish noonday heat had been replaced by the bitter cold of night. There was a scratchy blanket over his bandaged torso, but he didn't need it, for he was burning with the fever of infection, and a thirst worse than the pain.

He thought of his home in Wales, and wondered if he would ever see the lush green hills again. Probably not; a surgeon had once told him only one man in three survived a serious wound.

There was a certain peace in the prospect of dying. Not only would it bring surcease from pain, but he had, after all, come to Spain with the bitter knowledge that death would free him from an impossible dilemma. He had wanted to forget both Caroline, the woman he had loved more than honor, and the terrible promise he had made, never thinking he might be called upon to fulfill it.

With vague curiosity, he wondered who would miss him. His army friends, of course, but they were used to such losses. Within a day, he would have become "poor old Kenyon," simply one more of the fallen. No one in his family would be sorry, unless from irritation at having to put aside their finery to wear mourning black. His father, the Duke of Ashburton, would utter a few pious platitudes about God's will, but he would be secretly pleased to be free of his despised younger son.

If anyone would feel real grief at his passing, it would be his oldest friends, Lucien and Rafe. And there was Nicholas, of course, but he could not bear to think of Nicholas.

His bleak thoughts were interrupted by a woman's voice, as cool and clear as a Welsh mountain spring. Strange to hear an English lady in such a place. She must be one of the intrepid officers' wives who chose to "follow the drum," accompanying their men through all the hardships and danger of campaign life.

Softly she asked him, "Would you like water?"

Unable to speak, he nodded assent. A firm arm raised his head so he could drink. She had the fresh thyme and lavender scent of the Spanish hills, discernible even through the stench of injury and death. The light was too dim to see her face, but his head was resting against a warm curve. If he could move, he would bury his face against her blessedly soft female body. Then he would be able to die in peace.

His throat was too dry to swallow, and water spilled from his mouth and ran down his chin. She said matter-of-factly, "Sorry, I shouldn't have given you so much. Let's try again."

She tilted her vessel so that only a few drops trickled between his cracked lips. He managed to swallow enough to ease the burning in his throat. Patiently she gave him more, a little at a time, until the excruciating thirst was gone.

Able to speak again, he whispered, "Thank you, madame. I'm . . . most grateful."

"You're very welcome." She lowered him to the straw, then rose and went to the neighboring pallet. After a moment, she said sorrowfully, *"Vaya con Dios."* Go with God. It was a Spanish farewell, even more appropriate for the dead than the living.

After she moved away, Michael dozed again. He was vaguely aware when orderlies came and removed the body on the next pallet. Soon after, another casualty was laid in the space.

The new arrival was delirious, mumbling over and over, "Mam, Mam, where are you?" His voice revealed that he was very young and terribly afraid.

Michael tried to block out the wrenching pleas. He was unsuccessful, but the steadily weakening words showed that the boy was unlikely to last much longer. Poor devil.

Another voice sounded from the foot of Michael's pallet. It was the Scottish surgeon saying, "Bring Mrs. Melbourne."

"You sent her home yourself, Dr. Kinlock," an orderly said doubtfully. "She was fair done up."

"She'll not forgive us if she learns that boy died like this. Go get her."

An indefinable time later, Michael heard the soft, distinctively feminine rustle of petticoats. He opened his eyes to see the silhouette of a woman picking her way through the barn. Beside her was the doctor, carrying a lantern.

"His name is Jem," the surgeon said in a low voice. "He's from somewhere in East Anglia. Suffolk, I think. The poor lad is gutshot and won't last much longer."

The woman nodded. Though Michael's vision was still blurred, he thought she had the dark hair and oval face of a Spaniard. Yet her voice was that of the lady who had brought water. "Jem, lad, is that you?"

The boy's monotonous calling for his mother stopped. With a quaver of desperate relief, he said, "Oh, Mam, Mam, I'm so glad you're here."

"I'm sorry it took so long, Jemmie." She knelt beside the boy's pallet, then bent and kissed his cheek.

"I knew you'd come." Jem reached clumsily for her hand. "I'm not afraid now that you're here. Please . . . stay with me."

She took his hand in hers. "Don't worry, lad. I won't leave you alone."

The surgeon hung the lantern from a nail above the boy's pallet, then withrew. The woman—Mrs. Melbourne—sat in the straw against the wall and drew Jem's head onto her lap. He gave a deep sigh of contentment when she stroked his hair. She began to sing a gentle lullaby. Her voice never faltered, though tears glinted on her cheeks as Jem's life slowly ebbed away.

Michael closed his eyes, feeling better than before. Mrs. Melbourne's warmth and generous spirit were a reminder of all that was good and true. As long as earthly angels like her existed, life might be worth living.

He drifted into sleep, her soft voice warming him like a candle defying the darkness.

The sun was inching above the horizon when Jem drew his last, labored breath, then became still. Catherine laid him back in the straw with a grief beyond tears. He was so young.

Her cramped legs almost failed when she got to her feet. As she leaned against the rough stone wall and waited for her muscles to recover, she glanced at the man on her left. His blanket had slipped, exposing the stained bandages swathing his broad chest.

The air was still chilly, so she leaned down and drew the blanket up to his shoulders again. Then she laid her hand on his forehead. To her surprise, the fever had broken. When she had given him water, she would not have given a ha'penny for his chances. But he was a tall, powerful-looking fellow; perhaps he had the strength to survive his wounds. She hoped so.

Wearily she made her way toward the door. During her years following the drum, she had learned a great deal about nursing and more than a little surgery, but she had never become inured to the sight of suffering.

The austere landscape was peaceful after the deafening clamor of the day before. By the time she reached her tent, much of her tension was gone. Her husband, Colin, had not yet returned from duty, but her groom, Bates, was sleeping outside, guarding the captain's womenfolk.

Tired to the bone, she ducked inside the tent. Amy's dark head popped up from her blankets. With the nonchalance of an old campaigner, she asked, "Is it time to march, Mama?"

"No, poppet." Catherine kissed her daughter's forehead. After the horrors of the field hospital, it was heaven to hug the child's healthy young body. "I expect we'll stay here today. There's always much to be done after a battle."

Amy regarded her sternly. "You need to sleep. Turn around so I can untie your gown."

Catherine smiled as she obeyed. Her qualms about taking her daughter on campaign were countered by the knowledge that the life had produced this miracle of a child: resilient, wise, and capable far beyond her years.

Before Amy could undo the stained gown, hoofbeats sounded outside, followed by the jingle of harness and the staccato sound of her husband's voice. A moment later, Colin barreled into the tent. He had a cavalry officer's energetic personality, and one was always aware when he was in the vicinity.

" 'Morning, ladies." He ruffled Amy's hair carelessly. "Did you hear about the cavalry charge yesterday, Catherine?"

Not waiting for an answer, he dug the roast leg of a

skinny chicken from the hamper and took a bite. "It was the prettiest maneuver I've ever been in. We went roaring at the French like thunder and swept them from the field. Not only did we take thousands of prisoners and dozens of guns, but two eagles were captured! There was never anything like it."

The gilded French regimental standards called eagles were patterned after those of imperial Rome, and capturing two was a stunning feat. "I heard," Catherine replied. "Our men were magnificent." And she had spent the night tending the price of victory.

Having stripped the meat from the drumstick, Colin tossed the bone out the tent flap. "We went after the Frenchies, but no luck. One of those damned Spanish generals disobeyed Old Hookey's order to set a garrison at the river, then didn't have the courage to admit his error."

Catherine ignored the profanity; it was impossible to shield a child who lived in the midst of an army from strong language. "One can see the general's point. I shouldn't like to confess a mistake like that to Lord Wellington."

"Very true." Colin peeled off his dusty jacket. "What else is there to eat? I could down one of the dead French horses if it were roasted properly."

Amy gave him a reproachful look. "Mama needs to rest. She was at the hospital almost all night."

"And your father fought a battle yesterday," Catherine said mildly. "I'll go make breakfast."

She moved past her husband to go outside. Under the odors of horse and mud was the musky scent of perfume. After the pursuit of the French was called off, Colin must have visited his current lady friend, a lusty widow in Salamanca.

Her maid-of-all-work was the wife of a sergeant in Colin's company and would not arrive for at least an hour, so Catherine knelt by the fire herself. She laid twigs on the embers, wearily thinking how her life had turned out so differently from her dreams. When she'd married Colin at the age of sixteen, she'd believed in romantic love and high adventure. Instead she had found loneliness and dying boys like Jem.

Impatiently she got to her feet and hung the kettle over the fire. There was no place in her life for self-pity. If there was sorrow in her nursing work, there was also the satisfaction of knowing she was doing something that truly mattered. Though she didn't have the marriage she had hoped for, she and Colin had learned to rub along tolerably well. As for love—well, she had Amy. A pity she would never have any other children.

Mouth tight, she told herself what a lucky woman she was.

Chapter 2

Penreith, Wales
March 1815

Michael Kenyon neatly ticked off the last item on his list. The new mining machinery was working well, his recently hired estate manager was doing an excellent job, and his other businesses were running smoothly.

Since he had accomplished his other goals, it was time to look for a wife.

He rose from his desk and went to gaze at the mist-shrouded landscape. He had loved this dramatically beautiful valley and weathered stone manor from the moment he had seen them. Still, there was no denying that Wales in winter could be a lonely place, even for a man who was finally at peace with himself.

It had been more than five years since he had been involved with a woman. Five long, difficult years since the sick obsession that had destroyed every claim he had to honor and dignity. The madness had been useful during his warrior years, but it had warped his soul. Sanity had returned only after he had come perilously close to committing a deed that would have been truly unforgivable.

His mind sheered away, for it was painful to remember how he had betrayed his deepest beliefs. But the people he had wronged had forgiven him freely. It was time to stop flagellating himself and look to the future.

Which brought him back to the subject of a wife. His expectations were not unrealistic. While he was no paragon, he was presentable, well-born, and had a more than adequate fortune. He also had enough shortcomings that any self-respecting female would itch to improve him.

He wasn't looking for a grand passion. Christ, that was

the *last* thing he wanted. He was incapable of that kind of love; what he had thought was a grand passion had been a warped, pathetic obsession. Instead of seeking romance, he would look for a woman of warmth and intelligence who would be a good companion. Someone with experience of life. Though she must be attractive enough to be beddable, great beauty was not necessary. In fact, based on his experience, stunning looks were a liability. Thank God he was past first youth and the idiotic susceptibility that went with it.

Personality and appearance were easy to assess. More difficult, but more vital, she must be honest and unflinchingly loyal. He had learned the hard way that without honesty, there was nothing.

Since this corner of Wales had few eligible females, he must go to London for the Season. It would be pleasant to spend a few months with no goal but pleasure. With luck, he would find a comfortable woman to share his life. If not, there would be other Seasons.

His reverie was interrupted by a knock. When he called permission to enter, his butler entered with a travel-stained pouch. "A message has arrived for you from London, my lord."

Michael opened the pouch to find a letter sealed with the signet of the Earl of Strathmore. He broke the wax with anticipation. The last time Lucien had sent such an urgent message, it had been a summons to join an intriguing rescue mission. Perhaps Luce had come up with something equally amusing to liven the late winter months.

Levity vanished when he scanned the terse lines of the message. He read it twice, then got to his feet. "Make sure Strathmore's messenger is properly taken care of, and tell the cook I might not be back for dinner. I'm going to Aberdare."

"Yes, my lord." Unable to restrain his curiosity, the butler asked, "Is there bad news?"

Michael smiled without humor. "Europe's worst nightmare has just come true."

His mind was so full of the news that Michael scarcely noticed the chilly mist as he rode across the valley to the grand mansion that housed the Earls of Aberdare. When he reached his destination, he dismounted and tossed his reins to a groom, then entered the house two steps at a time. As always when he visited Aberdare, he felt a sense of wonder that once again he could breeze into Nicholas's home as casually as when they had been schoolboys at Eton. Three or four years earlier, such ease had been as unthinkable as the sun rising in the west.

Since Michael was virtually a member of the family, the butler sent him directly to the morning room. He entered to find Lady Aberdare sitting beside a magnificently carved crib that held her infant son, Kenrick.

Michael smiled at the countess. "Good day, Clare. I gather that you can't bear to let Viscount Tregar out of your sight."

"Hello, Michael." Her eyes twinkled as she extended her hand. "It's very lowering—I feel exactly like a mother cat standing guard over her kittens. My friend Marged assures me that in another month or two, I shall become more sensible."

"You're always sensible." He kissed her cheek with deep affection. By her mere existence, Clare was an example of all that was good and true about womankind. Releasing her hand, he glanced into the crib. "Incredible how tiny fingers can be."

"Yet he has an amazing grip," she said proudly. "Give him a chance to demonstrate it."

Michael leaned over the crib and gingerly touched the baby's hand. Kenrick gurgled and locked his miniature fist forcefully around Michael's fingertip. Michael found himself unexpectedly moved. This minute scrap of humanity was living proof of Clare and Nicholas's love, with his father's wickedly charming smile and his mother's vivid blue eyes. Named for his paternal grandfather, Kenrick was a bridge from past to future.

There might have been a child of Michael's, who would have been almost five now. . . .

Unable to bear the thought, he gently disengaged his finger and straightened. "Is Nicholas home?"

"No, but he should be back anytime now." Clare's brows drew together. "Has something happened?"

"Napoleon has escaped from Elba and landed in France," Michael said flatly.

Clare's hand went to the crib in an instinctive gesture of protection. From the doorway, there came the sound of a sudden intake of breath. Michael turned to see the Earl of Aberdare, his dark hair beaded with moisture from riding in the mist.

His mobile features uncharacteristically still, Nicholas said, "Any word on how the French people are receiving him?"

"Apparently they are welcoming him back with wild acclaim. There's an excellent chance that within the next fortnight, King Louis will run for his life and Bonaparte will be sitting in Paris and calling himself emperor again. It isn't as if Louis has endeared himself to his subjects." Michael pulled the letter from his pocket. "Lucien sent this."

Nicholas read the letter with a frown. "In a way, it's a surprise. In another way, it seems utterly inevitable."

"That was exactly how I felt," Michael said slowly. "As if I'd been waiting to hear this news, but hadn't known it."

"I don't suppose the allied powers will accept this as a fait accompli and let Napoleon keep the throne."

"I doubt it. The battle must be fought once more." Michael thought of the long years of war that had already passed. "When Boney is defeated this time, I hope to God they have the sense to execute him, or at least exile him a good long way from Europe."

Clare looked up from the letter, her gaze level. "You're going to go back to the army, aren't you?"

Trust Clare to guess a thought that had scarcely formed in Michael's mind. "Probably. I imagine that Wellington will be recalled from the Congress of Vienna and put in charge of the allied forces that will be raised to oppose Napoleon. With so many of his crack Peninsular troops still in America, he's going to need experienced officers."

Clare sighed. "A good thing Kenrick will be christened in two days. It would be a pity to do it without his godfather. You'll be here that long, won't you?"

"I wouldn't miss the christening for anything." Michael smiled teasingly, wanting to remove the concern from her eyes. "I only hope that lightning doesn't strike me dead when I promise to renounce the devil and all his works so I can guide Kenrick's spiritual development."

Nicholas chuckled. "If God was a stickler about such things, every baptismal font in Christendom would be surrounded by charred spots."

Refusing to be distracted, Clare said in a tone that was

almost angry, "You're glad to be going to war again, aren't you?"

Michael thought about the tangle of emotions he had felt on reading Lucien's letter. Shock and anger at the French were prominent, but there were also deeper, harder-to-define feelings. The desire to atone for his sins; the intense aliveness experienced when death was imminent; dark excitement at the thought of practicing again the lethal skills at which he excelled. They were not feelings he wanted to discuss, even with Clare and Nicholas. "I've always regretted that I was invalided home and missed the last push from the Peninsula into France. It would give a sense of completion to go against the French one last time."

"That's all very well," Nicholas said dryly. "But do try not to get yourself killed."

"The French didn't manage it before, so I don't suppose they will this time." Michael hesitated, then added, "If anything does happen to me, the lease of the mine will revert to you. I wouldn't want it to fall into the hands of outsiders."

Clare's face tightened at his matter-of-fact reference to possible death. "You needn't worry," he said reassuringly. "The only time I was seriously wounded was when I wasn't carrying my good-luck piece. Believe me, I won't make that mistake again."

Intrigued, she said, "What kind of lucky piece?"

"It's something Lucien designed and built at Oxford. I admired it greatly, so he gave it to me. In fact, I have it here." Michael pulled a silver tube from inside his coat and gave it to Clare. "Lucien coined the word 'kaleidoscope,' using the Greek words for 'beautiful form.' Look in that end and point it toward the light."

She did as he instructed, then gasped. "Good heavens. It's like a brilliantly colored star."

"Turn the tube slowly. The patterns will change."

There was a faint rattle as she obeyed. She sighed with pleasure. "Lovely. How does it work?"

"I believe it's only bits of colored glass and some reflectors. Still, the effect is magical." He smiled as he remembered his sense of wonder the first time he had looked inside. "I've always fancied that the kaleidoscope contains shattered rainbows—if you look at the broken pieces the right way, eventually you'll find a pattern."

She said softly, "So it became a symbol of hope for you."

"I suppose it did." She was right; in the days when his life had seemed to be shattered beyond repair, he had found comfort in studying the exquisite, ever-changing patterns. Out of chaos, order. Out of anguish, hope.

Nicholas took the tube from Clare and gazed inside. "Mmm, wonderful. I'd forgotten this. If Lucien hadn't had the misfortune to be born an earl, he'd have made a first-class engineer."

They all laughed. With laughter, it was easy to ignore what the future might bring.

Chapter 3

Brussels, Belgium
April 1815

The aide-de-camp gestured for Michael to enter the office. Inside he found the Duke of Wellington frowning at a sheaf of papers. The duke glanced up and his expression lightened. "Major Kenyon—glad to see you. It's about time those fools in Horse Guards sent me someone competent instead of boys with nothing but family influence to commend them."

"It was a bit of a struggle, sir," Michael replied, "but eventually I convinced them I might be of use."

"Later I'll want you with a regiment, but for the time being, I'm going to keep you for staff work. Matters are in a rare shambles." The duke rose and went to the window so he could scowl at a troop of Dutch-Belgian soldiers marching by. "If I had my Peninsular army here, this would be easy. Instead, too many of the British troops are untested, and the only Dutch-Belgians with experience are those who served under Napoleon's eagles and aren't sure which side they want to win. They'll probably bolt at the first sign of action." He gave a bark of laughter. "I don't know if this army will frighten Bonaparte, but by God, it frightens me."

Michael suppressed a smile. The dry humor proved the duke was unfazed by a situation that would dismay a lesser man.

They talked a few minutes longer about what duties Wellington had in mind. Then he escorted Michael out to the large anteroom. Several aides had been working there, but now they were gathered in a knot at the far end of the room.

The duke asked, "Have you found a billet, Kenyon?"

"No, sir. I came straight here."

"Between the military and the fashionable fribbles, Brussels is bulging at the seams." The duke glanced down the room. When a flash of white muslin showed between the officers, he said, "Here's a possibility. Is that Mrs. Melbourne distracting my aides from their work?"

The group dissolved, and a laughing woman emerged from the center. Michael looked at her, and went rigid from head to foot. The woman was beautiful—heart-stoppingly, mind-druggingly beautiful. As stunning as his mistress, Caroline, had been, and seeing her affected him the same way. He felt like a fish who had just swallowed a lethal hook.

As the lady approached and gave the duke her hand, Michael reminded himself that he was thirty-three years old, well past the age of instant infatuation with a pretty face. Yet the woman was lovely enough to cause a riot in a monastery. Her sleek dark hair was pulled back with a simplicity that emphasized the classic perfection of her features, and her graceful figure had a sensual lushness that would haunt any man's dreams.

To Wellington, she said drolly, "I'm sorry to have disturbed your officers. I merely stopped by to deliver a message to Colonel Gordon. But I shall leave directly, before you have me imprisoned for aiding and abetting the enemy!"

"Never that," Wellington said gallantly. "Kenyon, did you ever meet Mrs. Melbourne on the Peninsula? Her husband is a captain in the 3rd Dragoons."

Amazed at how calm his voice was, Michael replied, "I'm afraid I've never had the pleasure. The cavalry and the infantry don't always have much to say to one another."

The duke chuckled. "True, but Mrs. Melbourne was also known as Saint Catherine for her work nursing the wounded. Mrs. Melbourne, Major Lord Michael Kenyon."

She turned to Michael. Something flickered in her eyes, then vanished as she gave him her hand and a friendly smile. Her eyes were as striking as the rest of her, a shade of light, clear aqua unlike any he had ever seen.

"Mrs. Melbourne." As he bowed over her hand, the duke's words snapped a fragment of memory into place. Good God, could this elegant, frivolous female be the woman he had seen in the hospital after Salamanca? It was hard to believe.

As he straightened, the duke said, "Major Kenyon has just arrived in Brussels and is in need of a billet. Do you and Mrs. Mowbry have room in your ménage for another officer?"

"Yes, we have space." She made a comically rueful face. "That is, if you can bear living in close quarters with three children and a variable number of pets. Besides my husband and Captain Mowbry, we have another bachelor, Captain Wilding."

This time he recognized the low, soothing voice that had crooned a dying boy to his final rest. This sleek creature really was the lady of Salamanca. Remarkable.

The duke remarked, "Wilding is a friend of yours, isn't he?"

A warning sounded in Michael's head, saying he would be a damned fool to stay under the same roof with a woman who affected him like this one did. Yet he found himself saying, "Yes, and I rather like pets and children as well."

"Then you're welcome to join us," she said warmly. "The way the city is filling up, we'll have to take in someone else sooner or later, so it might as well be now."

Before Michael had a chance for second thoughts or polite refusal, Wellington said, "It's settled, then. I'll expect you here in the morning, Kenyon. Mrs. Melbourne, I hope to see you next week at a small entertainment I shall be holding."

She smiled. "It will be my pleasure."

As the duke returned to his office, Mrs. Melbourne said, "I'm on my way home now, Major. Shall I take you to the house? It's on the Rue de la Reine, not far from the Namur Gate."

They came out the front of the building. Neither carriage nor maid waited for her. He said, "Surely you're not walking alone?"

"Of course I am," she said mildly. "I enjoy walking."

He supposed that to a woman who had followed the drum, Brussels seemed very tame, but no woman so lovely should walk alone in a town full of soldiers. "Then let me escort you."

His groom and orderly were waiting nearby on horseback

with his baggage, so he stopped to instruct them to follow. As he and Mrs. Melbourne set off along the Rue Royale, she tucked her hand in his arm. There was nothing flirtatious in the gesture. Rather, she had the easy manner of a comfortably married woman who was accustomed to being surrounded by men.

Deciding it was time to stop acting like a stunned ox, he remarked, "It's very good of you to let me share your billet. I suspect that good quarters are hard to find."

"Kenneth Wilding will be glad to have another infantryman under the same roof."

He grinned. "Surely you know that one infantryman is easily a match for two cavalry officers, Mrs. Melbourne."

"Just because the British cavalry is famous for chasing the enemy as wildly as they run after foxes, there's no reason to be caustic," she said with a laugh. "And please, call me Catherine. After all, we shall be living together like brother and sister for the indefinite future."

Brother and sister. She was so unaware of the paralyzing impact she had made on him that he began to relax. He had shared billets with married couples before, and he could do so now. "Then you must call me Michael. Have you been in Brussels long?"

"Only a fortnight or so. However, Anne Mowbry and I have shared quarters before, and we have the housekeeping down to a science." She gave him a humorous glance. "We run a very good boardinghouse, if I do say so. There's always food available for a man who has worked odd hours. Dinner is served for anyone who is home, and there's usually enough for an unexpected guest or two. In return, Anne and I request that any drunken revels be held elsewhere. The children need their sleep."

"Yes, ma'am. Are there any other house rules I should know?"

She hesitated, then said uncomfortably, "It will be appreciated if you pay your share of the expenses promptly."

In other words, money was sometimes tight. "Done. Let me know how much and when."

She nodded, then glanced at his green Rifleman's uniform. "Are you just back from North America?"

"No, I sold out last year after Napoleon abdicated and have been living a quiet civilian life. However, when I heard that the emperor had bolted again . . ." He shrugged.

"A civilian life," she said wistfully. "I wonder what it would be like to know one could stay in one house forever."

"You've never had that?"

She shook her head "My father was in the army, so it's the only life I've ever known."

No wonder she had learned to create comfort wherever she went. Her husband was a lucky man.

They fell into an easy conversation, for the Peninsular years had given them experiences in common. It was all quite casual—except for the fact that he was acutely conscious of the light pressure of her gloved fingers on his arm.

Deciding that he should mention their first encounter, he said, "We did meet three years ago after a fashion, Catherine."

She frowned, an enchanting furrow appearing between her brows. "I'm sorry, I'm afraid I don't remember."

"I was wounded at Salamanca. At the field hospital, you gave me water when I was desperately thirsty. I've never been so grateful for anything in my life."

She turned and studied his face, as if trying to recall.

"There was no reason for you to remember me among so many. But you might recollect the boy on the pallet next to me. He was calling for his mother, and thought you were she. You stayed with him until he died."

"Ahh . . ." She exhaled, her lighthearted charm dropping away to reveal the tenderness of the woman who had comforted Jem. "Poor boy. There was so little I could do. So *damnably* little." She turned her face away. "I suppose I should have become accustomed to such scenes, but I never did."

Her beauty had struck him like a blow to the heart. Her compassion struck a second, harder blow, for years of war had made him treasure gentleness. He took a deep, slow breath before replying. "Callousness is easier. Yet even though it hurts more, there is much to be said for remembering the uniqueness and worth of each person whose life touches ours."

She gave him a measured glance. "You understand, don't you? Most soldiers find it better not to." More briskly, she continued, "Our destination is that house on the corner. Rentals are low in Brussels, so we were able to get a place with a nice garden for the children, plenty of stable room, and even a carriage for a ridiculously low amount."

The large, handsome house was surrounded by a wall. Michael opened the gate for Catherine, then beckoned to his servants, who were ambling quietly behind them. His young batman, Bradley, had eyes as large as saucers as he stared at Catherine. Michael could hardly blame him when he himself felt the same way.

Calmly ignoring the boy's smitten expression, Catherine described the household, then waved the two men toward the stables behind the house. The vulnerability she had shown earlier was gone, leaving her a well-organized army wife again.

As she led Michael inside, three children and two dogs came sweeping down the stairs in a stampede of small but astonishingly noisy feet. A bright soprano said, "We've finished our lessons, Mama, so can we please play in the garden?"

While the children and a long, low-slung dog swirled around Catherine, the other dog, a splotchy beast of indeterminate ancestry, began barking at Michael. Laughter in her voice, Catherine said, "Silence, please, or we'll drive Major Kenyon to another billet. Clancy, stop barking."

Michael's opinion of her went still higher when not only the children but the dog fell abruptly silent.

Catherine put an arm around the taller girl, who appeared to be about ten. "This is my daughter, Amy. Amy, Major Lord Michael Kenyon. He will be staying here."

He bowed gravely. "Miss Melbourne."

The girl gave a graceful curtsy. She had her mother's striking aqua eyes and dark hair. "A pleasure, Major Kenyon."

Catherine continued, "And this is Miss Molly Mowbry and Master James Mowbry."

Both children had red hair and lively expressions. Mary must be eight or nine, her brother a couple of years younger. Like Amy, they had impeccable manners.

After curtsying, Molly said, "You're a lord?"

"It's only a courtesy title," he replied. "My father is a duke, but I won't be a real lord, since I have an older brother."

"Oh." Molly digested that. "Captain Wilding is teaching us to draw. Do you know anything useful?"

Amy elbowed her and hissed, "Don't ask such questions."

Molly blinked her large hazel eyes. "Was that rude?"

Michael smiled. "Only because I'm afraid I don't have any interesting skills."

"No?" she said with disappointment.

He tried to think what might interest a child. Certainly not mining or investment strategy. "Well, I can tell when a storm is coming, but I don't think I can teach it to anyone else."

Her face brightened. "You could *try*."

Catherine intervened. "The major needs to get settled. You three go outside, and take Clancy and Louis the Lazy with you."

Michael watched in bemusement as the children and dogs obeyed. "Louis the Lazy?"

A voice from the stairs said, "He's the long, lethargic hound. Mostly he sleeps. It's his only talent."

He looked up to see a small-boned, pretty redhead descending the steps. With a smile, she said, "I'm Anne Mowbry."

After the introductions, they talked for a few minutes, until Anne said candidly, "Please excuse me. I'm in the family way again, and at the stage where all I want to do is sleep."

Michael was amused by her frankness. She was attractive, friendly, and charming. And, blessedly, she didn't scramble his wits the way Catherine did.

After Anne took her leave, Catherine began to ascend the stairs. "Your room is up here, Michael."

She led him to a sunny chamber that looked on to the side street. "Kenneth is across the hall. There's already fresh linen on the bed, since we knew it would be occupied soon."

She turned to face him. The movement brought her into the sunshine that poured through the window. Limned by light, she was like a goddess, too beautiful to be of the earth. Yet she also had a warm ability to create peace and happiness around her that reminded him of Clare.

Behind her was the bed. He had a brief, mad fantasy of stepping forward, taking her in his arms, and sweeping her down across the mattress. He would kiss those soft lips and explore the hidden riches of her body. In her arms, he would discover what he had been yearning for. . . .

Her gaze met his and there was a strange moment of awareness between them. She knew that he admired her. Yet though she was surely used to male appreciation, she quickly looked down and concentrated on peeling off her gloves. "If you need anything, just ask Anne or me or Rosemarie, the head housemaid."

He forced himself to look at the gold band that glinted on her left hand. She was married. Untouchable. The wife of a brother officer . . . and he must get her out of his bedroom *now.* "I'm sure I'll be very comfortable. I won't be here for dinner tonight, but I look forward to meeting the rest of the household later."

Not looking at him, she said, "I'll send a maid with a house key later." Then she vanished into the hall.

He carefully closed the door behind her, then dropped into the armchair and rubbed his temples. After the disaster of Caroline, he had sworn that never, under any circumstances, would he touch another married woman. It was a vow he was determined to keep at any price. Yet Catherine Melbourne might have been designed by the devil to tempt him.

The sheer egotism of the remark brought a reluctant smile to his lips. If there was a lesson in his meeting Catherine, it was a reproach for his own smugness. He had been so sure that age and experience would protect him from the follies of infatuation. Not for him the idiocy of becoming entranced by a lovely face.

Obviously, he'd been a damned fool to think himself immune. Yet while it might not be possible to control his reaction to Catherine Melbourne, he could, and would, control his behavior. He would say no word, make no gesture, that could be interpreted as improper. He would behave toward her as he did toward Clare.

No, not like that—there could be no casually affectionate kisses or hugs between him and Catherine. This billet was unlikely to last more than a few weeks, and certainly he could control himself that long. After all, by tomorrow afternoon he would be too busy for infatuation.

Yet a sense of disquiet lingered. He rose and went to stare out the window. All soldiers had a streak of superstition, a belief in the unseen. Perhaps the lovely Catherine really was a test. He had thought he'd come to terms with the past, but maybe some divine judge had decreed that he must confront the same situation in which he had come to grief before, and this time master his dishonorable impulses.

On one thing he was grimly determined: he would not make the same mistake he had made before.

Chapter 4

Catherine walked slowly down the hall, not noticing her surroundings. After all her years among soldiers, she should be used to the fact that almost every man was handsome in a uniform. When Colin was in full dress regimentals, susceptible young girls had been known to swoon in admiration.

Even so, there was something particularly attractive about Major Kenyon. The dark green Rifleman's uniform was more austere than the garb of other regiments; however, it did wonderful things for his eyes, which were a rare, striking shade of true green. The uniform was equally complimentary to his broad shoulders, chestnut hair, and lean, powerful body. . . .

But he was more than merely good-looking; like Wellington, he had the kind of compelling presence that enabled him to dominate a room without saying a word. She suspected that quality came from bone-deep confidence.

Though she had enjoyed talking to him, he was unsettlingly perceptive. She must take care that Major Kenyon did not get a chance to see below the polished surface she had worked so hard to perfect.

Odd that she was thinking of him so formally. Usually she preferred being on first-name terms with the officers around her. Her instincts must be saying that she should not let him get too close. Luckily she was an expert at keeping men at a safe distance.

Shaking her head, she went to her bedroom to work on a basketful of mending. There was nothing like darning to bring one down to earth.

Catherine was about to go downstairs to check on the progress of dinner when her husband came in.

"There are several new horses in the stables." Colin took

off his black leather helmet and tossed it onto the bed. "Good ones, too. Have we acquired a new billet mate?"

She nodded and made a small, precise stitch. "Major Lord Michael Kenyon of the Rifles. He sold out last year, but Napoleon's escape persuaded him to return. He's on the duke's staff, at least for now."

Colin's brows rose. "One of the high-born officers that Old Hookey likes because they can dance as well as they fight." He took off his jacket and shirt. "Could be a useful man to know. Did he act like he might go all soft over you?"

She looked down and bit off a knot, wishing Colin wasn't quite so blatant in his self-interest. It was true that an attractive wife was an asset to an officer, but she hated it when he urged her to flirt with his superiors. The first time he had done that, she had balked. He had been quick to point out that it was a wife's duty to promote her husband's career. The unspoken implication was that she was an unsatisfactory wife in other ways. After that, she had done as he wished.

Though Lord Michael had obviously admired her looks, she was reluctant to expose him to Colin's speculations. Casually she said, "Major Kenyon showed no sign of being smitten by my infamous charms. I don't know about his dancing skills, but he fought in most of the major Peninsular campaigns."

"Sounds like a good addition to the house. Be extra charming—I'm overdue for promotion to major, and Kenyon must have influence with the duke."

"You'll get your promotion soon." She sighed. "There should be ample opportunities for glory in the next few months."

"I certainly hope so." As Colin began changing into his dress uniform, his brow furrowed. "Kenyon . . . The name is familiar." He snapped his fingers. "Now I recall. After the Battle of Barossa, he had a commemorative medal struck for the men he commanded. Said they had done such an outstanding job that they deserved to be honored." Colin laughed. "Can you imagine doing such a thing for a company of drunken soldiers?"

Catherine gave him a cool glance. "I think he's right—exceptional bravery should be celebrated. The Rifles are some of the finest troops in the army, and part of the reason is because officers are encouraged to know and respect their men."

"Common soldiers aren't like us. His precious troops probably sold the medals for drink." Her husband ran a comb through his light brown hair. "I'm going to dine with friends. It will probably run late, so I won't be back tonight."

She wondered with detachment who the woman was. The ladies of Brussels were most hospitable to the allied officers who had come to save them from having to endure the emperor's yoke again.

She rose and collected his crumpled shirt and linen for the laundry basket. "Have a pleasant evening."

"I will," he said cheerfully.

She didn't doubt it.

Michael dined with army friends who were posted in the area. It was good to see them, though he took considerable ribbing over the fact that he couldn't seem to stay away from the army.

Predictably, conversation centered around the military situation. While officially there was still peace, no one doubted that as soon as Bonaparte had consolidated his position in Paris, he would march against the allies.

Michael returned to his new billet late and let himself in quietly. Candles had been left in the foyer and the upstairs hall. Catherine and Anne definitely ran a fine boarding-house.

A crack of light showed below the door opposite his, so he knocked there instead of entering his own room. Kenneth Wilding's familiar baritone told him to enter.

Michael did, and found his friend busy with a sketch pad. Kenneth was a first-rate caricaturist and draftsman, a skill which had aided his work as a reconnaissance officer in Spain.

Kenneth's eyes widened when he looked up from his drawing. "Good God, where did you spring from?"

Michael chuckled. "Didn't our lovely landladies tell you that I'm now occupying the room opposite yours?"

"No, I only got home a short time ago and everyone had already gone to bed." Kenneth rose and took Michael's hand. "Damn, but it's good to see you."

Dark, broadly built, and craggy, Kenneth Wilding looked

more like a laborer than an officer and gentleman. He was one of the rare officers who had been promoted from the ranks, an honor generally reserved for acts of suicidal bravery. While still a sergeant, he had kept Michael out of trouble when Michael had been a very green subaltern with his first command. Friendship had grown from mutual respect.

Michael studied his friend's face as they shook hands, glad to see that some of the terrible tension left by the Peninsular campaign had faded. "I've some whiskey across the hall. Shall I bring it over?"

"I haven't had any of that rotgot since you left Spain," Kenneth said, humor lurking in his gray eyes. "I've rather missed it. Whiskey makes brandy seem overcivilized."

Michael went for the bottle, almost tripping over Louis the Lazy, who was sprawled in front of his door. When he returned to Kenneth's room, the dog followed, flopping so that his jaw rested on Michael's boot. He studied Louis with amusement. "Does this beast welcome all newcomers this way, or am I just unlucky?"

Kenneth produced two glasses and poured each of them a drink. "Consider yourself blessed. With Louis on guard, any potential assailant will die laughing."

After they had exchanged news, Michael said, "Are Catherine and Anne real, or products of my fevered imagination?"

"Aren't they amazing? I had the luck to share a chateau with them in Toulouse. When I found they were in Brussels, I came on bended knee to ask if there was room for a Rifleman. They are experts in the art of keeping men warm, well fed, and happy."

Knowing he shouldn't be so interested, Michael asked, "What are their fortunate husbands like?"

Kenneth swallowed a mouthful of whiskey. "You'll like Charles Mowbry. Quiet, but very capable and with a droll sense of humor."

"What about Melbourne?"

Kenneth hesitated until Michael remarked, "There is something ominous in your silence."

His friend studied his whiskey glass. "I don't know Melbourne well. He's a bluff cavalryman to the core. You know the sort—not unintelligent, but sees no reason to use his mind. Still, he's a good officer, from what I hear. Quite fearless."

"In the cavalry, courage is common. It's judgment that's rare. Is he worthy of the admirable Catherine?"

"I'm not in a position to say." Kenneth leaned over and scratched behind Louis's floppy ears. "She obviously thinks so. In Spain, she acquired the nickname Saint Catherine as much because of her virtue as for the nursing work she did. Half the men she meets fall in love with her, but she's never so much as looked at anyone other than her husband."

That put Michael in his place; he was merely one of a large crowd. Still, he was glad to hear that she was as good as she was beautiful. Once he had not believed such women existed.

He wondered what Kenneth wasn't saying, but enough questions had been asked. He lifted his friend's sketchbook from the desk. "May I?"

"If you like."

Michael smiled at the caricature Kenneth had been working on. "Clever the way you drew Bonaparte as a leering gargoyle. You should sell this to a print shop so it can be reproduced."

Kenneth shrugged off the suggestion. He invariably dismissed compliments by saying that his talent was no more than a minor knack for drawing.

Michael flipped through the pages of the sketchbook. After several architectural studies of a richly baroque guild hall, he found a drawing of Amy Melbourne and the Mowbry children playing. With a few swift lines, Kenneth had caught the fluid motions of a running game, plus the character of each child. It never ceased to amaze Michael that his friend's large hands could draw with such subtlety and grace.

"This is a nice sketch of the children." As he turned the page, he added, "The first thing Molly said was that you were teaching them how to draw."

Kenneth smiled a little. "Both girls are good students. Jamie isn't interested in anything that doesn't have four hooves, a mane, and a tail."

After more sketches of the children and one of Anne Mowbry, Michael turned the page and found himself looking at Catherine Melbourne. His heart constricted at the image of her standing on a rocky shore, her expression otherworldly. A sea wind unfurled her dark hair like a banner and molded her classical tunic to the curves of her splendid figure.

He studied the picture hungrily, in a way that would have been rude with the real woman. Trying to sound casual, he said, "A good drawing of Catherine. Is she meant to be a Greek goddess, or perhaps the legendary Siren whose songs lured men to their doom?"

"The Siren." Kenneth frowned. "The picture isn't that good, though. Her features are so regular that she's difficult to draw. Also, there's a sort of haunted look in her eyes that I didn't manage to catch."

Michael looked at the picture more carefully. "Actually, you did get some of that. What would haunt a beautiful woman?"

"I have no idea," Kenneth replied. "In spite of her easy manners, Catherine doesn't reveal much of herself."

There was definitely something his friend wasn't saying, for the very good reason that Catherine Melbourne's private life was none of Michael's business. Yet as he turned to the next page, he said offhandedly, "If you ever do a sketch of her you don't want, I'll be happy to take it off your hands."

Kenneth gave him a sharp glance, but said only, "Take that one if you like. As I said, I wasn't satisfied with it."

Michael removed the drawing, then continued paging through the sketchbook. He was a damned fool to ask for the picture of a woman who could never be part of his life. Yet when he was old and gray, if he lived that long, he would want to remember her face, and the way she had made him feel.

Wellington was right that the situation was a shambles. As soon as Michael appeared at headquarters the next morning, he was thrown a mountain of work involving supplies and equipment. As the duke said tartly, Major Kenyon might not be a quartermaster, but at least he knew what fighting men needed.

The work required total concentration, and by the end of the day, Michael's intense reaction to Catherine Melbourne was no more than a hazy memory. He headed back to the house on the Rue de la Reine for dinner, thinking it would be good to see her again. She was a charming, lovely woman, but there was no reason for him to behave like a love-crazed juvenile. A second meeting would cure him of his budding obsession.

Catherine had mentioned that the house custom was to gather for predinner sherry. After changing, Michael went down and found Anne Mowbry and a gentleman already in the drawing room.

"I'm glad you could be here for dinner tonight, Michael." Anne turned her head, setting her auburn curls dancing. "This is my husband, Captain Charles Mowbry."

Mowbry greeted him with a friendly handshake. "I've been admiring your horses, Major Kenyon. It doesn't seem fair that such first-rate mounts should be wasted on an infantry officer."

Michael chuckled. "No doubt you're right, but I have a friend who's half Gypsy, and the horses he breeds are marvelous. I'm fortunate that he let me buy two. Usually he'll give them up only in return for a man's firstborn son."

Mowbry glanced teasingly at his wife. "It would be worth trading Jamie for that chestnut, wouldn't it?"

She rolled her eyes. "Don't ask me that today. After the trouble Jamie has been, I'm ready to consider any offers!"

They all laughed. Soon they were chatting like old friends. Then Catherine Melbourne appeared in the doorway in a shimmering sea-green gown that emphasized her remarkable eyes. "Good evening, everyone," she said lightly.

Michael glanced toward her, and his confident belief that he was immune to her beauty shattered into flinders. The best that could be said was that the shot-in-the-heart feeling he experienced was no longer a surprise.

He studied Catherine as she crossed the room toward the others. Her appeal was beyond beauty and warmth, though she had those in abundance. Kenneth, with his artist's eye, had seen the haunted vulnerability beneath her dazzling surface, and now Michael could see it, too. Catherine was that most dangerous of creatures: a woman who aroused as much tenderness as desire.

"Good evening." He had learned as a child how to conceal his emotions, and now he invoked a lifetime of self-control so that no one, especially not her, would suspect how he felt. "I'm thanking my lucky stars that I found this billet. It's the only one I've ever had that included a dog to sleep on my bed."

Her eyes sparkled mischievously. "Interesting. If I were a dog, I should think twice about pestering you. Obviously Louis knew better. He already has you wrapped around his paw."

While Michael wondered if he appeared that intimidating, the Mowbrys began offering Louis the Lazy stories. Clearly he was a dog who made an impression wherever he went.

Kenneth was not returning to dine, but a few minutes later Colin Melbourne appeared. The man was very handsome, with the confidence that came of a complete lack of self-doubt. Catherine went to her husband and took his arm. The two made a striking couple. "Colin, I want you to meet our newest resident."

After the introduction, Melbourne said heartily, "Good to meet you, Lord Michael. As long as that room was empty, there was a risk someone unsuitable might be billeted here. Another so-called officer who was promoted from the ranks, for instance."

The Mowbrys and Catherine shifted uncomfortably, but Michael's anger was tempered with relief. He had feared that he might dislike Melbourne for being Catherine's husband. Instead, he would be able to dislike the man for his blatant snobbery. No wonder Kenneth had been guarded in discussing him. Voice edged, Michael said, "Someone like Kenneth Wilding, for example?"

Suddenly cautious, Melbourne said, "No slur intended. For a man of his class, Wilding does a good job of aping gentlemanly manners. Still, there's no substitute for breeding. As a son of the Duke of Ashburton, surely you would agree."

"I can't say that I've ever seen a strong correlation between breeding and character. After all, Kenneth had the poor taste to go to Harrow. One would have hoped for better from the only son of Lord Kimball." Michael downed the last of his sherry. "Still, even an old Etonian like me has to admit that Harrovians usually give the appearance of gentlemen."

Melbourne's jaw dropped. Since Harrow was as prestigious as Eton, even a bluff cavalryman couldn't miss the sarcasm.

Rallying, Melbourne said with disarming ruefulness, "Forgive me—I just made a bloody fool of myself, didn't

I? I've never spoken with Wilding much, and I made the mistake of assuming he was no more than a jumped-up sergeant."

It was well done, though Melbourne's charm did not quite outweigh his boorishness. Michael replied, "It probably appealed to Kenneth's antic sense of humor to let you keep your preconceptions."

Melbourne's brow furrowed. "If he's actually the Honorable Kenneth Wilding, why did he enlist as a private?"

Michael knew the answer, but it was none of the other man's business. He said only, "Kenneth likes a challenge. He was my sergeant when I was a raw subaltern. I was fortunate to have him. After he and his squad captured three times their number of Frenchmen, I recommended him for a field promotion." He set his glass on a table with an audible click. "I was amazed the army actually had the sense to make him an officer."

His comment produced a lively discussion about the idiocies of the upper ranks of the army, a topic that occupied the group well into dinner. It was a pleasant meal, with excellent food and good conversation. Even Colin Melbourne wasn't bad company, though he'd obviously never had an original thought in his life.

Yet when dinner was over, Michael could not recall a single bite he had eaten. What he remembered was Catherine's elegant profile, her rich laughter, the creamy smoothness of her skin.

He resolved to dine out whenever possible.

Chapter 5

It was well past midnight when Michael opened the door to the kitchen. He stopped in his tracks. "Sorry, I didn't expect to find anyone here."

Catherine Melbourne glanced up from the hearth where she was feeding the fire. "No reason why you should—all sane citizens are in bed." She rose and brushed off her hands. "The duke must be keeping you busy. You've been here a week, and I think I've only seen you once."

It might be wiser to retreat, but it would also be unpardonably rude. Michael entered the kitchen. "Most evenings I've been showing the flag at entertainments given by the English fashionables who have come to Brussels in hopes of excitement."

"I suspected as much. Wellington has always liked having his senior officers attend important social functions, and that must be particularly true now, when he doesn't want the civilians to become too alarmed over the military situation." She gave a teasing smile. "I'm sure you're much in demand to add your aristocratic luster to all of the routs and balls."

Michael made a face. "I'm afraid so. But why haven't I seen you? Wellington is also fond of the company of attractive ladies, so I would think you and Anne and your husbands would be on the prime guest lists."

"We're usually invited, but Colin is often . . . otherwise occupied." She lifted a wooden spoon and stirred a pot simmering on the hob. "When Anne and Charles attend, I usually go with them, but she has been feeling too tired for socializing, so I haven't been out lately. Except for the duke's own entertainments, of course. Everyone goes to them."

Michael hesitated before making the offer that would be

automatic and uncomplicated with any other woman. "If you need an escort, I would be honored to oblige."

Her head came up quickly and she studied his expression. Apparently satisfied with what she found, she said, "Thank you. There are events I would enjoy, but I'd rather not go alone."

"Fine. Tell my batman, Bradley, which functions you wish to attend and I'll be at your disposal." He covered a yawn with his hand. "Today, though, I rode to Ghent and back. I haven't eaten since breakfast, so I decided to raid the larder. Have you also come in search of a late meal?"

She tossed her long braid over her shoulder as she straightened from the pot. Tendrils of glossy dark hair curled against her slim throat. "I couldn't sleep. I came down to heat some milk, but this soup smelled so good I changed my mind."

The pale edge of a nightgown showed above her light-weight blue cotton robe. Though the garments covered her more thoroughly than a regular dress, the effect was destractingly intimate. Worse, the kitchen was lit only by two candles and the fire, and the shadowy darkness was rather like a bedroom. . . .

He looked away. "Is there a household protocol for late-night pantry theft?"

"Not really—whatever you can find is fair prey. There's generally soup simmering on the hob. This one is a rather nice chicken and vegetable concoction." She gestured toward the pantry. "There are also cold meats, cheeses, and bread. Help yourself while I set a place for you."

"You shouldn't be waiting on me."

"Why not?" She went to a cupboard and removed heavy white servants' dishes. "I know my way around this kitchen, and I haven't had as hard a day as you."

"I thought raising children is the hardest work there is."

Her brows rose. "Men aren't supposed to know that."

"A female once broke down and disclosed the secret to me."

She eyed him thoughtfully. "I imagine that women are always telling you secrets."

Preferring to keep the conversation impersonal, he took his candle into the pantry. "The local cheeses are wonderful, aren't they? And the breads, too."

"The food is so good it's easy to understand why the

French believe the country should be part of France. Would you like wine? There's a jug of very decent vin ordinaire here."

"Sounds wonderful, though I warn you, two glasses and I'll fall asleep on the table."

"If that happens, I'll tuck a blanket around you," she said serenely. "This is a very pragmatic household."

By the time Michael emerged from the pantry, the pine table was set and steaming bowls of soup were in place. Kenneth was right—Catherine was an expert at keeping men happy and well fed. She would be a rare prize even if she weren't beautiful.

As he started to slice the cheese, he heard a canine whimper. He glanced under the table and found Louis regarding him with mournful hound eyes. He grinned and tossed a small piece of cheese to the dog, who deftly snapped it out of the air. "For a beast called Louis the Lazy, he is remarkably good at turning up wherever people or food are found."

Catherine laughed. "He's from an old French hunting breed called *basset* because they're so low. Like the French soldiers in the Peninsula, he's a first-rate forager. He and the kitchen cat are always competing for the best bits."

A polite meow announced that a plump tabby had materialized beside Michael's chair. In the interests of fairness, he gave her a sliver of ham before applying himself to his meal.

Silence reigned for the next minutes. Yet despite his consumption of an embarrassing amount of food, he was intensely aware of Catherine on the other side of the table. Even the movement of her throat when she swallowed was erotic. Yet paradoxically, her presence was restful. His mistress, Caroline, had been many things, but never restful.

Noticing his bowl was empty, Catherine asked, "Would you like more soup?"

"Please."

She picked up the bowl and went to the fireplace, which was large enough to roast a calf. As she bent to the soup pot, her lush breasts swayed fluidly beneath the soft material of her robe. He went rigid, unable to look away.

Louis lurched to his feet and followed her hopefully. "Go away, hound," she said firmly as she ladled soup into the bowl.

Ignoring the order, Louis whined and reared up on his hind legs, banging his head into the bowl. It tilted and soup splashed onto the hearth. She jumped backward, then said severely, "You're due for a review lesson in manners, Louis." The dog hung his head with comical guilt.

Michael smiled at the byplay. He was enjoying himself more than at any of the glittering social events of the last week, and his attraction to Catherine was not getting out of hand.

Catherine refilled the bowl and turned toward him. With all his attention on her face, it took him a moment to notice that flames were licking up the left side of her robe. His heart jerked with horror. Christ, when she stepped back, her hem must have brushed the blazing coals.

He sprang to his feet and whipped around the table. "Catherine, your robe is burning!"

She looked down and gave a gasp of sheer terror. The bowl crashed to the floor and Louis bolted away, but Catherine didn't move. Paralyzed, she stared at the yellow-orange flames as they consumed the light fabric with ever-increasing hunger.

In the seconds it took Michael to leap across the kitchen, the fire had flared almost to her elbow. He untied her sash with a yank and dragged her robe from her shoulders, almost knocking her from her feet. Steadying her with his left hand, he hurled the burning garment into the fireplace with his right. A fountain of sparks shot up the chimney.

Ignoring his singed knuckles, he pulled her away from the hearth and turned her to face him. "Are you all right?"

A stupid question; she was in shock, her face as white as her nightgown. Fearing she would collapse, he drew her into his arms. Her heart was hammering so hard he could feel it against his ribs, and she seemed barely aware of him.

"You're safe, Catherine," he said sharply. "You're safe."

She hid her face against his shoulder and began sobbing. He held her close and murmured words of comfort. Her dark silky braid slid seductively across the back of his hand. He was guiltily aware of every inch of her length pressed against him—and her rosewater scent, and the pressure of her soft breasts against his chest.

This was as close to her as he would ever be. Yet he could not savor it because it was impossible to take real pleasure in her nearness when she was distraught.

Her tears gradually faded, but she was still chilled and her breathing was quick and shallow. Gently he guided her into a chair. She buried her face in her hands, exposing the fragile curve of her nape.

As he removed his jacket, he saw that the areolas of her breasts were dimly visible under her white muslin nightgown. The tantalizing sight caused him to begin to harden.

Good God, what kind of animal was he, to feel desire for a woman shaking with fear? As much for decency as for warmth, he draped the heavy wool jacket over her shoulders. The garment was far too large, so he crossed the braided panels double over her chest, painfully careful not to brush her breasts with his fingers. She stared at him numbly, still not speaking.

He knelt in front of her and took her hands in his. The dark green jacket intensified the hue of her aqua eyes. "Should I go for your husband?"

She said unsteadily, "Colin isn't home tonight."

"Do you want me to wake Anne?"

"Really, I'm fine." She tried to smile. "There's no need to disturb anyone else."

"Liar." He started chafing her cold fingers. "Seldom have I seen anyone who looked less fine."

She gave a watery chuckle. "I'm a disgrace to the army, aren't I?" Her hands knotted into fists. "I'm usually fairly levelheaded, but . . . well, my parents died in a fire."

He winced, understanding her shattering reaction to the accident. "I'm so sorry. How did it happen?"

"I was sixteen," she said haltingly. "My father's regiment was posted to Birmingham. We rented a charming old cottage that was covered with roses all summer. I thought it would be lovely to live there forever. Then winter came, and one night the chimney caught on fire. I awoke smelling smoke. I screamed to wake my parents, but the fire was already out of control. My bedroom was on the ground floor and I was able to escape out the window." She closed her eyes and shuddered. "My parents were upstairs. I kept screaming until half the village was there, but . . . Mama and Papa never woke."

He squeezed her hands, then stood. "Is there brandy in the cabinet in the dining room?"

"Yes, but really, it's not necessary."

Ignoring her protest, he said, "Will you be all right while I get the bottle?"

Feeling a shadow of humor, she said, "Believe me, I'm not going anywhere for a while."

He scooped the kitchen cat from under the table and set it on her lap. "Here. There are few things more comforting than a purring cat." Then he took a candlestick and left with long, soundless strides.

Catherine leaned back in the chair, stroking soft feline fur. It was a good thing Michael had given her the tabby, because her fragile peace of mind vanished along with him. She had not realized how safe he had made her feel until he was gone.

When she glanced down and saw the scorched hem of her nightgown, panic began rising again. She pulled Michael's jacket closer around her shoulders. It still carried his body heat. When he had wrapped the garment around her, the tenderness of the gesture had brought her near tears again. She had not felt so cared-for since she was a child.

Tartly she reminded herself that she had escaped unscathed and there was no excuse for hysteria. A towel was draped over the arm of her chair, so she lifted it and blew her nose. Then she concentrated on soothing the nervous cat. By the time Michael returned, the tabby was purring and Catherine had regained a semblance of calm.

"Drink up. You need this." He splashed brandy into two glasses and gave her one, then settled in the opposite chair. He sat casually, one arm resting on his upraised knee, but his watchful gaze was on her face.

"Thank you." She sipped the brandy, grateful for the way it warmed her bones. "Since we couldn't live without fire, I've had to suppress my fear of it. I didn't know how much terror was lurking inside me. If you hadn't been here, I probably would have stood like a frightened rabbit while I burned."

"You're entitled to your fear," he said quietly. "Quite apart from your parents' tragedy, far too many women have died or been horribly injured in accidents exactly like yours."

"Thanks to you, that didn't happen." She leaned back in her chair, rubbing the cat's chin with one finger as she drank.

Odd how the fire that had terrorized her was now so pleasant, its ruddy glow finding auburn highlights in Michael's hair. At their first meeting, she had found his austere good looks unsettling. He had reminded her of a finely honed sword, a quality she had glimpsed in other men who were born warriors. Very quickly she had discovered his humor, but it had taken near-catastrophe for her to recognize his kindness.

She did not realize that she had emptied her glass until he rose and poured more for both of them. She regarded the brandy doubtfully. "You're going to get me tipsy."

"Perhaps, but with luck you'll sleep soundly."

She thought of the nightmares she had experienced after her parents had died, and took a deep swallow. Wanting to talk about something safe, she said, "Charles Mowbry mentioned that you were a member of a group called the Fallen Angels. It that a club?"

He made a deprecating gesture. "It's only a foolish label that fashionable society slapped on four of us who have been friends since Eton. It originated in the fact that two of us have archangel names, and the other two, Lucien and Nicholas, acquired the rather sinister nicknames Lucifer and Old Nick."

She smiled. "I've known a lot of young officers over the years, and from what I've observed, I'd bet that you enjoyed having diabolical reputations."

Laughter showed in his eyes. "We did, actually, but now that I am respectably adult I don't like to admit it."

"Are you all still friends?"

"Very much so." His expression was wry. "Nicholas's wife, Clare, said we adopted each other because our families were less than satisfactory. I suspect she was right. She usually is."

The oblique comment made Catherine wonder what Michael's family was like. Now that she thought of it, when his noble relations were mentioned, he was always curt to a point just short of rudeness. But it wasn't hard to see him as a fallen angel, handsome and dangerous. "What are your friends like?"

He smiled a little. "Imagine a great long wall blocking the path as far as one can see in both directions. If Nicholas came to it, he would shrug and decide he didn't really need to go that way. Rafe would locate whoever was in charge of the wall and talk his way past it, and Lucien would find some stealthy way to go under or around without being seen."

"What about you?"

His smile turned rueful. "Like a mad spring ram, I would bash my head into the wall until it fell down."

She laughed. "A good trait for a soldier."

"This is actually my third go-around in the army. I first bought a commission at twenty-one. The military situation was very frustrating, though, so I sold out after a couple of years."

She made mental calculations from what he had told her of his battle experience. "You must have bought another commission after Wellington went to the Peninsula."

He nodded. "It was appealing to know that real progress was finally being made against Napoleon." His expression became opaque. "And there were . . . other reasons."

Painful ones, from his expression. "So you sold out when the emperor abdicated, then returned yet again." She tilted her head to one side. "Why do men fight?"

He gave her a bemused glance. "Having spent your life among soldiers, surely you know the answer to that."

"Not really."

"Well, the army and navy are honorable careers for gentlemen, particularly younger sons like me who need something to keep us out of trouble," he said dryly.

"Yes, but that doesn't explain why many men take pleasure in what is so terrible." She thought of the army hospitals she had worked in, and shivered. "Half the soldiers I know are panting for another chance to be blown to bloody bits."

He swirled his brandy as he thought. "There is no greater horror than war. Yet at the same time, one never feels more alive. It's both a heightening of life and an escape from it. That can become a drug."

"Did it for you?"

"No, but there was a danger that it would. It's one reason I sold out." His expression changed. "Why am I prosing on like this? You must be bored senseless."

"Not at all. You've taught me more about the essence of war than I've learned in a lifetime surrounded by soldiers." She sighed. "Your answer explains why there are always more men yearning to fight, even at the risk of death."

As silence fell, she leaned her head against the high chair back, idly studying Michael's fire-washed features. He really was extraordinarily attractive, all lean, pantherish muscle. She could watch him for hours, memorizing the fine lines at the corners of his eyes, and the way his white shirt emphasized the breath of his shoulders. As his long, tanned fingers fondled Louis's ears, she wondered what they would feel like on her. . . .

With a shock, she realized that the languid warmth in her limbs was desire. She had forgotten what it felt like.

Luckily she did not have a passionate nature. Even at sixteen, when she had thought herself in love with Colin, her common sense had been firmly in control of her behavior. After marriage taught her that passion was a wicked trap, she had never once been tempted to respond to the men who wanted to coax her into immorality.

She had learned early that her appearance could incite men to behave like idiots, which was not only embarrassing but potentially dangerous. Twice Colin had challenged men for distressing his wife. Fortunately the men in question had given apologies and no duels had resulted, but the incidents had made her realize that she must find a way to make men behave.

By the age of nineteen, she had learned the trick. A reputation for unswerving virtue was part of her method, coupled with a sisterly manner and a total absence of flirtatiousness. Realizing that they could never be lovers, men either left her alone or became friends and protectors. It had been years since a man had given her real trouble, and Michael was too much a gentleman to change that.

Wanting to hear his deep voice again, she said, "You mentioned that one of your Fallen Angel friends had married. Do the others have wives also?"

"Lucien married this past Christmas Eve." Michael smiled fondly. "His wife, Kit, is like a gazelle, all long legs and shy eyes. But she has a mind like a rapier, and the courage of a lioness. I don't know if Rafe will ever marry. I think he prefers his life exactly the way it is."

"What about you?" She was immediately sorry she had spoken. Only the amount of brandy she had consumed could explain why she had asked such a personal question.

Unperturbed, Michael answered, "I was going to spend the spring in London with an eye to surveying the marriage mart, but Napoleon played ducks and drakes with my plans."

"He ruined the plans of many people."

Michael shrugged. "There will be other Seasons."

The thought of Michael seeking a wife among the brightest belles of society gave her a strange twist of regret. She had met Colin shortly before her parents' death, and married him a month after the double funeral, thinking his strength and love would support her in her grief. It had not taken long to realize that his emotions did not run deep, and that she was stronger than he in most ways.

She had no right to complain—but there were times when she longed to have someone to lean on. Instinctively she knew that if she had married a man like Michael, she would have a husband who would share the burdens of life—a man who could support her when she felt too tired to carry on.

Knowing she must not think of such things, she rose and gently deposited the cat in the middle of the warm chair seat. "I'd better go to bed while I can still manage the stairs."

She took a step, then wavered, her head spinning.

Instantly Michael was on his feet steadying her. She leaned against his shoulder until her head cleared. "Sorry," she murmured. "I haven't much of a head for brandy."

He guided her to the stairs with a hand on her elbow. "I'm the one who must apologize for corrupting you with strong drink."

His touch gave her a sudden, sharp memory of what it had felt like when he held her in his arms. How could she remember so clearly now when she had been weeping her eyes out then?

Striving for lightness, she said, "Nonsense. They call me Saint Catherine, you know. I'm quite incorruptible."

He smiled appreciatively, his green eyes alight with amusement. The intimate warmth of his expression almost knocked her from her feet again. With a sinking sensation in her stomach, she realized that she had never been so drawn to a man, not even when she was sixteen and infatuated with Colin.

Thank God that Michael had no improper designs on

her. He might admire her looks, but he was one of those honorable men who had no interest in married women. She guessed that when he married, he would also be a faithful husband. His future wife was a lucky woman.

Since she and Michael could never be lovers, she must make him her friend. In the long run, that would be better, for friendship lasted longer and hurt less than passion.

Yet as he escorted her to her room, she knew that if any man could lead her astray, it would be this one.

Chapter 6

The next evening Michael decided to dine at home to see how Catherine was faring. He arrived late at the sherry hour.

Anne Mowbry smiled and offered her hand when he entered. "I can't believe it! Every one of our stalwart officers is here tonight. I'd begun to think I had imagined you, Michael."

"I thought I had better put in an appearance before you forgot my existence and gave my room to someone else."

She chuckled, then turned back to Kenneth Wilding. Michael went to Catherine, who was dispensing sherry and looking as calm as always. As he accepted a glass, he asked quietly, "Any ill effects from last night?"

"A headache for my excesses, but no nightmares." She glanced at the coals burning in the fireplace. "And I can look at flames without going into a flat panic."

"Good."

He was about to move away when she said, "Is the offer of escort still good? Lady Trowbridge is giving a musicale tomorrow, and I'd like to attend. She assured me that the string quartet she has engaged is quite extraordinary."

"It would be my pleasure."

As they set on a time, dinner was announced. The meal passed smoothly. Michael was becoming used to the ache of yearning he felt whenever he was near Catherine. Thank God she saw him only as a friend. If there had been the least hint of reciprocal interest on her part, the situation would be impossible. He would have had to find another billet even if it meant living in a woodshed.

After dinner he had to put in an appearance at two receptions, but he left both as quickly as possible. He needed a solid night's sleep. The previous night had been haunted by painfully vivid thoughts of Catherine. Whenever he closed his eyes, he had seen her candid aqua eyes, smelled the intimate fragrance of rosewater and woman on her satin skin, felt the seductive pressure of her body against his.

Finally he had fallen into a restless sleep, only to dream of making love to her in a world where she was free and they could be together without dishonor. He had woken exhausted and depressed. Why the hell couldn't he become obsessed with a woman who was eligible?

Because he had never done anything the easy way in his life. His friend Lucien had pointed that out upon several occasions.

The house on Rue de la Reine was still, though a scattering of lamps provided dim light. He was about to go upstairs when he heard a man's voice. Thinking it sounded like Kenneth, he turned down the hall that bisected the house. He came to the cross passage and looked left. Then he halted, feeling as if he had been punched in the stomach.

In the shadows at the end of the passage, Colin Melbourne was embracing his wife, his mouth devouring and his hand up her skirt. Catherine was flattened against the wall, invisible except for her dark hair and the pale folds of her gown. As Michael watched, paralyzed, Colin unbuttoned his breeches, then thrust into her. She whimpered with pleasure.

Michael suddenly had trouble drawing enough air into his lungs. No doubt the Melbournes should be envied for having such a passionate relationship after so many years of marriage, but seeing them together nauseated him. Thank God they were so engrossed in each other that neither had noticed his presence.

He was retreating when a female voice giggled. "*Ah, mon capitaine, mon beau Anglais . . .*"

He stopped dead, then swung around. Colin's forehead was pressed against the wall, revealing his partner's face. The woman was not his wife, but one of the Belgian maids, a dark-haired wench about Catherine's height. Her head was thrown back and her mouth was open, revealing large, irregular teeth.

Michael's sick feeling vanished in a flood of pure rage. How could the filthy bastard betray and humiliate his wife like this, and under her own roof? He deserved to be horsewhipped.

It took all of Michael's control to turn away. Blood

throbbing in his temples, he climbed the stairs two at a time. He had intended to go to his room, but there was light under Kenneth's door. He knocked, then walked in without waiting.

His friend looked up from a letter he was writing. "What happened? You look like murder."

"I feel like it." Michael slammed his shako onto the bed, almost breaking the plume. "Colin Melbourne is down in the west hall humping one of the maids. Christ, has the man no decency?"

"Not much," Kenneth said calmly. "I've heard he'll mount anything in skirts. He's usually fairly discreet, but if a wench is willing, he wouldn't say no, even in his own house."

"How can he?" Michael growled. "How could any man with a wife like Catherine look elsewhere?"

"I wouldn't presume to guess. But why are you so shocked? Society is full of men with the morals of tomcats, and women who are no better."

Michael stalked across the room, knowing Kenneth was right, but still outraged. "Does Catherine know how her husband behaves?"

"I'd be very surprised if she didn't. She's an intelligent woman, and she knows the world. In this case, rather better than you do. If you're thinking of telling her what you saw, don't. She wouldn't thank you for it."

"I suppose you're right," Michael said reluctantly. "But Catherine deserves better than a womanizing, narrow-minded oaf."

"Whatever his failings, Melbourne manages to keep his wife satisfied. It's none of your business if he has a regiment of dollymops, Michael." Kenneth's brows drew together. "Perhaps I should repeat that. *It's none of your business.*"

Michael stared out the window into the night. Again, Kenneth was right. No outsider could really understand a marriage, and he had no right to interfere, even for well-intentioned reasons. God knew, his good intentions had led him to hell before.

But this time was different. Was it, or was he merely demonstrating his dangerous talent for self-deception? Saint Michael, going off to slay all the wrong dragons.

Behind him, Kenneth said softly, "She's married, Michael."

"Do you think I'm not aware of that every moment?" he said tightly. He took several deep breaths before turning to his friend. "Don't worry—I'm not going to lay a finger on her, or on him, for that matter. I just wish for her sake that her husband was decent and honorable, like Charles Mowbry."

"Maybe she's the sort of good woman who finds a wicked man irresistible," Kenneth said dryly. "I've never seen a hint that she regrets her choice of husband."

Michael smiled humorlessly. "There's a poker by your fireplace. Do you want to hit me over the head with it, in case I haven't gotten the message yet?"

"I'll refrain, unless I see you going after Melbourne with blood in your eye." Kenneth dipped his pen in the inkstand and absently sketched a tiny weasel in the margin of his letter. "Speaking of which, Melbourne has been amazingly polite to me the last few days."

Michael sank into a chair. "My fault. He irritated me so much that I told him about your noble birth. Sorry."

Kenneth's mouth tightened. "You've really got to do something about that temper."

"I thought it was under control, but Colin Melbourne seems able to make mice feet of my good intentions."

"Ah, well, it's amusing to watch him try to overcome past rudeness in the hopes that I might be useful to him someday. Little does he know what a waste of time that is."

Needing to get his mind away from Catherine and her husband, Michael asked, "Have you and the other intelligence officers learned what Bonaparte is up to?"

"Hell knows. Not being allowed to set a foot on French soil is damned limiting. I wish someone would declare war and make everything official. Do you have any good headquarters gossip?"

"The duke doesn't share his thoughts with underlings, but it doesn't take a genius to see trouble on all sides." Michael frowned. "The Prussians are being difficult. Prince Blücher is sound, but many of his staff are suspicious of the British, which is why their headquarters are a good fifty miles from Brussels. It creates a serious weak point between the armies."

"One which the emperor will be quick to exploit if he decides to invade Belgium."

"Exactly. My personal opinion is that Napoleon will

march north very soon. So many French veterans have flocked to fight under the imperial eagles again that Boney's army will probably be larger than Wellington's, as well as vastly more experienced."

"The combined allied forces will greatly outnumber the French," Kenneth pointed out.

Michael raised his brows sardonically. "Do you think Boney will give the Allies a chance to assemble into one great army? He's always preferred attack, and in his present situation audacity is his only hope. The longer he delays, the more time Wellington will have to whip this ragtag army into a real fighting force and to get his veterans back from America."

"In any equal battle, I'd back Wellington over Napoleon hands down," Kenneth agreed. "But now the duke is in the damnable position of trying to make bricks without straw."

"That was true on the Peninsula, too, and the duke never lost a battle." Michael smiled a little. "I'm about to become a handful of straw myself. I'm being breveted to lieutenant colonel and given a regiment of green troops with orders to make of them what I can."

"It's a better use of your abilities than being a staff galloper. What's the regiment?"

"A provisional outfit called the 105th. It's made up of a handful of experienced British regulars who are being thrown in to season a mix of green soldiers and half-trained militiamen. The duke hopes the veterans will provide enough starch to make the whole regiment effective."

"You'll have your work cut out for you."

"I don't have to teach them anything difficult, like skirmishing or scouting. All they'll have to do is stand in one place and shoot their muskets, preferably not at each other."

"While cannonballs are tearing off the heads of their comrades, imperial guards are marching toward them to the beat of the death drums, and dragoons are charging on huge, iron-hooved horses. What could be simpler?" Kenneth said ironically.

"Exactly. Nothing at all complicated about the business."

Compared to restraining himself around Catherine, turning raw recruits into soldiers would be dead easy.

After dressing with extra care, Catherine went downstairs to go to the musicale. Michael was waiting for her in the foyer. The dark green Rifleman uniform fitted like a glove, and she'd never seen another man who looked so good in it. Trying not to stare, she said, "I'm looking forward to this evening. Except for events given by the duke, I've hardly been out in weeks."

"It's my pleasure." He offered his arm, and a smile that started deep in his eyes. "You look very fine tonight."

She took his arm and they went out to the carriage. Michael's long legs brushed hers as he folded himself into the cramped space. A slow burn of attraction began humming through her veins. This time she recognized it immediately. Familiarity made it less disquieting than the night in the kitchen. In fact, she found it possible to enjoy the sensuality since she knew her companion would not drop a hand on her thigh or try to force a kiss on her. Her desire was simply like a craving to eat fresh strawberries—real, but not dangerously powerful.

Lady Trowbridge's town house was not large, and the receiving line was in the same salon where guests were talking and laughing before the music program. The high-ceilinged chamber shimmered with candles, flamboyantly costumed officers from half a dozen nations, and almost equally colorful ladies.

"A brilliant scene," Michael remarked. "Brussels has gone mad for all things military."

"Once peace returns, the army will go out of fashion again," Catherine said tartly. "There is nothing like danger to make everyone love a soldier."

He gave her a glance of rueful understanding. "Yet when Napoleon is defeated, officers will be retired on half pay and common soldiers will be thrown back into civilian life with little to show for their service except scars."

"Until the next war." Catherine studied the crowded salon more closely. "Perhaps it's my imagination, but the atmosphere seems strange tonight—a hectic kind of gaiety."

"It's like this throughout fashionable Brussels, and the fever mounts with every day," Michael said quietly. "People are waltzing on the lip of the volcano. As in war, the possibility of danger heightens the intensity of living."

"But the danger is an illusion," Catherine said, her voice edged. "If Napoleon were to approach Brussels, most of these glittering people will fly back to their safe homes in

Britain. They won't stay to face the guns, or nurse the wounded, or search the battlefield for the bodies of their loved ones."

"No," Michael said, his voice quieter yet. "Few people have the courage of you and the other women who follow the drum. You belong to an elite sisterhood, Catherine."

She looked down at her gloved hands. "I'm proud of that, I suppose. Yet it's an honor I won't mind forgoing."

Their turn had come to greet the hostess. Lady Trowbridge exclaimed, "How lovely to see you, Catherine. Your admirers will be in ecstasy. How *do* you manage to look so beautiful?" She gave Michael a droll glance. "Catherine is the only diamond of the first water I know who is genuinely liked by women as well as adored by men."

"Please, Helen, spare my blushes," Catherine begged. "I am not such a paragon as all that."

Lady Trowbridge rolled her eyes. "And modest as well! If I was not so fond of you, Catherine, I swear I would hate you. Be off, now. I shall see you later."

Cheeks flushed, Catherine took Michael's arm and moved on. "Helen does rather exaggerate."

"She seems to have spoken the truth," Michael said as several guests of both sexes started to move eagerly toward them. "It doesn't look as if I'll be needed until it's time to go home. Do you mind if I leave you?"

"I'll be fine," she assured him. "Enjoy yourself."

He inclined his head, then moved away. She sent a wistful glance after him. She wouldn't mind more of his company, but it was wise of him not to hover over her. That might have caused talk, even about "Saint Catherine." Society loved clay feet.

Several of her officer friends arrived and swept her into a lively conversation. Soon she was enjoying herself thoroughly. Perhaps it was foolish not to come to functions like this alone, but when she had tried that, she had felt pathetic.

A few minutes later, Lady Trowbridge approached with a man on her arm. "Catherine, do you know Lord Haldoran? He has just arrived from London. Lord Haldoran, Mrs. Melbourne."

Haldoran was a handsome man of about forty with the powerful build of a sportsman. As Helen turned away,

Catherine offered her hand. "Welcome to Brussels, Lord Haldoran."

"Mrs. Melbourne." He bowed over her hand with practiced grace, and with an equally practiced meaningful squeeze.

Knowing from experience that she must make her position clear immediately, she removed her hand and gave him her best frosty look. As he straightened, she saw that her message had been received and understood. For a moment, she thought that he was going to make a heavy-handed compliment. Instead, his languid expression changed to a stare that bordered on rudeness.

Catherine said sweetly, "Is it so obvious that my gown has been remade several times?"

He collected himself. "Forgive me, Mrs. Melbourne. A woman of your beauty could wear sackcloth and no man would notice. I was merely startled by your eyes. They are so unusual—neither blue nor green, and as transparent as gemstones."

"I've heard that before, but since my parents' eyes were the same, I think of mine as nothing out of the common way."

Something flickered across his face before he said gallantly, "Nothing about you could be common."

"Nonsense," she said coolly. "I am merely an officer's wife who has followed the drum, learned to keep household when pay is months in arrears, and taught my daughter how to recognize the best chicken in a Spanish market."

He smiled. "Fortunate husband, and fortunate daughter. Do you have other children?"

"Only Amy." Preferring less personal conversation, she asked, "Are you in Brussels in the hopes of excitement, my lord?"

"Naturally. War is the ultimate sport, don't you agree? As a lad I considered asking my father to buy me a commission in the 10th Hussars. The uniforms were very dashing and the hunting was excellent." He inhaled a pinch of snuff from an enameled box. "However, I changed my mind when the regiment was transferred from Brighton to Manchester. It is one thing to risk one's life for one's country, and quite another to be exiled to Lancashire."

The flippant remark was in keeping for someone who had wanted to join the 10th Hussars, the most fashionable and expensive of cavalry regiments. Yet in spite of his banter, Haldoran was studying Catherine with disturbing intensity.

"A pity you didn't join when the regiment was sent to the Peninsula," she said dryly. "I'm sure you would have found it grand sport to pursue creatures that could shoot back. So much more exciting than foxes."

He laughed. "You're right. Hunting Frenchmen would have suited me right down to the ground."

It was true that hunting had been a popular pastime in the Peninsula. Catherine knew for a fact that once Wellington had been conferring on horseback with a Spanish general when a pack of hounds went by after a hare. The duke had instantly turned and joined the pursuit. After the kill, he had returned to the amazed Spaniard and resumed speaking as if nothing had happened.

Wellington, however, had earned his right to recreation. Lord Haldoran appeared to be the sort who had done nothing useful in his life, and done it very expensively.

Across the room, Lady Trowbridge announced that the concert was about to begin in the opposite salon. Haldoran said, "Shall we find a seat together, Mrs. Melbourne?"

"Thank you, but I've already arranged to sit with friends." She gave a wide, false smile. "It was a pleasure to meet you."

He bowed. "I'm sure we shall meet again."

Perhaps, but as she slipped into the crowd, she knew that she would not be sorry if that failed to happen.

Chapter 7

The spring weather was exceptionally fair, which added to the air of holiday that hung over Brussels. Catherine, however, liked the weather for more maternal reasons: it allowed the children to play outside. She was sitting under the chestnut tree in the back garden, mending and keeping an eye on her daughter and the young Mowbrys late one afternoon, when Michael Kenyon rode into the driveway. He was home early.

Catherine watched as he dismounted and led his horse into the stable. He moved beautifully, without a single wasted motion. She felt one of the odd lurches of the heart that occurred whenever he appeared.

In the past weeks, he had been her escort a dozen times. At balls, he would always claim a lively country dance—never a waltz—then keep out of her way until it was time to leave. Yet on the occasion when a drunken ensign had cornered her in an alcove and attempted to declare his love, Michael had appeared and removed the youth as firmly as an older brother would have.

A pity that her feelings weren't quite sisterly.

Michael came out of the stable and hesitated, then turned into the garden and walked toward her, his shako in his hand. The sun found glowing auburn highlights in his tangled brown hair. "Good afternoon, Catherine."

"Hello." She reached into her basket and pulled out a torn petticoat of Amy's. "You look tired."

"Commanding a raw new regiment is worse than digging ditches." He nodded toward the energetic game of hide and seek. "I heard the children and thought it would be pleasant to watch someone else do the running for a while."

In the distance, Amy emerged stealthily from behind one rhododendron and slipped behind another. "She does that well," Michael said approvingly. "It wouldn't take much to turn your daughter into a first-rate skirmisher."

"Don't tell her that! She's a dreadful tomboy—you should see her with a cricket ball. And she has had to be restrained from telling Wellington that women fought with the Spanish guerrillas, so why can't Englishwomen do the same?" Catherine began stitching a torn flounce. "How are your men shaping up?"

"I have grave doubts whether they know which end of a musket the ball comes out."

Catherine laughed. "Surely it's not that bad."

"I exaggerate, but only slightly. I've been trying to convince them that the most dangerous thing soldiers can do in battle is break and run, so they're better off holding their ground. If they learn that, they may be of some use. Thank God for my sergeants. If it weren't for them, I would give up now."

"I see you're still wearing your Rifleman uniform instead of infantry scarlet."

"The official reason is that I haven't had time to visit a tailor." His eyes gleamed with humor. "But that's only an excuse. The truth is I don't want to give up my Rifle green."

"A good thing the duke doesn't care an iota what his men wear. I swear, I've never seen two officers who were dressed exactly alike." She smiled reminiscently. "Remember how ragtag everyone looked after a few months on the Peninsula? One could tell a new man because his uniform could still be identified."

Suddenly Jamie Mowbry exploded from the bushes and pointed a branch at Michael. "Bang, bang!"

Because she was watching Michael, Catherine saw the instinctive response that in battle would have resulted in lethal action. It vanished as quickly as it had come and Michael collapsed dramatically on the grass. "I'm done for, lads. Take care of my horse Thor." He kicked a few times and lay still.

Jamie charged over, Clancy at his heels and his branch triumphantly aloft. "I got you, I got you, you filthy frog!"

As soon as the boy was within reach, Michael grabbed him and began tickling his ribs. "Who's got whom? Never trust an enemy to be as dead as he looks, Jamie."

Flushed and shrieking with delight, the boy rolled around

in the grass with his former prey. Catherine watched in amusement, surprised at how easily Michael had entered the child's world.

The wrestling match ended when Amy raced up. "Hello, Colonel Kenyon." She tagged Jamie. "You're it now!" She dashed off with Jamie and Clancy at her heels.

Michael stayed sprawled on the grass. "Lord, it feels good to lie down in the sun and not have to do anything for the next hour." He closed his eyes and unbuttoned his jacket.

Catherine said, "The weather has been lovely, hasn't it? But I keep thinking that it is like the calm before the storm."

"And black clouds are gathering just over the horizon."

Michael's remark reduced them both to silence. For all they knew, Napoleon was already marching north to reclaim his empire.

Louis the Lazy, who had been snoozing by Catherine, hauled himself onto his stubby legs and went to flop beside Michael. "I'm jealous," she said teasingly. "Louis is only willing to be my friend when you're not around."

"Nonsense," Michael said without opening his eyes. "The contrary beast is trying to ruin my reputation. Since dogs and their owners are said to resemble each other, it will be assumed that I am as lazy and useless as he is. Tell him to go away."

His order was undercut by the way he ruffled the dog's ears. Louis moaned with pleasure and rolled onto his back, holding his broad paws in the air.

She laughed. "If that is how you command your troops, Colonel, the 105th is in trouble."

Out of sight at the end of the garden, Molly squealed and Jamie shouted, "Got you!"

Michael's eyes opened. "Jamie looked rather pale. Has he been ill?"

"He suffers from asthma sometimes," Catherine replied. "Anne says the attacks are terrifying. He had a bad one yesterday. Apparently spring is the worst time for him."

"I had occasional asthma attacks as a child, but in time I pretty much outgrew them. No doubt Jamie will, too."

She studied his rugged frame. "I'll tell Anne that. It will make her feel better to know that an asthmatic boy can grow up into a strapping fellow like you. What causes the attacks?"

"I don't know if anyone is sure," he said slowly, "but I think it's usually a combination of things—dampness, food or plants that don't agree with one." He laid his arm across his eyes, blocking the sun and concealing his expression. "I believe there's an emotional component as well."

"Do you mean getting too excited? Jamie is high-strung."

"That, or being frightened or distressed. Painful emotions can sometimes trigger an attack in a matter of moments."

"I see." She would have liked to know more, but his tone forbade questions.

He continued, "How is Anne feeling these days?"

"Much better. She's napping at the moment, but she says she's almost at the stage of pregnancy where she will go from exhaustion to boundless energy. In another week, she'll be eager to be dancing again." Catherine knotted and cut her thread. With Anne as a companion, she would no longer need Michael's escort. She would miss spending time with him. She would miss it a great deal. "Then you won't have to squire me around."

"Escorting you has been a pleasure, not a burden. When Charles isn't available, I can take you both. I'll be the envy of every man in Brussels."

He covered a yawn and lapsed into silence. In spite of the noise of the children and the wagons rumbling along the road that ran through the Namur Gate, he dozed off, his breath becoming slow and steady. There was a precious intimacy to the situation.

Catherine continued sewing. She was very good at concealing her feelings, and not even the most suspicious observer would suspect the quiet joy in her heart. Michael's presence fed a part of her soul that had been starving for years.

Perhaps she should feel guilty about her improper feelings, but she didn't. No one would be hurt, and soon their paths would diverge, probably forever. But when that happened, she would have the memory of a few golden hours to carry in her heart.

She finished Amy's petticoat and folded it into her basket, then began darning Colin's socks. When she had done two, she allowed herself to study Michael's tanned right hand, which lay relaxed in the grass only two feet from her.

The fingers were long and capable. A thin, long-healed saber scar curved across his palm and up the wrist.

She experienced a nearly overpowering urge to lay her hand over his. To touch him, if only in the most superficial way. To feel the vivid life pulsing through his powerful body. What would it be like to lie alongside him, to feel his warm length against her?

Face heated, she reached for another sock. She hoped that when she met Saint Peter, her life would be judged by her deeds, not her thoughts.

After she finished her mending, she packed her scissors and thread away and leaned back against the trunk of the chestnut, watching Michael from under half-closed lids.

Peace was shattered by piercing screams from the children and an anguished howl from Clancy. Catherine sat bolt upright, recognizing that it was not the sound of normal play. Simultaneously, Michael's eyes snapped open.

Amy shouted, "Mama, come quickly!"

Michael leaped up and grabbed her hand to help her. As soon as she was on her feet, they raced across the garden, her heart pounding with fear at what they might find.

The children were by the stone fountain, where a dancing porpoise gushed water into a small pool. Catherine's heart spasmed as she saw the blood splashed across both girls. Blood was pouring from a gash in Molly's scalp. Amy had taken off her sash and was valiantly trying to stanch the flow.

Jamie stood a few feet away, his face ashen under his red hair as he watched his sister's wild sobbing. Clancy jumped around anxiously, getting in the way and adding to the confusion with his sharp yips.

Catherine dropped beside Molly and took over the job of trying to stop the bleeding. "Amy, what happened?"

"Jamie shoved Molly and she fell against the fountain."

"I didn't mean to!" Jamie gasped. His quick, shallow breaths began whistling eerily. Michael, who had been calming the nervous dog, looked up sharply at the sound.

Catherine ordered, "Amy, go get Anne."

As Amy ran to obey, Molly asked with ghoulish curiosity, "Am I going to die?"

"Of course not," Catherine said briskly. "Head wounds bleed dreadfully, but this one isn't deep. You'll be fine in a few days. Any scar will be hidden by your hair."

"I didn't mean it!" Jamie cried with anguish. Suddenly he bolted away, his limbs flailing frantically.

Catherine's instinct was to follow, but she couldn't, not with Molly still bleeding in her arms. She gave Michael an agonized glance. To her relief, he was already going after the weeping child, but he was slowed by the necessity of untangling himself from Clancy and having to circle the fountain.

Jamie tripped and went sprawling on the turf. The walled garden echoed with the sound of his hideous wheezing.

Shocked out of thoughts of her own injury, Molly tried to stand up. "Jamie is having one of his attacks!"

Catherine held the little girl still. "Don't worry, Colonel Kenyon will take care of your brother." She prayed that her words were the truth, for she herself did not know what to do.

Before Michael could reach Jamie, the child regained enough breath to scramble to his feet. He began running again, his eyes wild with terror as he plunged through a thicket where an adult couldn't follow. He emerged on the other side and collapsed, struggling desperately for air. Even fifty yards away, Catherine could see that his face was a horrible bluish shade.

Jamie was feebly trying to clamber to his feet when Michael rounded the thicket and scooped the boy up in his arms. "It's all right, Jamie," he said soothingly. "Molly isn't badly hurt."

Though Michael's expression was grim, his voice was calm as he brought the child back to the fountain. "It was an accident. We know you didn't mean to injure your sister."

Supporting Jamie in a sitting position, Michael pulled out his handkerchief and soaked it in the fountain. Then he patted the child's contorted face with cool water, all the while keeping up a stream of reassuring words. "You can breathe, Jamie, you've just forgotten how for a minute," he said softly. "Look in my eyes and remember how to breathe. S-l-o-w-l-y in. Relax. Then s-l-o-w-l-y out. Spell the words with me. B-r-e-a-t-h-e, space, i-n . . . Come on, you can do it."

Catherine watched, mesmerized, as Jamie's lips began silently forming the letters along with Michael. Gradually his breathing evened out and color began to return to his face.

By the time Anne ran from the house with Amy, Catherine had a crude bandage on Molly's head and Jamie was almost back to normal. Anne's face was so pale that faint, ghostly freckles showed on her cheekbones as she said, "Goodness, you two certainly get into a quantity of trouble."

She knelt between her children and pulled them to her. Jamie burrowed against her side and wrapped his arms around her waist. Molly also snuggled as close as she could get.

In the sudden silence, hoofbeats sounded clearly. A moment later, Charles Mowbry called from outside the stable, "Trouble?"

"A little," Anne replied, relief on her face. "Molly cut her head and Jamie had an attack, but everything is fine now."

As Catherine got to her feet, she saw Charles and Colin coming toward them, their scarlet coats brilliant against the grass. They had had a regimental drill today, she recalled.

Charles arrived first, his expression under control, except for his stark eyes. When he reached his family, he bent and lifted Jamie, hugging him tightly. "You all right, old man?"

"I couldn't breathe, but Colonel Kenyon reminded me how," his son offered. "Then it was easy."

"That was good of him," Charles said huskily. "Will you remember how to do it yourself next time?"

Jamie nodded vigorously.

Anne and Molly got to their feet. Charles smoothed his daughter's hair, careful not to disturb the blood-soaked bandage. "I know you don't like this dress, but wouldn't it be better to get rid of it by ripping rather than bleeding?"

A smile lit her teary face. "Oh, Papa, you're *so* silly."

Concealing a smile, Catherine wondered what the men in Charles's company would think if they heard that.

"Time to get you two inside and cleaned up." Anne gave Catherine and Michael a heartfelt glance. "Thank you both for being here."

As the Mowbrys headed to the house, Catherine put an arm around her daughter's shoulders. "Amy was splendid, Colin. She tended to Molly's injury, then went to get Anne."

"You're like me and your mother," he said approvingly.

"A good soldier *and* a good nurse." He glanced at Catherine. "Can I take Amy for an ice as a reward for bravery?"

It was really too close to dinner, but Amy had earned a treat, and she had seen little of her father lately. "Fine, but Amy, change your dress first. Have a maid put it in a bucket of cold water so the blood doesn't set."

Amy nodded and bounced off with her father.

Alone with Michael, Catherine sank onto the rim of the fountain and buried her face in her hands for a moment. "Please excuse me while I have hysterics."

"I'll join you." Wearily he settled onto the fountain beside her. "It's always worst when the crisis is over, isn't it?"

"I turn into quivering aspic every time." She tried to laugh. "Family life requires nerves of steel."

"Your husband was right, though. Amy behaved splendidly."

"Isn't she amazing? I used to wonder if it was wrong to take her to the Peninsula, but she thrived on it." Catherine smiled wryly. "She's like her father that way. I'm more of a cowardly homebody myself."

"You may think so," he said, warm affection in his voice, "but if I ever need nursing, I hope you're available."

She glanced away before her eyes could reveal too much. "And you're a good man to have around during domestic disasters, of which we have had more than our share lately. Fire, blood, asthma. Anne was right that the attacks are terrifying."

"They feel even worse, like iron bands around the lungs. The harder you try to breathe, the less air you take in. The worst part is the panic, which can destroy every shred of sanity and control you have. I remember doing exactly what Jamie did—running till I dropped, then getting up and running again as soon as I could stagger to my feet." He grimaced. "How do Anne and Charles stand it? It must be ghastly to see your child struggling to breathe."

"They do it because they have to, just as your parents did."

"They were cut from different cloth," he said dryly. "In fact, most of my attacks were triggered by my father. When I had one in my mother's presence, she left me to the care of the nearest maid. The sight was too distressing for one of her delicate constitution." The planes of his face hardened. "If I hadn't been shipped off to Eton, I probably wouldn't have made it to my tenth birthday."

Catherine winced. "I see why you never mention your family."

"There isn't much to say." He trailed his fingers through the fountain, then flicked a few drops of water at Louis, who was snoozing at his feet again. "If my father had to choose between being God and being Duke of Ashburton, he would ask what the difference is. My mother died when I was thirteen. She and my father despised each other. Amazing that they produced three children, but I suppose they felt obliged to keep going until they had an heir and a spare. My sister, Claudia, is five years older than I. We scarcely know each other and prefer it that way. My brother Stephen is Marquess of Benfield and heir to the noble Ashburton title and extravagant Kenyon wealth. We know each other a little, which is rather more than either of us wants to."

His expressionless words sent a shiver up her spine. She remembered what he had said about how he and his Fallen Angel friends had become a family because they had all needed one. With sudden passion, she wished she had the right to take him in her arms and make up for everything he had been denied.

Instead, she said, "I've always regretted not having a brother or sister. Perhaps I was lucky."

"If you like, you can borrow Claudia and Benfield. I guarantee that within two days you'll be thanking your lucky stars for being an only child."

"How did you survive?" she asked quietly.

"Sheer stubbornness."

She rested her hand on his for a moment, trying to wordlessly convey her sympathy, and her admiration for the strength that had enabled him to endure. Instead of bitterness, he had learned compassion.

He laid his other hand over hers, enfolding her fingers. They did not look at each other.

She was acutely aware of the long length of his leg only inches away from hers. It would be so natural to lean forward and press her lips to his cheek. He would turn and his mouth would meet hers. . . .

With horror, she recognized how close she had come to the fire. She lifted her hand away, knotting her fingers into a fist to prevent herself from caressing him. Her voice was distant in her own ears when she asked, "When did you outgrow the asthma?"

There was a brittle pause before he said, "I don't know if one ever really does completely—I've had several mild attacks as an adult—but there were very few after the age of thirteen." His face tightened. "The worst one took place at Eton. That time I knew—absolutely *knew*—I was going to die."

"What triggered it?"

"A letter from my father." Michael rubbed his temple, as if he could erase the memory. "It informed me that my mother had died suddenly. There was a strong implication of . . . good riddance." He closed his eyes and took several deep, slow breaths. "The attack began immediately and I collapsed, wheezing like a blown plow horse. There's something particularly horrible about dying fully conscious but helpless, unable to move. Luckily my friend Nicholas's room was next door and he heard me. He came and talked me through it, as I did with Jamie. The trick is to break through the victim's panic and get him to concentrate on breathing successfully."

Surprised, she said, "Your friend must be about your age. Did he know what to do because he had asthma also?"

Michael smiled a little. "There has always been something a little magical about Nicholas. He's half Gypsy and knowledgeable in their traditional ways of healing. He taught us all how to whisper horses and tickle fish from a stream."

Glad to see his expression ease, she said, "It sounds as if he has been a good friend to you."

The words must have been a mistake, for Michael's clasped hands went rigid, the tendons showing in the wrists. "He has. Better than I have been to him." He shook his head. "Lord, why am I telling you all this?"

She hoped it was because she was special to him. "Because you know I care, and that I will honor your confidence."

"Perhaps that is the reason." Not looking at her, he said quietly, "I'm glad to have met you, Catherine. When I think of Brussels in the future, I might forget the balls and the rumors and the frantic gaiety, but I will always remember you."

The air between them seemed to thicken, becoming so palpable she feared he must be able to feel the beating of her heart. Haltingly she said, "Your friendship means a great deal to me, too."

"Friendship and honor are perhaps the two most important things in life." He bent and picked a daisy from the grass. "Friendship so that we are not alone. Honor because what else does a man have left at the end of the day except his honor?"

"What of love?" she asked softly.

"Romantic love?" He shrugged. "I haven't the experience to comment."

"You've never fallen in love?" she said skeptically.

His voice lightened. "Well, when I was nine, my friend Lucien's sister proposed to me and I accepted with enthusiasm. Elinor was a quicksilver angel."

Seeing the warmth in his eyes, she said, "Don't discount your feelings simply because you were young. Children can love with a kind of innocent purity that no adult can match."

"Perhaps." He rolled the daisy between thumb and forefinger. "And because Elinor died two years later, the love between us was never tested."

Nor had it had a chance to fade away naturally. Somewhere inside Michael, she suspected, there must still be the dream of finding a quicksilver angel. "If you loved like that once, you can again."

His hand clenched spasmodically on the daisy, crushing it. There was a long silence before he said in a barely audible voice, "I once loved—or was obsessed by—a married woman. The affair destroyed friendship and honor both. I swore I would never do that again. Friendship is safer."

For a man like Michael, failing to meet his own code of honor would have been devastating. Such a catastrophic mistake also explained why he had never said or done anything improper with her. Now she knew that he never would.

"Honor is not the exclusive province of men," she said quietly. "A woman can have honor, too. Vows must be kept, responsibilities must be met." She got to her feet and looked down into his fathomless green eyes. "It is fortunate that honor and friendship can coincide."

They looked at each other for a suspended moment as

everything and nothing was said. Then she turned and walked toward the house, her steps steady so that no one would guess that her eyes were blurred with tears.

Michael sat in the garden for a long time, his eyes unfocused, his breathing slow and deliberate. Sometimes it was convenient to have to pay close attention to the air moving in and out of his lungs, because the effort kept pain at bay, at least for a little while.

It was easy to be obsessed by Catherine. Not only was she beautiful, but she was truly admirable. His mother, sister, and Caroline combined could not have equaled a fraction of her warmth or her integrity. She was perfect in every way, except that she was unattainable. Married beyond redemption.

Yet there was something real between them. Not love, but an acknowledgment that under other circumstances matters might have been very different.

He wondered if there had been a different path he might have chosen when he was younger, one that would have led him to Catherine on the terrible day when she was orphaned. Like Colin, he would have been quick to offer his protection. Unlike Colin, he never would have turned from his wife to other women.

Such speculations were nonsense. He had never seen a path except the one he had taken, which had led him to a warped love that had stained his soul. He got to his feet, feeling as drained as if he'd just fought a battle. Yet under the pain, he was proud that he and Catherine had forged something pure and honorable from what could have been sordid and wrong.

Of course, her husband was a soldier on the brink of war. . . .

He shied away from the thought, appalled that it had even crossed his mind. It would be obscene to hope for the death of a fellow officer. It was also ridiculous to try to look beyond the next few weeks. When battle came, he was as likely to be killed as Melbourne. There were no certainties in life, love, or war.

Except the fact that whether the rest of his life was measured in days or decades, he would never stop wanting Catherine.

Chapter 8

Catherine was dressing for dinner the next evening when Colin entered the bedroom. Instead of ringing for her maid, she asked, "Could you fasten the back of my gown?"

"Of course." His fingers were deft and passionless. She was struck by the sheer strangeness of the way they inhabited the same house, the same marriage, yet never touched emotionally. Their relationship was woven of law, courtesy, convenience, and habit. They almost never fought, because each of them knew exactly how much—and how little—to expect of the other.

After Catherine's gown was secured, Colin moved away and began changing his own clothing. He looked uncomfortable in a way that she recognized. She asked, "Is something wrong?"

He shrugged. "Not really. But . . . well, I lost a hundred quid at whist last night."

"Oh, Colin." She sank down into a chair. There was never enough money, and a hundred pounds was an enormous sum.

"Don't look at me like that," he said defensively. "I actually did rather well. I was down three hundred before I won most of it back."

She swallowed, trying not to think what they would have done if he had lost so much. "I suppose I should be grateful, but even a hundred pounds will cause problems."

"You'll manage. You always do," he said carelessly. "It was worth losing a little. I was playing with several officers of the Household Guards—men from families with influence."

"Influence may be useful for the future, but we must pay our share of the household expenses *now*."

"Ask your friend Lord Michael for more—everyone knows the Kenyons are as rich as nabobs." Colin removed his stock and tossed it onto the bed. "The way he's been squiring you around, he obviously fancies you. Has he tried to bed you yet?"

"Nonsense," she snapped. "Are you suggesting that I have behaved improperly?"

"Of course not," he said with bitter amusement. "Who would know that better than I?"

There was sudden, sharp tension as the room pulsed with all of the issues that divided them. Realizing she had overreacted to Colin's casual remark, Catherine said evenly, "Michael is pleasant, but he has escorted me from courtesy, not because he's trying to bed me." And if her words were not quite the whole truth, they were close enough.

Accepting her statement at face value, Colin said, "See if you can turn him up sweet in whatever time is left in this billet. I've been doing some thinking about the future."

Her brows drew together. "What do you mean?"

"After Boney is defeated, the government will cut the army to a fraction of its present size. There's a good chance I'll be retired on half pay. It's time to start looking for another occupation, preferably a nice government post that pays well and leaves plenty of time for hunting." He pulled on a fresh shirt. "Getting such a position will require influence. Luckily, Brussels is teeming with aristocrats this spring. When you're hobnobbing with 'em, be extra charming to anyone who might be helpful when the time comes."

"Very well." The idea did not enthrall her, but since their future would depend on Colin finding a decent post, she must do her part. "Are you going to be dining here?"

"No, I'm meeting friends."

She sighed. "Try not to lose any more money. I can make a shilling stretch until it squeaks, but I'm not a miracle worker."

"There won't be any gaming tonight."

Which meant he would be with one of his women. She wished him a pleasant evening and went downstairs. It was early and Kenneth was the only person in the salon. He was gazing out the window, his shoulders as broad as those of a blacksmith.

"Good evening, Kenneth," she said lightly. "You've been as busy as Michael. I'm beginning to think the infantry works harder than the cavalry."

He turned to her. "Of course—everyone knows that."

She smiled. "You're as bad as my father. He was in the infantry, you know."

Kenneth looked horrified. "The devil you say! How come a nice lass like you married a dragoon?"

"The usual reasons." She poured two glasses of sherry and joined him at the window. The sun was hidden behind the trees, but it gilded the clouds with ocher and crimson and turned Brussels' graceful church spires to dramatic silhouettes. "A lovely sky. At times like this, I wish I could paint."

He sipped his sherry. "So do I."

"You don't? I assumed you must, since you draw so well."

He shrugged. "Drawing is a mere knack. Painting is quite another matter, one I know nothing about."

She glanced at his stern profile. Something in his tone suggested that he regretted that, but an army on campaign would have presented few opportunities to learn, particularly in the years before he received a commission.

Outside, the colors were fading and indigo clouds were gathering on the horizon. How quickly the night was falling. "It's not going to be much longer, is it?" she said softly.

He knew exactly what she meant. "I'm afraid not. The emperor has sealed France's northern borders. There's not a stagecoach, fishing boat, or document getting across—except for the false information Napoleon's agents are merrily spreading, of course. They say the authorities don't expect the campaign to begin before July, but I think war could come at any time."

"I have this sense that . . . that we're all living in a glass bubble that's about to shatter," she said intensely. "Everything seems larger than life. These last two months feel like a special time that won't come again."

"All times are special, and none ever comes again," he said quietly.

Yet it was human to try to hold back the night. On impulse, she asked, "Could you do a favor for me?"

"Of course. What would you like?"

"Could you do drawings of everyone in the household? Anne and Charles, Colin, the children. The dogs. You. Michael." Most of all, Michael. Seeing Kenneth's quizzical glance, she added quickly, "I'd pay you, of course."

His brows rose. "Really, Catherine, you know better than that."

She stared into her sherry glass. "I'm sorry. I suppose that sounded rather insulting, as if you were a tradesman."

The lines around his eyes crinkled. "Actually, it was a compliment—it would be my first professional drawing commission, except that I can't accept it."

"Of course not. I'm sorry, I shouldn't have asked."

He cut off her apology with a quick gesture. "I didn't say I wouldn't make the sketches. In fact, I already have a number that would do, but you must take them as a gift."

When she tried to thank him, he said, "No thanks are necessary. You and Anne have the gift of taking an assortment of misfit pieces and creating a home from them." He gazed out at the nearly dark sky. "It's been a long time since I've had a home. A very long time."

His wistfulness made her lay her hand over his, a gesture that was as easy with him as it was complicated with Michael. "When you do the sketches, don't forget the self-portrait."

"If I try to do one, the paper might spontaneously disintegrate," he said dryly.

"As Molly would say, you're *so* silly."

They both laughed. Removing her hand, she went on, "Are you going to the Duchess of Richmond's ball next week? It's supposed to be the grandest entertainment of the spring."

He gave an elaborate shudder. "No, thank heaven, I'm not important enough to rate an invitation. I'll be at the duke's ball on the twenty-first, though. Since he's commemorating the Battle of Vitoria, he'll expect his officers to be there."

She smiled teasingly. "I shall expect a dance with you."

"Absolutely *not.* I am quite willing to give you my drawings or my life, but dancing is quite another matter."

They laughed again. Turning from the window, she saw Michael standing in the doorway. When he saw her looking at him, he entered the room, his expression impenetrable. She ached to go to him and take his hands. Instead, she put on her Saint Catherine face and went to pour another sherry.

It was easier to be a saint than a woman.

* * *

That evening Kenneth went through his drawings, selecting ones he thought Catherine would like. He was surprised at how many he had done. Only one or two more would be needed. He set aside several for Anne as well. There was one of the Mowbry family together in the garden that was really quite good.

Idly he took his pencil and began sketching the lovers Tristram and Iseult. Tristram, the mighty warrior, and Iseult, the healer princess who was wed to Tristram's uncle. It had ended tragically, of course; it wouldn't be much of a legend if they'd settled into a cottage and she'd had nine children and he'd turned into a red-faced hunting squire.

He did not realize what he was doing until the picture was done. Then he saw that the tormented warrior wore Michael's face, and the dark-haired princess in his arms had the haunted sweetness of Catherine Melbourne.

He gave a soft whistle. So that was how the wind was blowing. It wasn't the first time his drawings had revealed something he had not consciously recognized. Damnation, hadn't Michael suffered enough? Or Catherine, for that matter, paying endlessly for the foolish marriage made when she was sixteen.

Having learned to his bitter cost that happiness was fleeting, he would throw morality to the winds and seize what joy he could if he were in love. He would like to believe Michael and Catherine were doing exactly that, but they were both too damned noble. They were probably concealing their feelings from each other, perhaps even from themselves.

He tossed the drawing into the fireplace and held a candle to the edge until the paper flared. As he watched the picture crumble into ash, he hoped they would get their reward in heaven, for it wasn't likely to happen on earth.

The day before the Duchess of Richmond's ball, Michael and Kenneth attended a dinner to welcome several officers of the 95th who had just arrived from America. Inevitably, the conversation turned to Peninsular days. It was a good evening, but Michael said dryly as he and Kenneth rode home, "There is nothing like distance to make bad food, bad wine, and bad housing look romantic."

"The real romance is that we were young, and we survived." Kenneth chuckled. "Lord, remember the time we held the Rifles anniversary banquet on the bank of the Bidassoa?"

"Sitting with our legs in trenches and using the turf as both table and chair is not the sort of thing one forgets."

They turned into the Rue de la Reine, moving at a quiet walk. As he dismounted and opened the gate, Michael said slowly, "There's a bad storm coming in the next few days."

Kenneth looked at him sharply. "Literal or metaphorical?"

"Perhaps both." Michael unconsciously rubbed his left shoulder, which ached before major changes in the weather. "It's going to be an almighty thunderstorm. That may be all—but remember how often storms hit before battles on the Peninsula?"

Kenneth nodded. "Wellington weather. It was uncanny. Perhaps you should tell the duke."

Michael laughed. "He'd throw me out of his office. He's a man who deals in facts, not fancies."

"No doubt he's right—but I'll tell my batman to make sure my kit is ready to go in case we have to move out quickly."

"I intend to do the same."

They led their horses into the stable. A lamp was lit inside, and its light showed Colin Melbourne sprawled in a pile of hay, snoring heavily. His mount, still saddled and bridled, was standing nearby, looking bored. Kenneth knelt and examined the sleeping man. "Drunk as a lord," he reported.

"I beg your pardon?" Michael said icily.

Kenneth grinned. "Very well, he's as drunk as some lords. I've never seen you that far gone."

"No, and you never will."

"Give the man his due, though. He was able to stay in the saddle long enough to get home. A credit to the cavalry."

After bedding down his own horse, Michael did the same for Melbourne's mount. No sense in the beast suffering because its master had overindulged. When he finished, Kenneth hauled their drunken companion to his feet.

Colin came alive, asking blearily, "Am I home yet?"

"Almost. All you have to do is walk to the house."

"The bloody infantry to the rescue. You fellows do have

your uses." Colin took a step and almost pitched to the floor.

Kenneth grabbed him barely in time. "Give me a hand, Michael. It's going to take both of us to get him inside."

"We could leave him here," Michael suggested. "The night is mild, and the condition he's in, he won't mind."

"Catherine might worry if she's expecting him home tonight."

Since that was undoubtedly true, Michael pulled Melbourne's right arm over his shoulders. There was a heavy scent of perfume underlying the smell of port. The bastard had been with a woman.

He tried not to think of the fact that this drunken dolt was Catherine's husband. That he had the right to caress her, to possess her with his own promiscuous body . . .

Gritting his teeth, he took his share of Colin's substantial weight and supported the man through the stable doors. Revived slightly by the fresh air, Colin turned his head and blinked at Michael. "It's the aristocratic colonel. Much obliged to you."

"No need," Michael said tersely. "I'd do the same for anyone."

"No," Colin corrected him. "You're doing it for Catherine 'cause you're in love with her."

Michael went rigid.

"Everyone's in love with her," Colin said drunkenly. "The Honorable Sergeant Kenneth, the faithful Charles Mowbry, the damned duke himself dotes on her. Everyone loves her because she's perfect." He belched. "Do you know how hard it is to live with a woman who's perfect?"

Kenneth snapped, "That's enough, Melbourne!"

Relentlessly Colin continued, "I'll bet your noble lordship would like nothing better than to roll Catherine into the hay and make a cuckold of me."

Michael stopped in his tracks, his fists knotting with fury. "For Christ's sake, man, shut up! You insult your wife by suggesting such a thing."

"Oh, I know she wouldn't go," Colin assured him. "It's not for nothing they call her Saint Catherine. Know why the original Saint Catherine was made a saint? Because the silly bitch—"

Before he could finish the sentence, Kenneth pivoted and gave Colin a short, sharp punch to the jaw.

As the man's dead weight sagged between them, Kenneth said dryly, "I thought I had better do that before you murdered him."

Kenneth saw too damned much. Grimly Michael continued his part of the job of hauling Melbourne inside and up the stairs to his bedroom. When they got there, Kenneth rapped on the door.

A minute passed before Catherine opened it. Her dark hair was loose over her shoulders and she wore a hastily tied robe that revealed too much of the nightgown beneath it. She looked soft and slumberous and infinitely beddable. Michael dropped his gaze, blood throbbing in his temples.

"What happened?" she asked.

"Don't worry, Colin isn't hurt," Kenneth said reassuringly. "A bit drunk, and I think he bruised his chin falling in the stable, but nothing serious."

She stood back, holding the door open. "Bring him in and lay him on the bed, please."

As they carried Colin into the room, Michael saw her nostrils flare slightly as the scent of alcohol and perfume wafted toward her. In that moment, he realized that Kenneth had been right: Catherine knew about her husband's other women, but whatever his failings, she accepted them with dignity. Michael admired her even as he wanted to beat Colin to a bloody pulp.

They tilted Melbourne onto the bed and Kenneth pulled off his boots. "Can you manage the rest, Catherine?"

"Oh, yes. This isn't the first time." She sighed, then said with forced good humor, "Luckily, it doesn't happen often. Thank you for bringing him up."

Her words were for both of them, but she did not look directly at Michael. Ever since that day in the garden, they had avoided meeting each other's gazes.

The men said good night, then left the room and walked silently toward the other wing. Privately Michael acknowledged that his fury had not been merely because Melbourne's comments had been crude, vulgar, and unbefitting a gentleman.

The really upsetting part was that everything the bastard had said was true.

Chapter 9

Early the next morning, Michael was finishing a quick breakfast when Colin entered the dining room. Since no one else was there, it was impossible to ignore the man.

Colin headed straight for the coffeepot. "I have no memory of it, but my wife says that you and Wilding brought me in last night. Thank you."

Glad the other man didn't remember, Michael replied, "Your horse deserves most of the credit for getting you home."

"Caesar is the cleverest mount I've ever had." Colin poured a cup of steaming coffee with an unsteady hand. "My head feels as if it was hit by a spent cannonball, and I deserve every ache. At my age I should know better than to drink beer, brandy, and wine punch the same night."

His expression was so ruefully amused that Michael could not help smiling back. He was struck by the uncomfortable realization that if Colin were not married to Catherine, Michael would like him well enough. At least, he would have been tolerant of the other man's failings. Trying to treat Colin as if Catherine didn't exist, he said pleasantly, "It sounds like a wicked combination. You're lucky to be moving this morning."

"No choice." Colin put sugar and milk in his coffee and took a deep swallow. "I have to get out to the regiment, then back here in time to take my wife to the Richmond ball."

It was, after all, impossible to forget about Catherine. Michael said in a neutral voice, "She'll be glad you can attend."

Colin made a face. "I dislike such functions, but it's too important to miss."

"I'll see you there, then." Michael finished his own coffee and left the dining room. It was ironic that he wanted to despise Melbourne, yet for Catherine's sake he must hope that her husband was kind, decent, and reliable. Why did life have to be such a damned muddle of grays? Blacks and whites were easier.

Outside, he looked up at the fair morning sky and rubbed his left shoulder. The storm was drawing nearer.

The footman intoned, "Captain and Mrs. Melbourne. Captain and Mrs. Mowbry."

Catherine blinked as they stepped into the ballroom. The scene was dizzying, the light from the brilliant chandeliers reflecting from the richly colored draperies and rose-trellised wallpaper, then spilling through the open windows to the Rue de la Blanchisserie outside. Beside her, Anne murmured, "The air fairly burns with tension."

"By this time, everyone in Brussels has heard of the three different dispatch riders that came galloping into the duke's headquarters this afternoon," Catherine replied. "Obviously something is happening. The question is what, and where?"

The best guess was that Napoleon was invading Belgium. Even now, his army might be marching toward the capital. They would all know the truth soon enough. She glanced at her husband. He was strung as tightly as harp wire, almost quivering with anticipation of the action to come. He was never more alive than when in battle. Perhaps the pursuit and conquest of women was his way of capturing some of the same thrill in mundane life.

After arranging later dances with Colin and Charles, she set herself to enjoying the ball. God only knew if there would ever be another such occasion. Every important diplomat, officer, and aristocrat in Brussels was present, so there was no shortage of partners. Catherine even discovered Wellington's surgeon, Dr. Hume, lurking in a corner. Since he was an old friend from the Peninsula, she coaxed him onto the floor.

Expression martyred, Hume said, "I would do this only for you, Mrs. Melbourne, and only because you're such a fine nurse."

"Liar," she said affectionately. "You're enjoying yourself."

He laughed and agreed just before the figures of the

dance separated them. When they came together again, he said, "Your friend Dr. Kinlock arrived in Brussels today."

"Ian's here? How splendid! But I thought he'd left the army after two years in the Peninsula."

Hume's eyes twinkled. "He went to Bart's Hospital in London, but he can't resist the prospect of a lovely assortment of wounds. Several other surgeons have come over with him."

Catherine had to smile. "I should have guessed. You surgeons are such *ghouls*."

"Aye, but useful ones." Hume's expression became sober. "We'll need every man who can wield a knife soon enough."

It was another reminder of war in a night that was saturated with a sense of impending doom. As the evening advanced, Catherine noticed officers from more distantly placed regiments quietly slipping away. But the man she most wanted to see had not come. Even when she was dancing, she unobtrusively searched the room for Michael. He had planned to attend, but what if he had already left to join his men? She might never see him again.

Lord Haldoran, the sporting gentleman who had decided against the army rather than go to Manchester, came to claim her for a dance. She still found him disquieting, and not only because of the predatory expression she had sometimes seen in his eyes. However, he had made no improper advances and his anecdotes were amusing, so she gave him a polite smile. Fanning her heated face, she said, "It's dreadfully warm in here. Would you mind if we sat this one out?"

"I'd be glad to," Haldoran replied. "The servants are sprinkling water on the flowers to keep them from wilting. It's most unkind of the duchess not to do the same for her guests."

Catherine chuckled as she seated herself on a chair near an open window. "Wellington should be here soon."

"When the French may already be in Belgium?" Haldoran whisked two glasses of champagne from the tray of a passing footman and presented one to Catherine before sitting down beside her. "Surely the duke should be in the field, with his army."

"Not really. By coming here, he shows confidence and allays panic among the civilian population." She took a sip of the chilled, bubbly wine. "Also, with all of the top commanders at the ball, it will be easy for him to confer with them quietly."

"A good point." Haldoran's brows drew together. "The emperor is known for striking with great speed. If he advances on Brussels, are you and Mrs. Mowbry planning to withdraw to Antwerp?"

"My place is here. Besides, the question is moot. The duke will never permit Napoleon to reach the city."

"He may not have a choice," Haldoran said, his expression sober. "You are a brave woman, Mrs. Melbourne, but will you expose your daughter to the hazards of an occupying army?"

"The French are a civilized people," she said coolly. "They do not make war on children."

"No doubt you are right, but I would not like to see harm befall you and Mrs. Mowbry and your families."

"No more would I, Lord Haldoran." Catherine studied the tentlike draperies that fell in great swoops of gold and scarlet and black, and wished Haldoran would stop talking about her own secret fears. Though she didn't believe she was endangering her daughter, the uncertainty was enough to make any mother nervous.

The music ended and Charles Mowbry approached to lead her into the next dance. She rose. "Thank you for indulging my fatigue, Lord Haldoran. Until next time?"

He smiled and took her empty glass. "Until next time."

Charles was not only one of Catherine's dearest friends, but an excellent dancer. Their cotillion was a pleasure. They had just finished when the air was pierced by the skirl of bagpipes. "Good God, those devils in skirts are coming!" Charles exclaimed.

Catherine laughed with delight. "That sound always makes my blood stand up and salute." They turned to see soldiers from two Highland regiments marching into the ballroom, kilts swinging and feathered bonnets nodding to the wild song of the pipes.

In a stroke of entertaining genius, the Duchess of Richmond had engaged the Highlanders to dance. The guests drew back to the sides of the room as the Scots began whirling and stamping through their traditional reels, strathspeys, and one stunning sword dance. The contrast of elegance and primitive splendor was one Catherine would never forget.

Yet even in the eerie magic of the moment, her restless gaze never stopped seeking Michael.

Preparing his regiment to march kept Michael busy through a long day. It was late when he reached the Richmond ball. The room buzzed with excitement. An island of calm, Wellington was sitting on a sofa chatting amiably with one of his lady friends.

Michael stopped a friend, an officer of the Household Guards who was about to leave the ball. "What has happened?"

"The duke says the army will march in the morning," was the terse reply. "I'm on my way to my regiment now. Luck to you."

Time was running out. Perhaps it was self-indulgent to come to the ball, but Michael had wanted to see Catherine one last time. He halted by a flower-twined pillar and scanned the crowd.

She was not hard to find. Because her clothing budget and jewelry were modest, she dressed with relative simplicity, maintaining a stylish appearance by expertly changing the trimming of her few gowns. As a result, no one looked at Catherine Melbourne and remarked on the splendor of her costume or the sumptuousness of her ornaments. What they saw and remembered was her heart-stopping beauty.

Tonight she wore ice-white satin and lustrous pearls that set off her dark glossy hair and flawless complexion to perfection. In a room full of brilliantly colored uniforms, she stood out like an angel on loan from heaven.

Colin stood next to her, a proprietary hand on her elbow. It was obvious from his smug expression that he was aware of how other men envied him for possessing the most beautiful woman in a room full of beautiful women.

Face set, Michael began working his way through the crowded ballroom. After paying his respects to his hostess, he went to Catherine. Colin had moved away, but the Mowbrys had joined her.

Her eyes lit as he approached. "I'm glad you could come, Michael. I thought perhaps you had already been called away."

"I was delayed, but I would never miss such a splendid

occasion." As the music began, he said, "May I have this dance with you, Anne, and the one after with you, Catherine?"

Both women agreed, and Anne gave him her hand. There was strain in her eyes as he led her onto the floor, but years as an army wife had taught her control.

As they took their places for a reel, he said, "You look very fine in that gown, Anne. This isn't too tiring?"

She smiled and shook her auburn curls. "I shall bubble with energy for another six or eight weeks, until I become the size and shape of a carriage."

They kept up an easy stream of talk as the pattern of the dance drew them together and apart. Yet as soon as he returned Anne to Charles, she forgot everything but her husband. Gazes locked, they moved together onto the floor. Michael uttered a silent prayer that Charles would survive the coming campaign; a love as strong and true as theirs deserved to last.

He turned to Catherine and gave her a formal bow. "I believe this is my dance, my lady?"

She smiled and swept a graceful curtsy. "It is, my lord."

He did not realize that he had claimed a waltz until the first bars of music were played. He had deliberately avoided the intimacy of waltzing at previous functions, but tonight it seemed right, for this would likely be their last dance.

She came into his arms as if they had waltzed a thousand times before. Together they flowed into the music, her eyes drifting half shut. She followed his lead as lightly as the angel he had thought her, yet he was intensely aware that she was a woman, a creature of the earth, not the heavens.

Dark tendrils of hair clung damply to her temples as they circled the floor without speaking. The pulse in her slim throat was beating rapidly from exertion. He wanted to press his lips to it. The delicate curve of ear showing below her upswept hair was an invitation to dalliance, and the tantalizing swells of her breasts would haunt his dreams for as long as he lived.

More than anything on earth, he wanted to sweep her into his arms and take her to the fairyland beyond the rainbow where they could be alone, and there would be no tormenting issues of war and honor. Instead, he had a bare handful of moments that were spilling away like cascading grains of sand.

Too soon, the music came to an end. As he let her go, her long lashes swept upward. Her expression was stark. "Is it time for you to go?" she said huskily.

"I'm afraid so." He looked away, fearing that his yearning must be showing. Across the room, Wellington caught his eye and gave a faint nod. Michael continued, "The duke wants to speak with me. By the time you return home, I will probably be gone."

She caught her breath. "Please—be careful."

"Don't worry—I'm cautious to a fault."

She tried to smile. "Who knows? This may all be a false alarm and everyone will be back in our billet by next week."

"Perhaps." He hesitated before adding, "But if my luck runs out, I have a favor to ask. In the top drawer of the dresser in my room, I've left letters to several of my closest friends. If I don't make it through the campaign, please post them for me."

She bit her lip. Tears were sparkling in her aqua eyes, making them seem even larger. "If . . . if the worst happens, do you want me to write to your family?"

"They will learn all they need to know from the casualty lists." He lifted her hand and kissed her gloved fingertips. "Good-bye, Catherine. God bless and keep you and your family."

"Vaya con Dios." Her fingers tightened convulsively. Then she released his hand a fraction of an inch at a time.

Wrenching his gaze from hers, he turned and crossed the ballroom. It was warming to know that she cared for him. The pleasure of that was not diminished by the knowledge that she also cared for Charles and Kenneth and other men. It was her capacity for caring that made her so special.

Wellington had abandoned his sofa to talk to his officers one at a time. To Michael, he said tersely, "Napoleon has humbugged me, by God. The French have captured Charleroi."

Jarred out of his reverie, Michael exclaimed, "Damnation! Charleroi isn't much more than thirty miles away."

"It could have been worse," the duke said with a wintry smile. "The road from Charleroi to Brussels was virtually undefended. If it hadn't been for damned good luck and a first-rate show put on by Prince Bernhard and his troops at Quatre-Bras, Marshal Ney could have marched straight into the city."

As Michael swore under his breath, Wellington said, "Tell me, Kenyon, will those green troops of yours stand?"

A fortnight before, Michael would not have known how to answer. Now he could say, "They may not be the fastest shots or the best at maneuvering, but put them in a line or square with veterans nearby and they will stand."

"I hope to God you're right. We're going to need every soldier we've got." The duke rapped out several orders, then turned his gimlet gaze on the crowd to collect another officer.

Before Michael left, his gaze sought out Catherine one last time. It was easy to find her with the ranks of guests thinning so rapidly. She was on the far side of the room with her husband, who was speaking excitedly. The Mowbrys joined them and both couples turned to leave.

His breath coming with great effort, Michael went out into the warm night. She was not for him, he reminded himself bleakly. *She would never be for him.*

Michael glanced across his horse's back. "Bradley, did you pack my greatcoat? It was in the back hallway."

The batman flushed. "No, sir. I'll go get it."

Michael bit off an oath. Though the boy wasn't as well organized as an officer's servant should be, he tried hard. "Be quick about it. We need to be off."

As Bradley left the stable, Colin Melbourne entered. Michael said, "Are you and Charles heading out to your regiment now?"

Melbourne nodded, his eyes shining. "You heard that Boney is at Charleroi? By God, we'll see some excitement now!"

"I don't doubt it." Michael was about to lead his horse out when he saw that Melbourne was saddling a nondescript cavalry hack rather than Caesar, his usual mount. Casually he said, "You're going to lead Caesar to keep him fresh?"

"No, I'm leaving him here. I'll ride Uno and keep Duo for reserve." Melbourne indicated a bay gelding as unimpressive as the one he was saddling.

Michael stared at him. "You're not riding your best horse into battle?"

"I don't want to risk him," Melbourne replied. "Besides the fact that I'm devilishly fond of the beast, if he were to be killed, the amount paid by the government compensation fund wouldn't begin to cover his value."

"For God's sake, man, it's folly to try to save a few pounds at the risk of your life!" Michael exclaimed. "In battle, a horse's stamina can be the difference between surviving and being speared like a rabbit."

"It may seem like only a few pounds to you," the other man said tartly. "Not all of us have your financial resources."

Michael bit back an oath. Melbourne was acting like an idiot and deserved whatever he would get. Yet for Catherine's sake, Michael must try to prevent the other man's folly. "If money is the issue, take Thor." He stroked the chestnut's sleek neck. "His stamina is outstanding, and I've given him cavalry training so he'll be able to do whatever is needed."

Melbourne's jaw dropped. "I can't possibly take your horse. You'll need him yourself." He gazed at Thor longingly. "If he were killed, I'd never be able to replace him."

"A horse isn't as critical in the infantry as the cavalry. My other mount will do well enough. I hope Thor comes through safely, but if not, I'll settle for whatever you receive in compensation." Michael unbuckled his saddle. "If all goes well, you can return him to me in Paris. If I don't come through, he's yours."

"You make it impossible to refuse." Melbourne smiled boyishly. "You're a good fellow, Kenyon."

As Michael transferred his gear to his second horse, Bryn, he wondered if Melbourne would be so cheerful if he knew how Michael felt about Catherine. Probably he wouldn't care, since his wife's fidelity was beyond question.

Michael collected his servants and rode into the night. For honor's sake, he had done what he could to help Catherine's husband survive. All else was in God's hands.

Chapter 10

Catherine packed her husband's personal belongings while Colin readied his horses. All too soon, she, her husband, and the Mowbrys were in the stable yard. Two torches illuminated ten saddled horses, two servants for each of the officers, and Catherine's groom, Everett, who had come down to help.

Charles had just come from kissing his sleepy children good-bye and his expression was strained. Anne went straight into his arms. They held each other tightly, neither of them speaking. Catherine envied her friends their closeness even as she grieved for their distress. It would be worth the pain to have such love.

Turning to her husband, Catherine said, "Are you sure you don't want to see Amy?"

"No need to disturb her." Colin had the bright, impervious expression that meant he was thinking about the action that lay ahead. "It won't be long until you'll both be joining me."

She blinked back the tears that threatened, knowing that Colin would hate it if she became weepy. Yet it was impossible to live with a man for a dozen years and not care about him. In an ideal world, perhaps it would have been Michael she had met and married, leaving Colin free to chase foxes, women, and the French without the responsibilities of a family. But that hadn't happened. In the real world, she and Colin had wed, and in spite of being grievously mismatched, they each in their own way had honored their marriage. She whispered, "Take care, Colin."

He gave a jaunty smile. "Don't look so worried. You know I share Wellington's magical immunity to bullets." He chucked her under the chin as if she were Amy's age. Then he swung onto his horse. "I'll see you in Paris, sooner if it's safe."

Then he and Charles and their entourage clattered out into the cobbled street. Catherine gazed after her husband. Sadly, she recognized that if he had loved her even a little bit, she would have loved him in spite of his women. Oh, he was rather fond of her. He enjoyed his comfortable home and took great satisfaction in the fact that other men envied him his wife. But she would lay long odds that he cared more deeply for his horse.

His horse. She blinked, only now registering what she had seen. Turning to her groom, she asked, "Was Captain Melbourne riding Colonel Kenyon's horse?"

"Aye," Everett replied. "The captain didn't want to risk Caesar, so the colonel said he could take Thor instead."

Oh, Lord, how typical of Colin to assume that his luck would carry him safely through a battle even on a mediocre mount. And it was equally typical of Michael to look out for another person.

Numbly she turned to Anne and they went into the house, going straight to the liquor cabinet in the dining room. Anne poured each of them a measure of brandy. After downing half of her drink, she said vehemently, "Why the devil didn't some sensible person assassinate Bonaparte? One bullet would have saved the world so much grief."

Catherine gave a humorless smile. "Men tend to think such things are dishonorable."

"Fools." Anne bent her head and rubbed her temples. "Saying good-bye doesn't get any easier with practice."

"I didn't get to say good-bye to Kenneth at all." Catherine sighed. "Did I mention that two days ago, I asked him to do some sketches of everyone in the household? I should have asked sooner. He was willing, but there wasn't enough time."

Anne raised her head. "Are you sure? There are a couple of portfolios on the table over there. I noticed them earlier, but I was too distracted to take a look."

They went to investigate. The top portfolio contained a note from Kenneth to Catherine. He apologized for the fact that he had not had the chance to give the drawings to her in person, and said that the other portfolio was for Anne.

Catherine gave the second folder to her friend, then paged through her own. The drawings were wonderful, particularly the ones of the children. A sketch of Amy swinging joyfully from a branch in the back garden caught her daughter's intrepid spirit perfectly. A laughing Colin was being nuzzled by his horse, Caesar. He looked confident and dashing and very handsome.

The drawing of Michael made her heart ache. In a handful of lines, Kenneth had caught the qualities of strength and humor, honor and intelligence, that stirred her so deeply.

Though Kenneth had included the self-portrait she had requested, it was the weakest drawing of the lot. The features were recognizable, but the overall effect was harsh and rather intimidating, revealing none of his imagination or dry wit. It must be hard to see oneself clearly.

Voice quavering, Anne said, "Look at this."

The drawing she held up showed her family in the garden. Jamie was gleefully astride his father's back as Charles played the part of cavalry horse. Molly sat by her mother, looking immensely superior from the pinnacle of her advanced years, while at the same time secretly feeding a cake to Clancy. Catherine laughed. "Bless Kenneth. To think he remembered to put these together for us when so much else was happening."

Anne studied a picture of Charles in his uniform, his plumed helmet tucked under his arm. He wore the grave expression of a man who had experienced war without being coarsened by it. "A century from now, future Mowbrys will look at this and know what kind of man their great-great-grandfather was."

"They'll be proud to be his descendants."

Anne drew the back of her hand across her eyes. "I won't cry again," she said fiercely. "I *won't.*"

There was a long silence, broken only by the harsh rhythm of distant drums. Hearing that, Catherine suggested, "Neither of us will sleep a wink. Let's go to the city center and watch the mustering of the troops."

Anne agreed and they went to change from their ball gowns to simpler garments. As Catherine prepared to join Anne, Amy poked her head from the door of her room. "Has Papa gone?"

Wishing Colin had taken the time to wake his daughter, Catherine said, "Yes. He didn't want to disturb you."

"I wouldn't have minded," Amy said with a scowl. "Are you and Aunt Anne going out to watch what's happening?"

When Catherine nodded, Amy pleaded, "Please, can I go with you? It's horrid to be alone and unable to sleep."

Catherine could sympathize with that. "Very well. Put on a warm dress and come with us."

It was only a week until the summer solstice, and the sky was already lightening in the east as the three walked along the Rue de Namur. The drums were louder now. Their thunder was overlaid by strident trumpets calling assembly. Allied soldiers were billeted all over Brussels, and the streets boiled with activity as men responded to the summons, buttoning their jackets and dragging on their packs as they stumbled from the houses.

A British infantry regiment swung past them, marching toward the Namur Gate to the harsh rumma-dum-dum of the drums. The hammering rhythm entered the blood, as exciting as it was alarming. Catherine studied the tramping soldiers, wondering if the regiment might be Michael's. It was too dark to identify the uniform markings, and she could not see his erect form among the officers who rode alongside their troops. No matter; even if it was his regiment, they had already said their good-byes. To do so again, in front of Anne and Amy, would be excruciating.

The Place Royale was sheer chaos. Soldiers from half a dozen nations searched for their companies, sometimes with weeping women beside them. A few veteran campaigners slept with heads on their packs, oblivious to the racket of horses, cannons, and wagons clattering across the stones.

Amy's hand crept into Catherine's. "Boney doesn't have a chance, does he?"

"Not against Wellington. The duke has never lost a battle in his life," Catherine said, trying to sound confident.

They made their way from the Place Royale to the nearby park. It was about four o'clock, and the summer sun was edging above the horizon. Oblique rays of light caught the spires of the Cathedrale St. Michel. Catherine smiled wryly at the sight. Reminders of Michael were everywhere.

In the park, the fierce, blunt Welsh General Picton was mustering his division. Anne said, "The Rifle Brigade is with Picton, isn't it? Perhaps we can find Kenneth."

They scanned the seething mass of green-jacketed Riflemen, looking for officers. Amy's sharp eyes found him. "Look!" she said excitedly. "Captain Wilding is over there."

He was on horseback, snapping orders to his junior officers, but he turned when Catherine called his name. She went to him and reached up to clasp his hand. "I'm so glad we found you, Kenneth. It didn't seem right not to wish you Godspeed."

He gave the rare smile that turned his craggy face handsome. "You're very kind, Catherine."

"You've become family. If you're wounded, be sure they bring you home, so we can take care of you properly."

His face tightened. Not wanting to embarrass him further, she added, "Thank you for the drawings. They're splendid."

"I will keep mine forever," Anne said vehemently.

"I'll rest easier for knowing I have achieved immortality of a sort," he said with a faint smile. "But what makes a picture interesting is the subject, so it is you and your families who deserve the credit."

"Come back soon," Amy added. "Molly and I haven't gotten the trick of drawing perspective yet. We need more lessons."

"I'll do my best, but now I must go. Take care." He touched his forehead in a salute and turned back to his company.

Catherine and the others withdrew to one side and watched as order emerged from what had seemed hopeless confusion. Soon Picton's troops were striding away, the heavy tramp of boots reverberating through the park.

The division included the Highland regiments that had entertained the Duchess of Richmond's guests. The soldiers marched so smoothly that the plumes on their bonnets scarcely stirred. The bagpipes that had seemed exotic in the ballroom had a fierce rightness as they sang the kilt-clad Scots to war.

Following in the division's wake, the three women retraced their steps to the Rue de la Reine, picking their way around mounds of equipment and lines of heavily laden baggage animals. As the city emptied of troops, the citizens of Brussels returned to their beds. By the time they reached home, fatigue had drained away Catherine's nervous energy. Perhaps now, she thought wearily, they would all be able to rest.

But sleep eluded her. She rose heavy-eyed in midmorning. In Spain, she had usually been close enough to the action to have some idea what was happening. Here there was no news, and it made the day one of the longest of her life.

Sensing the tension, the children were quarrelsome. The servants gathered in knots to talk in hushed whispers, and one of the Belgian maids asked for her wages so she could return to her family in a village north of the city.

As Catherine and Anne ate a late luncheon, the distant rumble of cannons rolled ominously across the countryside. Battle had been joined. They stared at each other, not daring to speak, before silently returning to their bowls of soup.

When they could bear the inactivity no longer, they went up onto the city ramparts, taking all three children and Anne's pretty young Scottish nursemaid. Hundreds of others were gathered on the walls, staring to the south. Rumors were flying, but of solid news there was none.

At ten o'clock that night, a sharp rap on the door brought Catherine and Anne at a run. Anne swung the door open and found her husband's dust-covered batman, Will Ferris, standing on the steps. She went white. "Oh, my God! Is Charles—"

"No, ma'am!" he said swiftly. "Just the opposite. The master sent me to say that he and Captain Melbourne are fine."

As Catherine ushered Ferris toward the kitchen, he continued, "There's been a nasty fight against Marshal Ney at Quatre-Bras, but the cavalry didn't arrive until the very end, so we were hardly touched. They say the duke was almost captured by a party of French lancers. Had to leap a ditch full of Gordon Highlanders to save himself." Ferris shook his head. "The Highland regiments were cut to pieces, poor devils."

Catherine laid out cold meats and ale, thinking sorrowfully of the gay young Scots who had danced the night before. How many still lived? "What was the outcome of the battle?"

Ferris shrugged cynically. "I don't know if either side

won, but at least we didn't lose. They say Napoleon himself went after the Prussian army. Blücher had more men, so if he and his lads did well, the French may be retreating by now."

"I hope you're right," Anne said fervently. "What about the Rifle Brigade? And Colonel Kenyon's regiment?"

"The Rifles were in the thick of it, but Captain Wilding came to no harm." Ferris paused for a swig of ale. "Nor did the 105th—they were held in reserve and never got into the fight."

Probably that was because of the regiment's inexperience. Catherine hoped the 105th would continue to be used as reserves rather than frontline troops. Perhaps Michael and his men would find that disappointing, but she would not.

After eating, the batman excused himself to visit Elspeth McLeod, Anne's young Scottish nursemaid. The two were courting. He spent half an hour with his sweetheart, then saddled up again for the long ride back to the army.

Catherine's spirits were heavy when she went to bed. It would be wonderful to believe that the French had been broken, but in her heart, she knew the worst was still to come.

The proof of the previous day's battle came the next morning, when Molly looked out an upper window and called excitedly, "Mama, there are wounded soldiers in the street!"

Her cry brought most of the household running. From the vantage point of the upper window, they could see into the Rue de Namur. Injured men who had walked through the night were beginning to stumble into the city through the Namur Gate.

White-lipped, Catherine said, "I'll get my medical kit."

"They'll want water." Anne looked down at her children, who were pressed against her skirts. "Molly, it was very clever of you to see the soldiers. Jamie, may I borrow your wagon so I can take out buckets of water?" He nodded gravely.

Elspeth said, "I'll come, too, ma'am. I have six brothers, so I know something of fixing injuries." The other servants also volunteered to do what they could.

Anne ordered her children to stay in the house with the

cook. Older and more determined, Amy did not bother to ask if she could help; she simply accompanied Anne with the little water wagon. Catherine considered telling her to go home, but decided against it. Her daughter was no stranger to painful sights.

By the time their party reached the Rue de Namur, the street had turned into an impromptu hospital. Besides the walking wounded, wagonloads of injured men were rumbling through the gate. Citizens of Brussels and foreigners poured from their homes to work side by side to alleviate the suffering in any way they could. Some helped wounded men to their billets while others provided blankets, straw, and parasols to shield men from the hot sun. Catherine saw a nun and a girl who looked like a streetwalker aiding a Belgian boy who had collapsed against the railings of a house. The pharmacies freely gave away supplies.

Catherine's Peninsular experience stood her in good stead as she cleaned and dressed less serious wounds. After the horrible suspense of the previous day, it was a relief to be able to do something. Since Amy was a reliable dispenser of water, Anne fetched a notebook and took last message and mementos from dying men who wanted word sent to their families.

Catherine was picking fragments of fabric and gold lace from a gory, mangled arm when a familiar Scottish voice said, "Trust you to be in the middle of this, lassie."

She looked up to see the prematurely white hair and blood-stained shirt of her surgeon friend, Ian Kinlock. "And trust you to come all the way from London for the chance to see more carnage," she said unsteadily. "Thank heaven you're here, Ian. This sergeant needs more than I can do."

Kinlock knelt beside her and examined the wound. "You're in luck, Sergeant. There are two balls in your arm, but no bones are broken, so amputation isn't necessary. Catherinc, hold him while I take the balls out." He pulled instruments from his bag.

Catherine braced the injured right arm. The sergeant gave one anguished gasp and sweat covered his face, but he scarcely moved during the long minutes it took to locate and extract the balls. When the probing was over, Catherine sponged the sergeant's face with cool water while Ian bandaged the wound.

"It's grateful I am to you both," the sergeant said with a rich Irish brogue. He pushed himself to a sitting position with his good arm. "If you'll help me up, sir, I'll be on my way."

"You'll do, Sergeant," Ian said as he complied with the request. "Are you going to the hospital tent over by the gate?"

The Irishman shook his head. "I've a billet where they'll take care of me. Don't understand a word they say, but they treat me like a prince." Before the sergeant had taken ten steps, an elderly priest came to help him to his destination.

Noticing that it had darkened, Catherine glanced up to see heavy clouds covering the sky. The wind was rising and lightning flickered on the horizon. "Lord, a thunderstorm is coming. That's all we need."

"And coming fast. A good thing the hospital tents are up." Ian repacked his instruments. "That will give these poor fellows some shelter."

Catherine looked around and found that the street was almost empty. The first wave of wounded had been tended or moved under cover. Anne had left half an hour earlier, gray with fatigue.

The lightning crackled much closer, illuminating the street with garish brilliance. As Catherine stared numbly at the fat raindrops splashing onto her stained skirt, the surgeon asked, "How long have you been working out here?"

"I don't know." She wiped water from her brow. "Hours."

"Go home," he ordered. "You can come to the hospital tent when you've had some rest."

"Will you be working there?"

"Aye." He smiled wryly. "Sleeping there, too, I expect."

"Stay with Anne and me." Catherine pointed out her house. "We have ample space, and you'll rest better than in the tent."

"I'll take you up on that, most gratefully."

Lightning blazed across the sky, followed immediately by a deafening roll of thunder. As the rain intensified to a torrent, Catherine grabbed her medical kit and went to collect Amy.

Her daughter loved storms, and now she was staring raptly at the sky. "Wellington weather, Mama," she said, raising her voice above the thunder. "There's going to be a battle."

"Very likely." Catherine took Amy's hand. "But now let's go inside before we drown!"

Catherine took Amy to the nursery. Then she changed to dry clothing and came down to the hot tea and sandwiches Anne had ordered. They were just finishing when a knock sounded at the front door. A minute later, the parlor maid brought Lord Haldoran into the morning room. Water cascaded from his greatcoat, and his fashionable detachment had been replaced by urgency.

"Mrs. Melbourne, Mrs. Mowbry." He made a quick bow. "Have you heard the latest news?"

"I'm not sure," Anne replied. "Please tell us."

"Yesterday the Prussians were badly mauled at Ligny. They had to retreat almost twenty miles, so Wellington is falling back also to maintain his lines of communication. I understand he's setting up his headquarters at a village called Waterloo."

"Dear God," Anne whispered, her face white. "That's only ten or twelve miles from here."

"Napoleon is on Brussels' doorstep," Haldoran said bluntly. "It's anybody's guess whether Wellington will be able to stop him with his ragtag assortment of troops. Every foreigner who can leave the city is going or gone."

Catherine set down her teacup carefully. "I would put my money on the duke, but this is not good news."

"I didn't come only to frighten you," Haldoran said more moderately. "Last week I took the precaution of hiring a barge to take me to Antwerp if the fighting went badly. There's room for you and your children and a servant each. But if you wish to come, we must leave right away."

Catherine gave him a startled look. It was a remarkably generous offer. Perhaps she had misjudged him.

"I . . . I can't abandon my husband." Anne unconsciously pressed her hand to her swelling abdomen. "What if Charles is wounded and he is brought home?"

"If matters go well, you can return in a few days." Haldoran's gaze went from Anne to Catherine. "But if they don't, would your husbands want you to risk the lives of your children?"

Catherine bit her lip. She was willing to take her chances,

but dare she do that with her daughter? "There is a solution." When the other two looked at her, she said, "I have more nursing experience and Anne has more children, so I'll stay here and keep the house open while Anne takes the three children to Antwerp."

Anne exhaled with relief. "If you're willing, that would be perfect. Though I hate leaving, we'd be fools to pass up a chance to take the children to safety when the French are so close. Lord Haldoran, it will take half an hour to get everyone ready. Is that acceptable?"

Catherine saw a flash of sharp irritation in Haldoran's eyes, and realized that his offer had been less generous than it appeared on the surface. It was her that he wanted, probably with the hope that the distraught officer's wife might be in need of comfort. No matter; his help was welcome, and he was too much of a gentleman to withdraw it merely because Catherine wasn't coming.

Quickly concealing his irritation, he said, "Half an hour will be fine, though I wish you were coming also, Mrs. Melbourne. Brussels might be dangerous." He got to his feet. "I'll write down the address of my bankers in Antwerp. You can reach me through them if necessary."

"Thank you. It's very good of you to go to such lengths for people you've only known for a few weeks," she said with a hint of dryness.

"It would be criminal to waste the space on the barge," he said piously. "With both of your husbands risking their lives for their country, it seems right to extend my protection to you."

The next half hour passed in a flurry. When told she was going to Antwerp, Amy begged, "Please, Mama, let me stay. You've said often what a help I am."

"You are, my love. But I will not be able to stop myself from worrying about what might happen to you." Catherine smiled ruefully. "I can't help it, I'm a mother. When you have children of your own, you will understand."

Amy capitulated, with the stipulation that she be allowed to return as soon as it was safe.

The pretty young nursemaid Elspeth McLeod also asked to stay. Knowing the girl wanted to be near Will Ferris, Anne agreed, taking Catherine's maid to help with the children.

Exactly half an hour after Haldoran's offer, the travelers

assembled in the front hall. Catherine hugged Amy fiercely, then turned to embrace Anne.

Her friend said in a choked voice, "If the fortunes of war separate us, you know the address of Charles's mother in London. And if . . . if anything happens to you and Colin, I will raise Amy as if she were my own."

"I know." Catherine swallowed hard. "And if necessary, I will nurse Charles as you would."

Anne took a deep breath, then said calmly, "Time to go, everyone."

Catherine watched out the window as the party hastened through the rain to the carriages. She was glad to see that Haldoran had several large, dangerous-looking male servants to protect the party.

She watched until the carriages disappeared from sight. Then she turned from the window, tears trickling down her cheeks. She had never been separated from Amy before. "Damn Napoleon," she whispered. *"God damn him to hell."*

Chapter 11

One of the first military lessons Michael had learned was that an officer must always appear composed under fire. That was particularly true when hours of lethal French cannonading had already killed or wounded a quarter of his regiment, and more than half of the officers. The pummeling din and the clouds of black smoke were enough to unnerve even experienced soldiers.

The regiment was formed into a hollow square for defense. Ranks of armed soldiers faced in all four directions while officers, supplies, and the wounded sheltered in the center of the formation. Less seriously injured men retired from the field, while the dead were ruthlessly thrown from the square to make room for the living. Michael strolled around inside the formation, talking to his men, offering what comfort he could to the wounded, and sharing an occasional wry joke.

Trying not to inhale the acrid, stinging smoke too deeply, Michael walked to the center of the square where the two regimental flags, called the colors, were standing. By tradition, they were carried by the most junior officers in the regiment and guarded by experienced sergeants. The youngest ensign, Thomas Hussey, was only sixteen, so Michael kept a close eye on him.

As he approached, a cannonball struck soggily near the colors. Luckily no one was hit. The ball rolled slowly across the soft ground. Tom Hussey handed his flag, the Union Jack, to one of the color sergeants. "Since the French have provided us with the means," he called gaily, "shall we have a game of football?"

He ran toward the ball with the obvious intention of kicking it. Michael barked, "Don't touch that! A cannonball might look harmless, but it could take your foot off. I've seen it happen."

The ensign skidded to a halt. "Thank you, sir." Face a little pale, he returned to his flag. Michael gave a faint, approving nod. Though green, the boy had the cheerful courage that would make him a good officer, if he survived.

Michael raised his spyglass to see what little he could of the battle. His view consisted mostly of shoulder-high fields of rye. Earlier in the day, there had been a French infantry assault to the left. The rye and the foglike smoke obscured everything more than a few hundred feet away, so Michael had tracked the attack by the sounds of muskets, shouts, and marching music. The French had been beaten back, but he knew nothing beyond that.

Another cannonball struck several men in the rear of the square. Captain Graham, the highest ranking uninjured officer after Michael, went to survey the damage. Expression grave, Tom Hussey said, "May I ask a question, Colonel Kenyon?"

"Go ahead."

"What is the point of standing here and being cut to pieces? There is no fighting in this section of the lines. Surely we could withdraw to a safe distance until needed."

"We *are* needed—to do exactly what we are doing," Michael said soberly. "If we weren't here, Napoleon's men would drive right through and the battle would be lost. The cavalry may race back and forth across a battlefield, but it is the infantry that takes possession." He kicked the soft earth. "As long as one member of the 105th lives, this is British soil. The death of our fellows is tragic, but it isn't meaningless."

The ensign nodded slowly. "I see, sir."

Though his explanation was true, this long and bloody day was a vivid reminder of why Michael preferred the swift, fluid combat of the Rifle Brigade. It felt better to be a moving target than a stationary one. He wondered how Kenneth and the 95th were faring. They were probably spending the day skirmishing with the French between the lines. He envied them.

He began ambling around the square again. He was talking with a lieutenant when he realized that he could hear his own voice. The ceaseless thunder of artillery had made speech and thought almost impossible. Now the cannon had stopped shelling their section of the lines. Knowing what that meant, Michael called, "Prepare for attack! They've stopped the artillery so they won't hit their own men."

Numbed soldiers came sharply alert. Sergeants barked at their men, firming the lines with curses and exhortations to check the loading of muskets. The air quivered with tension, for this could be the regiment's first taste of face-to-face combat.

At first the straining eyes of the regiment saw only ghostly shapes moving forward through the veils of smoke. Then a line of horsemen emerged, the misty figures gradually taking the shape of French cuirassiers. Their gleaming steel helmets and breastplates made them seem eerily like medieval knights. Large men on large horses, they were the heavy cavalry, designed to crush all opposition, and they were heading directly at the 105th and the two neighboring squares.

The massive hooves of the horses flattened the stalks of grain into the muddy ground as the cuirassiers moved inexorably up the slope. Seeing the front line of the square waver, Michael moved swiftly forward from his position in the center of the square. "Stand firm!" he shouted. "Horses won't charge directly at a square, and we have more guns than they do. Hold your fire until I give the word. Then aim for the horses!"

The oncoming riders were within forty paces when Michael ordered, "Ready. Level. *Fire!*"

His front rank discharged their muskets in a deafening blast. There was a shriek of wounded horses and a weird, metallic rattle like hailstones as balls ricocheted from the steel breastplates. Half a dozen horses and their riders fell, forcing those behind to swerve to the sides.

As his first rank reloaded, Michael gave the order for the second rank to fire. The ragged salvo brought more attackers down. In spite of the furious efforts of the riders, the horses sheered away, flowing around the square, which brought them under fire from the muskets on the flanks.

The cavalrymen churned chaotically around the square, firing their pistols and being fired on in return. Finally seeing the futility of the maneuver, their commander ordered a retreat.

The horses were cantering down the slope when a fallen rider called desperately for help. One of his comrades wheeled and came back. As he caught his friend's hand to pull him onto his mount, two British soldiers raised their muskets and took aim.

"No!" Michael barked. "Don't kill a brave man for helping his friend!"

After a startled moment, the men nodded and lowered their weapons. Courage deserved respect even in the enemy.

During the lull that followed, Michael scanned the field with his spyglass. He could see little beyond the neighboring squares, but it sounded as if the French cavalry was attacking along a wide section of the allied lines.

A shout warned that the cuirassiers were returning. Michael said wryly, "Enjoy the cavalry charges, gentlemen. They're a lot less dangerous than the cannonade."

Laughter rippled around the square. This time the firing was steadier. A barrier of dead or wounded horses began to build around the square, making it harder for the riders to approach.

Michael was moving toward the left side of the square, which was under the heaviest fire, when a ball struck him in the left arm. The impact spun him around and knocked him to the ground.

Captain Graham rushed over to him. "Are you hurt, sir?"

Dazedly Michael pushed himself to a sitting position. A wave of pain almost caused him to black out. When he saw the alarmed expressions around him, he forced himself to his feet. "It's not serious," he said tightly. "Get someone over here to bandage it."

The regimental surgeon had been killed and his assistants seriously wounded, so a corporal who had been a barber was doing what he could for injuries. After tightly binding the wound and fashioning a sling, the corporal offered a canteen. "Have a drink of this, sir, but slowly."

Heeding the warning, Michael took a swallow from the canteen. It contained straight gin. His eyes watered, but the spirits certainly distracted him from the pain in his arm. "Thanks, Symms. Generous of you to share your medicine."

Symms grimaced as he closed the canteen. "Need to keep you fit, sir, 'cause we're running short of officers."

The cavalry withdrew while Michael was being tended. Though the 105th had stood fast, injuries were thinning the ranks. Michael gave the order for the square to close up, and prepared for the next attack.

Catherine went early to work in the hospital tent. In midafternoon, she took a short break, carrying a glass of water to Ian Kinlock's operating table. A canvas wall separated it from the pallets of the wounded men. He was also taking a break, so she handed him the water, saying, "Perhaps the armies haven't engaged yet, Ian. There's no sound of firing today."

He swallowed deeply, then shook his head. "Wind's from the wrong direction. Anything could be happening, and probably is."

They both fell silent. Nearby, a church bell rang. Catherine said soberly, "I'd forgotten that today is Sunday. A bad day for a battle."

"They're all bad days." He wiped the sweat from his face, then said to the orderlies, "Bring the next one."

Catherine returned to work, giving water and changing dressings. But though she had a smile and a soft word for everyone, part of her heart was with the men who were fighting, and perhaps dying, only a few miles away.

The cavalry attacks swirled in again and again, like waves breaking against the rocks. Michael had lost track of the number. Ten? Twelve? But the regiment had gained confidence. As the third assault had lumbered up the hill, he'd heard a North Country voice drawl, "Here come those damned fools again."

The current attack was the worst. The cuirassiers had been circling for most of an hour, firing their pistols, brandishing their sabers, and doing their best to break the allied squares. They failed. Not only were they outgunned, but their horses continued to shy away from the British bayonets and muskets.

The 105th stood as firmly as if they were rooted to the soil. Wellington had taken heed of Michael's words the night of the ball and positioned the regiment between veterans. To the left was the British 73rd Infantry, to the right Hanoverians of the King's German Legion, who had fought with honor in the Peninsula. Michael's men had a fierce determination to prove themselves equals to their neighbors, and they were succeeding.

A ragged shout went up behind Michael. Hearing disaster in the cry, he whirled and saw a dying horse crash into one edge of the square. The beast screamed and fell thrashing, knocking down a swath of British soldiers and tearing a hole in the line.

Seeing their chance, other cuirassiers drove their horses toward the gap. Michael swore furiously, for the freak accident was virtually the only way that cavalry could break a square. Already the line was crumbling as panicky soldiers scrambled away from the massive charging horses.

He dashed forward to rally his men. When a terrified youth with a powder-blackened face tried to bolt past him, Michael struck him with the flat of his sword. "Stand and fight like a man, goddammit! Running is the quickest way to die!"

The terror in the boy's eyes abated and he turned back, raising his musket with trembling hands. The other surviving officers and several sergeants also moved in to prevent the square from collapsing. A vicious struggle began as the British tried to force back the French cavalrymen.

For Michael, time slowed, turning the hand-to-hand combat into an unearthly dance. The leisurely tempo meant he could see and exploit every enemy error. A damned nuisance that his left arm was unusable, but the lack did not seriously impede him. A cuirassier slashed at him wildly with his saber. Michael easily turned the stroke aside with his sword. In the same fluid, rising motion, he buried his blade in the precise center of the Frenchman's throat.

Without pause he wrenched his sword away and dodged a horse that was about to run him down. He dropped beneath the level of the rider's blade and severed the horse's right front tendon, crippling it. The rider was hurled to the ground and bayoneted by a burly Irish soldier.

A bellowing cuirassier drove straight for the company colors, determined to seize one. The six-foot flags were a regiment's heart and spirit, and losing one in battle would be an irreparable source of shame.

Seeing the danger, Tom Hussey and his two color sergeants rushed the Union Jack to safety. The guardians of the blue regimental flag were less fortunate. One sergeant was already down. The other raised the pike that was his badge of office. He was struck by a shot from the cuirassier's pistol before he could use the pike, leaving the ensign and his banner undefended.

The ensign, Gray, tried to protect the standard, but the Frenchman rode him down and seized the staff of the flag in one hand. With a hoarse shout of triumph, he spurred his mount to escape the square.

Blood rage swept through Michael at the sight. He dropped his sword and threw himself at the charging horse. His left arm was useless, but he managed to grab the staff with his right hand. The sharp yank almost dragged his arm from its socket. He hung on grimly, his weight slowing the cuirassier.

Seeing that Michael was utterly defenseless, the Frenchman jerked his saber up, slicing his assailant's ribs. He was preparing to deliver a lethal blow when the wounded color sergeant lurched to his feet and drove his pike through the armhole of the breastplate, spitting the Frenchman. Michael dizzily clung to the staff as the rider's body fell past him.

Chest heaving, he scanned the square and saw that the 105th's savage defense had closed the gap. Two cuirassiers were trapped inside. Neither survived to return to his own lines.

The wounded sergeant and bruised ensign reclaimed the color, leaving Michael to endure the bandaging of his ribs. Though he had not felt pain during the white heat of action, it exploded with full force when the danger had past.

His wounds were serious enough that no one would blame him if he retired from the field, but he daren't leave. No other officer had a fraction of his experience. Graham, next in line for command, was brave, but he had come from a county militia regiment and seen no fighting before today. If Michael did not stay, God only knew what would happen during the next crisis.

Though gin was no substitute for blood, a few mouthfuls did dull the pain.

A cockney voice yelled, "Blimey! Here comes Old Hookey!"

A cheer went up. Michael returned the gin canteen and turned to see Wellington and an aide racing toward his square, pursued by a dozen French lancers. The square opened to admit the duke and his companion, then closed again. A volley of musket balls drove off the lancers.

Wellington was famous for always being where the fighting was fiercest. Unperturbed by the nearness of his escape, he pulled up his horse. "Good show here, Kenyon."

Michael forced himself to stand straight. "The regiment has done itself proud, sir. How goes the battle?"

The duke shook his head. "We're taking a pounding. Blücher swore he'd come, but the rain turned the roads to mud, so God knows when we'll see him. If the Prussians don't get here soon . . ." His voice broke off. "I must be on my way. Stand steady, Kenyon."

As Wellington prepared to leave, a soldier yelled, "When can we go at the frogs, sir?"

The duke smiled faintly. "Don't worry, lads, you'll have your chance at them." Then he cantered out of the square toward the beleaguered Chateau de Hougoumont, where the Guards had been fighting the French all day in a vicious battle-within-a-battle.

It was early evening, Michael supposed, but time had lost all meaning. Hard to believe that two days before, he had been waltzing with Catherine in a room full of light and elegance.

As he waited for the next attack, he tried to remember what it was like to have her in his arms. But detail was impossible to recall. The only thing he could conjure up was the warmth in her aqua eyes, and the bittersweet joy of holding her close.

The menacing beat of French drums began the signal for an infantry attack. Michael's lips thinned. He raised his spyglass, balancing it awkwardly with his good hand. Through the heavy smoke, he saw a vast French column advancing toward the allied lines. Luckily it would hit to the right of the 105th, so his tired men would have time to recover.

A bandage on his thigh, Captain Graham limped up. "May I borrow the spyglass, sir?"

Michael passed it over. The captain muttered an obscenity as he identified the red plumes and high bearskin hats. "So Boney is finally sending in his Imperial Guard."

"Precisely. They've never failed in an attack, and after spending the day in reserve, they're as fresh as if they were on parade in a park," Michael said grimly.

It was the last grand throw of the dice. With the Imperial Guard, Napoleon would regain or lose his empire.

* * *

At suppertime, Catherine forced herself to go home. Though activity was infinitely preferable to waiting, she must conserve her strength. It had been confirmed that another battle was being fought, so there would be a new wave of wounded in the morning. Intensely she prayed for the lives of her friends.

Catherine collected Elspeth, who was also helping in the hospital. The girl was proving herself a stalwart Scot, but her face was gray and dark circles shadowed her eyes.

Together they walked the short distance to the Rue de la Reine. Most of the Belgian servants had returned to their families, leaving only the cook and Catherine's groom. A good thing Everett was there, or the horses might have been stolen.

After washing up, the two women ate together in the kitchen. Catherine found it impossible to swallow more than a few mouthfuls of soup. Wearily she added a generous dash of brandy to her tea and took it to the morning room.

The portfolio of sketches was still there. She leafed through them again, wondering if the men in the pictures were still safe and whole. Was Colin glorying in what must be the battle of a lifetime? Would Charles live to see his unborn child, or Kenneth survive to draw other laughing families?

She came to the last picture, and quickly closed the portfolio, her throat tight. It would be a pity to ruin the drawing of Michael with her tears.

The Imperial Guard fell back, shattered by the fierce resistance of the allied troops. Michael was almost too dazed to appreciate the enormity of it. France's finest troops had broken and turned into a mob instead of an army.

But it wasn't over yet. How much longer would the battle last? How much longer *could* it last? The 105th had suffered over forty percent casualties, half of whom had died outright. Other regiments had fared even worse.

Then Graham cried jubilantly, "Look, sir!"

An elm tree at the crest of the ridge, where two roads intersected, was Wellington's command post when he was not riding the lines. The spot was barely visible through the smoke. Now the duke was there, his lean form silhouetted against the evening sky as he stood in his stirrups and waved his cocked hat forward three times. It was the signal for a general advance. A thunderous cheer went up in the regiments nearest the duke and rolled down the allied lines in a swelling roar.

Fierce exultation burned through Michael, searing away his weakness. In his bones, he knew that this battle was won. The long years in the army, the brutal hours of being cut up by French artillery, had come down to this moment. Raising his sword in the air, he shouted, "Follow me, 105th!"

"Aye, Colonel! To hell, if you'll lead us there," a voice boomed back.

The regiment formed into companies and boiled down the slope over the matted, blood-soaked rye, muskets and bayonets at the ready. All along the ridge, the action was being echoed by the other allied troops under command of any officers who survived. They swooped down onto the plain, leaving behind them unmoving scarlet lines of dead and wounded.

Vicious skirmishing began across the two-mile width of the battlefield. Though much of the imperial army was in full flight, pockets of French soldiers still resisted gallantly.

The 105th split into smaller groups, some men pushing forward after the fleeing enemy, others engaging in fierce hand-to-hand combat with those Frenchmen who still fought. All was chaos. Light-headed from blood loss, pain, and fatigue, Michael was in a dark, fierce place where there was no past or future or fear. Only instinct and will and the madness of war, where any moment might be his last.

Reality was a collection of feverish, disconnected images. A tangle of fallen French guards, their limp bodies intertwined like tree roots. An abandoned horse peacefully cropping a mouthful of grass. A dying hussar, his belly ripped open, pleading for death. Michael spoke a prayer in French, then cut the poor devil's throat.

He thought his own death had found him when a cuirassier charged, sword swinging. Michael braced himself, but knew that in his present condition he had no chance against a mounted man.

Then the Frenchman's gaze went to Michael's sling. He raised the hilt of his sword to his forehead in a salute and swerved away in search of other targets. Michael touched the hard ridge of the silver kaleidoscope, which was tucked inside his coat. His lucky charm had not failed him yet.

They were moving up the opposite slope of the valley when Michael pushed through a gap in a ragged hedge and found Tom Hussey being attacked by two Frenchmen. As one stabbed a bayonet through the ensign's shoulder, Michael leaped forward with a murderous shout. He sliced one assailant's chest, then turned snarling on the other. Unnerved by his attack, both men fled.

Tom wiped his forehead with a grimy sleeve. "How does one learn to fight like you, sir?"

"Practice and a bad temper." Michael's fury subsided, leaving him panting. He indicated the blood seeping between the ensign's fingers. "You should get that taken care of."

"There will be time for that later." Tom's eyes were bright with the intoxication of fighting and surviving.

There were only two good hands between them, but together they managed to bind the bayonet wound. Then they moved forward again. Michael tried to keep an eye on the boy, but a flurry of advancing Hanoverians separated them.

Death in battle can come in an instant, or with excruciating slowness. For Michael the end came swiftly. He heard a snarled French curse, and turned to see the men he had driven away from Tom Hussey. Both were aiming their muskets from less than fifty feet away. They fired. Two balls slammed into him almost simultaneously, one in the thigh, the other in his abdomen. When he crumpled to the muddy earth, he knew he would not rise again.

He lay there, barely conscious, until he felt the vibration of galloping hooves drumming through the soil. He raised his head to see half a dozen French lancers racing toward him in mindless panic. Though he knew the effort was pointless, he tried to crawl toward a ragged hedge that might offer some protection. He did not reach it in time. The lancers rode over him, the hooves of the horses rolling him across the ground. One lancer slowed long enough to stab his lance into Michael's back.

Pain was everywhere, so intense it blacked out the red setting sun and the clamor of battle. With each shuddering breath, he hoped that dying with honor would redeem the times when he had not lived with it.

He felt himself floating away, disconnected from his battered body. Catherine was there, her presence more vivid than the devastation around him. She smiled and dissolved his pain with gentle hands.

With the final shreds of awareness, he knew that he had died well, and that he had been privileged to know a woman worthy of being loved. Then he spiraled into darkness, his spirit at peace.

Chapter 12

As the evening passed, Catherine knew with nerve-searing certainty that something was terribly wrong. She and Elspeth sat together in the morning room, the dogs at their feet. There was nothing unusual about Louis sleeping, but even Clancy's high spirits were subdued.

It was almost a relief when the knocker banged in an eerie echo of two nights before. Both women dashed to the front door to find Will Ferris again. His face was haggard and blackened by powder, but apart from a bandage around his right forearm, he was uninjured. With a cry, Elspeth flew into his arms.

Catherine envied them, wishing her own life was so simple. She gave them a few moments before asking, "What news, Will?"

Still holding Elspeth, he said in staccato sentences, "The battle is won. Bloodiest thing I ever saw. Your husband isn't hurt, but Captain Mowbry was injured. I came to tell his wife."

"She took the children to Antwerp. What are his injuries?"

"A ball shattered his left forearm. He was knocked from his horse and likely would have died if not for your husband, ma'am. Captain Melbourne turned around, took him up, and brought him back to our lines."

Thank God for Colin's indomitable courage. "I must bring Charles home. Do you feel strong enough to take me to him now, or will you need to rest first?"

Ferris looked alarmed. "I'm well enough, but I can't take you to Waterloo, ma'am. Every house in the village is full of dying men. It's no place for a lady."

"I promised Anne I would care for Charles as if I were her, and by God, I will," she said flatly.

When Ferris tried to protest again, Elspeth said in her

soft burr, "Don't worry, Will. Mrs. Melbourne can manage *anything.*"

Outnumbered, Ferris surrendered. Everett was called from his room above the stables to prepare the small cart that was used for household hauling. The groom covered the flat bed with straw and Elspeth brought blankets while Catherine packed her medical kit, including her laudanum. Rather than travel in the cart with Everett, she donned the breeches she had sometimes worn in Spain and rode Colin's horse, Caesar.

As they set off through the Namur Gate, she asked Ferris about the fate of other friends. He knew nothing about infantry officers like Michael and Kenneth; however, he was well informed about the cavalry regiments. The litany of casualties was brutal. Men Catherine had known for years were dead or grievously wounded. Though the Allies had carried the day, they had paid a bitter, bitter price.

The road passed through a dense forest. It was a lovely drive during normal times, but as they neared the village of Waterloo the way became clogged with wagons, dead horses, and spilled baggage. Luckily their cart could squeeze through where a larger vehicle would have been stopped.

It was after midnight when they reached their destination. Leaving Everett with the cart and horses, Catherine followed Ferris to the house-turned-hospital where Charles had been taken. An irregular mound lay beside the door. With a shudder, she recognized it as a pile of amputated limbs.

Inside the house were the groans and stoic suffering that she knew all too well. A strangled cry came from the salon at the left. She glanced in and saw that the dinner table was being used for operating. A frowning Dr. Hume bent over it.

Ferris led her through the crowded house to the small side room where Charles lay. He was conscious, though obviously in pain. When he saw her, he said huskily, "What are you doing here, Catherine?"

"Substituting for Anne. When the outcome of the fighting looked chancy, Lord Haldoran offered to take her and the children to Antwerp until the danger was past. In return, I promised to care for you. Which means a kiss, though not quite the one Anne would give you." She bent over and touched her lips to his forehead. "We've come to take you home."

He smiled faintly. "I'd like that. I believe it's almost my turn for the cutting room. After my arm comes off, we can go."

His eyes drifted shut. She studied his drawn face, then gave a nod of satisfaction. The arm would certainly have to be amputated, but if there was no infection, he would pull through.

Softly she said to Ferris, "Since we'll be here for a bit, why don't you lie down and get what rest you can?"

He rubbed his face, smearing the powder marks. "A good idea. I noticed an empty corner in the next room. I'll doss down there until you're ready to leave."

A few minutes later, a boyish voice murmured, "Ma'am, could . . . could you get me some water, please?" The speaker was an ensign on the next pallet. There was a bandage around his head and another around his shoulder. He was heartbreakingly young.

"Of course." She went in search of a pitcher of water and a glass, finding them in the kitchen. The ensign accepted the drink gratefully. She was giving water to a man on the other side of the room when Colin's bemused voice said, "Catherine?"

She looked up to see her husband standing in the doorway. He was filthy and exhausted, but intact. "I'm so glad to see you." She rose and went to him. "I've come to take Charles back to Brussels."

"Good. I stopped by to see how he was." Colin put an arm around her and drew her close in a gesture that was as much fatigue as affection. "Lord, what a fight it was! There's not a man who came through who won't be proud to have taken part, but it was a near-run thing. Damned near-run." For a moment he rested his chin against her hair. Then he released her.

"You were right about your magical immunity to bullets," she said. "Ferris told me you saved Charles's life."

"The credit must go to Michael Kenyon for insisting I take his horse. During the afternoon, we made the grandest cavalry charge I've ever seen. It was magnificent." His eyes brightened at the memory. "We sent the French flying, but we went too far into their territory, then had to retreat with their cavalry after us. The ground was muddy from the rain. If I'd been riding Uno or Duo, they would have caught me."

He grimaced and ran a hand through his tangled hair. "That's exactly what happened to Ponsonby, the Union Brigade commander. Like me, he didn't want to risk his best mount, so he was riding a second-rate hack. Because of the heavy soil, the beast became blown during the retreat. Ponsonby was run down and killed by lancers. I was spared his fate only because Kenyon's horse has incredible stamina. Saved Charles and me both."

"Then I'm very glad Michael insisted on the exchange." She hesitated, then asked, "Do you know how he fared in the battle?"

"I've no idea." Colin's brows drew together. "Did you come here on Caesar? If so, I'll take him and you can ride Thor back to Brussels. Because the Prussians missed most of the battle, they took charge of the pursuit, but tomorrow I imagine we'll go after the French, too. I'll need a fresh horse."

Catherine described where Colin could find Caesar. "Is the fighting over?"

Her husband shrugged. "If Napoleon manages to regroup, there could be another battle."

"Dear Lord, I hope not," she said with a glance at the wounded men surrounding them.

"Perhaps it won't come to that. I don't imagine I'll see you again until we're in Paris. Take care." Colin kissed her cheek absently and left.

A few minutes later, orderlies came to take Charles to Dr. Hume. Catherine accompanied him. The exhausted surgeon greeted her with no show of surprise. After a careful examination, he said, "You're in luck, Captain. I'll be able to leave you the elbow. Do you want a piece of wood to bite?"

Charles closed his eyes, the skin tightening across his cheekbones. "That shouldn't be necessary."

Catherine moved forward and took hold of his right hand. His fingers clamped around hers and sweat showed on his brow when Hume sawed off the injured arm, but he uttered no sound. Hume had the swiftness that was essential to a good surgeon, and the operation was over in minutes.

An orderly was taking away the severed limb when

Charles said hoarsely, "Wait—before you toss that out. There's a ring my wife gave me on our wedding day. I'd like it back, please."

The orderly looked startled. Then he tugged the ring from the dead finger. Not knowing whether to laugh or cry, Catherine took the ring and slid it onto the third finger of Charles's right hand. He whispered, "Thank you."

Catherine said, "Dr. Hume, I want to take him back to Brussels. Will that be all right?"

"He'll be better off there than here," the surgeon said. "Give him some laudanum so the jarring of the cart won't distress him too much. You know how to change dressings."

"Yes, and I've also got Ian Kinlock staying at my house, when he has time to rest."

Hume laughed, his expression lightening. "Trust you for that. Mowbry's a lucky man—he'll have the best of care."

The surgeon returned to his operating table. Catherine instructed the orderlies to take Charles back to his former pallet. She gave him laudanum, then sat back to wait for the drug to take effect. A few minutes later, she again heard a surprised male voice say, "Catherine?"

When she looked up, it took a moment for her to recognize the man in the doorway because of the sticking plaster that covered most of his cheek and curved into his dark hair. But the burly build was unmistakable.

"Kenneth!" She rose and took his hands. His Rifle Brigade uniform was almost unidentifiable and one epaulet had been shot off, but he was blessedly alive. "Thank God you came through." She glanced at the sticking plaster. "A saber slash?"

He nodded. "I'll be even uglier when it heals, but it's nothing serious. Are you here for your husband?"

"No, Colin is well. Charles Mowbry was injured, and I'm going to take him back to Brussels. He lost his lower left arm, but his condition is good otherwise." Her heart began beating faster. "Do . . . do you know anything about Michael Kenyon?"

Kenneth looked grim. "I'm here looking for him. He's not with his regiment, nor in any of the other temporary hospitals."

It was the news Catherine had been dreading. She pressed her knuckles to her mouth. It might be wrong to care more for Michael than for her other friends, but she could not help herself.

Seeing Catherine's expression, Kenneth said, "Michael could be alive on the field, so there's still hope."

She frowned. "Are many wounded still out there?"

"After ten hours of battle, Wellington's entire army has collapsed and is sleeping like the dead," Kenneth said heavily. "I would be doing the same if I didn't want to find Michael." More to himself than her, he added, "I owe him that."

The ensign who had earlier asked for water interrupted diffidently. "Begging your pardon, sir, ma'am, but are you talking about Colonel Kenyon of the 105th?"

Catherine knelt beside the boy's pallet. "Yes. I'm a friend of the colonel's. Do you know what happened to him?"

"I don't know if the colonel is alive or dead, but I saw him fall. I might be able to find him." The ensign pushed himself upright. "I was trying to reach him when my skull was creased by a ball. By the way, I'm Tom Hussey of the 105th, ma'am."

Kenneth said, "Tell me where he is and I'll go search."

Tom shook his head. "I think I can find the place, sir, but it would be hard to describe. I'll have to go with you."

"Can you manage that?"

"For the colonel, I can manage." Expression resolute, the ensign lurched to his feet.

"I've got two men and a cart with me," Catherine said. "I'll get them, a litter, and my medical kit."

Kenneth looked startled. "You can't go onto the battlefield, Catherine."

"Try and stop me," she snapped, her voice vibrating with emotion. "If Michael is alive, he'll need medical help."

He indicated Charles's sleeping form. "What about Mowbry?"

"He's resting quietly from the laudanum. It won't hurt him to wait a little longer. It might even be beneficial."

"Come along, then." Kenneth smiled wearily. "I haven't the strength to fight both Napoleon and you on the same day."

Ferris rose to join the search. Everett drove the cart while the others rode. Colin had exchanged horses and saddles, so Catherine rode Michael's gelding. Thor was weary and a bullet had grazed his flank, but he carried her without complaint. She stroked the chestnut neck, blessing him for saving two lives.

The 105th had been positioned near a road, so the first part of the trip went quickly. The nightmarish journey made Catherine grateful for the darkness. Bodies and wrecked equipment were everywhere. When she heard groaning, she forced herself to ignore it. They could not help everyone. She wondered how many wounded men would die during the night, but understood why the exhausted survivors had not even tried to help. In the morning, the task of aiding the casualties would seem less overwhelming.

They followed the road until they were as close as possible to where Tom Hussey had last seen his colonel. Rather than risk the cart becoming bogged down in the muddy earth, they left Everett on the road and cut off across country. Their pace slowed, for the ground was scattered with broken swords and bayonets that could cripple a horse.

Tom dismounted and began leading his horse. The others did the same, Kenneth and Ferris carrying the lanterns while the ensign studied the landscape. They zigzagged several times before he said hesitantly, "I think he was by that hedge."

After they followed the line of the hedge for a hundred yards, the lantern light suddenly washed over two men in peasant dress who were leaning over the limp form of a fallen soldier. Growling an oath, Kenneth pulled out his pistol and fired into the air. The peasants fled into the night.

"Looters," he said with disgust as he reloaded.

Catherine was unsurprised. In Spain, sometimes the dead and wounded had been robbed even when a battle was in progress. Her pace quickened and she went to the fallen man. The height and lean, muscular build were right, the dark jacket . . .

Heart pounding, she dropped to the muddy ground beside the man. Kenneth was right behind her. His lantern illuminated the sharply planed features of Michael Kenyon. His face was pale as a death mask and his uniform saturated with dried blood.

Fearfully she touched his throat, seeking a pulse. She could not find one, and he was cold, so cold. Her vision blurred as grief swept over her.

Kenneth asked harshly, "Is he alive?"

His voice pulled Catherine back from her near-faint. Lips dry, she said, "I don't know." She lifted Michael's arm. It moved easily. "I can't find a pulse, but there's no rigor." She pressed her hands to her temples. What should she do?

She must think of Michael as a patient, not as a man she cared for. "Do you have something highly polished, like a watch?"

Tom Hussey said, "Take this, ma'am." He pressed a silver locket into her hand. She held it in front of Michael's mouth. A faint film of moisture appeared.

Dizzy with relief, she sat back on her heels. "He's breathing, though only just."

"We'll have to move him," Kenneth said.

"Let me examine him first."

When Catherine returned the locket, the ensign said, "The sling is from a ball that went through his arm—a flesh wound. His ribs were slashed by a saber."

There was a deep gash in his back, perhaps from a lance. It had bled, but the earlier bandage had afforded some protection. There was also a messy flesh wound in his thigh, with the bullet still buried. She bound it, then turned him onto his back.

Her heart contracted when she saw the ragged hole above his waist. Abdominal wounds were invariably fatal. She pulled the blood-crusted fabric away so she could see how much damage had been done. To her surprise, her fingertips touched the coolness of metal. She traced the shape, then removed a flattened silver tube with a lead ball embedded in it. "This thing, whatever it is, stopped a bullet from going into him."

"It's a kaleidoscope," Kenneth answered. "It makes changing patterns of colored glass. He called it his good-luck charm."

"Good luck, indeed." She dropped the object into her medical case.

Her examination confirmed that none of his injuries were necessarily fatal. What worried her most was that there was no active bleeding, indicating that he had already lost massive amounts of blood. She had a jug of water in her bag, so she spooned some between his dry lips. He couldn't swallow. She stopped, fearing he might choke, and got wearily to her feet. "I've done as much as I can here. We must get him to a surgeon."

Kenneth and Ferris carefully lifted Michael onto the litter and Catherine covered him with a blanket. Then they set off across the fields to the waiting cart. The sky was lightening in the east. The endless night was almost over.

Michael was alive. But would that be true in an hour?

Chapter 13

It was late morning when Catherine and her two patients arrived back in Brussels, escorted by Everett and Ferris. Kenneth and Ensign Hussey had returned to their regiments. She had promised to send news of Michael's condition, but from their bleak expressions, she knew they expected the worst.

The journey had been made slowly to minimize the jolting of the unsprung cart. Catherine had ridden behind, watching her patients like a hawk. Even with laudanum, the trip was hard on Charles, though he had born the pain stoically. Michael had been so still that she feared they were carrying a corpse.

As soon as they reached home, she had dismounted and checked Michael for vital signs. His skin was bluish and clammy and his pulse and breathing were almost nonexistent, but he still lived.

A rumpled but rested Elspeth emerged from the house and hugged Will Ferris. "How is Captain Mowbry?"

"He's doing well," Catherine replied. "When the men have settled him in his room, will you administer a dose of laudanum and sit with him?"

Ferris said, "I'll stay with the captain, ma'am."

"Not until you've slept," Catherine said sternly. "You fought a battle yesterday and have had no rest since."

He started to protest, but Elspeth gave him a look. "To bed with you, Will, or I'll send you there myself with a skillet over your stubborn Sassenach head."

Ferris gave in with a tired smile. As he and Everett placed Charles on the litter, Catherine said to Elspeth, "Colonel Kenyon is in a bad way. Is Ian Kinlock here?"

"Aye, he's sleeping. He came in a little after you left."

"Please wake him, and ask him to come to the colonel's room as soon as possible."

Elspeth nodded and left. After Everett and Ferris took Michael inside, Catherine dismissed the two men and began cutting off Michael's ruined coat and shirt. He had not taken time to change the night of the ball, so he was still wearing his dress uniform. He had looked so splendid then. So alive.

As she pulled pieces of garment out from under him, he gave a faint, breathy moan. She touched his cheek. "Michael, can you hear me?"

His lids fluttered once, but he did not wake. Trying to sound confident, she said, "You're going to be all right, Michael. The best surgeon I know will be here in a few minutes."

She turned her attention to his battered body. He was bare from the waist up, except for the stained bandage around his ribs. His torso was a mass of bruises and abrasions. Long-healed scars were overlaid by new wounds, and there was an enormous purple-blue bruise where the musket ball had rammed the kaleidoscope into the muscles of his abdomen.

She had seen many men's bodies in the course of her nursing work, but never had she felt such tenderness. She skimmed her fingers over Michael's collarbone, thinking that it was criminal that a beautiful, healthy body had been so abused. Once more, she damned Napoleon Bonaparte and his insatiable ambition.

Then she set her emotions aside and began the laborious process of cleaning the wounds. She was picking bits of scorched cloth from the hole in his arm when the surgeon joined her.

Ian looked like a wrinkled, unshaven beggar, but his blue eyes were alert. "An emergency?"

She nodded. "Colonel Kenyon is a particular friend. He was billeted here. We found him on the battlefield last night."

Ian moved to the bed and studied the patient. "Why weren't his injuries dressed in Waterloo?"

"We took him there, but Dr. Hume said that . . . that there was no point. Other men needed him more." The words had fallen on her heart like a death knell. "I decided to bring him here in the hopes that you would treat him."

"I see why Hume decided not to waste the time—the fellow is more dead than alive. Still, since he's a friend of yours . . ." Ian began an examination. "Hmm, I worked on him somewhere in the Peninsula—I recognize the wounds. Grapeshot, very messy. I'm surprised he survived. Get my instruments. I left them drying in the kitchen after washing them last night."

Kinlock's insistence on cleanliness when possible produced much teasing from other surgeons. He had always smiled and said his Scottish mother had been a demon for washing, and surely it did no harm. Perhaps because Catherine was a housewife, clean instruments made perfect sense to her. She suspected that they were one reason why Ian's patients did so well.

By the time Catherine had retrieved the instruments from the kitchen, Ian had finished the examination and removed the rest of Michael's clothing. He began to clean and dress the wounds with the combination of strength and dexterity essential to a good surgeon. Catherine handed him what he needed and took away what he didn't. The lengthy process made her thankful Michael was unconscious.

Even so, when Ian was probing for the ball buried in his thigh, Michael made a hoarse sound and tried feebly to pull away. Catherine caught his knee and hip to immobilize the limb. Embarrassingly aware of his nakedness, she averted her gaze. No matter how much she tried, she could not make herself think of him as an ordinary patient. "Is his reaction a good sign?"

"Perhaps," the surgeon said noncommittally. There was a dull scrape as his forceps closed around the lead ball. He tugged the ball free with painstaking care and dropped it in the basin Catherine held. Then he took a different kind of forceps and began removing fragments from the gaping wound. "Your friend was lucky again. The ball missed the major blood vessels and only chipped the thigh bone without causing serious damage. Half an inch either way and he would have died on the field."

With such luck, surely Michael was not intended to die. Yet all the humor and vivid intelligence were gone from his face, leaving an austere mask. Her eyes ached with unshed tears.

Ian finished and pulled blankets over Michael's chilled body. Fearing the answer, Catherine said, "What are his chances?"

"Damned poor," Ian said bluntly. "The wounds are survivable, even though it looks like half the French army used him for target practice, but he's bled out." He shook his head with regret. "I've never seen a man so deep in shock recover."

Catherine pressed her fist to her mouth. She would not cry. She *wouldn't.* Ian had only said what she already knew. It was not wounds that would kill Michael, nor infection, for he would not live long enough for that. Loss of blood would be the cause. She stared at his still body, her mind racing desperately through all of the medical theories she had ever heard.

Kinlock was cleaning his instruments when the idea struck her. "Ian, didn't you tell me once that occasionally blood has been transferred from one person to another?"

"Aye, and from animals to humans, but only experimentally. It's a chancy business at best."

"You said that sometimes the procedure helped."

"*Seemed* to help," he corrected. "Perhaps the patients that survived would have lived anyhow."

"And the ones who died might have died." She ran nervous fingers through her hair. "Would blood transfusion help Michael?"

"Good God," Ian said, horrified. "Do you want to kill the poor devil?"

"What are his chances if nothing is done?"

Ian sighed and looked at the man on the bed. "Almost nil."

"Might more blood be the difference between life and death?"

"It's possible," he admitted reluctantly.

"Then let's do it. You know how, don't you?"

"I've seen it done, which isn't quite the same thing." Ian scowled. "The patient died in the case I saw."

"But sometimes patients survive. Please, Ian," Catherine said softly, "give Michael a chance."

"The Hippocratic oath says doctors should first do no harm," he protested. "Besides, where would we get a donor? Most people would rather face Napoleon's cavalry than a surgeon's knife."

"I'll be the donor."

Shocked, he said, "I can't allow you to do that, Catherine."

Frayed by fatigue and anxiety, she exploded, "I'm so tired of men saying 'Oh, Catherine, you can't do that.' I'm a healthy, strapping wench, and I can certainly spare some blood."

"That's the first time I've ever seen you lose your temper." He surveyed her with a faint smile. "I don't usually think of you as a strapping wench, but I suppose there's no reason why you shouldn't give your blood. There's little danger for the donor."

"So you'll do the transfusion?"

"He's a tenacious man, or he would never have survived this long." Ian lifted Michael's wrist, frowning as he felt for the pulse. There was a long pause before he said decisively, "In for a penny, in for a pound. Very well, we'll try. A transfusion might just give him the extra strength he needs."

She felt almost dizzy with relief. "What do you need?"

"A couple of clean quill pens, one a little larger than the other, and an assistant. You'll be in no position to help."

Catherine went to enlist Elspeth, leaving the cook to sit with Charles. Thank God the girl had stayed; her own maid would have shrieking hysterics if asked to do such work.

Kinlock's preparation didn't take long. He trimmed the goose quills and ran a wire through them to ensure that they were clear. Then he fitted the large end of one into the large end of the other and sealed the joint with sticking plaster.

When he was satisfied, he said, "Catherine, lie next to the colonel, facing the other direction. I'm going to make the incisions inside the elbows."

Catherine pulled Michael's bare arm from under the blanket and rolled up her right sleeve. Then she lay down on top of the covers, feeling a nervous twinge at the intimacy of sharing a bed with Michael even under such bizarre circumstances. Ian laid down towels to absorb spilled blood, then made adjustments until he was satisfied with the positions of their arms.

She tried to relax, but it was difficult when she was acutely aware of Michael's nearness. His life seemed like a frail spark that could be extinguished with a single puff of breath. Yet in spite of the odds, he still lived. She clung to that fact.

"It's a simple process, really," Ian said conversationally

as he lifted a lancet. "I'll expose a vein in his arm and an artery in yours and tie ligatures around the vessels to control the flow of blood. Then I'll insert one end of the quill apparatus into the colonel's vein, tie it in place, and do the same to your artery. After that, it's only a matter of loosening tourniquets and ligatures so the blood can flow."

Catherine laughed shakily. "You make it sound easy."

"In a way, it is. The hardest part will be finding and opening one of his veins when they're almost collapsed. Close your eyes, now. You don't want to see this."

She obeyed, following what was happening by sound. Ian's muttering confirmed the difficulty of finding Michael's vein and sliding in the quill. Success was signaled when he said, "Hold the quill in place, Miss McLeod."

Then he laid a hand on her arm. "Ready, Catherine? It's not too late to change your mind."

If Michael died when she could have done something to help, she would never forgive herself. "Cut away, Ian."

The razor-edged blade sliced into her arm. It hurt, of course. It hurt a lot. When Ian tied off her artery in two places with waxed thread, she bit her lip to prevent herself from whimpering. She stopped when she noticed a metallic taste in her mouth, thinking a little hysterically that it wouldn't do to waste blood that might be of use to Michael.

The lancet cut again, more deeply. Ian swore and there was a strangled moan from Elspeth. Catherine opened her eyes to see blood spraying from her arm and Elspeth weaving, her face ashen.

Ian barked, "Damn it, lassie, you don't have my permission to faint! You're a Scot, you can do this." Swiftly he stopped the splattering blood. "Close your eyes and breathe deeply."

Elspeth obeyed, gulping for air. A little color returned to her face. "I'm sorry, sir."

The crisis past, he said soothingly, "You're doing fine. I've seen strong men drop like felled timber after a single incision. Don't look again. All you have to do is hold that quill in Kenyon's arm."

"I will, sir," Elspeth promised.

Feeling faint herself, Catherine closed her eyes, not wanting to watch as the narrow end of the quill was inserted into her artery. A good thing she was lying down. After securing the quill, Ian loosened the ligatures and tourniquet. He gave a murmur of satisfaction. His hands stayed on her arm, holding the crude apparatus in place.

She opened her eyes a slit and saw that the translucent quill had turned to dark crimson. Her blood was flowing into Michael. Now, when it was too late, she questioned the arrogance of demanding a procedure that might kill him. She had no right—yet what else could she do? As a nurse, she recognized approaching death, and it had been in Michael's face.

Curiosity overcoming her queasiness, Elspeth asked, "How can you tell how much blood has been transferred, Dr. Kinlock?"

"I can't, any more than I can tell how much the donor can spare," he said harshly. "Catherine, how do you feel?"

She licked her dry lips. "Fine."

"Let me know the moment you start to feel dizzy or unwell."

Coldness crept through her body. She was acutely aware of the beating of her heart, the pumping that forced her blood into his veins, and with it, her love. *Live, Michael, live.*

"Catherine?" Ian's voice seemed very remote.

"I'm all right." Surely she was a long, long way from the blood depletion that Michael had suffered. "Continue."

Numbness was spreading up her arm and into her body. She opened her eyes again and saw Ian frowning. He touched the ligature, as if preparing to stop the transfusion.

She summoned every shred of her will to make her voice strong. "Don't stop too soon, Ian. There's no point in doing this if he's not going to get enough blood to make a difference."

Reassured, the surgeon held his peace.

Her mind began wandering. She thought of the first time she had seen Michael. He had been attractive, certainly, but many men were. When had he become special, his life as dear to her as her own? She could no longer remember.

"Catherine, how are you feeling?"

She tried to answer, but couldn't. There was no sensation in her cold lips.

Swearing again, Ian tied off the vessels and ended the transfusion. As he sutured her arm, he muttered about pig-headed females with less sense than God gave the average flea. She would have smiled, but it was too much effort.

"Miss McLeod, get a pot of tea," the surgeon ordered. "A large one, and a goodly amount of sugar."

The soft sound of footsteps, then the closing of the door. Catherine felt movement beside her, and realized it was from Michael. She moistened her lips, then whispered, "Is he better?"

Ian finished his bandaging, then laid his hand over hers. It seemed feverishly warm on her cold flesh. "His pulse and breathing are stronger, and there's a little color in his face."

"Will . . . will he survive?"

"I don't know, but his chances have improved." Ian squeezed her hand, then released it. "If Kenyon does live, he'll owe it to you. I hope he's worth the risk you took."

"He's worth it." Catherine gave a faint smile. "Confess, Ian. You're glad to have had an excuse to try a new procedure."

Amusement in his voice, he said, "I must admit that it's been interesting. I'll be curious to see the results."

Catherine let her eyes drift shut. She had done what she could. The result was in God's hands.

It was dark when she woke. Disoriented, she raised her hand and felt a sharp stab of pain inside her elbow. The events of the afternoon rushed back to her. The transfusion had left her near collapse. Ian had poured several cups of hot, sweet tea down her, then carried her to bed. After giving orders for her to rest at least until the next day, he had left Elspeth in charge and gone back to the hospital tent.

Catherine sat up cautiously and swung her legs to the floor. If she exercised care, she should be able to walk. She rose and pulled on a robe, needing the warmth, then went out.

Charles and Anne's room was across the hall from hers, so she peered in. A lamp showed Ferris sleeping on a pallet beside the bed. Charles was breathing easily and his color was good. It grieved her to see the stump of his left arm, but the loss was not one that would destroy his life. He would manage. In the morning she must ask Elspeth if a letter had been sent to Anne, who was surely half out of her mind with worry.

Then she made her way to the other end of the house, one hand on the wall for balance. Michael's room was also lamplit, though there was no one with him. Perhaps Elspeth had felt there was nothing she could do for someone so ill, or perhaps she was simply too tired. She had worked like a Trojan for days.

Michael turned restlessly. His breathing was strong; if anything, too strong. Unsteadily she crossed the room and put her hand on his brow. It was heated and he was sweating. She supposed some fever was inevitable, but it still disturbed her.

His eyes flickered open, but there was no awareness in them. Hoping to rouse him, she said, "Michael? Colonel Kenyon?"

He began to move spasmodically, trying to get up. "I'm coming," he muttered hoarsely. "Steady on, now. Steady on . . ."

His action brought him alarmingly close to the edge of the mattress. Fearing he might fall and break open his wounds, she caught his shoulders and pressed him back to the bed.

"No, Michael, you must rest," she said soothingly. "You're safe now. You're going to heal and be as good as new."

Though he was too weak to break away, he continued to struggle mindlessly. Frustrated by her weakness, she climbed onto the bed and drew him into her arms, cradling his head against her breasts. Her embrace calmed him a little, but not enough. He reminded her of Amy as a feverish infant. The thought gave her an idea. She began to croon a lullaby. *"Sleep, my child, and peace attend thee, all through the night . . ."*

She stroked his head as she sang every lullaby she knew. His rough breathing slowed, but when she stopped, he became agitated again. She sang old songs she had learned as a child. "Greensleeves" and "Scarborough Fair," "The Trees They Grow So High," and, rather shyly because it was a love song, "Drink to Me Only with Thine Eyes." Anything with a gentle tune.

She included some of the lovely ballads she had learned from Irish soldiers on the Peninsula. One was the haunting "Minstrel Boy." Without thinking, she started, *"The minstrel boy to war has gone./ In the ranks of death you'll find him./ His father's sword he has girded on,/ and his wild harp slung behind him . . ."* She stopped, throat tight, unable to bear the images of war, then started a wordless rendition of "A Londonderry Air."

She sang until her voice was hoarse and she was so tired she could barely open her mouth. Gradually Michael's restlessness stilled and he fell into what seemed like natural sleep.

She knew she should leave, but it was hard to be concerned with propriety when Michael's life still hung in the balance. Besides, she doubted if she could walk as far as her room.

With a sigh, she settled into the pillows. His unshaven chin prickled her breasts pleasantly through the thin muslin of her nightgown. His hair was damp, but he was no longer perspiring and his temperature seemed near normal. God willing, the crisis had passed.

He would heal, and soon he would be gone. She would have the satisfaction of knowing that somewhere in the world he was healthy and happy, but never again would they be so close.

Daring because he could not hear, she whispered, "I love you, Michael. I always will." Then she kissed him on the forehead, as she had done with Charles. Surely no one could condemn such a kiss too harshly.

Weary to the soul, she drifted into sleep.

Chapter 14

Having carried Catherine's face into the darkness, Michael was unsurprised to see her when he returned to consciousness. His first hazy thought was that the vision above him was an angel disguised as Catherine to make him feel welcome in heaven.

Yet surely heaven was not his most likely destination. He frowned, trying to understand. He was drifting in a sea of pain, so hell seemed more likely. Purgatory at the very least.

Catherine's soft voice said, "Michael?"

She sounded so real that he involuntarily reached out to her. The abstract sea of pain became shockingly personal, racking every inch of his body and darkening the veils that shrouded his mind. He gave a shuddering gasp.

She laid a cool hand on his brow and studied his face. Her eyes were shadowed and her hair was tied back carelessly. She was still the loveliest woman he'd ever seen, but if he were in the afterlife, he would surely remember her as she had looked the night of the Richmonds' ball. Amazingly, he must be alive, though not for long, considering the wounds he had received.

He tried to speak and managed a hoarse, "Catherine."

"Finally you're awake." She gave him a shining smile. "Can you swallow some of this beef broth? You need nourishment."

He gave a faint nod. It seemed like a waste of time to feed a dying man, but perhaps moisture would make speech easier.

She sat on the edge of the bed and raised his shoulders a little, supporting him as she spooned broth between his lips. Even that small motion produced an explosion of new pain. In a world of agony, her yielding body was the only balm. Softness and the scent of roses, and a haunting dream of music.

When he had swallowed as much as he could, she laid him back against the pillows. Then she changed her seat to a spot where he could see her easily. Though movement of the mattress hurt, it was worth it to have her so close.

Voice stronger, he asked, "The battle?"

"We won. That was three days ago. Allied troops are now pursuing what's left of Napoleon's army into France. If they prevent the French from regrouping, the war might be over."

He blinked. "Three days?"

She nodded. "Kenneth is well—he and Ensign Hussey from your regiment found you on the field after the battle." She hesitated. "Kenneth sent your groom and baggage here, but I've heard nothing about your orderly, Bradley. Was he killed?"

He nodded bleakly. Bradley had been a cheerful young Irishman. At least his death had been mercifully quick. "Your husband and Charles Mowbry?"

"Colin came through without a scratch. He said to thank you because your horse, Thor, saved Charles and him both. Charles is here. He had to have his left forearm amputated, but he's doing well." She smiled wryly. "Much better than you."

He was glad to hear that her husband had survived. Colin Melbourne's death would have produced deep, wholly irrational guilt because Michael had wished the other man didn't exist.

"Surprising . . . I'm still breathing." His hand went feebly to the spot where the bullet had plowed into his abdomen. It was impossible to separate that pain from myriad others.

"You were insanely lucky." She reached into the nightstand and brought out his kaleidoscope, now badly mangled. "You have three major wounds and half a dozen minor ones, but this saved you from the one bullet that would surely have been fatal."

He stared at the lead ball and the ruined silver tube. "Shattered rainbows, in truth."

She looked at him quizzically. "Shattered rainbows?"

"That's what the kaleidoscope contained—pieces of dreams and rainbows. A lovely thing. A gift from a friend." He smiled faintly. "My lucky charm."

"Obviously."

He reached for it, but could not raise his hand. Pain again, like red-hot knives. "Not . . . lucky enough."

"You're not dying, Michael," she said emphatically. "In the process of being shot, slashed, trampled, and kicked by horses, you lost about as much blood as a man can lose and still live. For that reason, you're going to be horribly weak for some time to come—months, perhaps. But you are *not* dying."

She sounded so sure that he was half convinced. He had felt almost equally awful after Salamanca, and he'd survived that.

Her brows drew together. "I'm talking too much. You need rest." She got to her feet. "One more thing. You wanted letters sent to your particular friends if you died. Do you want me to write them to say how you're doing? When they see your name on the casualty lists, they'll be worried."

"Please. And . . . thank you." He tried to keep his eyes open, but the brief conversation had exhausted him.

"I'll write this afternoon and give the letters to a military courier so they'll reach London quickly." Catherine pressed his hand. "You're going to be fine, Michael."

Having seen how state of mind could affect a man's recovery, she intended to repeat her assurance often. She got to her feet wearily. Though she'd lost only a fraction of the blood Michael had, she still felt feeble as a newborn kitten.

She took the three letters from Michael's dresser so she could copy the addresses. Her brows rose a little as she looked at them. The Duke of Candover, the Earl of Strathmore, the Earl of Aberdare. High circles indeed. She guessed that the men were the other "Fallen Angels" Michael had known since school days. What had he called them? Rafe, Lucien, Nicholas. She envied them for having had his friendship for so many years.

Catherine was not there the next time Michael awoke. Instead, a pretty brunette was shyly laying her hand on his shoulder. After a moment, he recognized her as Elspeth McLeod, the Mowbrys' nursemaid. He murmured, "Hello."

"Good morning, Colonel. I have some gruel for you. Dr. Kinlock says we must feed you at every opportunity."

"Gruel," he said with as much loathing as he could get

into a whisper. But he submitted meekly. He couldn't have eaten real food even if it were offered.

After he finished, Elspeth laid him back and straightened the covers. "I don't mind saying I didn't expect you to survive. When Catherine brought you home, you looked ready for planting."

He frowned, not understanding. "Catherine brought me home? She said Kenneth Wilding found me."

"Aye, but she was with him. She went to Waterloo to get Captain Mowbry, and ended up going onto the battlefield with Captain Wilding." The girl shivered. "Better her than me."

Michael had known Catherine was intrepid, but even so, he was amazed. "I owe her even more than I realized."

"That you do," Elspeth agreed. "You were bled out and the next thing to dead, so she talked Dr. Kinlock into letting her give you some of her blood. I helped. 'Twas the strangest thing I've ever seen. It worked, though. Dr. Kinlock says you would have died if not for the transfusion."

He frowned, confused. "How could she give me her blood?"

"Through a pair of goose quills, from her arm to yours." Elspeth rose. "The doctor said not to tire you, so I'll leave. With you and Captain Mowbry ill, there's much to be done."

After the door closed behind her, Michael raised his hand a few inches and stared at the shadowy vessels pulsing beneath the thin skin inside his wrist. Catherine's blood was literally running in his veins. It was an intimacy so profound that his mind could not encompass it. Saint Catherine indeed, not only brave but modest, and the most generous woman he had ever known.

She would have done the same for any friend, perhaps even for a stranger. Yet the knowledge that she had shared her lifeblood moved him profoundly. For as long as he lived, something of her would be part of him. He closed his eyes against the sting of tears. It was damnable to be so weak.

The Earl of Strathmore was frowning over the letter he had just received when a footman entered. "Lord Aberdare is here, my lord. I've shown him into the drawing room."

Lucien rose to greet his friend. Trust Nicholas, the intuitive Gypsy, to come all the way from Wales because he sensed trouble on the wind. After shaking hands, Lucien said, "I just received a letter from Brussels about Michael. He was badly wounded, you know."

"I know—Clare and I have seen the casualty lists," Nicholas said tersely. "But I've been worried about Michael for weeks. Since I was nervous as a cat on a griddle, Clare told me to come to London because news would arrive here more quickly."

Lucien handed him the letter. "A Mrs. Melbourne wrote this. Michael was billeted with her family this spring, and now she's caring for him. Apparently his chances of recovery are good."

Nicholas scanned the page. "He mentioned Catherine Melbourne in several of his letters. Her husband is a dragoon captain." He gave a low whistle as he read the letter. "Michael was carrying that kaleidoscope you gave him all those years ago and it blocked a bullet to the belly?"

"Apparently. Mysterious are the ways . . ."

"Thank God he had it with him." Nicholas frowned. "It's obvious that even if Michael doesn't take a turn for the worse, it will be a long convalescence. You know everyone, Luce. Where can I find a really comfortable yacht?"

Lucien's brows rose. "You mean . . . ?"

"Exactly." Nicholas neatly refolded the letter. "Clare has already given me my marching orders. I'm to go to Belgium and bring Michael home."

Chapter 15

Amy's dark head peered around Michael's door. "Today's newspaper has arrived, Colonel. Shall I read it to you?"

"I would enjoy that very much."

He smiled as Amy entered and sat down with a graceful swirl of skirts. The house was much livelier since Anne and the children had returned from Antwerp. Charles had regained much of his strength, and most of the Belgian servants were back.

Life had returned to normal for everyone except Michael. Though the pain had lessened, he was still maddeningly weak. The brisk Dr. Kinlock had assured him that his condition was normal after such blood loss, but the knowledge did not increase his patience. He particularly hated having Catherine see him in such a pathetic state. The fact that she was an experienced nurse and not in love with him did not assuage his tattered male pride.

His condition had one advantage: he was too feeble to feel desire. Instead, his yearning was of the heart, not the body. He had not realized how deeply he cared for Catherine until now, when passion no longer obscured more subtle feelings.

Amy read the main stories of the day, translating from French to English. Michael knew French, of course, but listening to English was less effort. Besides, he enjoyed her company. If he ever had a daughter, he hoped she would be like Amy.

She turned the page. "Here's a nice story. The French army surgeon, Baron Larrey, the one who invented the field ambulance? He was captured by the Prussians after Waterloo. Marshall Blücher was going to have him executed, but a German surgeon who had heard Baron Larrey lecture went to Blücher to plead for his life." She looked up, her eyes shining. "And guess what?"

"Blücher changed his mind, I hope?"

"Not only that. It turned out that Blücher's own son had been woumded and captured in a skirmish with the French, and it was Larrey who had saved his life! Isn't that wonderful?" She looked back at the paper. "Now Marshal Blücher is sending Baron Larrey back to France with a Prussian escort."

"That's a very good story," Michael agreed. "The world needs all the healers it can get."

As Amy refolded the newspaper, her mother entered. "Time to go upstairs for your lessons, my dear."

After grimacing elaborately, Amy dropped an elegant curtsy. "So good to see you again, Colonel Kenyon. Until tomorrow?"

"Until tomorrow, Mademoiselle Melbourne. Thank you for the gift of your presence."

Her dimples flashed as she skipped out, a tomboy again.

Catherine said with mock severity, "What, pray tell, is Louis the Lazy doing on your bed?"

"Sleeping, of course." Michael rested his hand on the dog's back. "Does he ever do anything else?"

"He eats. Sometimes he scratches. It's a narrow range." Catherine ruffled the dog's silky ears. "Do you mind if I do my knitting here? This is the quietest room in the house."

"You're always welcome, if you can bear my snappish temper."

"Actually, you're surprisingly good-natured for a man who is probably being driven mad by inactivity." Catherine took a seat and removed embroidery from her work bag. Now that she was less busy, she spent hours sitting quietly with him, doing needlework or writing letters. It was healing to have her near.

"I don't have the strength to throw a really good tantrum," he said wryly. "Not when my great achievement of the last week has been managing complete sentences again."

"Ian Kinlock says you're making excellent progress." She looked up with a stern glance. "As long as you don't bring on a relapse by trying to do too much, too soon."

"I can't lie here like a limp cravat forever," he said reasonably. "You're very patient, but surely you want to join your husband in Paris. Life will be much gayer there."

Her gaze dropped and she made a precise stitch. "A

letter came from Colin today. He said that since he owes you his life, I must stay in Brussels until you're well."

Michael's mouth tightened. "There is a limit to how much charity I can accept."

"There is no charity involved." She selected a new skein of silk thread. "Having spent an exhaustingly brilliant spring in Brussels, I'm in no hurry to frolic in the fleshpots of Paris. Besides, with Charles leaving the army and taking his family back to London, heaven knows when I'll see the Mowbrys again."

He released his breath in a slow sigh. Perversely, he was simultaneously glad not to be a burden and regretful that he was not more important to her.

Footsteps were heard approaching along the hall. After a perfunctory knock, Anne opened the door. "Michael, are you well enough for a visitor? A friend of yours has just arrived from England." She stepped aside and ushered in Nicholas, then left.

"Good Lord," he said blankly. "I'm dreaming."

"No such luck. I've tracked you down." Nicholas clasped Michael's hand, the hardness of his grip belying his casual air. "Clare sends her love. She would be here if not for the baby."

Michael tried to think of some witty response, but he failed. After swallowing hard, he said, "Catherine, meet the Earl of Aberdare. Nicholas."

The earl turned and gave a warm smile. "Sorry, I didn't see you there. I'm glad to meet the legendary Saint Catherine."

The obvious affection between Michael and his friend made Catherine feel forlorn and excluded and not at all like a saint. Disliking her reaction, she rose and offered a smile in return. "The pleasure is mine. How did you get to Brussels so quickly?"

"A good yacht and captain." The earl glanced at Michael again. "Both courtesy of Rafe, who sends his best wishes, and a severe scold for being fool enough to get yourself shot."

A smile crossed Michael's gaunt face. "Knowing Rafe, the scold probably came first."

"Yes, but I'm too tactful to admit that." Aberdare reached inside his coat and pulled out a shining silver tube. "Lucien sent this, to replace the one that was destroyed."

"Does it include the same good luck?"

"Guaranteed." Aberdare gave him the kaleidoscope.

Michael held it to his eye and turned it slowly. "This version is a little larger than the other, and even lovelier. Catherine, you never saw the original before it was smashed, did you? Take a look."

She accepted the tube and pointed it at the window. Inside was a brilliantly colored star-shaped pattern. She gave a sigh of delight. "Enchanting."

The figure changed as she turned the tube and the colored fragments realigned. They really did look like pieces of rainbow. Lowering the device, she said to the visitor, "It was good of you to come. Are you on the way to Paris?"

Aberdare shook his head. "No, I've come to take Michael back to Wales. That is, if he wants to go and can be moved."

Fighting back a ridiculous urge to say that he was hers and she wouldn't let him leave, Catherine said, "It's up to the doctor, of course, but surely that's a long, exhausting trip even for a healthy person."

"I'll take him to the coast by barge," the earl said. "Then the yacht will sail around Britain to the port of Penrith, only a few miles from home. Not a fast trip, but going by water all the way should make it fairly painless. Also, I brought a nurse handpicked by Lucien's wife to take care of Michael on the trip."

"Home." Michael's eyes closed for a moment. "I'd like that. Very much."

"Then it will be done." Aberdare regarded him thoughtfully. "It's time to leave. We're tiring you."

His eyes opened again, looking very green. "Not really. I'm this useless all the time."

"True, but Mrs. Melbourne will surely have my head if I don't let you rest." Aberdare briefly laid his hand on Michael's. "Until later."

Catherine and Aberdare left the room. As soon as the door closed, the earl exhaled roughly and covered his eyes with his hand. Concerned, Catherine asked, "Are you unwell, my lord?"

"Please, call me Nicholas." He lowered his hand, revealing a strained expression. "We knew he had been gravely wounded—that's why I came. But it's still a shock to see him like this. He's always been so strong. He must have lost two stone, and he looks like his own ghost. It brings home how close we came to losing him."

"He's fortunate to have such friends," Catherine said as she led the way downstairs. "You've gone to a great deal of effort for him."

"Michael is family, really. He lives just across the valley from us. He's godfather to my son." Nicholas ran tense fingers through his black hair. "We've been friends since our school days. I'm half Gypsy, not the best ancestry for a snobbish place like Eton. Michael was the first boy willing to make friends. I've never forgotten that." He gave Catherine a slanting glance. "I promise we'll take good care of him, Mrs. Melbourne."

Wondering uncomfortably how much the earl had seen in her face, Catherine said, "You must call me Catherine." They entered the drawing room. "Where are you staying?"

"Nowhere yet—I came directly here." Nicholas made a dismissive gesture. "With everyone gone to Paris, it should be easy to find rooms in a hotel."

"You can stay here—the room across from Michael's is empty, and there is room for three or four servants."

"Thank you." He gave a tired smile. "You're very kind."

Catherine smiled back, but underneath, her heart ached. Though she had known she would lose Michael, she had not expected it to be quite so soon.

It took Nicholas only two days to complete the arrangements to return to Wales. Michael was not surprised; having known Nicholas for twenty-five years, he was well acquainted with the efficient, razor-sharp mind concealed beneath the casual charm.

By the day of departure, Michael had progressed to sitting up, though doing so was painful. As they waited for the coaches to come, he fingered the edge of his robe restlessly. "Is that rumble outside the departing Mowbrys?"

Nicholas glanced out the window. "That was the baggage wagon leaving. The coach is being delayed while that overexuberant canine called Clancy is being corraled. Anne Mowbry is looking understandably harassed. Ah, Charles is exerting his authority as an officer and gentleman and ordering the beast into the carriage. It looks like they are finally on their way."

"It doesn't take long for a home to come unraveled."

Michael wondered if Catherine would come to say good-bye. It might be easier if she didn't, yet he hated the thought that he might not see her again. Perhaps she would say a public farewell, when he was being carried out on a litter. He hated that thought also. "This really was a home for several months."

"Credit going to Anne and Catherine, I assume. I like them both immensely." Nicholas gave his friend a shrewd glance. "Especially Catherine."

There were advantages to learning to control one's emotions from infancy. "They're both a credit to the female half of the race. I'll miss them and the children. I'll even miss Louis the Lazy, who is surely the most inert dog on God's green earth."

Nicholas laughed. "The carriages I hired to take us to the barge will be here soon. Are you ready?"

"As ready as I can be." Michael sighed. "I had hoped that when the time came, I would be able to walk out of the house, but that's obviously impossible."

"All in good time. From what Dr. Kinlock said before he returned to London, within a few months you should be entirely recovered, barring some colorful new scars."

"He also said I must lie about doing nothing for weeks to come." Michael's fingers drummed on the coverlet. "Patience has never been my strong point."

"True, but don't worry about whether you can be still for that long," Nicholas said pleasantly. "If you try to push yourself too hard, I will nail you to the bed."

Michael smiled, knowing full well that his friend's words were not a joke. He would have a leisurely convalescence whether he wanted it or not.

A soft rap on the door heralded Catherine. "Nicholas, your carriages have arrived."

The earl glanced from her to Michael. "I'll go and supervise the baggage loading." Tactful as a cat, he left.

Catherine's hair was drawn back simply, emphasizing the fine bones of her face. Her cheekbones were more prominent than when they met. She had lost weight, much of it because of the work and worry he had caused.

Eyes not meeting his, she said, "I hate good-byes, but I suppose they're necessary."

"They make it clear when something is over," he agreed. "When are you and Amy leaving for Paris?"

"Tomorrow. The house will seem empty tonight with everyone gone." She drifted to a window and gazed out at the ramparts. "It's strange. You and I became good friends, yet much of that was a result of being in the same place at the same time."

Was that what she thought of the complicated, undefined feelings between them? "I would like to think we would be friends under any circumstances."

"I'm sure we would be." A pulse was beating hard in her throat. "Perhaps what I meant was that our paths would not have crossed if not for the war. Since you're selling out of the army, we probably won't meet again."

He was painfully aware of that fact. "If you and Colin should ever wish to tour Wales, you would be very welcome at Bryn Manor. You would enjoy Nicholas's wife, Clare."

"Nicholas is wonderful," she said with a quick smile. "He could charm the fish from the sea. What is his wife like?"

"Very down to earth. Clare was a village schoolmistress before her marriage. She says there is nothing like teaching thirty children to make one practical." He spoke almost at random, all of his attention on the lithe figure silhouetted against the window. Even though passion was beyond him at the moment, he knew the memory of Catherine's provocative curves would haunt him through sleepless nights the rest of his life.

One thing must be said before he left. "A simple thank-you seems inadequate when you saved my life several times over. I am deeply in your debt, Catherine."

"And you saved Colin and Charles."

"Lending a horse is hardly in the same category with what you did," he said dryly.

"All women are nurses when necessary," she said with an embarrassed shrug.

"Oh?" He held out his hand. Uncertainly she came forward and clasped it. He pushed her sleeve up with his free hand, revealing the small, not yet healed scar inside her elbow. "This is hardly normal nursing. Elspeth told me. Why didn't you?"

Her mouth curved ruefully. "I was ashamed of my presumption. Though the transfusion worked out well, it might easily have killed you."

"Instead, it saved my life," he said quietly. "You gave

me your heart's blood. I will never receive a more precious gift."

"Given for selfish reasons." Shimmering tears made her aqua eyes enormous. She blinked them away. "I don't like my patients to die. It's bad for my saintly reputation."

His hand tightened on hers. "Catherine, if ever you need any kind of help, come to me. I will do anything in my power."

Her gaze shifted away. "Thank you. I'll remember that."

He raised their joined hands and kissed her fingertips, then released her. "See that you do."

"Good-bye, Michael. I'm very glad our paths crossed." She touched his cheek with gossamer lightness, then turned and left the room. She swayed gracefully, a sensual saint.

He wanted to call her back, to lock her in his arms so she could never escape. He wanted to plead with her to leave her husband and live with him no matter what the consequences. To prevent that, he clenched his teeth so hard that his jaw ached.

Perhaps he might have asked her to leave her husband if he had not once before urged a woman to do exactly that. He had already used his lifetime's supply of folly.

The door closed behind her. As he listened to her retreating footsteps, he felt the tightening of his lungs that heralded an asthma attack. Bands of fire constricted his breathing and the first tendrils of fear clawed into his muscles.

He lay back and forced himself to inhale and exhale very slowly. In and out, in and out, until the air was moving smoothly again. The scorching pressure and fear faded away.

Drained, he stared at the ceiling. It was the closest he had come to an asthma attack in years. Since Caroline had died.

He closed his eyes. He had done the right thing. Someday he would be proud of that, but now he felt only anguish.

Catherine was the most remarkable woman he had ever known. And he hoped to God that he would never see her again.

BOOK II

The Road to Heaven
Spring 1816

Chapter 16

The door of the London town house was opened by a neatly dressed housemaid. Catherine said, "Is Mrs. Mowbry home? If she is, please tell her that Mrs. and Miss Melbourne are here."

The housemaid glanced curiously at their travel-stained clothing before going to obey. A minute later, Anne came swiftly into the vestibule. "Catherine, how wonderful to see you! I thought you were still in France." She hugged both of her visitors.

Catherine noticed that Amy was now almost as tall as Anne, and Anne had regained her figure after the birth of her second son. Much can happen in a year. Too much. "We've only just arrived in England." She took off her dusty bonnet. Her temples were throbbing with a rare headache. "Is Charles home? Or your mother-in-law?"

"They're both out." After a shrewd glance at Catherine's face, Anne continued, "Amy, would you like to join Molly and Jamie? I believe they are about to have tea in the nursery."

Amy brightened. "Oh, yes, I'd like that. I've so much to tell them. I want to see Clancy and Louis, too."

After the housemaid took Amy off, Anne ushered her friend into the small drawing room. As soon as the door closed, she said, "It isn't polite to say this, but you look downright haggard. Are you ill, or simply tired by the long journey?"

Catherine sank onto the sofa. Now that she had reached a safe haven, she didn't know if she would ever be able to move again. "Colin is dead."

"Dear God." Anne's eyes widened with shock. "What happened?"

Catherine peeled off her gloves and crumpled them into a ball. "He was murdered."

"Oh, Catherine, how horrible! After he had survived so many battles without a scratch."

"It happened on the street late one night. He had just left a friend's house." Catherine pressed her fingers into her forehead, remembering the horror and disbelief she had experienced when Colin's commanding officer came to break the news. "He was shot in the back. It . . . it was over in an instant. A violet scarf and a note saying *'Vive le empereur'* were left beside him. Apparently he was killed by a Bonapartist, for no better reason than because he was a British officer."

Wordlessly Anne sat and gathered Catherine into her arms. Her friend's sympathy released the tears that Catherine had been holding back ever since she'd learned of Colin's untimely death. When her tears had finally run dry, she said in a raw whisper, "It almost made me wish he had been killed at Waterloo. That was the death he would have wanted. To die at a coward's hand was damnable."

"He died for his country as much as if he had died in battle," Anne said softly. "At least it was quick. Now he will never grow old. Colin would not have liked aging."

That was true, but little comfort. Colin had been a long way from old age. On the verge of tears again, Catherine sat up and groped for the handkerchief in her reticule.

Anne frowned. "I'm surprised that the news of his death hasn't reached England. Did it just happen?"

Catherine's mouth twisted. "The authorities feared that if his death became widely known, public opinion would be roused against France. As you know, the moderate treaty that came out of last summer's conference was hard won. The British ambassador personally informed me that a public scandal over the murder of a heroic army officer might endanger the peace."

"So Colin's death has been hushed up."

"I wasn't exactly forbidden to speak of it, but there were several earnest requests that I be discreet. Scarcely anyone knows outside of the officers of the regiment."

"I suppose that makes sense. We certainly don't need another war." There was a long silence as each of them remembered the high price of battle. Shaking her head against the thought, Anne asked, "Are you planning to take a house in London, or would you prefer a quiet place like Bath?"

"Neither," Catherine said grimly. "I must find work. I knew that Colin was bad about money, but I didn't realize how serious things were until after his death. My dowry, the income he inherited from his father—everything is gone. Not only that, but he left a mountain of debts. Thankfully, most of his creditors are officers in the regiment. I don't think any of them will try to send Amy and me to debtors' prison."

Shaken, Anne said, "I had no idea." After a long silence, she said, "No, that's not true. I'd almost forgotten that he owed Charles a hundred pounds. We'd given up hope of seeing it."

"Oh, no!" Catherine stared at her friend in dismay. "You, too? I should never have come here."

"Don't be ridiculous. Colin's irresponsibility has nothing to do with you and Amy. Besides, Colin risked his life to save Charles. That's worth infinitely more than a hundred quid."

Comforted by the reminder, Catherine said, "Colin had his failings, but lack of courage wasn't one of them."

"He was a good soldier. But what is this nonsense about looking for work? You shouldn't have to do that." Anne hesitated before adding, "I know it's too soon to be saying this, but you're a beautiful, charming woman. You'll marry again. Any eligible officers in the regiment would marry you in a minute."

In fact, several of them had offered before Catherine had left France. Trying to keep the revulsion from her voice, Catherine said, "I will never remarry."

"I don't wish to speak ill of the dead, but . . . well, Colin was not always an ideal husband," Anne said quietly. "Not all men are like him."

Catherine appreciated her friend's delicacy in not mentioning Colin's affairs, but the issues were far deeper than that. In fact, in his careless way, Colin had been a more tolerable husband than most men would be. But the subject was not one that could be discussed with anyone, ever.

"I will never remarry," she repeated. "Since I have no relatives who can help, that means working for wages. I can be a housekeeper or a nurse companion for an invalid. I'll do anything as long as I can keep Amy with me."

"I suppose you're right," Anne said reluctantly. "And if

you change your mind, there will be no shortage of men eager to cherish you for the rest of your life."

Not wanting to discuss the subject further, Catherine glanced around the cramped drawing room. "You had said we could stay here if we ever came to London, but the house is not large. Is there really room? Be honest—I can make other arrangements."

"Don't even think of leaving. We'll be a bit crowded, but there's a nice, sunny little bedroom that you and Amy can share. Charles's mother is a darling—he got his easy disposition from her. She'll be delighted to provide a home for the woman who nursed her only son after Waterloo."

"How are things with you? Has Charles found a position?"

Anne's face tightened. "Not yet. There are not enough jobs, and too many other former officers looking for similar positions. A pity that neither Charles nor I have influential relatives, but he will find something in time."

"How does Charles feel?"

"It's hard on him, of course. He's adjusted to the loss of his arm, but he's used to being busy. Being in this small house with not enough to do, and no good prospects . . ." Anne turned her palm upward. "He never complains, of course."

Catherine smiled ruefully. "We're in a fine fix, aren't we?"

She had first used the phrase on the Peninsula one night when the baggage mules had escaped, the children were sick with measles, and the mud hut she and Anne were sharing had dissolved in a rainstorm. Ever since then, the words had made them laugh and count their blessings.

Anne's expression eased. "Things will get better—they always do. We won't starve, we have a roof over our heads, and I won't ever have to see another blasted baggage mule in my life!"

Her words triggered a storm of giggles as they traded frightful memories of the Peninsula. Afterward, Catherine felt better. Things would, indeed, improve. All she needed was a decent job and her daughter. Surely that wasn't too much to ask.

Anne leaned back on the sofa. "Lord Michael Kenyon is in town for the Season. I've seen discreet references to him in the society columns. He's staying with Lord and Lady Strathmore and doing the social rounds."

"Really? Then he must be fully recovered. I'm glad." Catherine concentrated on straightening her twisted gloves. "His family certainly has influence. Have you considered going to him? I'm sure he would be happy to help Charles find a position."

"The thought has occurred to me," Anne admitted. "But it would seem dreadfully forward. He's the son of a duke, while Charles and I are the offspring of a barrister and a vicar."

"Michael wouldn't care about that."

"If worse comes to worst, I'd go to him, but we're not that hard up yet." Anne gave her an oblique glance. "Will you let him know you are in town? You and he were such good friends."

An overpowering desire to see Michael lanced through Catherine. To have him hold her comfortingly as he had the night her robe had caught fire. To see the warmth in his eyes, and hear the laughter in his voice . . .

She looked down and saw that she had crumpled her gloves again. "No, I shan't call on him. It would be hard not to feel like a supplicant."

"He would be happy to help. After all, you did save his life, and he's a generous man."

"No!" Realizing how sharp her tone was, Catherine said more moderately, "Like you, I would call on him in extreme need—I won't let Amy suffer because I have too much pride to beg. But I don't want to presume on a passing wartime friendship."

Particularly not with the man she loved. Would his offer of aid extend to proposing marriage so he could take care of her and Amy? It might. They were friends, he found her attractive, and he felt a strong sense of obligation. The combination might very well elicit an offer if his heart was not engaged elsewhere.

Her lips tightened. She had not thought twice about turning down the other proposals she had received, but with Michael, she might be tempted to accept. And that would be disastrous for both of them.

Catherine found it harder than she had expected to secure work. There were few positions and many applicants.

She went to every respectable employment agency in London and answered advertisements in the newspaper. Having a child disqualified her from some positions, lack of experience from others. Several agencies flatly refused to consider a female who was "a lady," claiming it would make clients uncomfortable to have a servant who was better born than themselves. Apparently they did not realize that even ladies must eat.

Several times she was interviewed by women who looked her up and down, then dismissed her without asking questions. A kindly agency owner explained that few women would want a housekeeper who was beautiful. As Catherine trudged home through Hyde Park one day, she cursed the face that had caused her so many problems. What men considered beauty had been a blight on her life. The only offer of employment she had received had been from a man whose lascivious stares had made it clear what her duties would include.

With a sigh, she decided to stroll around the Serpentine. Looking at the ducks put her in a better mood. Though it was depressing to be turned down for work so often, her situation was not dire. In Paris she had sold the pearls left by her mother. She'd felt a pang, but the money gave her a little security now. Anne and Charles and his mother had been wonderful, and Amy, with the versatility of the young, was perfectly happy to be with her friends. Something would turn up in time.

It was nearing the fashionable hour, so she studied the elegant people riding and driving through the park. She was smiling to herself over the costume of a truly ridiculous dandy when suddenly she saw Lord Michael Kenyon driving toward her in a curricle. Her heart began pounding and her hands clenched spasmodically.

Because the day was fine, he was hatless, and the sun caught russet highlights in his windblown hair. He looked wonderful, with so much vitality that it was hard to remember how weak he had been when they had parted in Brussels. He had written to her from Wales to assure her of his safe arrival and complete recovery, but it was good to see the proof.

He would not notice her in the afternoon crowd. It was all she could do not to wave and call out. She would love to talk with him, but in her present state, she might be unable to conceal her feelings.

She was glad for her restraint when she noticed the young woman sitting beside him in the curricle. The girl was pretty and very appealing, with a slim figure and shining brown hair visible beneath her fashionable hat. Her delicate face showed warmth and wit, and character as well.

Michael glanced at his passenger and made a laughing remark. She joined in and briefly laid her gloved hand on his arm in a gesture of quiet intimacy.

Catherine swallowed hard and slipped into a group of nursemaids and children. The references to Michael in the society columns had hinted that he was looking for a wife. One paper had suggested that an "interesting announcement" was expected soon. From the looks of Michael and his companion, the issue was already settled, if not yet officially announced.

She took one last hungry look as the curricle passed. If she had not known him, that austerely planed face might seem intimidating. As it was, he was simply Michael, whose kindness and understanding had touched hidden places in her heart.

Wearily she made her way from the park. Now that she was a widow, she would be shamelessly throwing herself at Michael—if she were a normal woman. But she wasn't.

She thought of the ruined kaleidoscope buried among her possessions at Anne's house. In Brussels Michael had told her to throw it away. Instead she had kept the twisted silver tube, cherishing it as a memento of what had been between them even though it was useless at the task for which it had been designed. But it was no more useless than she had been as a wife.

She quickened her pace. Another marriage was unthinkable. That being the case, she should be happy that Michael seemed to have found a partner worthy of him. He deserved that.

If she worked at it long enough, perhaps she really would be so generous.

When she reached the Mowbrys' house, Catherine was still debating whether or not to mention that she had seen Michael in the park. She decided against it. Though Anne and Charles would be interested, Catherine would not be able to sound suitably casual.

When she entered the front door, Anne called from the drawing room, "Catherine, is that you? There's a letter for you on the table."

She opened it incuriously, assuming it was another discouraging missive from an employment agency.

It wasn't. In brief, formal terms, the letter stated that if Catherine Penrose Melbourne would call on Mr. Edmund Harwell, solicitor, she would learn something to her advantage.

She reread the note three times, the hair at her nape prickling. It might be nothing. Yet she could not escape the feeling that her luck was about to change.

Chapter 17

Michael was starting his second cup of coffee when his host and hostess joined him in the breakfast room. He did not look at Lucien and Kit too closely. Luce's arm was around his wife's waist, and their expressions had a lazy contentment that made it obvious what they had been doing before they rose from their bed.

Her glossy brown hair loose over her shoulders, Kit gave his arm a friendly pat as she passed on her way to pouring coffee for her husband and herself. "Good morning, Michael. Did you enjoy Margot's party last night?"

He glanced up from the newspaper. "Very much. The fact that it was all friends, with scarcely an eligible female in sight, meant I could relax. A pleasant change after being hunted like a fox by every ambitious mother and daughter in London."

Lucien laughed. "You're giving the hounds a good run. But there was at least one unmarried female there—Maxima Collins, the American girl who is staying with Rafe and Margot. You seemed to enjoy talking with her."

"She may be unmarried, but she is definitely not eligible. Robin Andreville acted like a cat in a catmint patch when he was around her, and she didn't seem to mind one bit." Michael thought about the young lady in question with a trace of regret. Her wit and directness made her the most attractive girl he'd met all spring. "Even if Miss Collins were available, she's too short for me. We would both have sore necks all the time."

"True," Lucien agreed. "You'd do better with someone of Kit's height." To demonstrate the convenience, he tilted his wife's chin up to give her a light kiss.

Michael smiled at the raillery, but he couldn't suppress a twinge of sadness. All his old friends had married, even Rafe, the confirmed bachelor.

For a moment, Catherine's image glowed in his mind. He forced it away. God knew he was trying his best to forget her. He had come to London with the idea of undertaking the search for a mate that had been delayed by Napoleon's escape from Elba. He had danced with countless females, called on the more promising ones, taken a few for a ride or drive. There were none he could imagine living with for the rest of his life.

He had thought the search for a wife would be easy if he didn't insist on love, but he couldn't even find a decent companion. He found far more pleasure in talking with Kit or Margot, Rafe's delightful wife.

He was turning a page when a footman entered. "Lord Michael, a messenger from Ashburton House brought this for you."

Michael's face went blank as he accepted the letter and tore it open. The message inside was brief and to the point.

Lucien asked, "Trouble?"

"It's from my brother." Michael rose to his feet, pushing his chair back brusquely. "Benfield says that the most noble Duke of Ashburton has had a heart seizure and is about to shuffle off this mortal coil. My presence is commanded."

Lucien regarded him gravely. "You don't have to go."

"No, but deathbed vigils are the done thing," Michael said cynically. "Who knows? Perhaps my father will have a last-minute change of attitude. Apologies, repentance, eleventh-hour reconciliations. Could be quite amusing."

Neither Lucien nor Kit were deceived by his brittle humor, but they made no comments. There really was nothing to be said.

The truly depressing thing, Michael realized as he prepared to leave, was that in his heart, he could not prevent himself from hoping that his ironic words would come true.

Edmund Harwell rose as his clerk ushered Catherine into the office. He was a thin, neat man with shrewd eyes. "Mrs. Melbourne?" Then he blinked, disconcerted. "Island eyes."

Catherine gave him a quizzical glance. "I beg your pardon?"

"Please, take a seat. My first task was going to be verification that your maiden name was Catherine Penrose and you are the only child of William and Elizabeth Penrose." He smiled faintly. "However, the proof of your bloodlines is in your eyes. I've never seen that shade of blue-green except on people from the island."

"What island?"

"The Isle of Skoal, off Cornwall."

"Everyone there has aqua eyes?"

"About half do. Locally they are called island eyes." Harwell hesitated, as if gathering his thoughts. "How much do you know about your parents' background?"

She shrugged. "Very little. They were from somewhere in the West Country. They married against their families' wishes and were disowned as a result. They never spoke of the past, so that's all I know." Yet suddenly, as clear as a church bell, she could hear her mother's voice referring to "the island." Curiosity aroused, she asked, "My parents were from Skoal?"

"Your mother was the daughter of a smallholder and your father was the younger son of the twenty-seventh Laird of Skoal. The laird, Torquil Penrose, asked me to communicate with you."

Her brows rose. "After all these years, this grandfather is suddenly interested in me?"

"Very much so."

Catherine's eyes narrowed. "Why?"

The solicitor said obliquely, "Are you familiar with Skoal?"

Catherine searched her memory. Though she had heard of the place, her knowledge was minimal. "It's a feudal domain like Sark in the Channel Isles, isn't it?"

"Precisely. Though nominally English, Skoal has its own laws, its own customs, its own citizens' assembly. There is a strong Viking influence, and a goodly dash of Celt as well. The laird is technically a British baron with a seat in the House of Lords, but on Skoal he is the sovereign of a tiny kingdom. Your grandfather has ruled the island for almost fifty years. Now his health is failing and he is concerned for the future."

Beginning to understand why she was summoned, Catherine said, "My father was the younger son. What of other children?"

"Therein likes the problem. There were only the two boys. Your father is dead, and the elder, Harald, and his son recently died in a sailing accident. That leaves you and your daughter as the laird's only legitimate descendants."

"You're saying I am heir to a feudal island?"

"Not necessarily. Your grandfather has the legal right to leave Skoal to anyone he chooses, or even sell it outright. However, he would prefer the island to stay in the family. That is why he wishes to meet you and your husband now."

"Me and my husband?" she repeated stupidly.

"Your grandfather does not believe a female would be equal to the task of governing the island and its enterprises." Harwell cleared his throat. "Also, since a wife's possessions legally belong to her husband, Captain Melbourne would become the laird if you became the lady."

Harwell didn't know Colin was dead. That wasn't surprising; few people did. She asked, "If I were a single woman—unmarried or widowed—would my grandfather consider me unacceptable?"

"I imagine he would insist you marry a man of whom he approved before he would designate you as heir. Luckily, that is not the case." Harwell pursed his lips. "May I speak frankly?"

"Please do."

"The laird is a very . . . forceful man, with strong opinions about the way things should be. I think he regretted disinheriting your father. He followed William's career from a distance. He knew of your marriage and the birth of your daughter." The solicitor cleared his throat. "He grieved deeply when he learned of the death of your parents."

Disliking the knowledge that she had been under observation all of her life, Catherine said coolly, "In other words, my grandfather is a stubborn, pigheaded tyrant."

Harwell almost smiled. "There are some who would say so. But he takes his duty seriously, and he is determined to leave the island in good hands. There is a distant cousin who would like to be the next laird. He's an accomplished gentleman who maintains a home on the island, but your grandfather would prefer the heir to be his own flesh and blood."

Harwell's tone implied that he did not approve of the cousin, but Catherine knew he would not say more. "I'm not sure if I want an unknown grandfather to judge my life."

"It would be worth your while to meet him. Besides the title and the estate, there is an income of about two thousand pounds a year." He gave a dry little cough. "Captain Melbourne is a distinguished officer, but a military career is seldom lucrative, especially in peacetime."

She bit her lip, knowing she should reveal Colin's death. Yet if her grandfather would only consider her as half of a married couple, telling the truth would lose her this heaven-sent opportunity for financial security. The alternative, taking another husband, was unthinkable, even if it would gain her ten thousand pounds a year. Temporizing, she asked, "Is my grandfather in London now?"

"Oh, no, he hasn't left the island in years. As I said, his health is failing." Harwell looked troubled. "That is an understatement. He is bedridden, and his physician believes that he will not last out the summer. Though his will is strong, his body is very frail. That is why he wants you to travel to Skoal with your husband immediately."

"What if he doesn't like what he sees?"

"He needn't leave you a penny." The solicitor smiled. "But there is no reason to suppose he will disapprove of his granddaughter. He has heard of Saint Catherine and her work on the battlefields of Spain. He is anxious to meet you."

"The feeling is not mutual," she said tartly. "What kind of man would disinherit his son for marrying a woman as fine as my mother?"

"A stubborn man," Harwell said quietly. "And a lonely one. I can appreciate your doubts, but please, consider carefully. The laird is your blood kin. If you walk away from him, you disinherit not only yourself, but your daughter, and any other children you might bear. More than that, you cut yourself off from your own unique heritage."

Hearing a yearning note in the solicitor's voice, she asked, "Do you know the island well?"

"My father was born there. He was the laird's London agent before me. I've visited the island often over the years. It's a wild, beautiful place." The solicitor gave a faintly embarrassed smile. "One might almost say magical."

Once more Catherine heard her mother's voice, this time saying, "The daffodils will be out now on the island." There had been a pause before her father replied, "Soon they will be out here." She had been too young to recognize the wistfulness in the mundane comments. Suddenly she wanted to see the island that shaped her parents. And, if possible, she wanted to win the inheritance that would give her and Amy financial freedom.

She rose to her feet. "You've given me much to think about. I will let you know my decision tomorrow."

"Excellent." The solicitor also stood. "Bring your husband as well, since he is intimately involved in your decision."

Blindly she went out into the sun. Such a legacy would solve all her problems. But one thought was blazingly clear. She needed a husband, and she needed one fast.

Chapter 18

It had been years since Michael had set foot in Ashburton House, but it hadn't changed. It was still enormous, grand, stifling. The butler, Riggs, had acquired a few more gray hairs, but his face was still supercilious.

Michael handed over his hat. "I presume the death watch is in the duke's suite?"

"Yes, Lord Michael."

He turned and went to the majestic staircase. As he climbed the polished marble steps, he remembered sliding down the sweeping banisters. He had gotten into trouble every time he was caught, but that had never stopped him.

Though the mansion had not changed outwardly, he felt a subtle difference in the atmosphere. It was charged with the hush of a household waiting for death. A footman in powdered wig and knee breeches stood outside the duke's chambers. Recognizing a Kenyon, he opened the door with a bow.

Michael took a deep breath, then entered, crossing the sitting room to his father's bedchamber. He tried to remember if he had ever set foot in it before; he didn't think so. He and his father had never been on intimate terms.

The bedroom was claustrophobically dark and heavy with the scents of medicine and decay. It was a shock to see his father's wasted body lying in the bed, dwarfed by the velvet hangings and massive carved posts. Abruptly it hit home that the ogre of his childhood was dying. As a soldier, he respected the power and finality of death, and he found himself feeling some compassion. The fourth Duke of Ashburton had finally found an enemy he could not bully into submission.

A dozen people were clustered uneasily around the room: his brother and sister and their respective spouses, the duke's valet and secretary, several physicians. His sister, the Countess of Herrington, scowled at Michael. "I'm surprised to see *you* here."

His mouth tightened. "If my presence is unwelcome, Claudia, that can be remedied."

His brother frowned at the byplay. "This is not the place for squabbling. I invited Michael because Father wants to see him." Though all of the Kenyons were tall, with dark chestnut hair and chiseled features, the Marquess of Benfield had the cold eyes and flinty authority of a man who had been raised to be a duke. There were times in their childhood when the brothers had gotten on fairly well. There were only two years between them, and as a child Michael had called his brother Stephen.

It had been decades since he had used any name but Benfield.

"Is that Michael?"

The hoarse whisper caused everyone to turn to the bed.

"Yes, sir. I've come." Michael stepped close and looked down at his father.

The duke was a shadow of his former self, all strained bones and will, but in his eyes, anger still smoldered. "Everyone leave. Except for Michael and Benfield."

Claudia started to protest. "But Father—"

The duke cut her off. "Out!"

There was a shuffling as people left the room. Though Claudia's face was stiff with anger, she dared not disobey.

Michael glanced at Benfield, but his brother gave a slight shake of the head, as much in the dark as Michael.

The duke said in a thin, rasping voice, "You want to know why I called you here."

It was a statement, not a question. Michael braced himself; he'd been a damned fool to think there was a chance of an eleventh-hour rapprochement. There could be no reconciliation where there had never once been harmony. Wondering what parting shot his father had in store, he said, "It isn't unreasonable for a father to wish to see all of his children at such a time."

The duke's face twisted. "You are not my son."

Every nerve in Michael's body went taut. "As you wish, sir," he said coolly. "It doesn't surprise me to be disinherited, though I'll be damned if I know what great crime I've committed. I've never understood."

The age-paled blue eyes blazed. "*You are not my son!*

Can I say it any more clearly than that? Your whore of a mother admitted it freely."

Michael felt his lungs constrict until he could scarcely breathe. As he struggled for control, he looked from the duke to Benfield, seeing the same bones and coloring that faced him in the mirror every morning. "With all due respect, I look very much like a Kenyon. Perhaps she lied in order to anger you." God knew that the duke and duchess had fought like pit vipers.

The duke's face reddened with a fury that had festered for decades. "She spoke the truth. You were fathered by my younger brother, Roderick. I found them together myself."

Benfield sucked his breath in, his face showing the same shock that must be on Michael's.

"She didn't like my affairs, so she decided to pay me back in kind," the duke continued. "Said she'd always fancied Roderick—that he was better looking and better in bed. That I should be grateful to her, because if anything happened to Benfield and you inherited, the duke would still be a Kenyon. Grateful! The bitch—the treacherous, bloody-minded bitch. She knew I had no choice but to accept you, and she reveled in it."

He went into a fit of coughing. Hastily Benfield offered him a glass of water, but the old man waved it away. "Roderick had always resented me for being the elder. Georgiana gave him not only the chance to cuckold me, but the possibility that Roderick's son would inherit. Vicious, the pair of them."

Michael felt numb from head to toe, and his lungs were barely capable of expanding. Strange to think that he had been brought into existence to serve as a pawn between a man and a woman who despised each other. No wonder his childhood had been saturated with hatred. "Why did you choose to tell me now?"

"A man has a right to know who his father is." The duke's mouth twisted. "And since Benfield will be head of the family, he should know the truth. Maybe now he'll get busy and sire a son. Besides, he's soft and might treat you like a member of the family if he doesn't know better."

"You needn't worry," Michael said, unable to conceal his bitterness. "He's never been very brotherly in the past."

"You're just like Roderick," the duke snarled, ancient

fury vivid in his expression. "The same damned green eyes. Smart, strong, arrogant, better at everything than my own son." Ignoring a choked exclamation from Benfield, he finished, "I should have exiled you to the Indies, as I did Roderick."

Michael wanted to lash out, to wound the man who had tormented him all his life, but what was the point? The duke was dying, and the hatred he had nurtured had been its own punishment. "I suppose I must thank you for finally being honest with me. Good day, sir. I wish you a peaceful death."

The duke's bony fingers bit into the coverlet. "I despise the fact of your existence, yet I . . . I couldn't help but respect you. You served with honor in the army, and you built a fortune from no more than a younger son's portion. I would have liked an heir like you." He gave Benfield a contemptuous glance, then looked back at Michael. "I wanted another son. Instead, I got *you.*"

"I would have been your son if you had wanted me to be," Michael said tightly. Feeling on the verge of dissolution, he turned and walked toward the door.

An ashen Benfield intercepted him, catching his arm. "Michael, wait!"

"For what? The duke has said everything worth saying." Michael jerked his arm away. "Don't worry, I'll never darken any of your doors again. I wish you much joy of your inheritance."

Benfield started to speak, then stopped, silenced by the ice in Michael's eyes.

He swung open the door to the duke's sitting room. Claudia and the others stared, trying to divine what had happened. Looking neither right nor left, he walked across the room and into the hall. Down the polished stairs, one hand on the banister because he was less steady than he pretended. Past the butler, then outside into the blessedly cool air. It soothed the suffocating heat in his lungs.

So he was a bastard. It explained everything: the duke's obvious loathing, the smug way his mother had petted and spoiled him when she was in the mood. Claudia and Benfield had sensed the duke's attitude and become contemptuous in their turn. What should have been a family had become a holocaust.

He had never known Roderick, who had died in the West

Indies when Michael was an infant. He had vague memories of being told by the elderly Kenyon nurse that he was just like his poor dear uncle. She had been more accurate than she knew.

Instead of returning to Lucien's house, he deliberately went in the opposite direction. Now that the first shock was over, the news of his birth was curiously liberating. *It hadn't been his fault.* He had done nothing to justify his father's—no, the duke's—ruthless criticisms and savage whippings. When he was sent to Eton instead of Harrow, the traditional Kenyon school, it was not because of his personal failings.

All of his attempts to be the best, to prove himself worthy, had been doomed to fail, because nothing could have made the duke accept him. Yet the struggles had not been valueless, for they had shaped his character, made him what he was. Feeling like an outsider, he had developed an empathy for other outsiders that was unusual in someone raised as the son of a duke. That empathy had led him to befriend Nicholas and Kenneth and others, greatly enriching his life.

Though the news was jarring, it was of no real significance. He was still the man he had always been, both his flaws and his strengths. If he ever told the truth to his closest friends, they would not care. They had provided shelter, both literally and emotionally, when he was growing up, and they would not abandon him now. He had become a wealthy man through mining and investments to prove that he did not need the duke's help. Because of those efforts, now it didn't matter that he would inherit nothing.

He thought back, reinterpreting the past in the light of this new knowledge. He had not lost his family, because he had never really had one. Oddly, he found that he no longer hated the duke. A better man might have treated his wife's bastard more kindly, but the duke had never had much kindness in him. It was characteristic of the duke's cruelty that he could be so disdainful of his own son in front of Benfield's face. Pride and propriety were his ruling passions, and it could not have been easy to be continuously confronted with the proof of his humiliation.

After Michael walked his way to peace, he returned to Strathmore House. It was better to know the truth than to remain in ignorance. Nonetheless, he felt almost as exhausted as during his long convalescence after Waterloo. Thank God for Nicholas and Clare, who taken him into their own home and cared for him like a brother. With such friends, he didn't need a family.

His tranquillity lasted until the footman handed him a card. "There is a lady waiting to see you, my lord."

Her heart pounded when she heard the salon door open and his familiar footsteps. She donned the serene expression of Saint Catherine, then slowly turned from the window.

Michael had seemed younger, more carefree, that time she had seen him in the park. Now that she was closer, she saw that the lines at the corners of his eyes had deepened, and he seemed strained. But there was warmth in his voice when he said, "Catherine?"

Dear Lord, would she be able to carry through such a deception? Throat tight, she said, "I'm sorry to bother you, Lord Michael."

"Are we on such formal terms, Catherine?" He crossed the room and gave her a light, friendly kiss. "It's good to see you. You're as lovely as ever."

Releasing her hands, he asked, "How is Amy? And Colin?"

"Amy is wonderful. You'd scarcely know her. I swear she's grown three inches since last spring. Colin—" she hesitated, searching for words that would be partially true, "is still in France."

Unsuspicious, Michael said, "I'm forgetting my manners. Please, sit down. I'll ring for tea."

Knowing she must speak before she lost her nerve entirely, Catherine said, "I'd better state my piece first. I need some rather unusual aid. You—you may want to throw me out when you hear what it is."

Michael's expression became serious and he studied her face. "Never," he said quietly. "I owe you my life, Catherine. You can ask anything of me."

"You give me more credit than I deserve." She swallowed hard and reminded herself of why she must lie. "I'm afraid that . . . that I need a husband. A temporary husband."

Chapter 19

Michael stared at Catherine, wondering if he had heard properly. The obvious, vulgar interpretation could not be true. Perhaps he'd fallen from his horse and landed on his head and this whole day was a fever dream. "I beg your pardon?"

"I'm sorry, my thoughts are rather scrambled." She sat down and drew a deep breath. "I've just come from a solicitor's office, where I learned that I'm the only granddaughter of the Laird of Skoal. My grandfather wishes to look me and my husband over to see if we are worthy of inheriting the island. According to Mr. Harwell, the laird is very ill, so it must be done soon. It would take weeks to notify Colin so he could return from France. By that time, my grandfather might be dead and this opportunity lost."

"You can reach Skoal from London in two or three days."

Catherine smiled mirthlessly. "Alone, I'm not good enough. Mr. Harwell said the laird wants to approve my husband as well as me. Otherwise, the island may be left elsewhere." Her eyes slid away. "Since Colin can't possibly get here in time, could . . . could you come with me for a few days and pretend to be my husband?"

In its way, this request was as shocking as the duke's announcement. "You're joking."

"I'm afraid not." She bit her lip. "I know this is an outrageous request, but I can think of no better solution."

There was definitely a God, and He had a very strange sense of humor. Michael said carefully, "In other words, you'd like me to take part in a charade to deceive your grandfather."

"It sounds dreadful, doesn't it? I hate the idea of deceit. Yet, to be blunt, the legacy would be welcome. Very welcome indeed." Her mouth twisted wryly. "To be even more blunt, my grandfather might approve of you more than Colin. I gather that the laird is looking for reliable hands in which to leave Skoal."

And Colin Melbourne was not the steadiest of men. Remembering the signs of financial strain in Brussels, Michael could understand why this legacy was vitally important to her.

Catherine continued, "It's not as if the deception will cause any harm. A woman can run an estate as well as a man, and I will learn whatever is necessary."

He wondered if she feared that Melbourne would refuse to live such an isolated life. Or perhaps she could no longer accept her husband's infidelities and wanted to build a life of her own. Whatever her reasons, he could not ask. But there were other questions that must be answered. "The mere thought of telling a lie has tied you in knots. Are you a good enough actress to successfully pass me off as your husband?"

She closed her eyes for the space of a dozen heartbeats. Then she opened them and said easily, "I'm an excellent actress, Colin. I can do whatever I need to do."

She was serene Saint Catherine again, and her voice was so convincing when she called him by her husband's name that he felt chills. Were all women born deceivers? A good thing she was nothing like Caroline, or she would be dangerous.

Perhaps she could carry off the charade, but could he? They would have to spend a great deal of time together. In public, they would have to mimic the physical and verbal intimacy of a long-married couple. In private, he must keep his distance. Feeling about her as he did, the combination would be sheer hell.

Of course, she did not know how he felt about her. She also had the innocence of a long-married, monogamous woman. She had forgotten what unruly beasts men could be, if indeed she had ever known. Yet he could not say no. Not only because he had given her a carte blanche for help, but because he could not resist the opportunity to be with her. He was as much a fool as he had ever been. "Very well. You have yourself a temporary husband."

She gave a sigh of relief. "Thank you so much. There is no one else I could trust to do this."

Because her other male friends had more sense, Michael

thought dourly. "If time is of the essence, shall we leave for Skoal tomorrow?"

"If you can get away so quickly, that would be ideal." Her brow furrowed. "But don't you have social commitments?"

He shrugged. "Nothing that can't be canceled."

"Bless you, Michael. I don't know what I would do without you." She got to her feet. "I'll go back to Mr. Harwell's office and tell him we'll be going to Skoal. No doubt he'll have instructions for me. Also, he said he would advance me the money for travel expenses if I decided to go."

"No need. I'll take care of the costs."

"I can't possibly let you do that."

"Why not? I'm your husband, after all," he said lightly. "Also, if your grandfather is the bullying sort, you will feel at a disadvantage if you have accepted his money." Growing up in the household of the Duke of Ashburton, Michael had become an expert on the politics of power and money.

"I hadn't thought of that." She considered. "I would certainly rather be obligated to you than an unknown grandfather, but I will repay you as soon as I can."

"Very well." Michael opened the salon door for her. "I'll take you to the solicitor."

"That's not necessary."

He arched his brows in the way he had used to intimidate young ensigns. "I expect my wife to obey my wishes."

She laughed, looking years younger than when she had come in. "I shall strive to be more conformable, my dear."

"Don't try too hard. I like you the way you are."

For a long moment their gazes held. He wondered if she realized how dangerous this masquerade was. He had sworn to behave honorably where she was concerned, but he was only flesh and blood.

She trusted him. He must remember that.

Feeling equal parts relief and guilt, Catherine climbed into Michael's curricle. Lying to Michael was despicable when he was helping her so much. Yet for the life of her, she could see no alternative. Even to Anne, she could not explain why remarriage was unthinkable. Neither could she chance the possibility that he might feel obligated to solve her problems by giving her his name. He deserved better; he deserved that lovely girl in the park with her shining hair and warm, intimate smile. He deserved a real woman, not a shameful fraud like Catherine Melbourne.

Locking away her guilt, she relayed what she had learned about her parents and Skoal as Michael threaded his curricle through the heavy afternoon traffic.

When she finished, he frowned. "Your grandfather sounds like a tyrant. A good thing you're not going there alone."

She agreed. Spending so much time with Michael might be difficult, but she would feel safer with him beside her.

He continued, "Since the lawyer and your grandfather have so much information on you and your family, you'd better tell me about Colin's background so I don't make any mistakes."

Catherine thought a moment about what Michael would need to know. "Colin's father was an American loyalist who stayed with the British army after the revolution. His mother was also American, so he had no close English relatives. Growing up with the army meant there was no particular place he called home. He went to school at Rugby before joining the regiment. By the time I met him, his parents were dead." She felt a wave of sadness as she recounted the bare bones of Colin's life. Blinking back tears, she continued, "Though you don't really resemble each other, luckily you both fit the general description of being tall, brown-haired, and of military bearing."

"That's a simple history to remember, and since British officers usually don't wear uniforms when off duty, I won't have to find myself dragoon finery overnight." Michael expertly guided the curricle between two stopped drays. "Are you taking Amy to Skoal? I presume your grandfather wants to meet the next generation."

Catherine shook her head emphatically. "I won't take her into a situation that is so uncertain. The laird might be a complete monster. Besides, it wouldn't be right to ask her to participate in a deception."

"Quite right. Deception is for adults," he said dryly. "Do you have someone to look after her? If not, I'm sure the Strathmores would be glad to have her as a guest."

"No need. We're staying with the Mowbrys. Anne and Charles are living with his widowed mother, if you recall." She chuckled. "Amy is delighted to see Clancy and Louis the Lazy again."

He smiled involuntarily. "I miss the beast myself. How is Charles?"

She paused a moment, wondering if she dared ask for more help, and decided that for the sake of her friends, she would dare. "Charles has recovered well from his wounds, but he's having trouble finding work."

"Many former soldiers are in similar straits." Michael's brows drew together thoughtfully. "As Duke of Candover, my friend Rafe owns an enormous range of estates and businesses. Just last night he mentioned that the gentleman who has been a sort of general manager for the last thirty years is nearing retirement. Rafe asked if I knew someone who could work with old Wilson and eventually take over. Besides intelligence, honesty, and efficiency, the position requires someone who knows how to command men, which is why Rafe thought a former officer would be a good choice. I think he and Charles would get on very well."

"That sounds *perfect*. You are so good, Michael."

He shrugged away her thanks. "Rafe will be glad to find someone of Charles's abilities. I'll tell him to expect Charles to call at Candover House within the next few days."

They had reached their destination. Michael drew up and tossed a coin to a boy to hold the horses, then climbed down and helped Catherine from the carriage. She gave him a nervous smile. "The first act of the masquerade is about to begin."

The mischievous light in his green eyes drew her in, making them partners against the world. "I'll say as little as possible," he promised. "That should keep me out of trouble."

The meeting went smoothly. Mr. Harwell was delighted with Catherine's decision, and he obviously liked what he saw of her "husband." When they were safely in the curricle again, Catherine gave a sigh of relief. "That was a favorable omen, don't you think?"

"So far, so good. Shall I take you home now?"

Uneasily she realized she could not let him meet the Mowbrys. If anyone mentioned Colin's death, her deception would go up in flames and Michael would be understandably angry. Eventually he would learn that she had been widowed, but because of the way the government was hushing up the death, she should be able to obscure the actual date. Dear God, but she was walking a tightrope! "Well, almost home. It would be better if you leave me off a street or two away."

"You don't want Anne and Charles to see us together?" He gave her a slanting glance. "If you're concerned about appearances, it will be difficult to manage this charade."

"Any woman who has crisscrossed Spain with an army doesn't worry overly about propriety," she said lightly. "But the fewer people who know about this escapade, the better."

"Which means no servants for either of us." He shook his head. "That part is easy, but do you have any idea how many potential complications you are setting up for the future?"

Knowledge of the complications was knotting her stomach. Trying to sound calm, she said, "I've thought about it. All I can do is deal with the problems when they appear. That's another thing I learned in Spain—don't worry about tomorrow's crisis until you've solved today's." She offered a tentative smile. "And with your help, today's crisis has been overcome."

"Intrepid woman." He returned her smile, his eyes warm. "It's a mad business, but I must say that I'm looking forward to our marriage."

So was she; too blasted much.

As soon as Michael stepped into Strathmore House, the butler said that the earl wished to see him. Wondering what else would happen on this lunatic day, Michael went to his friend's study.

Lucien got to his feet when Michael entered, saying gravely, "This letter arrived a little while ago."

The paper was black-bordered. Understanding why his friend had wanted to hand it over in person, Michael broke the seal and scanned the message. "It's from Benfield," he said expressionlessly. "The Duke of Ashburton is dead. He must have given up the ghost very soon after I left his house."

"I'm sorry," Lucien said quietly. "No matter how difficult the relationship, losing a parent has to be a blow."

"The end of an era, certainly, but don't waste your sympathy on me." Michael stared at the scrawled lines. Benfield was a responsible fellow; he would make a good duke.

Better than the bitter old man he was succeeding. He had even politely requested a meeting, saying they had matters to discuss.

Unable to think of anything the two of them might say to each other, he touched the corner of the letter to a burning candle on the desk. The paper blackened, then burst into flame.

I would have been your son if you had wanted me to be. His chest constricted as painful regret washed through him. If the old duke had wanted filial love and loyalty, he could have had them so easily. Michael had desperately wanted to love; perhaps that was why later he had loved so unwisely.

Before the flames could scorch his fingertips, he threw the burning scrap into the fireplace. "I'll be going out of town tomorrow, probably for a fortnight or so."

"I presume the burial will be at Ashburton."

"No doubt, but that's not where I'm going. Some other business has come up."

"You're not attending your father's funeral?" Lucien could not keep shock from his voice, but then, he had loved his father.

"My presence would be unwelcome." Not ready to explain, even to Luce, Michael watched the paper crumble to ash. With luck, it was the last connection he would ever have with the Kenyon family.

He raised his head. Lucien had the worried expression Michael had seen before on his friends, though not in the last two years. He wanted to assure Luce that there was no need for concern, but he was too drained to find the right words. He said, "I'm not expecting anything urgent, but if you should need to reach me, I'll be staying on the Isle of Skoal under the name Colin Melbourne."

His friend's brows rose. "What are you up to? Deception is usually my specialty."

"Merely a bit of dragonslaying." Michael halted, suddenly remembering his childhood nurse. Fanny had been a good-natured country girl, the closest thing he'd had to a mother. In her bedtime stories, she had combined Saint George and the Archangel Michael into one swashbuckling, heroic figure called Saint Michael. Michael would dream of slaying dragons, saving maidens, and performing other great feats. If he did that, surely he would win the approval of his father, and the hand of the most beautiful princess in the world.

But his father was not his father, and the beautiful princess was married to another man. A pity that Fanny hadn't been educated enough to tell him about Don Quixote, who was the real model for Michael's life. Face set, he began describing a steam engine company he was considering for investment. Lucien tactfully accepted the change of subject, and there was no more discussion of the late, unlamented Duke of Ashburton.

It wasn't until he went to bed that night that Michael realized how lucky he was. Helping Catherine was the perfect antidote to what would otherwise be a bleak time.

I wanted another son. Instead, I got you.

Chapter 20

"There's a post chaise outside," Amy reported. She glanced over her shoulder. "Are you *positive* I can't come with you?"

"Positive. I want to be sure this new grandfather deserves to meet my daughter." Catherine hugged Amy. "But if he behaves himself, just think—someday you may be the Lady of Skoal!"

"It does sound rather grand," Amy admitted. "If you like the old gentleman, send for me and I'll come right away."

"We'll see. I promise I won't be gone too long."

Catherine went outside, accompanied by the whole family and both dogs. As the driver packed the baggage away, Anne said, "I wish you weren't traveling alone."

"I'm not alone with a driver and a postboy. Besides, this is England, not Spain. I'll be safe." More guilt; now she was lying to her best friend. It was a relief to be on her way.

Half an hour later, the chaise stopped at a busy coaching inn to collect Michael. After his baggage was stowed, he swung into the vehicle, saying, "If you don't mind traveling long hours, we should be at Skoal tomorrow evening."

"I hope so. I'm very curious about this grandfather of mine." The chaise was spacious and very comfortable, but Michael was still too close for her peace of mind. She had forgotten the aura of leashed power that emanated from him.

They spoke little, each of them absorbed in private thoughts. Though they were servantless, Michael's natural authority produced instant deference and the best available horses whenever they stopped. They made excellent time.

Michael knew the road well, and Catherine found out why when they reached a village called Great Ashburton, in Wiltshire. It was market day, and the chaise slowed to a crawl as they went through the town square. Drowsily she asked, "Does this village have a connection with your family?"

He looked unseeing out the window. "Ashburton Abbey, the family seat, is about two miles down that road we just passed."

"Good heavens." She sat up, her sleepiness gone. "This is your home?"

"I was born and raised here. My home is in Wales."

Fascinated, she said, "You bought sweets at that shop?"

"Mrs. Thomsen's. Yes."

He was as terse as if confessing to murder. Since he didn't wish to discuss the past, she studied the village and tried to imagine a young Michael dashing through the streets. It seemed to be a pleasant, prosperous community. Then she frowned. "There are black ribbons on many of the doors."

"The Duke of Ashburton died yesterday."

She stared at him, sure she must have misheard. "Your father died yesterday and you said *nothing*?"

"There was nothing to say." He was still gazing out the window, face like granite.

She remembered the time he had discussed his family in Brussels, and her heart ached for him. His hand was clenched on the seat between them. She rested her palm on the knotted fist. "I'm even more grateful that at a time like this, you have the generosity to help me."

He did not look at her, but his hand turned and convulsively clasped hers. "On the contrary, it is I who should be grateful."

Though neither of them spoke again, their hands stayed locked for a long time.

They traveled until it was full dark, then stopped at a coaching inn. There were two bedchambers available, for which Catherine was grateful. After refreshing themselves, they dined in a private parlor. They both relaxed under the influence of good food, good conversation, and a fine bottle of Bordeaux.

When the last of the dishes had been cleared away, Michael produced a small book. "I stopped at Hatchard's and found a guidebook to the West Country that mentions the Isle of Skoal. Shall we find out what awaits us?"

"Please. My ignorance is almost total."

He thumbed through the pages to the correct entry. "The island is about two miles by three and is divided into Great Skoal and Little Skoal. They are almost two separate islands, connected only by a natural causeway called the Neck. The writer strongly suggests that visitors not attempt to cross the Neck at night, for fear of the 'awesome toothed rocks jutting from the sea more than two hundred feet below.' "

She took a sip of wine, enjoying the sound of his deep voice. "I'll bear that in mind."

"There are approximately five hundred residents, and more gulls than the writer wants to think about," he continued. "Fishing and farming are the main occupations. It has been inhabited since 'time immemorial,' and is 'noteworthy for the blend of Celtic, Anglo-Saxon, Viking, and Norman customs.' It is also one of the few feudal precincts left in Western Europe."

She rested her chin on her hand and admired the dramatic shadows that candlelight cast on Michael's face. "What does that mean in practical terms?"

"I hope you like pigeon pie. The laird is the only one allowed to have a dovecote."

Catherine laughed. "That is the extent of feudal privilege? I'm disappointed."

He consulted the book. "Well, the laird pays feudal homage to the King of England, which is rare in these boring modern days." He scanned the next pages. "No doubt there's more, but the author prefers to wax enthusiastic over the spectacular cliffs and sea caves. I'll let you read the details yourself."

"Thank you." His fingertips brushed hers as he passed the volume over. Her skin prickled with aliveness. The intimacy of this meal was exactly what she had feared when she decided to ask him to help her. Too much closeness. Too much yearning.

She finished her wine in a swallow and got to her feet. "I'll retire now. It's been a long day."

He emptied his own glass. "Tomorrow will be even longer."

As they went upstairs, he held her arm in an easy, husbandly way. But if they were really wed, she would be used to his quiet courtesy and intense masculinity. She would not feel a giddiness more suitable to a girl of sixteen than a widow of twenty-eight.

They reached her bedchamber, and Michael unlocked the door. When he stepped back so she could enter, she looked into his eyes and knew she should not have had a second glass of wine. Not that she was tipsy; merely relaxed. It would be simple, and friendly, to raise her face for a good-night kiss. And, oh, how good it would be to have his arms around her.

Unhappily she recognized that desire was flowing through her like warm syrup, sweet and melting. Desire, her treacherous enemy. She swallowed hard. "By the way, I forgot to mention that Elspeth McLeod and Will Ferris have married. They're living in Lincolnshire and expecting their first child."

"I'm glad. They seemed well suited." Michael smiled down at her. "Elspeth was almost as intrepid as you."

The warmth of his admiration almost destroyed what sense she had left. Hastily she said, "Good night, Michael."

He touched a warning finger to her lips. "Don't use my real name," he said quietly. "I know it will be difficult, but you must think of me as Colin."

Hesitating, she said, "It will be easier to call you by some endearment." And such a term would safely express her secret longings. "Sleep well, my dear."

He put the room key in her hand. This time his touch did not tingle. It burned.

She swung the door shut and locked it, then sank onto the bed. Her tongue touched her lips where his finger had made that feather-light contact. Though she could conceal her love, it was far harder to suppress her sensual responses.

She clenched her hands and thought of the reasons why desire must be resisted.

Because Michael thought her an honorable married woman.

Because of that lovely girl in the park, who had made Michael laugh.

Most of all, because she herself could not endure the inevitable consequences of passion.

Such good reasons. Why couldn't they cool the fever in her blood as she tossed and turned throughout the night?

* * *

The small port of Penward was the gateway to Skoal. They drove directly to the waterfront, where half a dozen fishing boats were moored in the bay. Catherine climbed from the chaise gratefully, sore from two days of being jostled at high speed.

Together they approached the only person in sight, a sturdily built man who sat on a stone wall and puffed a clay pipe as he gazed out to sea. Michael said, "Excuse me, sir. We wish to go to Skoal. Do you know someone who could take us there?"

The man turned, his gaze passing over Michael and coming to rest on Catherine. "You'd be the laird's granddaughter."

She blinked in surprise. "How did you know that?"

"Island eyes," he said succinctly. "Word came from London this morning that you would be here soon. The laird sent me over to wait for you. You made good time." He got to his feet. "I'm George Fitzwilliam. I'll take you across."

Catherine and Michael exchanged a glance. The solicitor had wasted no time in notifying the laird. From now on, they would be under constant observation.

The baggage was transferred to Fitzwilliam's boat and the chaise dismissed. They set out across the choppy water. Shortly after the mainland disappeared behind them, the captain said, "Skoal," and gestured to the southwest.

Catherine studied the dark, jagged shape on the horizon. The sun was low in the sky, making it hard to see details. Slowly the island resolved into cliffs and hills. Seabirds wheeled above with slowly beating wings, their cries mournful in the empty sky. Occasionally one plunged arrow-straight into the sea after its prey.

They sailed partway around the island, close enough to see waves crashing against the base of the cliffs. The guidebook had been right about the spectacular scenery, but Skoal's first impression was forbidding. Catherine found it strange to think that this remote spot might become her home.

Michael's arm went around her. She didn't know if he was responding to the temperature or her nerves. Either way, she was grateful.

A break showed in the cliffs and the boat turned into it. She held her breath as they sailed between jagged pillars of rock. At night or in a storm, this would be a dangerous passage.

Inside was a small bay with three docks and several moored boats. As they approached the shore, an odd, low carriage pulled by a team of ponies rattled into view from behind two sheds. It halted and the door swung open. A tall, lean man with a weathered face climbed out and walked without haste to the dock where Fitzwilliam was mooring his boat.

Michael jumped to the dock, then turned and took Catherine's hand to help her from the bobbing boat. Releasing his clasp with reluctance, she turned to the newcomer. He was in his mid-thirties and dressed casually, more like a clerk than a gentleman, but he had a quiet air of authority.

He inclined his head. "Mrs. Melbourne, I presume."

She opened her mouth to reply, then paused, struck by his clear, blue-green eyes. They were the brilliant shade she had seen only in her parents and daughter. She offered her hand. "Yes. Seeing your eyes makes me understand why I was identified so easily by the solicitor in London and Captain Fitzwilliam."

He smiled as he took her hand. "You'll grow accustomed to it. Half the people here have the island eyes. I'm Davin Penrose, constable of Skoal. I'll take you to the laird's home." He had a soft, rolling accent unlike any she'd ever heard.

"Penrose," she said with interest. "Are you and I related?"

"Almost everyone on Skoal is—there are only five family names in common usage. Penrose, Fitzwilliam, Tregaron, De Salle, and Olson."

Names as diverse as the island's heritage, she noted. Taking Michael's elbow to bring him forward, she said, "Mr. Penrose, this is my husband, Captain Melbourne."

It was the first time she had introduced Michael with Colin's name. It felt very strange.

Unperturbed, Michael said, "A pleasure, Mr. Penrose. What does it mean to be constable?"

"That's the Skoalan name for the laird's steward, though I have other duties as well." Davin shook hands, then gave orders for the luggage to be loaded. A few minutes later they were rumbling toward the sheer cliffs that surrounded the bay.

Michael said, "There's a tunnel?"

Davin nodded. "It was cut through the cliffs about fifty years ago by miners from Cornwall. This is the best bay on the island, but it was useless before the tunnel."

Catherine glanced out and saw that the road climbed steeply until it disappeared into a dark opening in the cliff. The light diminished sharply when they entered the crudely cut tunnel. The shaft was barely large enough for the carriage. "The ponies are strong to pull us uphill at such an angle."

"They have to be," the constable replied. "The only horses belong to the laird. Everyone else uses oxen and ponies."

They emerged into the light and the road leveled out. The few trees visible were stunted and twisted by the wind, but masses of gorse surrounded them. The yellow blossoms glowed golden in the setting sun.

As they drove toward the center of the island, they passed scattered farms of rugged gray stone and carefully tended fields. Once they descended into a small valley lush with taller trees and a blue haze of wild hyacinths. Catherine's heart lifted. It would not be hard to love a place that looked like this.

The sun had dropped below the horizon by the time they reached the laird's residence. The massive building was crowned with battlements and clearly had begun as a castle, though additions had been added later. Davin climbed from the carriage first and helped Catherine out.

As she straightened her skirts, a middle-aged woman emerged from the house. "Hello, Mrs. Melbourne, Captain Melbourne. I'm the housekeeper, Mrs. Tregaron. Your baggage will be taken to your room, but the laird will see you right now."

Michael said, "We've had a very long journey. My wife might prefer to refresh herself before meeting her grandfather."

The housekeeper's brows drew together worriedly. "The laird was most particular that you come up right away."

"It's all right." Catherine bit back Michael's name, which she had almost said aloud. "No doubt he's as curious about me as I am about him."

He studied her face, then nodded. "As you wish."

His concern for her was warming. She took his arm and

they set off after Mrs. Tregaron. The house was a warren, with the jumble of furnishings characteristic of very old houses. Sheraton chairs sat next to carved Jacobean oak chests, and shabby tapestries hung next to paintings of stiff Elizabethans. Catherine glanced at one of the portraits and saw aqua eyes staring out at her.

The route twisted and turned, but stayed on the ground floor. Finally they came to a heavy oak door. Mrs. Tregaron knocked, then swung the door open. "They're here, my lord."

A deep voice said gruffly, "Send them in."

Catherine raised her chin. The main act of the masquerade was about to begin.

Chapter 21

Intensely grateful that Michael was with her, Catherine entered her grandfather's bedchamber. A pair of lamps illuminated the stern features of the man propped against the pillows of the massive four-poster bed. She caught her breath, startled by the familiarity of the long, lined face under the thick silver hair. If her father had lived to such an age, he would have looked very like the laird.

Her appearance appeared to be equally surprising. The old man's veined hands curled into the counterpane as he stared at her. "You've a look of your grandmother about you."

"I'm sorry I never knew her, but I'm glad to be meeting you." She moved to the side of the bed and took his hand. The bones felt brittle under the thin skin, but his eyes still burned with will. His aqua island eyes. She squeezed his hand, then released it. "Grandfather, this is my husband, Colin Melbourne."

Michael bowed respectfully. "A pleasure to meet you, sir."

The laird's eyes narrowed. "I'm not sure that's mutual. From what I've learned, you're an irresponsible rascal."

"There's some truth to that," Michael said mildly. "A really responsible man would not have allowed his wife and child to campaign through Spain." He smiled at Catherine. "But I defy any man to resist my wife when she has made up her mind."

The warmth in his voice when he said "my wife" made her throat ache. If only she were different . . .

The laird asked, "Where is my great-granddaughter?"

"Amy is with friends in London," Catherine replied.

He scowled as he waved them to chairs near the bed. "You should have brought her."

"The trip is long and tiring, and I didn't know what Skoal would be like."

"It didn't have to be so tiring," he said acidly. "You came quick enough when you learned there was a legacy in the offing."

His tone made her feel like a greedy fortune hunter. Well, she was one. "I'll admit that the possibility is welcome, but I was also interested in meeting you. Since Mr. Harwell said your health was poor, it seemed best to come quickly."

His heavy brows drew together threateningly. "Don't think that I'll automatically leave everything to you just because you have a pretty face. Your cousin Clive was born on the island, and he knows it well. Far better than you."

She guessed that her grandfather was deliberately baiting her. "The decision must be yours, of course. The responsibility for so many lives should not be given lightly."

"It won't be." His gaze went to Michael. "Much depends on you. I don't know if I'd trust my island to a soldier. My son William was mad to go into the army. He was selfish and disobedient. Unfit to rule a henhouse."

Catherine's face tightened. "I wish you would not refer to my father like that. He and my mother were brave and generous and the best of parents."

"I'll speak of them any way I please," the laird said harshly. "He was my son, until he ran off with that round-heeled farmer's daughter. Your mother set out to trap him and succeeded. Wrecked both of their lives."

Coldly furious, Catherine said, "I can't prevent you speaking as you choose under your own roof, but I don't have to listen. I understand now why my father left and never spoke of the place again." She stood and stalked toward the door.

"If you walk out of this room, you can say good-bye to being Lady of Skoal," the laird snapped.

She hesitated for a moment, remembering her dire financial situation. Then she shook her head; she would never be able to deal with her grandfather if he was so malicious about her parents. "Some prices are too high." She glanced at Michael. "Come, my dear. I suppose it's too late to leave tonight, so we must try to find an islander who will take us in."

The laird's voice rose. "Are you going to let your wife

throw away a fortune, Melbourne? How the devil did you manage to command a company when you can't control your own wife?"

"The decision is Catherine's," Michael said in a flinty tone. "I will not ask her to endure insults to her parents for the sake of an inheritance. We don't need you or your money—I am quite capable of supporting my family." He moved forward and put his hand at the back of her waist. The light touch helped counteract her fatigue and bitter disappointment.

Before they could leave, her grandfather gave a crack of laughter. "Come back here, girl. I wanted to see what you'd do. You're a Penrose, all right. I'd not have thought well of you if you groveled for the sake of money."

She said warily, "You won't speak ill of my parents?"

"No more than they deserve. You can't deny that your mother was reckless to elope and follow the drum, or that William was stubborn, since you obviously take after both of them."

She smiled a little and reclaimed her chair. "No, I can't deny it, though I'm usually considered quite reasonable."

"Except in the defense of those you love," Michael said quietly. "Then you are a lioness."

Their gazes caught and held. Her heartbeat accelerated. He was an excellent actor; anyone watching would think he was a man who loved his wife deeply.

The laird's voice ended the moment. "You've much to answer for, Melbourne. Twelve years of marriage and only one daughter to show for it? Surely you can do better than that."

Catherine's face flamed, but Michael said calmly, "War does not create the best conditions for building a family. But even if we never have another child, I won't feel a failure. No man could ask more than a daughter with Amy's wit and courage."

If Catherine had not loved him already, his statement would have won her heart. But it would be better to change the subject. "I know nothing about the Penrose family. Will you tell me about my relatives?"

Her grandfather looked suddenly tired. "Your grandmother died two years ago. She was a Devonshire girl, daughter of Lord Traynor, but she took to the island as if she were born here. My older son, Harald . . ."

He stopped and swallowed, the movement of his Adam's apple visible in his thin throat. "Last autumn, he and his wife and only son were sailing. He knew the currents and shoals as well as any fishermen, but a squall came up and blew the boat onto the rocks. They drowned within sight of the island."

She drew her breath in sharply. "I'm so sorry. I wish I'd had the chance to know them."

"Why? Their deaths put you in line for a fortune." His gruffness was belied by the gleam of tears in his eyes.

No wonder her grandfather's health had declined, when he had lost his whole family in such a short period of time. Gently she said, "I would rather have kinfolk than money."

"Then you're a damned fool."

Michael said pleasantly, "Do you try to antagonize everyone, Lord Skoal, or only relatives?"

The laird's face reddened. "I see that you are impudent as well as irresponsible."

"Like my wife, I do not enjoy hearing insults to those I care about," Michael retorted. "Catherine is the most selfless, caring person I've ever known. Even if you are incapable of love, she deserves your courtesy and respect."

"You're a prickly pair." The old man's tone was sharp, but he did not seem displeased.

Tired of verbal fencing, Catherine got to her feet. "We've been traveling for two days. For me, at least, a chance to rest and refresh myself would do wonders for my temper."

"I've ordered dinner for eight-thirty. I want you to meet the important people on the island, including your cousin Clive." The laird gave an edged smile. "I'm sure you're anxious to meet the competition."

"I'll look forward to it." She was surprised that the laird had the strength to sit at a table. Perhaps he was invigorated by the prospect of new people to hector.

"Until later, Grandfather." She and Michael left the room.

Mrs. Tregaron was waiting patiently in the corridor. "Would you like to go to your room now?"

Michael glanced at Catherine, his expression opaque. "Two adjoining rooms would be preferable. I'm a restless sleeper, and I dislike disturbing my wife."

Mrs. Tregaron looked worried again. "The laird believes

husbands and wives should sleep together. He says separate bedrooms are unnatural."

Catherine shared Michael's feelings, but dared not protest too strongly. If they had campaigned together on the Peninsula, they would be used to tight quarters. She gave her pretend husband a reassuring smile. "It will be all right, my dear. I don't mind being disturbed if it's by you."

Relieved, Mrs. Tregaron led the way along the corridor and up a winding stairway. Over her shoulder, she said, "Your room is on the next floor, but if you follow these stairs to the top, you'll reach the battlements. The view is quite lovely."

They followed her down another hall until she opened the door to a large bedroom with chestnut wainscoting and heavy Jacobean furniture. "Your luggage is here already. Since you brought no servants, I'll assign a maid to you, Mrs. Melbourne. It is the house custom to gather in the small salon before dinner. I'll send someone to show you the way a few minutes before eight-thirty. Is there anything else you would like?"

"A bath would be heavenly."

"I'll send hot water up directly."

"I'd like a key for the room." Michael gave Catherine a melting look. "My wife and I don't like our privacy to be interrupted unexpectedly."

Looking happily scandalized, the housekeeper said, "We don't use keys much on the island, but I'll try to find one."

As soon as Mrs. Tregaron left, Catherine sank into a chair. "My grandfather obviously doesn't believe in giving people a chance to rest before important encounters. What do you think of him?"

Michael shrugged. "A tyrant, partially redeemed by occasional flashes of humor and fairness." He prowled across the room to the window, his body taut and powerful. "He reminds me of the Duke of Ashburton, though not so cold, I think."

"I think that under the acid tongue, he's lonely."

"Not surprising, since he's probably bullied or alienated everyone he ever met. Power brings out the worst in many men," Michael said dryly. "If his heir hadn't died, he would never have summoned you here. He would have gone to his grave estranged from his only granddaughter."

"Perhaps, but I still feel sorry for him." She pulled the

pins from her hair and rubbed her tired temples. "It must be dreadful to be so weak after a lifetime of strength and power."

"You're more generous than he deserves." Michael smiled affectionately. "Saint Catherine still."

Her gaze dropped and her relief was replaced by unease. How the devil were they going to share a room and a bed?

By confronting the issue head-on. "It's strange," she said honestly. "I was raised with the army. I've been surrounded by men all my life, and married for a dozen years. Yet I feel horribly awkward now."

Michael's mouth quirked upward. "These are hardly normal circumstances—it would be surprising if we didn't feel strange. I'll sleep on the floor. Locking the door will prevent any chambermaids from discovering our guilty secret. We'll manage."

"I don't want you to be uncomfortable." Catherine glanced uneasily at the huge canopied bed. "Surely the bed is large enough for two people."

"I'd be far more uncomfortable in the bed." His gaze went over her, then slid away. "My intentions are honorable, but I'm only human, Catherine."

She winced. She didn't want him to desire her; the situation was too complicated already. "The floor it is, then." Trying to put more emotional distance between them, she went on, "By the way, I've been curious. According to Anne Mowbry, the newspaper society notes implied that you came to London in search of a wife. Have you had any luck?"

She wondered if he would mention the girl in the park, but he was too much a gentleman to discuss a lady behind her back. Coolly he said, "I'm a little surprised Anne reads such rubbish."

Catherine smiled and tossed his words back at him. "She's only human—and so am I. Women are always interested in matchmaking. But you must hate knowing that strangers are speculating about your private affairs."

"Indeed." He scanned the bedchamber. "At least there's a screen around the hip bath in the corner. It will offer some privacy for bathing and dressing. And this won't be for long. If the two of us continue speaking our minds, the laird will toss us out in a day or two."

She laughed. "That would simplify matters, but I don't think it will happen. He seems to enjoy being challenged."

"So he does." Michael gave her a level glance. "Though your grandfather is frail, he doesn't appear to be at death's door, as the solicitor implied. It won't be possible to maintain this masquerade indefinitely, you know. If you inherit and want to bring Colin here, you'll have to do some lively lying."

Not as much as Michael thought; she would merely tell the truth, that Colin had died suddenly. But it was true that the perils of her deception loomed much larger now that she was on the island. "That might not happen. My grandfather seems to prefer my cousin. I wonder what the mysterious Clive is like? Mr. Harwell said nothing critical, but I had the sense that he wasn't enthusiastic about the fellow."

A knock heralded two maids with coppers of steaming water. Michael let them in, then said, "I think I'll go up to the battlements for some fresh air. I'll be back in half an hour or so. That will leave enough time for me to bathe before dinner."

Catherine nodded, concealing her relief. The thought of being naked in the same room with Michael made her feel hot and confused, even though she would be safely behind the screen.

Safe? There would be no safety until this charade was over.

Mrs. Tregaron was right about the view from the battlements, even at night. A few lights were visible, most clustered in the nearby village. Because the castle stood on the highest point of the island, Michael could see beyond the shadowy fields to limitless expanses of moon-kissed sea. The irregular liquid beat of waves murmured in the distance. There would be no place on the island out of sound of the ocean.

The air on the battlements was blessedly cool, easing his tension. He sighed and braced his hands on the stone wall. A shared bedroom. Wonderful. It only needed that.

Though Catherine might think her grandfather inclined to choose her cousin as heir, Michael disagreed. No man was proof against her warmth and intelligence, and the laird was already beginning to soften. She would receive her legacy, as long as her pretend husband did not antagonize her grandfather. He should not have snapped at the old man. Still, no damage had been done. The laird seemed to like a bit of spirit in those around him, though real opposition would probably infuriate him.

He stared at the distant sea and tried not to think of Catherine washing herself in the hip bath. Soap sliding over her smooth, pale skin. Warm water trickling between her full breasts. His body tightened as his imagination pictured her in excruciating detail. Dear Lord, but it had been a long time since he had lain with a woman.

Yet, in a sense, it didn't matter how much time had passed. Even if he had spent the spring bedding every courtesan in London, he still would crave Catherine with painful intensity.

When half an hour had passed, he went down to their room. He found Catherine curled on her side on the bed, fast asleep. She had bathed and donned a blue evening gown, though her hair fell unbound over her shoulders. She looked exhausted. He would let her rest as long as possible.

Fresh hot water was waiting by the tub. He bathed quickly and changed into evening clothing, then went to wake Catherine.

Before he did, he studied her sleeping face. Nothing could make her bone structure less than exquisite, but there were shadows under her eyes. She must be weary of carrying all of the responsibility for her family. Colin wouldn't be much help.

Michael's gaze drifted downward. The evening gown was modest, but it could not conceal the lushness of her figure. The gentle rise and fall of her breasts riveted him. And the alluring curve of ear visible beneath the dark silk of her hair . . .

He took a slow breath. "Catherine, it's time to get up."

She sighed and rolled onto her back, but didn't wake.

He put a gentle hand on her shoulder and said more loudly, "Catherine, dinner will be served soon."

"M-m-m." She smiled a little and turned her head sleepily into his hand, her eyes still closed. Her mouth pressed against his fingers. Her lips were warm and luxuriantly soft.

Desire flared, hot, red, and blinding. He jerked his hand back as if he had been scalded. *Dammit, remember that she's a married woman!* Sharply he said, "Catherine, wake up! It's almost dinnertime."

Her dark lashes swept upward. She stared at him with shock, and something that was almost fear in the depths of her eyes.

Guessing that she was disoriented, he said, "We're in Skoal, and about to go for dinner with your alarming grandfather."

Her eyes cleared and she pushed herself upright with one hand. "I only meant to lie down for a few minutes, but I went out like a drowned candle."

"It's been a long day. Unfortunately, it isn't over yet."

"My grandfather must think that putting us through our paces when we're exhausted will reveal our true natures. He's probably right." She slid from the bed and went for her hairbrush. With a few swift strokes, she untangled the dark, glossy mass. Then she twisted it into a knot on her nape. Simplicity merely emphasized the graceful line of her slim throat.

A knock sounded and a shy voice called, "Sir, ma'am, I'm here to take you down to the salon."

Michael said quietly, "Ready for the next act?"

She raised her chin. "As ready as I'll ever be."

He opened the door and ushered her out. Sharing the intimacy of a married couple with Catherine was proving even more difficult than he had expected.

Catherine took Michael's arm as they followed the parlormaid down through the house, but she kept her eyes cast downward. She was still unnerved by the moment when she had woken to find his face above hers. She had been drifting in a marvelous dream, where she was normal, Michael was her husband, and they were looking forward to the birth of their first child. For a paralyzed instant, the dream had carried over into reality. Then it vanished, leaving only anguished regret.

The salon was in a newer section of the house. As Catherine and Michael entered, five pairs of curious eyes stared at them. The laird was in a wheelchair with a blanket tucked around his legs. Also present were Davin Penrose and a pretty blond who must be his wife, and an older couple.

The laird accepted her greeting with a nod. "You've met

the constable already. This is his wife, Glynis, and the Reverend and Mrs. Matthews." He gave a rusty chuckle. "Obviously Skoalan society doesn't glitter."

"How fortunate. I've found that glitter doesn't wear nearly as well as good sense and a good heart." Catherine gave a warm smile to her grandfather's guests, most of whom were regarding her with a certain wariness.

Determined to start on the right foot with people who might soon be her tenants and neighbors, Catherine accepted a glass of sherry and set out to put everyone at ease. Conversation flowed easily, but she wondered where her cousin Clive might be.

The sherry glasses were empty when the door opened again. "Please excuse my lateness, Uncle Torquil," a smooth, familiar tenor voice said. "What is this surprise you promised me?"

The hair had prickled on the back of Catherine's neck when she heard the voice. No, it couldn't possibly be . . .

A gleam of malicious amusement showed in the laird's eyes. "It's about time, Clive. Come meet my granddaughter, Catherine, and her husband, Captain Melbourne."

Catherine braced herself and turned to the newcomer. She had not mistaken the voice. Lord Haldoran, the languid, inscrutable gentleman who had flirted with her during the hectic spring in Brussels, was her own cousin.

Chapter 22

Catherine thought frantically as Haldoran crossed the room. Had he ever met Michael, who had escorted her so often in Belgium? Or Colin? She couldn't remember. But if he had, her deception would be exposed on the spot, and she had seen enough of her grandfather to know he would not be amused.

She thought her heart would stop when an odd expression—shock?—flickered in Haldoran's eyes at the sight of Michael. It vanished so quickly that she might have imagined it. He said genially, "How delightful to meet you again, Mrs. Melbourne."

He bowed to her, then offered his hand to Michael. "I believe I saw you with your wife at a number of those crushes in Brussels, but we were never properly introduced. I'm Haldoran."

Catherine did her best to conceal her relief as the men shook hands. It was ironic that Michael's consideration in escorting her now reinforced their charade.

The laird frowned. "You already know each other?"

"We met in Belgium last spring," Catherine replied. "When it seemed that Brussels might be overrun by the French, Lord Haldoran very kindly conveyed my daughter and the family who shared our billet to Antwerp."

"I'm glad you didn't turn tail and run," her grandfather said approvingly. "Being a woman is no excuse for cowardice."

"Au contraire," Haldoran said with a hint of mockery. "Your granddaughter was known throughout the army for her bravery. She earned the nickname Saint Catherine for her nursing work."

"I'd heard that," the laird said. "It made me think she might be strong enough to rule Skoal, even though she's female."

Catherine disliked being spoken of as if she were not present. Luckily, Michael caught her grandfather's attention by saying, "From what I've read, the islanders trace their ancestry to the Vikings and Celts, whose women were known for courage and independence. With such blood in her veins, it's not surprising that Catherine dared the battlefields."

"You're interested in history?" Not waiting for a reply, the laird began expounding his opinions about early Britain while Michael listened with apparent interest.

Catherine gave Haldoran a quizzical glance. "I haven't gotten over my surprise at finding you here. Did you know last spring that we were cousins?"

"I knew you must be of Skoalan descent, perhaps William's daughter, but I wasn't sure, so I thought it better not to speak." He accepted a glass of sherry. "However, when I returned to London I visited Edmund Harwell and said I'd met a charming officer's wife with island eyes. He confirmed your identity."

She remembered how disconcerted he had seemed the first time they met. Island eyes again. Had he concealed their kinship because of discretion, or because he did not want to alert a possible rival for Skoal? The uneasiness she had always felt with him intensified. Under his amiability, she sensed a kind of disdain, as if he felt superior to the mere mortals around him.

A footman entered to announce dinner. Davin Penrose unobtrusively stepped behind the wheelchair and pushed the laird into the dining room. As steward, he must work with her grandfather constantly, which would require tact as well as competence. The more Catherine saw of him, the better she liked him. She also liked his blond wife, Glynis, whose droll sense of humor was reminiscent of Anne Mowbry's.

"Catherine, sit at the other end of the table," her grandfather ordered. "Melbourne, you sit next to me."

She silently obeyed, realizing that he was giving her the position of hostess. Haldoran was seated on her right. She gave him a quick glance, wondering if he resented the laird's mark of favor. She couldn't read through his polished surface. As the first course was served, she said quietly, "My grandfather seems to want to set us against each other. I'm sorry."

His brows arched. "Well, we are in competition, aren't we? Only one of us can inherit Skoal."

She gave him a level look. "Before three days ago, I'd scarcely heard of the place. It must seem unfair to you that I have appeared from nowhere with a claim to what you must have believed would be yours."

He shrugged. "My expectations were not long-standing. Until last year, I assumed Harald would inherit. I must admit that the sheer feudal whimsy of being Laird of Skoal appeals to me, but that is offset by the dreary responsibilities that go with the title. The island is also hopeless for serious hunting. I shan't repine if Uncle Torquil prefers you."

It was a persuasive disclaimer. She wished she believed it. She swallowed a spoonful of lobster soup. "Exactly how are you and I related?"

"My grandfather was younger brother to your great-grandfather," he explained. "The island has few opportunities for younger sons, so my grandfather embarked on a very profitable career as a privateer. He used Skoal as a base during his active years, then retired to an estate in Hampshire and became so respectable that he was made a baron. However, he also kept a house on the island. I was born here and I visit regularly."

"So you are also a Penrose, and you know the island well." She finished her soup, feeling somewhat revived by the food.

He gave her another wide, unreadable smile. "Since we are cousins, you must call me Clive."

She nodded vaguely, though she really did not wish to be on terms of intimacy with her newfound cousin.

The Reverend Matthews, who was sitting on her other side, asked if she had ever met the Duke of Wellington. Everyone was interested in the hero of Europe, so the duke provided a safe, neutral topic for general conversation.

Catherine was eating a sliver of poached sole when Haldoran drawled, "Speaking of dukes, Melbourne, I understand that Lord Michael Kenyon, younger brother of the new Duke of Ashburton, was billeted with you in Brussels. I've some acquaintance with the duke. What is Lord Michael like?"

She choked on her fish. It seemed impossible that the question was innocent. Perhaps Haldoran was toying with her, waiting for the best moment to expose her deceit. Her helpless gaze went to her partner in crime.

Michael calmly broke a piece of bread. "Kenyon was a rather quiet fellow. Since he was busy with a new command, we didn't see much of him."

Haldoran said, "Quiet? I'd had the impression from his brother that Lord Michael was a rake, the family disgrace."

Michael's fingers tightened around the stem of his wineglass, but he kept his voice even. "Perhaps he was. I really couldn't say." He smiled at the vicar. "After all, the traditional choices for younger sons are the church or the army. I assume that the saints go for the church."

Matthews chuckled. "Even among men of the cloth, saints are in short supply." To Catherine, he said, "Will you be visiting the island church, All Souls? The crypt dates from the seventh century, when the first place of worship was built by missionaries from Ireland."

The vicar would want to be on good terms with her, since his post was held at the mercy of the laird. The prospect of having such power over a man's livelihood made her uneasy. Luckily, Mr. Matthews seemed kind and conscientious. Catherine tried to convey her approval in a smile. "I'd love to visit the church."

The laird gave a sharp nod. "You need to see the whole island. Tomorrow Davin will take you and your husband about. The sooner you start learning about the place, the better."

From the corner of her eye, she saw Haldoran's lips thin. She wondered if her grandfather was treating her as the likely heir in order to provoke Clive. She wouldn't put it past the old devil. It was far too soon to assume she would be his choice, and she suspected that premature gloating would be fatal.

After she and the constable set a time for the next morning, Haldoran said, "When you're done with the tour, stop by Ragnarok for tea. The setting is quite dramatic."

"Ragnarok?" she said, startled. "Isn't that the Nordic version of Armegeddon?"

"Exactly—the twilight of the gods," he said with cool amusement. "A melodramatic name for a house, but my grandfather wanted to honor the island's Viking past."

"Tea should bring the melodrama down to the mundane. We'll call tomorrow." She got to her feet. "Since the meal is over and I'm at the end of the table, I suppose it's my duty to give the signal for the ladies to withdraw so the gentlemen can have their port. Alas, I have no idea in what direction to withdraw."

Everyone laughed, and Glynis Penrose and Alice Matthews rose and led her to the drawing room. It was a relief to be with the women, who were both pleasantly down-to-earth. As they took seats, Glynis, the steward's wife, said candidly, "It's good to meet you, Mrs. Melbourne. Speculation has been running wild ever since your grandfather revealed your existence. It was feared you'd be a grand society lady with no use for folk like us."

"I am merely an army wife," Catherine replied as she settled into a chair. "There's nothing grand about me. But I feel as though ever since we reached Penward and met George Fitzwilliam, everyone knows more about my business than I do."

"It's like that in small communities," Alice Matthews said placidly. "But Skoalans have good hearts. With your island background, you'll soon be accepted."

Thinking this was a good time to ask questions, Catherine said, "I know nothing about my mother's family. Do I have any aunts or uncles, or other close relatives?"

Glynis and Alice shared a glance, as if wondering whether to reveal some secret. "Your mother was a De Salle," Glynis said. "She was an only child so you've no first cousins, but I was a De Salle, so you and I are related. Second cousins, I believe."

"How lovely. I think I'm going to like having relations." Catherine leaned forward in her chair. "Did you know my mother?"

"Aye, though I was just a tiny lass, I remember her well. She was the most beautiful girl, but then, you'd know that." Glynis smiled wryly. "Headstrong, too. It was plain to anyone who saw her with Will that they were meant to be together, but neither set of parents wanted to believe it. Too much difference in their stations, him being the son of the laird and her the daughter of a smallholder, not even a member of the council."

"What is the council?"

Looking surprised by Catherine's ignorance, Alice explained, "The original Norman charter said the laird must be able to field forty armed men to fight for his overlord, the Duke of Cornwall. The first laird assigned a plot of land to each of his men-at-arms. The land and the right to sit on the island council descend to the eldest son."

"I see. Is Davin a council member?"

Glynis glanced at Alice again. "No, but he was a bright lad, so he was sent to the mainland to study agriculture."

Catherine wondered what wasn't being said. Before she could pursue the point, the vicar and Davin joined the ladies. "The laird wished to speak privately with your husband." Amusement showed in Davin's eyes. "I don't think it will be fatal."

Poor Michael; he was paying dearly for the nursing care he'd received in Brussels. When he and her grandfather joined the others half an hour later, Catherine was not surprised that they both looked tired.

Michael came to her side. "Would you like to go onto the balcony for some fresh air?"

"That would be welcome." They went outside. After closing the French doors behind them, Michael draped his arm around her shoulders. "Since everyone can see us, we might as well put on a small show of spousely affection," he said under his breath.

She smiled, glad for an excuse to slip her arm around his waist. "Was my grandfather interrogating you?"

Michael rolled his eyes. "It was easier being a French prisoner. The laird seems to have heard of every wild thing Colin ever did. After throwing it all in my face, he announced I was not good enough for his granddaughter. Naturally I agreed with him instantly."

Half amused, half appalled, she said, "How dreadful. Did that mollify him?"

"Eventually. After I mumbled a lot of platitudes about how the horrors of war can make a man act recklessly, but that peace and my fortunate survival have made me reevaluate my life and vow to reform." He frowned. "I dislike deceiving him. Though he's difficult, his concern for his tenants is very real."

She bit her lip. "I'm sorry to have put you in that position. You were right at the beginning when you said there would be all sorts of unexpected consequences."

His arm tightened around her shoulders. "In this case, I think the end justifies the means. You'll make an admirable Lady of Skoal. But first we must convince your grandfather that we are reliable and very married. He has an old-fashioned belief that a woman must have a husband."

"Then it's time for more spousely affection." She stood on her toes and touched her lips to his.

She meant it as a gesture of thanks and affection, so she was unprepared for the intensity of his response. He made a choked sound and his mouth crushed into hers. Her lips opened under the force of the kiss. Sliding, languid richness. Fierce, consuming power. She felt strengthless, her body melting into his, yet at the same time she was blazingly alive, her fatigue seared away.

She had not known, never dreamed, that a kiss could be like this. Her hands opened and closed helplessly on his ribs. *This* was what she had wanted since the first time she met him. This dark masculine force that dissolved her fears, this flowering of desire that filled her heart and flooded her senses.

His palms kneaded her back, shaping her body and pressing it into his. Then the hardening ridge of male flesh against her belly shattered her mood and returned her to reality. She wanted to cry out and shove him violently away.

But the fault was hers, not his. She put her hands on his upper arms and stepped back, saying lightly, "That should convince everyone we're married."

She saw the shock of interrupted desire in his eyes, the rapid pulse in his throat, and despised herself. She had failed to keep her distance, and now he was paying for her weakness.

Because he was stronger than she, it was only a handful of moments before his feelings were masked behind cool, social amusement. "We might have overdone it. People who have been married for a dozen years seldom kiss like that in the middle of a dinner party. This would be more believable."

He raised her chin and his lips slanted across hers for an instant. She saw when he released her chin that he was unaffected by the caress. She was not so lucky; the swift, passing touch was enough to restore the fever in her blood. With despair, she wondered why life was so unfair. It would be far easier if she were incapable of desire.

Placing his palm in the small of her back, Michael guided her toward the French doors. "I think we've done our duty as guests and can honorably retire now. I'm so exhausted that I won't even be aware I'm sleeping on the floor."

Perhaps he wouldn't notice, but she would. She noticed every breath he took.

Michael spent half the night lying awake and feeling like an adulterer. Catherine's expression after that damnable, heedless kiss haunted him. Granted, she had initiated it, but her intentions had been innocent. He was the one who had turned a simple embrace into raging lust.

When she broke away, her eyes had been filled with dismay, almost fear. He had hated himself for doing that to her. She considered him a friend, and was trusting him in a situation vital to her future. But because of that kiss, she had watched warily when he locked the door of the bedchamber behind them. Her body had been stiff, as if she feared he would force unwelcome attentions on her, and she did not speak as she went behind the screen to change from her evening dress.

She had emerged in a nightgown that was large and shapeless and quite opaque. Nonetheless, she had looked utterly desirable as she slid under the bedcovers.

He had done his best to be matter-of-fact, as if sharing a bedroom with her was a perfectly normal business. The pallet he made up was as far from the bed as possible. He carefully dowsed the candles before changing into his nightclothes and lying down.

His behavior must have allayed her concern, for soon her breathing had become soft and regular. He envied her clear conscience, the result of being a saint rather than a sinner. Proof of his depraved nature was that he could not suppress the satisfaction of knowing that she had briefly responded to him with an intensity that matched his own. Though she was a good and virtuous wife, she, too, felt the sexual pull between them.

It would be safer if she did not. As he stared into the darkness and listened to the ceaseless rumble of the sea, he wondered if their honorable principles would be strong enough to prevent them from doing the unforgivable.

Chapter 23

Catherine threw back her head and laughed into the wind. "Beautiful!"

Silently Michael agreed, though his gaze was on her sunlit form, not the crashing waves far below at the base of the cliff. She looked eerily like the sketch that Kenneth had drawn of the diabolically beautiful Siren who stood on a wild, rocky shore, singing a lethal song to draw sailors to their doom. If the Siren was as lovely as Catherine, those ancient sailors had died happy.

Davin Penrose was giving the visitors a tour of Skoal, explaining the sights and introducing Catherine and her "husband" to the islanders. The Skoalans were reserved with the laird's granddaughter. Slow, thoughtful gazes would go from her to the constable to Michael, then back to Catherine. She would have to prove herself before she would be fully accepted.

Michael guessed that her beauty counted against her, for it was hard to believe a woman so lovely could also be serious of purpose. The islanders would learn in time.

Davin spoke again. "Even though the island is small, the edges are so rough that it's said the coastline is forty miles long." He indicated the rocky path that led down the cliff face. "Below is Dane's Cove. There's a small beach below. You might like to visit another day. It's a good place to picnic."

Catherine smiled. "If the seagulls don't steal one's food. I've never seen so many gulls."

"It's illegal to kill a gull on Skoal," Davin said. "In the fog, their cries warn sailors that land is near."

Michael shaded his eyes and peered into the sun. "Is that another island out there, or a mirage?"

"That's Bone, our sister island. It's almost as large as Skoal. You've not heard of it?"

"I'm afraid not," Catherine replied. "What an odd name."

"Not so odd," Davin said dryly. "Skoal meant 'skull' in the old Viking tongue. The warriors' toast of 'Skoal!' was drunk from the skull of an enemy. Since Vikings named this island, it makes sense that the neighboring one is called Bone." Having earlier received permission from Catherine to smoke when he wished, Davin took out a clay pipe and filled it with tobacco from his pouch. "Bone is part of the Bailiwick of Skoal, so it belongs to the laird."

Catherine gazed out over the white-capped waves. "Does anyone live there?"

"It's an unlucky place." Davin shielded the bowl of his pipe from the wind and lit the tobacco. "There's a huge seabird colony, and sheep and cattle graze there, but no man has lived on Bone for at least a hundred years."

"Why is it considered unlucky?" Michael asked.

"Irish monks built there as well as here, but one Easter they were murdered by Vikings while singing mass. It was a long time before Bone was settled again. Things were well enough at first. Then a plague killed every man, woman, and child. No one has wanted to live there since." The constable gazed pensively across the sea. "There are other problems. The landscape is rocky and the soil not so fertile as here. Also, though the islands are only a couple of miles apart, the waters are so rough and the currents so strong that crossing between is difficult."

Intrigued, Catherine said, "Is it possible to visit?"

"Oh, aye, with a good boatman and a calm day. We go over once or twice a year to shear the sheep and slaughter some of the cattle. Tough beef, but it means that more land on Skoal can be cultivated for crops."

"Skoal is a tiny kingdom, isn't it?" Catherine observed. "Almost entirely self-sufficient, every inch of land known and loved by people whose roots run centuries deep. You must be proud of your part in making it this way."

Davin's teeth clamped onto the stem of his pipe, and a muscle jerked in his jaw. Catherine didn't notice because she was still looking at Bone, but Michael saw, and was surprised. He wondered what caused such a reaction in a man who was usually so calm. One would think the constable would be pleased by the approval of a woman who might become his employer.

After a long silence, Davin removed the pipe from his mouth and said dispassionately, "I merely do my job. Everyone on Skoal contributes in his own fashion. We need and trust each other. There are no locked doors on this island."

As they went back to where their horses were tethered, Glynis Penrose and two young boys strolled into view from behind a stand of wind-gnarled trees. The constable's wife also carried an infant in a sling fashioned from a shawl.

She smiled sunnily at the visitors as the older children skipped up to greet their father. "Good day to you both. These are our boys, Jack and Ned." She grinned. "I think they saw you riding this way, and had hopes of a meeting. You two are the most exciting news on Skoal in years."

Jack and Ned bowed politely when they were introduced to Catherine, but their real interest was in Michael. Jack, about eight years old with vivid island eyes, said, "You were at Waterloo, Captain Melbourne?"

Michael affirmed that he was, and was instantly besieged with questions. Ned, two or three years younger and with blue eyes like his mother, favored the cavalry, while Jack hero-worshiped the Rifles. Obviously a child of outstanding intelligence.

As Michael answered the barrage of questions, Catherine said, "Who is the youngest member of the family?"

"This is Emily." Glynis lifted the baby from the sling. "Would you like to hold her?"

"Oh, yes." Catherine accepted the infant with enthusiasm. "What a pretty poppet. I'm your cousin Catherine. Are you your mama's favorite girl?" She rubbed noses with the child. "Your papa's little sweetheart?"

Emily squealed with delight and waved her plump arms. Soon the two were conversing in the nonsense sounds of baby talk.

The sight of Catherine's radiant face made Michael's throat tighten. She was everything he had ever idealized in a woman. The loving mother every child deserved, and few had. The irresistible woman who had captured his heart. The fiercely caring nurse who had risked her life to save his.

The wife who was not his own.

Yet he could not stop himself from wanting her. In a moment of bittersweet clarity, he recognized that he did not regret his desire, even though it made this mission so difficult. Simply being with Catherine was worth almost any price.

"What a darling," Catherine said as she handed the chortling baby back to her mother. "It's interesting—I've noticed that most islanders either have dark hair, like me and Davin and Jack, or blond hair, like you and Ned and Emily. Almost no one seems to be in the middle, with brown hair." She glanced at Michael with a smile. "Like you, who haven't a drop of Skoalan blood."

Actually, he had gotten more than a drop from her, but he supposed that it didn't count in this context.

"You're right," Glynis said thoughtfully. "I suppose our ancestors were mostly blond Scandinavians or black-haired Celts."

Her husband added, "There's an old legend that the island eyes came from a selkie—a magical creature that's a seal in the sea and a man on the land."

"It's a grand tale," Glynis said. "The selkie loved a lass with raven hair and an angel's smile. But he could only come to land on the full moon, and she could not join him in the sea. They became lovers and she bore him a child. But she was wed, and when her husband saw the sea in the baby's eyes, he took his longbow to Seal Rock and slew his rival. They say the selkie's ghost still calls for his love when the moon is full."

"The moral seems to be that adulterers come to a bad end," Michael said dryly.

Glynis gave him a glance of amused exasperation. "Anglo-Saxons have no romance in their bones."

"I'm afraid not," he agreed. And he was definitely against adultery.

The constable checked the time on his pocket watch. "Since Lord Haldoran invited you for tea, we should be getting on." He gave his wife a private smile. "I'll be home for dinner."

The touring party mounted and waved good-bye to Glynis and the boys. They followed the track along the cliff for half a mile. The fertile fields ended, replaced by tough, wind-scoured shrubbery. The path turned sharply and Davin pulled to a halt. "Lord Haldoran lives on Little Skoal. This is the Neck, the natural causeway that connects the two parts of the island."

Michael's brows went up as he surveyed the perilous ribbon of stone and the waves crashing on jagged rocks far below. "The guidebook mentioned that the Neck is only ten feet wide and hundreds of feet above the sea, but words don't do it justice."

"The writer exaggerated. The Neck is a good twelve feet across in some places," Davin said with dry humor. "But beasts get nervous here, so it's better to walk across."

They all dismounted and set off across the Neck, leading their horses. In the middle, Catherine paused and peered over the edge. The fierce wind whipped at her clothing and the sound of the waves was so loud she had to raise her voice. "Shouldn't there be railings?"

"It's not necessary," Davin replied. "Only one man has ever fallen, and he was drunk. Islanders know to be careful here."

She glanced at the rocks below doubtfully. If she became the Lady, railings would go up soon.

The constable added, "By the way, that islet there is Seal Rock, where legend says the selkie was slain."

Sure enough, one of the barren rocks in the distance was draped with the bodies of sunning seals. Catherine had a mental image of a seal emerging onto land under the silvery light of the full moon and turning into a man. If he were tall and lithe and strong, like Michael, and with equally mesmerizing eyes, it was understandable how a girl would forget honor and wisdom. . . .

With a sigh, she resumed her passage across the Neck. Her problem was not adultery, for she no longer had a husband. The insoluble dilemma lay within her.

Ragnarok was only a few minutes' ride beyond the Neck. It stood near the edge of the cliffs. Though the name was ancient, the house itself was relatively new. Its calm Palladian lines seemed almost incongruous in this wild, windswept setting.

Davin did not dismount when they reached the head of the driveway. "If you don't mind, I'll leave you here. I've work to do. Can you find your way back to the castle?"

"Don't worry," Michael said as he helped Catherine from her sidesaddle. "Skoal isn't large enough to get seriously lost."

The constable touched his hat brim, then trotted down the driveway again. Catherine watched him go. "I get the feeling he would rather not be Lord Haldoran's guest."

Before Michael could respond, a broad, muscular man with a scarred face emerged from the house. "I'm Doyle," he said laconically. "I'll take your horses to the stables."

Catherine studied Doyle curiously as she handed over her reins. He looked familiar. She guessed that she had seen him in Brussels, when he had been one of the brawny servants who had helped Haldoran convey Amy and the Mowbrys to Antwerp. Doyle's London accent marked him as a non-Skoalan, and his battered face made him seem like a ruffian. Like the house itself, he was an odd sight in this remote place.

They ascended the steps and were admitted to a gleaming marble foyer by the butler, another tough-looking Londoner. Apparently Haldoran liked servants who could double as guards.

Haldoran himself was descending the stairs. "Hello, Cousin Catherine, Captain Melbourne. What do you think of our island?"

"Unique and very beautiful." Catherine gave her hat and riding crop to the butler. "Not rich, perhaps, but well cared for. I saw no signs of want among the people."

"Everyone has a roof over his head, food in his belly, and shoes on his feet. That's more than can be said about most places on the mainland." He took her hand, holding it a moment longer than she liked, then ushered them into the morning room.

Conversation over tea and cakes was as bland as talk could be, with Haldoran encouraging Catherine to discuss what she had seen. Michael spoke little. Strange, she thought, how he could dominate a room without saying a word.

When they had finished eating, her cousin said, "Would you like a tour of Ragnarok? The views are exceptional."

Deciding she really should use his name, she said, "I'd love to see it, Clive."

Haldoran took them through the ground floor, talking amusingly about the house's history. Catherine enjoyed it more than she expected. Her cousin had excellent taste and a passion for collecting beautiful objects. The result was a treasure trove of polished furniture, Oriental carpeting, and fine art.

The tour ended upstairs in the back corner of the house.

As Haldoran swung the last door open, he said, "I think you'll find this interesting, Captain."

Inside was a gallery with wide windows overlooking the sea. Catherine thought it merely another handsome chamber until she realized it was a weapons room. The walls were covered with elaborate displays of ancient swords, halberds, and dirks, with glass-fronted cabinets for favored items.

Her mouth tightened as she looked around. Growing up with the army had given her no fondness for weapons. Quite the contrary. There was a strange dissonance between the brilliant sunshine washing through the windows and the metallic gleam of death on all sides.

"I've never seen such a collection outside a Highland castle," Michael remarked. "You have weapons unlike any I've ever seen."

Haldoran opened a cabinet and took out an unusual long pistol. There was sensuality in the way he stroked the brass barrel. "This has six chambers and is one of the first multishot guns ever made, almost two hundred years ago. Hard to load, terribly inaccurate, and prone to misfire, but interesting."

Michael examined the pistol with professional thoroughness and made appropriate comments before handing it back.

Haldoran returned the pistol to its cabinet. "I also have several superb swords. Are you familiar with Damascus steel?"

"If I recall rightly, it's beaten and folded on itself many times, like French pastry," Michael replied. "They say that Damascene blades take a sharper edge than any European weapon."

"They do." Haldoran pulled out a tinder box and lit a candle that stood on a cabinet. "Watch this."

He removed an elegant curved sword from a case of similar weapons. Grasping the handle with both hands, he snapped his wrists and the blade sliced through the candle with wicked speed.

Catherine gasped as the blade cut the wax so cleanly that the two pieces of the candle stayed together. The flame continued burning with scarcely a flicker. "That's incredible. I didn't know a sword could be so sharp."

"I'm glad I never had to face a Frenchman with a blade

like that," Michael added. "I wouldn't like to see what it would do to flesh and bone."

"It's not a pretty sight." Haldoran set the scimitar back in its cabinet, then took an unusual object from another case. "Have you ever seen an Indian thrusting knife, Captain? Setting the handle at right angles to the blade gives it phenomenal stabbing power. It's said to be deadly in close fighting."

As the men began discussing exotic daggers, Catherine drifted over to a window. There was something obscene about Clive's passion for weapons. She wondered if he would be so bloodthirsty if he'd ever fought in a real battle. War usually destroyed romantic notions about violence.

Since the house stood on a cliff, the gallery had a stunning view of the sea. Far below, water smashed relentlessly into the rocks. During her morning tour, she had seen several gentle beaches, but most of the island's perimeter was uncompromising stone. In the distance she could see the dark shape of Bone. Skull and Bone. Was this where she was to spend the rest of her life?

Behind her, Haldoran said, "What did you think of our noble constable, Catherine?"

She turned and leaned back against the windowsill. "Davin? He seems to know everything about the island worth knowing, and the tenants like and respect him. I think my grandfather is fortunate to have such an employee."

"I grant you he's competent, but that's not what I meant. Did you have no stronger feelings? No sense of kinship?"

Annoyed, she asked, "What are you trying to say? I like Davin, but I hardly know the man. Why should I feel kinship?"

Clive smiled maliciously. "Because good, sober Davin is your nearest relation—your only first cousin."

"I thought my mother was an only child."

"She was. Davin is on your father's side—Harald's bastard by an island girl."

Catherine stared at him. "You mean he's the laird's grandson? If that's true, does my grandfather know?"

"Oh, he knows. Everyone on the island knows. When Harald turned twenty-one, he announced that he wanted to marry his island sweetheart, from the peasant branch of the Penroses. The laird promptly packed him off on a

Grand Tour, but it was too late—the chit was already pregnant. She managed to conceal the fact from everyone, even her family, almost to the end. Then she died in childbirth, calling for her lover. The infant was left for her parents to raise." Haldoran's eyes sparkled, as if he found the tale amusing. "Harald never really forgave his father when he returned and learned what had happened. He took an interest in Davin, and saw that he was properly educated, but of course the boy was still a bastard."

Catherine's hand clenched on the windowsill behind her. No wonder Glynis and Alice Matthews had exchanged uneasy glances when discussing her relatives the night before. "In other words, if Davin were legitimate, he would be the next Laird of Skoal."

"Yes, but one could hardly expect the laird to publicly acknowledge his son's bastard." Haldoran smiled with spurious kindness. "I thought you should know, since everyone else does."

Michael, who had been listening quietly, said, "Do you think Davin resents my wife for being a possible heir?"

"A little, perhaps, but he's too stolid to cause trouble. If you keep him as constable, he'll serve you well." Dropping the subject as abruptly as he had raised it, Haldoran went to a gun rack and removed a long rifle. "This is an American Kentucky rifle. It looks plain, but it's the most accurate gun I've ever used. Watch."

He loaded the gun, then opened a window, admitting moist air and the sharp cries of wheeling gulls. His eyes narrowed with concentration as he aimed. When he fired, the discharge was deafening in the enclosed gallery. Catherine flinched as a distant seagull screamed, then dropped lifeless into the sea. The other gulls darted away, shrieking frantically.

"Good shooting," Michael said coolly, "but I thought it was illegal to kill gulls on Skoal."

"One more or less won't be missed." Haldoran turned, challenge in his eyes. "Of course, since you're a soldier, surely you are a better marksman than I."

"Not necessarily. The job of an officer is to lead, not kill the enemy himself."

"You are too modest. Go on, try this rifle. Skoal can spare another gull." Haldoran rammed another patch and ball down the barrel, then offered it to his guest.

Michael hesitated a moment. Then his expression hardened and he accepted the gun. After surveying the scene outside the window, he said, "Not being an islander, I don't feel free to break the law. I'll take the shrub on that headland as a target. The top branch."

Catherine squinted, barely able to see the shrub. "Surely it's impossible to be accurate at this distance."

The shrub was swaying in the wind, making the shot even more difficult. Out of the corner of her eye, she saw Haldoran smile.

Making it look easy, Michael sighted along the barrel of the Kentucky rifle and squeezed the trigger. Far out on the headland, the top branch of the shrub spun away and tumbled down the cliff into the sea.

Haldoran's expression froze. "Well done," he said tightly. "That was superb marksmanship."

"It's a good weapon," Michael said noncommittally as he handed it back.

"Are you as good at fencing as shooting, Captain?" Haldoran said with an edge to his voice.

Michael shrugged. "I know how to use a sword to defend myself, but I'm no expert."

Catherine watched uneasily. There was some kind of unspoken competition going on between the men, with Haldoran trying to engage and Michael resisting. What the devil was her cousin trying to prove? Not liking it, she said, "We should be leaving now. Thank you so much for inviting us, Clive."

"You mustn't rush off, Catherine." He went to another cabinet and removed two matching cavalry sabers. "I want to see another example of your husband's skill." He took one saber by the blade and tossed it hilt first to Michael, who pulled it deftly from the air.

Haldoran raised the other saber in a mocking salute. "*En garde,* Captain." With no further warning, he lunged forward in a lethal attack.

Chapter 24

Catherine's heart almost stopped when Haldoran thrust his saber toward Michael's chest. Before she could cry out, Michael had parried the other man's blade.

"Are you mad, Clive?" she cried. "It's insane to fence with unprotected blades."

"Nonsense." Her cousin struck again. There was a piercing metallic shriek as sword slid along sword. "This is merely sport. No injury will be done. Will it, Captain?"

"As harmless as playing charades," Michael said with ironic humor. He blocked another blow. "What sportsman could resist?"

"Glad you agree." Clive punctuated his words with teasing jabs to test his opponent's skill. "But the finest sport is hunting in the Shires. Have you ever done that?"

"I've never had that privilege, but good hunting can be found elsewhere." Michael gracelessly warded off the other man's saber. "I've had splendid runs in Spain with local greyhounds."

"That sounds rustic but amusing." Haldoran advanced and there was a noisy clash of blow and counterblow. Conversation flagged, replaced by harsh breathing as they fought up and down the center of the gallery. Clive was a first-rate swordsman, quick to take advantage of any weakness. Michael was slower, his moves almost awkward by comparison.

Catherine watched in suffocated silence. Though her cousin claimed this was sport, if Michael failed to defend himself well enough he might end up seriously wounded, or worse. It took time to recognize that he was deliberately holding back. His offensive blows might be ineffective, yet somehow his sword was always positioned to protect him from his opponent's blade. Though he retreated again and again, he was never cornered. It was a performance of consummate skill. Only someone who knew him well would guess what he was doing.

The fight ended when Haldoran suddenly broke through his opponent's guard. Catherine gasped when she saw the blade stabbing for Michael's throat. At the last possible instant, Michael jerked his saber up to ward off the blow. Clive's blade bounced and skidded downward. The tip grazed the side of Michael's wrist, leaving a trail of scarlet.

"My dear fellow, I'm so sorry." Haldoran stepped back, the point of his sword dropping. "I didn't mean to draw blood, but in the pleasure of engaging a worthy opponent, I forgot myself." His apology was belied by the triumph in his eyes.

"No harm done. It's a mere scratch." Michael set his saber on a cabinet and pulled out his handkerchief.

Heart pounding, Catherine swept across the gallery and inspected the damage. Luckily, it was as minor as Michael claimed. She bound his handkerchief around the shallow cut. When she had finished, she gave Haldoran a furious glance. "You have appalling ideas of sport, cousin."

"It won't happen again," he promised. "Next time, we can use the blunted foils. But it was a rare treat to cross swords with a skilled fighter. Once again you were unduly modest about your ability, Captain."

"I've merely learned to do what needs to be done." Michael tugged his sleeve over his bandaged wrist. "Thank you for an entertaining visit, Haldoran."

"The pleasure was mine. Society on the island is often rather flat." Clive sighed with what seemed to be genuine regret. "Unfortunately, tomorrow I'm going to London for a few days. I hope you're still here when I return."

"Do hurry back," Catherine said with a bright, false smile. The longer he stayed away, the happier she would be.

They collected their horses and set off along the track toward Great Skoal. She held her tongue until they were walking their horses across the Neck. Then she said icily, "Why the devil did you allow that to happen?"

"Allow? One doesn't have a choice when attacked by a man with a saber."

She gave him an exasperated glance. "You could have ended it sooner. You're a better swordsman than Haldoran, but you pretended otherwise."

"You guessed that? I'm not as good an actor as I thought." Michael's mouth curved in a humorless smile. "Your cousin is skilled with weapons, but he is an amateur, not a professional. Unfortunately, he does not like to lose. After I made the mistake of outshooting him, he was bound and determined to prove he could best me at something. The sooner I let him win, the sooner we could go."

"Letting him preserve his pride could have resulted in you being badly injured," she snapped.

His brows rose. "I think this is the first time I've seen you angry. I didn't know saints could lose their tempers."

"I never claimed to be a saint, and I have no patience with a man who blithely allows himself to be used as a pincushion."

"There was no danger of that." He gave her a slow, intimate smile. "You're being unreasonable. I rather like it."

The tenderness in his eyes disarmed her temper. He was right; she was overreacting to the incident. If she wasn't careful, she might realize how deeply her feelings were engaged.

She released her breath in a slow exhalation. "I couldn't bear it if you were hurt while helping me. I feel guilty enough about enlisting you in this mad scheme of mine."

"Don't waste your time on guilt," Michael said with a hint of bitterness. "It doesn't accomplish a damned thing."

They had reached the end of the causeway. He linked his hands together to help her into her saddle.

When she was back on her horse, Catherine said gravely, "Be careful around Haldoran. He's a strange man. I must be grateful for the way he helped us in Brussels, but I can't like him."

"I'm not fond of him myself. I've met similar would-be heroes in the army. They rarely lasted long." Michael mounted his horse. "You needn't worry that your cousin will provoke me into a fight. There's no one like an old soldier when it comes to avoiding unnecessary battles."

She smiled, her fears allayed.

Unfortunately, his own were not. During that impromptu duel, he had sensed that Haldoran would not have minded causing a lethal "accident." But why would the other man want to kill?

It could be from sheer bloody-mindedness, of which

Haldoran had more than his share. But there might be another motive. Michael had noticed a hungry possessiveness in Clive's eyes when he gazed at his beautiful cousin. Could desire have created a secret wish to see Catherine's alleged husband dead? Perhaps.

One thing was sure: Haldoran should be watched carefully.

When Catherine and Michael went into the castle, they came across the butler with a tea tray. Guessing it was for her grandfather, Catherine said, "Olson, may I visit the laird now?"

"I shall inquire," the butler said grandly.

After he left, Michael said, "Shall I go with you, or should I leave you to the lions while I take a bath before dinner?"

She considered. "It might be better if I go alone. I suspect that an old rooster like my grandfather feels the need to crow and proclaim himself king of the hill if there's another male around."

"A trait that runs in Penrose men."

"I've never seen you do that kind of posturing."

He gave her a wicked smile. "I don't have to."

She laughed, but after he left, she realized it was not really a joke. Michael had the quiet confidence that didn't need to prove anything to anyone.

Or did he? Remembering how he had looked when telling her of his father's recent death, she realized that his confidence lay in physical skills, at which he was a master. In the murkier areas of the emotions, he was less sure. She found the knowledge that he was vulnerable oddly endearing.

Soon Olson returned. "His lordship will see you, ma'am."

She followed him through the house to a sitting room that adjoined the laird's bedchamber. The butler gestured toward the French doors. Through the gauzy curtains, the outline of a wheelchair was visible. "His lordship is outside."

She stepped through the doors onto a sunny balcony with a fine view over the island. Her arrival was watched by both her grandfather and a large brown hound. The dog looked rather more friendly. Not bothering with pleasantries, the laird growled, "Here to see if I'm ready to turn up my toes?"

She smiled, less intimidated than she had been at their first meeting. "I'm pleased to see you, too, Grandfather." She settled in a straight-backed chair. "You're looking well today. Naturally I'm devastated by such signs of health, but I shall endeavor to hold up under the disappointment."

His jaw dropped. Then he gave a reluctant smile. "You've a wicked tongue, girl."

She grinned. "Who do you think I inherited that from?"

"A *very* wicked tongue," he muttered, but there was amusement in his eyes. "What do you think of my island?"

"There's an amazing amount of diversity for an area so small. Meadows, moors, wooded valleys. I was impressed at how nearly self-sufficient the island is."

"And the people?"

She turned her hand palm upward. "The ones I met were rather reserved, but that's only natural."

"As well they should be. Feudalism is a damned fine system, but everything depends on the character of the overlord. They'll want to know you a good deal better before they trust you."

"Speaking of feudalism, I was startled when we passed some men working on the road and Davin said every male over fifteen on the island owes the lord a fortnight of labor a year. I thought that sort of thing was abolished centuries ago."

"Why shouldn't men work to maintain their own roads and harbor?" her grandfather said. "The island's customs originated for good reasons. Only the laird can have a dovecote because pigeons eat the grain in the fields, endangering the crops. I'm also the only one permitted to have a bitch." The hound rose and rested her head on the laird's knee. He ruffled her long ears. "If anyone could have a bitch, the island would be overrun with dogs in no time. You'll understand it all eventually."

She tilted her head to one side. "Are you seriously considering me as your heir, or is your summons merely a game? After all, Clive is male and has known the island all his life. Surely he is the obvious choice."

"Yes, but . . ." Her grandfather glanced away. "This is not Clive's primary home. He has many other claims on his time. I would rather leave Skoal to someone who will put it first."

It was a good answer. Nonetheless, she sensed that the laird was not entirely comfortable with Lord Haldoran.

Abruptly the laird said, "Tell me about your parents."

She looked at him warily, not sure what he wanted to hear.

He plucked at the blanket that lay over his lap. "I didn't dislike your mother, you know. She was a delightful girl. But I didn't want to see William marry an islander. Skoal is too inbred. It needs regular doses of new blood."

That might explain why he had also opposed Harald's liaison with an island girl. "I can understand the need for new blood in theory, but my parents were very happy together," she said. "My mother loved following the drum. I suppose that's why it never occurred to me to do anything else."

She went on to describe her family's life. Her father's high reputation among his fellow officers and men, her mother's ability to make a home anywhere. How Catherine had learned riding from her father and nursing from her mother; the way both of her parents had loved the sea. Now that Catherine had seen Skoal, she understood why.

Her grandfather listened in silence, his gaze on the horizon. When she stopped speaking, he said, "A pity the boy was so stubborn. He didn't have to leave and never come back."

Having met the laird, she could understand why her father had assumed he would be unwelcome. Tactfully she said, "Their world was each other and the army. I was glad they died at the same time." Her voice broke. "It . . . it would have been hard for one of them to go on alone."

She blinked back tears, knowing they were grief not only for her parents, but for herself. She had wanted a marriage like her parents'. Indeed, she had assumed she would have it. That expectation made her failure all the more crushing.

Her grandfather cleared his throat. "Your husband isn't what I expected. He seems steady."

"Colin and I were very young when we married. I won't deny that he had a wild streak, but he has never failed in his duty to his family or his men." That was the truth. It was equally true when she went on, "If I were to become your heir, I promise that Colin would bring no harm to Skoal or its people."

"Davin says he had sensible comments about how my land is farmed, and what changes might be good."

"He has an impressive range of knowledge." Unlike Colin, Michael had grown up on a great estate, and apparently he had paid attention to how it was run. Wanting to get away from the subject of her husband, she went on, "Davin pointed out Bone and told its history. Is it really such an unlucky place?"

"Its past speaks for itself. Besides Viking raids and plagues, Bone has always been popular with pirates and smugglers. Have Davin get a good boatman to take you over for a visit. The largest sea cave in the islands is at the west end." He smiled reminiscently. "It's quite unusual. There's even a hot spring inside. Be careful, though. The cave can only be reached at low tide. If you stay too long, you'll be trapped until the tide falls again."

"Sounds interesting. I'm sure my husband would like to see it as well. I hope there's time to visit before we leave."

Her grandfather drummed his fingers on the arm of the wheelchair. "How long do you mean to stay."

"Perhaps a fortnight?" She gave a hesitant smile. "Unless you decide we're hopeless company and sling us out."

"A fortnight isn't very long. You've much to learn here."

More and more, it sounded as if he intended to designate her as his heir. Trying to conceal her pleasure, she said, "I'll study whatever you think necessary, but we can't stay indefinitely. Colin must return to duty."

His heavy brows drew together. "You can stay without him."

Her grandfather was lonely. It was a state she understood very well. "For now, my place is with my husband and daughter."

He scowled. "What if you inherited and Melbourne decided he didn't want to live in such an isolated place? Would you stay with him and let Skoal rot?"

She regarded him steadily. "If you make me your heir, I will put the island first. My duty to a whole community must come before my duty to my husband. But truly, you needn't worry that Colin will try to keep me away."

"See that you remember that." He leaned back in the wheelchair, his expression tired. "Get on with you, now."

She rose, then impulsively bent and kissed his cheek.

"Don't think you can turn me up sweet, girl," he growled. "I've been frightening everyone on this island for over fifty years, and I don't intend to stop now."

She laughed. "Grandfather, any woman who has been barked at by the Duke of Wellington is very hard to frighten. Wouldn't it be easier to become friends than to try to terrorize me?"

He stroked the hound, whose head still rested on his knee. "Dinner will be at six o'clock. See that you're on time."

She took her leave and made her way to her room. She was proud of the fact that she only got lost twice. Remembering that Michael had intended to take a bath, she knocked before entering. His deep voice called, "Come in."

She entered to find that he had finished bathing but was not yet fully dressed. His shirt hung loose over his pantaloons, the white linen emphasizing the power of his broad shoulders. Practically every inch of him was covered, so why was the effect so devastatingly intimate?

He asked, "How did you get on with your grandfather?"

Tendrils of damp mahogany hair curled around his neck. Darker strands showed at the V-shaped opening of his shirt. She looked down and carefully peeled off her gloves. "Quite well. Under that gruff manner, he's rather sweet."

Michael gave an eloquent snort.

She smiled. "He approves of you, which surprises him."

"It surprises me, too." Michael went to the mirror to tie his cravat. "I asked the footman who brought the hot water about the laird's health. The problem is his heart. He can walk, but he's easily exhausted and any kind of effort results in terrible attacks of chest pain."

Her brows drew together. "Angina pains are very debilitating, but not necessarily life-threatening."

"His continued existence might prove awkward," Michael said soberly.

"I know. Yet I'd hate to lose him so soon after finding him. I rather like the old scoundrel." She sank into a chair. "Now that he's met you, I think I could come with Amy for a visit every year and say that my husband is too busy to accompany us."

"With luck, that will work," Michael agreed.

She locked her hands in her lap and wished she could trust her luck.

Chapter 25

"Would you like some more ale?" Catherine asked.

"Yes, please." Michael opened his eyes a fraction so he could study his companion. He was sprawled on a blanket on the sand, as relaxed as a man could be. Except, of course, for the tension of being so close to Catherine. Lazily he admired the supple reflex of her body as she lifted a jug of ale chilling in a pool of seawater and poured a mugful. He sat up and took a long swallow. "It's nice to have an afternoon off from our labors."

She chuckled. "Intensive study of the history, laws, and agriculture of Skoal are not what I expected of this visit. It's all interesting, though. The island is so self-sufficient." She gestured at the remnants of their meal. "Island cheese and herrings, eaten with fresh island bread, drunk with island ale, followed by island apples."

"And carried in an island reed hamper. But they can't grow tea and coffee here."

"A grave lack. I guess Skoal can't secede from the rest of the world after all." She drew up her legs and linked her arms around her knees. Under the fluttering blue hem of her muslin gown, her feet were bare. "I wish Amy were here. She loves the sea. It's in her blood, I think."

He studied her exquisite profile. Ever since she had saved his life, he had become acutely aware of how often blood was used as a metaphor for connection and affinity. Perhaps the gift of life that joined them was the reason he felt so hopelessly connected to her, so aware of her every word and movement.

A puff of breeze molded her gown to her body, clearly delineating the entrancing fullness of her breasts. He looked away when his body involuntarily responded. His gaze went over the beach, a crescent of sand sheltered by towering cliffs. It was a private, sunny place. Damnably romantic. "Davin was right that this is a good spot for a picnic. In fact, he's always right. Another saint—clear proof that he must be your cousin."

She smiled. "That makes Davin sound boring, which he isn't. He and Glynis are both excellent company."

Michael rested his mug of ale on his knee. The tide was coming in, the small waves splashing only a few feet away. "You've been on Skoal for a week now. If your grandfather leaves you the island, do you think you could be happy here? It's a narrow life compared to what you've known."

"Yes, but it's also safe and comfortable. If it's offered, I can't afford to turn it down." She shrugged. "I don't know about happiness, but I can be content. That will be enough."

Giving in to impulse, he asked the question that had been haunting him since she asked for his help. "What about Colin?"

Her jaw tensed. "With Davin's help, I can run Skoal myself."

Michael caught his breath, wondering if her words meant that she and her husband might separate permanently. If they were already estranged, it would explain why she was not worried about how to bring Colin here later. His heartbeat accelerated as he thought of the implications. Would it be dishonorable to court a woman whose marriage was over, even if the legal bonds had not been dissolved? In fact, he realized with another jolt, it was possible that the bonds *could* be severed. Divorce was very rare, and it took money and influential friends to obtain one. However, Michael had both, and he would spend every penny he had to free Catherine if that was what she wanted.

The thought was stunning. Wondering if he was reading far too much into her words, Michael asked hesitantly, "Several times you've implied that Colin might not be part of your future. Are you considering leaving him?"

Her eyes squeezed shut. "Don't ask me about Colin," she whispered. "Please don't."

The wall of control he had erected with such painstaking care cracked. "Catherine." He laid his hand on her shoulder. Her skin was warm under the sun-baked muslin. "Catherine."

She drew an uneven breath, her lips trembling. Unable to bear the sight of her unhappiness, he slid his arm around her shoulders. With his other hand, he stroked her hair. Tears glimmered between her closed lids. Tenderly he kissed the fragile skin, tasting salt amid the prickliness of her lashes.

She made a choked sound in her throat and twisted, not away, but toward him. Her breasts compressed against his ribs and her arms circled his waist. He brushed back dark, gossamer strands of windblown hair and traced the delicate whorls of her ear with his tongue. She exhaled roughly, her full lips parting. She was unbearably alluring, a vulnerable Siren. He bent his head and covered her mouth with his.

She tasted of apples and ale, tangy and luscious. Her eyes remained closed, as if to deny the impropriety of this embrace, but her mouth answered his, hot and needy.

His heart began hammering, the clamor in his blood drowning reason. He pressed her back, the coarse sand crunching underneath the blanket. He had dreamed of her like this, her yielding body beneath his, the hard beat of her pulse visible under the pale skin of her throat. His hand shook as he cupped her breast. Soft, voluptuous, womanly.

Her dress was secured with a button on each shoulder. He unfastened them with clumsy fingers. Then he pulled down her bodice and the petticoat beneath, baring her breasts. Hoarsely he murmured, "You are beautiful, so beautiful."

He drew a velvet nub of nipple into his mouth. It hardened instantly, wickedly sweet. He wanted to suckle her essence into himself, to absorb the warmth and femaleness that he had craved all of his life.

She moaned and arched against him. He cradled her breasts and held them together, then rubbed his face between the warm, satiny curves, feeling the pounding of her heart. Her fingers slid into his hair, stroking through again and again.

He no longer gave a damn about marriage, husbands, wives. This was mating, savage and impossible to deny. In a just world, she would be his, protected by his strength and caring.

When had justice been part of his life? He would *make* her his own, now and forever.

His palm moved downward over the lithe curves of her torso, coming to rest on the mound at the junction of her thighs. Beneath the flimsy fabric was heat and the promise of musky welcome. As he caressed her, she became utterly still.

Her eyes snapped open and she cried out, "Oh, God, what am I doing?" Frantically she scrambled away from him, one hand holding her loose bodice over her breasts.

Taut and aching, he reached out to draw her back. "Catherine . . . ?"

She jerked away from his hand as if it were a serpent.

The stark fear in her sea-colored eyes shocked him back to sanity with the abruptness of ice water. *Bloody hell,* what had *he* been doing?

Breaking the most solemn vow he had ever made to himself.

"Christ, I'm sorry. So damned sorry." He buried his face in his hands. His whole body trembled, and not only from the frustration that burned viciously through his veins. "I didn't mean that to happen. I swear it."

Voice shaking, she said, "Neither did I. I'm sorry, Michael. The fault was mine."

It was true that she had not resisted. Quite the contrary. But he had taken advantage of her misery, the grief she felt about her marriage. Though he had not done so deliberately, it was still wrong. Sweet Jesus, would he never learn? He thought he had learned from past mistakes, but obviously not.

Escape from the island would be the wisest course. However, that would leave Catherine with difficult explanations and might endanger her future security. They must find a way to cobble up the ragged tears in their relationship.

He raised his head. She had refastened her dress and seemed poised to flee. An incoming wave slapped over his bare feet. He stood and rolled his trousers to his knees, then extended his hand to her. "Walk with me. Splashing along the beach should help clear our scrambled wits."

His matter-of-fact tone had the desired effect. Catherine stood and shyly gave him one hand, using the other to catch up her skirts. Her ankles were slim and shapely. He looked away and led her along the beach. Low waves broke on the sand and ran hissing forward to drench their feet, then retreated.

"Something like this was bound to happen," Michael said in a conversational tone. "It's not for nothing that society says men and women should not be alone together unless they're married. The way we've been living in each other's pockets is enough to strain even the best of intentions." He gave her a slanting glance. "It doesn't help that I think you're the most attractive woman I've ever known."

"Oh, Lord." Catherine stopped, paralyzed by dismay. "If I had known how you felt, I never would have asked for your aid. I've put you in an intolerable position."

"How were you to know? I did my damnedest to behave myself in Belgium." He tugged on her hand and got her walking again. "Even though our little charade has played holy hell with my self-control, I'm glad you came to me for help. Though I'll understand if your trust is gone. I deserve to be horsewhipped."

"Please, don't blame yourself," she begged. "This whole convoluted mess is my fault."

The knowledge that he was behaving honorably while she was deceiving him sickened her. For a moment, she teetered on the verge of telling him the whole truth: about Colin's death, and her own secret love. But the reasons for silence were as strong as ever. Stronger, if anything. "We must leave the island immediately. I'll tell my grandfather that I can't bear to be separated from Amy any longer."

"He'll tell you to send for her. He doesn't want you to leave, and I can hardly blame him. The least we can do is stay the full fortnight. I'll sleep up on the battlements. That will remove the worst of the temptation."

"You can't do that," she exclaimed.

"Of course I can," he said mildly. "I've slept beneath the stars many times before. I rather enjoy it."

She bit her lip. "I'm causing you so much trouble. I'm the one who deserves to be horsewhipped, not you."

His mouth curved ruefully. "Beautiful women are for kissing, not whipping. Which is why I'll sleep on the roof. We'll manage."

No doubt they would. Yet as she remembered the fierce pleasure of his lovemaking, she knew that what was preserving her virtue was not honor, but fear.

Anne Mowbry was in the parlor, teaching embroidery to Molly and Amy, when Lord Haldoran called. Since it was the maid's afternoon off, she answered the door herself.

Haldoran removed his hat. "A pleasure to see you again, Mrs. Mowbry. Is this a good time to visit?"

Why did visitors always come when she was wearing her third-best morning gown? "As good a time as any, my lord," she said philosophically. "Please, come in. It's kind of you to call."

The visitor stepped into the hall and was immediately surrounded by dogs and little girls. Anne concealed a smile at how taken aback he was. His lordship was obviously not a family man. Still, he greeted the girls politely and refrained from kicking an overexcited Clancy.

After the dogs had been shut away, she led him to the drawing room. As they went, he said, "Apart from the pleasure of seeing you, I have a mission on behalf of Mrs. Melbourne."

"I'm sorry, but Catherine is out of town at the moment."

"I know—she's on Skoal. I've just come from my house there. My family is from the island, and it turns out that she and I are cousins." He smiled. "I suspected it in Belgium, when I saw her eyes, but I didn't say so because I wasn't sure."

"Are you and I cousins, too?" Amy's voice piped up.

Anne glanced over and saw that the girls were sitting on the loveseat in the corner with their embroidery. In theory, they were dutifully working. In fact, they were eavesdropping shamelessly. "Yes, Lord Haldoran would be your cousin, also. But out with you both. You shouldn't be here."

"Actually, my visit concerns Amy. Since I was coming to London, Catherine asked me to bring her back to Skoal on my return journey. She wants her daughter to meet the laird."

"Really? I received a letter from her two days ago, and she mentioned nothing about that."

"She decided on impulse." He smiled tolerantly. "I suspect that the real reason is that she simply misses her daughter."

That had the ring of truth; Catherine had not liked going off without Amy. Anne said, "Did she give you a note for me?"

He shook his head. "As I said, she decided on impulse and came down to the harbor just as I was embarking. I had to leave quickly or miss the tide. I was pleased to be asked. After all, Amy and I are old traveling companions."

Anne thought of the anxious trip from Brussels to Antwerp. With Haldoran's escort, it had gone very smoothly. He had been patient under trying conditions. Letting Amy go with him now was hardly like turning the girl over to a stranger. Still ... "I don't know if I should let Amy go without word from her mother."

Haldoran's brows rose, giving him a faintly disdainful air. "You are a fine guardian, Mrs. Mowbry, but really. After all, Catherine is my cousin."

"Please, Aunt Anne," Amy said coaxingly. "Mama said she might send for me if the visit was going well."

"Naturally, I'll hire a maid to travel along with us to attend to the young lady's needs," Haldoran added. "We'll leave early tomorrow morning."

Besieged on all sides, Anne capitulated. "Very well, you can go, Amy. But you'll have to take your lessons with you."

"I will!" Amy said exuberantly. She whirled and dashed out of the drawing room, presumably to start packing. Molly followed more slowly, disconsolate that she would not be going along.

Anne's heart lifted. Their luck had turned. Because of Lord Michael's reference, Charles was now happily working for the Duke of Candover and earning an astronomical salary, and it sounded as if Catherine was making good progress toward becoming the Lady of Skoal. How very grand they would all become. With a smile, she turned back to Lord Haldoran to finalize the traveling plans.

Chapter 26

As Michael had suspected, there was tension between him and Catherine after the harrowing incident on the beach, but after a day it began to fade. She still tended to avoid his eye, and he had trouble looking at her and not remembering the taste and feel of her breasts. However, he was able to keep his hands off her, and that was what counted.

Three days later, they dined with the vicar and his wife. It was a pleasant evening, and Michael was feeling mellow when they returned to the castle. Another week and they would be safely back in London, beyond the reach of temptation. But in the meantime . . . he had another week with Catherine.

The front door was unlocked, like all Skoalan homes. They entered the foyer together. He was about to go upstairs when she glanced at a side table. "Some letters came for you, my dear." She handed him a small packet wrapped in oilcloth.

Michael felt a twinge when he saw the name "Captain Colin Melbourne." He really did not enjoy using Colin's identity. The parcel was certainly for himself, though; it was franked "Strathmore" in the corner and addressed in Lucien's hand. "I wonder what was important enough to be sent here."

"A matter of business, I expect." Catherine covered a yawn with her hand. "I think I'll go and say good night to my grandfather if he's still awake. I'll be up in a few minutes."

It was one of many such contrivances they used to give each other privacy for washing and changing clothing. He went to the bedroom and lit the lamps, then slit the oilcloth. Inside were several letters and a note from Lucien.

Michael—
Your brother sent a message that seemed to require forwarding. I'm including the other letters that have come for you. Hope the dragonslaying is going well.
Luce

Underneath was a letter franked "Ashburton." Michael held it in both hands, studying his name and the underscored word "Urgent." Though this Ashburton was his half-brother, not the man he had thought his father, the sight of the brusque signature aroused reflexive anxiety. The old duke had never written except to criticize or condemn. It was doubtful this letter would be any different. He tried to imagine what the new duke might have to say that Michael would want to hear, but he could think of nothing. Probably the letter concerned some legal business that he didn't give a damn about.

As in London, he held the corner of the letter in the candle flame and set it alight. That time he had been despairingly angry. Now he felt coolly determined to end the connection. After this, the new duke was unlikely to write again.

He tossed the burning letter into the fireplace and leafed through the other messages. As Catherine had guessed, most were business, but two were from Kenneth Wilding in France. In the one with the earlier date, Kenneth recounted news of the regiment and several amusing anecdotes about life with the army of occupation. The best bits were the tiny, wickedly satirical sketches that illustrated his stories.

Michael grinned at the end and set it aside. Wondering why Kenneth had written two letters so close together, he opened the second. It was a single scrawled page with no drawings.

Michael—
Forgive me if I'm going beyond the line of friendship, but it seemed in Brussels that your feelings for Catherine Melbourne were a good deal more than those of a friend. For that reason, I thought you would be interested to learn that several weeks ago Colin Melbourne was murdered on the street, apparently by a Bonapartist. A wretched business; they've still not found the

killer. The incident has been hushed up for fear of political repercussions. I only learned of it by accident, from a drunken officer of Colin's regiment. He said that after the funeral, Catherine took Amy back to England. I imagine Anne and Charles Mowbry would know her current location.

Of course it's bad form to pursue a widow when her husband is hardly cold in his grave, but Catherine is worth breaking a few rules for. Even if you have no romantic interest, you might want to see if she is in need of help. To no one's surprise, Melbourne died with his affairs in a shambles.

If you find Catherine and there is anything I can do for her, please notify me immediately.

Yours in haste, Kenneth

Michael stared at the page, feeling as if he had been kicked in the stomach. He read it again. Could Kenneth be wrong? Not likely. But why would Catherine lie to him? He had thought there was honesty and friendship between them.

It wouldn't be the first time a woman had made a fool of him.

He was staring numbly at Kenneth's letter when Catherine entered the bedchamber. As she closed the door, she said cheerfully, "The laird was tired, but he still had the energy to explain how the islanders pay an annual tax in capons on each chimney. Fascinating customs." She started to say more, then frowned. "What's wrong?"

"A letter came from Kenneth Wilding," he said tightly. "Is it true that Colin is dead?"

The blood drained from her face, leaving the perfect features as pale as marble. She caught the back of a chair to steady herself. "It's . . . it's true."

"Jesus bloody *Christ*!" He crushed the letter in his hand, feeling a shattering sense of betrayal. His beautiful, honest Saint Catherine was a liar. "Why the devil didn't you tell me?"

She brushed at her hair with a trembling hand. "Because I didn't want you to know, of course. I thought you might feel honor-bound to offer for me because I nursed you after Waterloo. It was simpler to let you think Colin was alive."

It was another blow, almost as hurtful as the first. "Is

the idea of being my wife so horrific that you had to hide behind a dead husband?" he bit out. "If you didn't want that, you could always have said no."

She dropped into the chair, her shoulders hunched and her gaze on her locked hands. "It . . . it wasn't horrific. It was appealing enough that I would be tempted to accept, so it was better if the question was never asked."

"Forgive my stupidity," he said icily. "If you thought I might propose, and you didn't dislike the idea, why the lies?"

"Because it's impossible! I will never—*never*—marry again. If I was fool enough to accept you, I'd make us both miserable," she said unevenly. "I can't be your wife, Michael. I have nothing left to give."

His anger vanished, displaced by despair. "So you loved Colin that much, in spite of his infidelities and neglect."

Her mouth twisted. "One can't spend twelve years married to a man without caring, but I didn't love him."

Michael could think of only one reason for her attitude. "Your husband abused you, so you've sworn off marriage," he said flatly. "If he weren't already dead, I'd kill him myself."

"It wasn't like that! Colin never abused me." Her hands clenched. "I wronged him far worse than he ever did me."

He studied her haunted expression. "That's hard to believe. Impossible, in fact."

"I know everyone blamed Colin and pitied me because of his womanizing, but I was the one who made a farce of our marriage," she said in a low voice. "He behaved with great forbearance."

"I'm very slow, apparently. Explain to me what you mean."

"I . . . I can't." She looked down, unable to meet his eyes.

Exasperated, he stalked across the room and put his hand under her chin to raise her face. "For God's sake, Catherine, look at me. Don't you think I deserve an explanation?"

"Yes," she whispered, "but . . . but I can't bear to talk about my marriage, not even to you."

Getting information from Catherine was like trying to drag oak roots from the ground. It was time for another approach. He curved his hand around her neck and bent to kiss her, hoping that desire might do what words couldn't.

For a moment she responded with desperate yearning.

Then she wrenched away, tears running down her face. "I can't be what you want me to be! Can't you simply accept that?"

In a distant corner of his mind, he began to have an inkling what this might be about. "No, I'm afraid I can't 'simply accept that,' Catherine. I've wanted you ever since we first met. God knows, I've tried to deny it and find someone else. But I can't. If I'm going to spend the rest of my life miserable because I can't have you, it will be easier if at least I understand why."

The starkness in her eyes showed how much she was affected by his words. Guessing that her resistance was breaking down, he said, "The problem was sex, wasn't it?"

Her eyes widened in shock. "How did you know?"

"There were hints in what you said." He knelt before the chair so he wasn't looming over her, and took one of her hands between both of us. Her fingers were cold and shaking. "And it would explain why you feel too humiliated to talk about it. Tell me why you consider marriage unthinkable. I doubt you can say anything that will shock me."

She crumpled into a ball in the corner of the chair, fragile as a child, her hands pressed to her midriff. "Marital intimacy is . . . is horribly painful for me," she said in a raw whisper. "It's damnably unfair. I find men attractive, I feel desire like any normal woman. Yet consummation is excruciating."

And feeling that she was abnormal must be even worse than the physical pain. He asked, "Did you ever consult a physician?"

She smiled bitterly. "I thought of it, but what do doctors know about how women are made? I couldn't bear the thought of being mauled by a stranger in return for the dubious pleasure of being told what I already know: that I'm hopelessly deformed."

"Yet you bore a child, so you can't be entirely abnormal," he said thoughtfully. "Did the pain lessen after Amy was born?"

She looked away. "I became pregnant very soon after we married, and I used that as an excuse to forbid Colin my bed. I . . . I was never a wife to him again."

"For twelve years you lived together without marital relations?" Michael exclaimed, unable to conceal his surprise.

She rubbed her temple wearily. "Colin deserved to be called a saint far more than I. We met when I was sixteen and he was twenty-one. It was a case of mutual calf's love, wildly romantic and not very deeply rooted. Ordinarily the affair would have burned itself out quickly. Colin would have become entranced with another pretty face, and I would have wept for a few weeks, then gone on with my life a little wiser."

She took a ragged breath. "But my parents died in the fire, leaving me alone in the world. Colin gallantly offered for me, and I accepted with never a second thought. I had assumed I would enjoy the . . . the physical side of marriage. Certainly I had enjoyed the stolen kisses that I had experienced. Instead . . ."

She thought of her wedding, and shuddered. After the usual drinking and ribaldry, Colin had come to bed hotly impatient to claim his husbandly rights. Though nervous, she had been willing enough. She had not expected such vicious, tearing pain, or the ghastly sense of violation. Nor had she thought she would cry herself to sleep while her new husband snored contentedly beside her. "The best that could be said for my wedding night was that it was over quickly."

Michael studied her face searchingly. "The first time is often painful for a woman."

"It didn't get any better. In fact, things got worse. The . . . the pleasures of the flesh were very important to Colin. He assumed that in return for surrendering his freedom he was getting a beautiful, lusty bedmate." Sadly she thought of the exciting time when she had just met Colin, and she had believed she was normal. "Based on how I behaved when we were courting, he had every reason to expect that. Instead, whenever he touched me, I began to cry."

"That must have been dreadful for both of you," Michael said with deep compassion.

"It was *horrible,*" she said vehemently. "I never refused him, but he found me so unsatisfactory that he soon stopped asking. We were both relieved when I became pregnant. Without ever discussing it, we devised a kind of silent pact that made our marriage tolerable."

"So you knew about his other women, but never complained?"

"Complain?" She gave a humorless smile. "I was grateful

for them. As long as he was happy, I didn't feel so guilty. I did my best to provide a comfortable home for Colin and Amy. In return, he supported us and didn't torment me about my failure. I got the better of the bargain, really. Colin was a decent husband and a father. He was careless in many ways, but he didn't abandon us, and he never allowed another man to bother me. No one ever knew what a farce our marriage was. Not until now."

"There were benefits for him," Michael said dryly. "Colin was a born womanizer. In you, he found the perfect wife—a beautiful, compliant woman who was the envy of every man he met. You never nagged about his philandering, and as a married man he never had to worry about other women trying to maneuver him into marriage. Some men would consider that heaven."

"Perhaps that's true. But the fact remains, I was the one who failed our marriage. I'm not fit to be a wife." Especially not the wife of the man she loved. She continued, "You see now why I can't marry you, or anyone. You can't possibly want a woman who cannot fulfill the most fundamental duty of a wife."

"Considering how much I desire you, that would be difficult. And yet . . ." Michael hesitated, then said slowly, "even so, I think I would marry you if you would accept me."

Her eyes widened. "You can't be serious."

"No?" He cupped her face with a warm hand. "I enjoy being with you, Catherine. As for the physical part—we may be able to work that out to our mutual satisfaction."

Her lips thinned. "I accepted Colin's infidelity, but I hated it. I won't have such a marriage again."

"Adultery was not what I had in mind." His fingers lightly skimmed her ear and throat, causing a shiver of pleasure to run through her. "Intercourse is not the only way to find physical satisfaction. I don't think you're cold by nature, so you might learn to enjoy some of the other possibilities."

"I'm not sure I understand." Heat rose in her face. "I'm ignorant as well as deformed."

"Ignorance can be cured, and it's possible that you're not deformed at all. The pain you experienced could have been the result of youth and inexperience, and a certain insensitivity on the part of a young husband." He searched for more words, then shook his head with exasperation. "Polite society doesn't discuss such matters, so forgive me if I say things that embarrass you. Bluntly put, if intercourse is forced too quickly, it will be uncomfortable for both partners, especially the woman. Once fear set in, you might have been caught in a vicious circle, with your body so dry and unyielding that you experienced pain again and again. The more the pain, the greater the fear."

"Surely it was more than that," she said doubtfully.

"Perhaps," he admitted. "But even if you were unusually small when you were sixteen, bearing a child causes permanent changes. It's quite possible that you will no longer experience the pain you felt when you first married."

It was a startling theory, almost terrifying in its implications. To be able to lie with a man without agony. To have another child. To be *normal.*

Not quite daring to hope, Catherine said, "You're about to say there is only one way to find out if you're right."

Michael gave her a long, level look. "I know I'm asking a great deal. Are you willing to try?"

"It was easier to go onto a battlefield during combat," she said with a shaky laugh. "But . . . dear God, Michael, I want so much to believe that you're right. That I'm a normal woman, that I'm capable of doing what almost every other woman in existence does."

He took her hand again. She looked down and saw the faint saber scar, and the sheer size and power of the warm fingers that engulfed hers. He was so large. So male.

The awareness triggered a sudden, ghastly memory of being a helpless *thing* trapped beneath a pounding masculine body. Of pain and violence that were degradingly personal. She pressed her fist to her mouth, her teeth biting into her knuckles. "But . . . the fear runs deep."

"Of course it does. It wasn't created in an hour, and it won't be healed in an hour," he said soothingly. "There are many, many kinds of sensual pleasure other than intercourse. You need to learn to enjoy them. Only when you've done that will it be time for the final intimacy."

She felt like a young bird being told it was time to leave the nest. All she had to do was jump from her nice safe bough and she would be able to fly. Unless, of course, her wings were inadequate, and she fell helplessly to the ground, smashing every bone in her body.

Seeing her indecision, he gently kissed the inside of her wrist. Her pulse accelerated under his warm lips, and heat curled insidiously through her.

"I swear I will do nothing—nothing at all—that you don't like," he said softly. "If you become uncomfortable at any time, simply tell me to stop. Can you trust me to do that?"

His green eyes burned with an intensity that touched cold, desolate places deep inside her. With a shock, she recognized that ever since they had met, he had suppressed his innate sensual power because he considered her beyond the pale.

That was no longer true. He desired her, and he was saying so with every subtle, voiceless lure a man could use to enthrall a woman. In the fact of his potent masculinity, she had no more will than a moth flying into the flame, seeking one transcendent moment of joy before being consumed.

"Yes, Michael, I trust you," she said huskily. "Do with me what you will."

Chapter 27

A smile started in Michael's eyes and spread across his face. "I'm so glad. I don't think you will regret it, either. We might as well begin tonight, before you have a chance to worry yourself into knots. Are you game?"

She immediately tensed. "Tonight?"

"First lesson only," he said reassuringly. "It will end whenever you wish."

He drew her from the chair into his arms, tenderly stroking her head where it lay on his shoulder. As his strong fingers kneaded her nape, she murmured, "That's very soothing."

"Since you like being petted, I think I'll treat you to what the French call a massage," he said thoughtfully. "Will you let me use your bottle of that lovely rose-scented skin lotion that makes you smell good enough to eat?"

"My Spanish lotion?" she said doubtfully.

He laughed, and she felt the rumblings of his levity under her ear. "You think I've gone mad, don't you? Don't worry, I promise you'll like this. We're going to turn this room into a delicious, and utterly painless, den of iniquity. First, a fire so the room will be warm enough for bare skin."

He released her and stood, then went to the fireplace. "Undress and wrap yourself in a sheet. And let your hair down."

Bemused, she did as he ordered. By the time she had brushed her hair out and emerged from behind the screen, swaddled in a sheet from the linen chest, the fire was burning steadily and Michael had made a soft pallet of folded blankets in front of the hearth. He had also changed to a green robe tied with a sash at the waist. It fell open loosely over his chest, revealing soft patterns of dark hair and hard planes of muscle.

She had come to know his body very well when she nursed him, but she had tried to make herself think of him only as a patient. For the first time, she allowed herself the pleasure of open admiration. He was beautiful, strong and well-made, utterly male. . . .

The thought of surrendering herself to that strength chilled her. She turned away and silently got her lotion from the dresser. He examined her face shrewdly as she handed him the bottle. "We have a long way to go, don't we? We'll start with a single small step. How far the journey goes is up to you." He held out his other hand.

Shyly she took it. He drew her forward for a kiss. Gentle and undemanding, it loosened the coiled fear inside her. Her taut muscles eased as his hand made slow circles on her back. "You taste wonderful," he murmured. "Like nectar. Like music."

She actually giggled. "That doesn't make sense."

"Sense is not welcome within these walls tonight." He slipped his arm around her waist and led her to the pallet. "Lie on your lovely front and I'll drape the sheet over you. Then I will massage you, starting with your back."

She stretched out on her stomach. He arranged the linen sheet over her, the weight of the fabric settling lightly on her bare skin. She felt tense, acutely aware of her nakedness and vulnerability.

"It's easy to tell when you feel anxious." He knelt beside her and moved the mass of her hair to the side of her head. Then he opened the lotion bottle, rubbing the rose-scented fluid between his palms. "You become as hard as a piece of army biscuit. A soldier of mine was spared when a ball struck a biscuit in his pocket. Even a French bullet couldn't penetrate the damned thing."

When she smiled, he drew the sheet to her waist and began rubbing her back with slow, powerful strokes. His large hands glided smoothly over her flesh, kneading and softening the taut muscles. He was right; she liked it. She liked it a lot.

He was so unlike Colin. Though her husband had never been deliberately cruel, he had been vigorous and uncomplicated, and he had liked women who responded with equal directness. He had never once touched her with such gentle sensuality.

The air was heavy with tropical warmth, the sweet tang

of the lotion, and the fragrance of the fresh flowers that were brought in every day. The world narrowed down to touch and scent and heat and the two of them. Michael varied his movements, sometimes working with his palms, other times using fingertips or heels of the hand to bring her body to tingly life. He paid special attention to her neck, easing away the iron strain.

She tensed again when he drew his hands along her arms, his thumbs brushing the sides of her breasts. Yet the light, tangential touches felt wonderful. When he didn't roughly grab for more, she relaxed again.

He massaged her hands, finger by finger. The pleasure was exquisite. He was right, there was an incredible range of sensual enjoyment of which she was totally ignorant.

She didn't flinch when he pulled the sheet farther down. "You have the loveliest body I've ever seen," he said, his voice not quite as even as it had been. His hands caressed her bottom. "A perfect pair of hips has a shape rather like a heart. All kinds of symbolism there, don't you think?"

He began to knead her buttocks, molding the curving flesh with his palms. He seemed to know exactly how hard to press and how to find hidden knots of tightness. The contrast of smooth surface strokes and deep compression turned her muscles to wax. "Where did you learn to do this?" she murmured. "Or would I be better off not knowing?"

"My teacher was a delightful French lady whom I met many years ago, when I was newly down from university. She had been in Turkey, and was much impressed with what she learned in the women's bathhouses there." He rubbed the small of her back with the heel of his hand. "Sophie considered it her mission in life to spread Oriental wisdom to the West.

"She was a lucky woman." Catherine stretched luxuriantly. "Not everyone gets to achieve such a noble goal."

He drew his hands down her legs in long strokes, all the way from her hips to her ankles. There was a distinctly sexual component to her enjoyment now. The desire that had been frightened out of her returned, flowing through her limbs like honey. Then his fingers brushed between her thighs with gentle intimacy. She froze, a thread of shivery excitement drowning in a flood tide of fear. "Please stop."

"Of course." He withdrew his hand and began massaging

down her calves until he reached her feet. She relaxed, and soon learned that her toes were as blissfully responsive as her hands.

When he had reduced her to the pliable consistency of bread dough, he drew the sheet up to her shoulders again. "Turn over if you would like the rest of you massaged."

An hour earlier, she would have been too embarrassed and fearful to expose herself. Now she rolled over. As she did, the sheet slipped and bared one breast. Michael didn't move, but his eyes narrowed and he became unnaturally still.

"I don't know how much further I can go tonight," she said quietly, "but I want to find out."

"Then let us continue." He swallowed as he drew the sheet down to her waist. "Your breasts are superb. Beautifully full and womanly." He started to say more, then shook his head. "We don't have enough words in English. There's nothing stronger than beautiful. And colors—we need more colors. What would you call the shade of these?" He took each nipple between thumb and forefinger and teased them with exquisitely judged pressure. "Tawny rose? Blush gold?"

Her nipples hardened and heat pulsed through her. "Tan. Pink. Plaid. I don't care as long as you touch me like that."

He took her at her word, massaging the tight nubs until her whole body pulsed with alarming pleasure. Huskily he said, "Would you mind terribly if I kissed you?"

"No," she whispered. "No, I wouldn't mind at all."

He leaned forward and claimed her mouth. The kiss was deep, deep, the heady stroke of his tongue fueling her fever. When he began to make feather kisses along her throat, she lifted her hands to his chest and shyly slid them inside his robe. He gasped and the muscles shivered under her touch.

As her hands stroked lower, hair tickled the heels of her hands and her fingertips found ridges of hard tissue. "You have more scars than anyone I know," she said ruefully. "It's a miracle you're alive and well."

"I wouldn't be if not for you." His lips slanted down her collarbone and over the creamy swell of her breast. The tug of his mouth on her nipple triggered a prickly yearning in the area between her legs that she tried never to think about. It was frightening, yet tantalizing as the serpent in Eden.

He shifted his position so that he was lying alongside her. Her quivery, fearful enjoyment turned abruptly to alarm when she felt the menacing jab of male flesh against her thigh. She tensed, unhappily reminded of where this was leading.

He muttered a curse under his breath and rolled onto his back. "I'm sorry, Catherine." Panting, he dragged his wrist across his forehead. "Damnation. I've about reached the limits of my control. If we are to go on, I'll have to remove the threat of this rude male organ of mine."

Her eyes shot open. "I beg your pardon?"

He laughed a little. "I don't have anything permanent in mind. The way I feel now, it will take very little to render me safe, particularly if you'll help. Can you do that?"

He was making it easy for her to refuse. But it was time she took some risks. For there to be real lovemaking, she must give as well as receive. "What do you want me to do?"

Silently he took her hand and brought it inside his robe, placing her palm on him. She wanted to jerk away when she felt the size and flagrant maleness of the throbbing flesh under her hand. *Pain, violation, a cruel and arrogant weapon.*

But this was Michael, not Colin, and he was a man, not a brusque, heedless youth. Slowly she squeezed.

The heated shaft jerked sharply and his whole body went rigid. "This . . . this won't take long at all," he gasped.

She had never realized that sex made a man as vulnerable as a woman, and she was startled to see how easily she could affect him. Her hand tightened on him with more confidence.

He arched against the pallet, sweat shining on his face as he tried to damp down his reaction. She closed her hand over the velvety head and squeezed again, at the same time rubbing the heavy rim with her thumb.

"Christ, Catherine!" A shudder went through him, and he jerked savagely in her hand. His fists clenched as his seed spurted into her palm. He was like a banked volcano, with suppressed violence in the tautness of his muscles, in the heaving of his chest and his harsh, panting breath.

Reflexive fear rose chokingly in her throat. Grimly she

fought it. There was no pain, no harm to her, she was not a victim. *There was no reason for fear.*

By the time the stiffness had faded from his long frame, she was composed again.

He brushed back her hair, then rested his warm hand on her shoulder. "Did you find that distressing?"

She wondered how many men would be as perceptive. "A little. Mating is a wild, primitive business." She squeezed him very, very gently. "But what seemed like a weapon a few minutes ago is now as harmless as a baby chick."

He grinned. "That puts me in my place."

She used a corner of the discarded sheet to dry them both. Her fear had gone, leaving a wistful sense of loss. This viscous fluid was the seed of life. If she had found the courage to truly mate with him, they might have made a baby. Though she would love any child, it would be pure joy to bear Michael's.

He drew her close, his hands soothing away any lingering distress. How had he learned such honesty and kindness? The hard way, she guessed. Hesitantly she said, "I assume that was what you meant when you said it's possible for a man to find satisfaction without intercourse."

"Yes, though it's not only for men." He rubbed her lower belly with the back of his hand. "Have you ever experienced the female equivalent of what happened to me?"

She gave him a quizzical glance. "How can anything like that happen to a woman?"

The amusement in his eyes showed that she had betrayed woeful ignorance, but his voice was tender when he replied, "Though the mechanics are different, I believe the feelings engendered are very similar."

She hid her face against his shoulder. "I've followed the army, borne a child, and nursed the dying. It's embarrassing to know so little about my own body."

"Lack of knowledge is easily cured," he said calmly. "Let me demonstrate."

He lowered his head for another kiss. The intermittent desire she had experienced earlier returned, this time without the undercurrent of fear. One thing she did know was that it took time for a man's sexual potency to return. That meant she could enjoy his caresses without anxiety.

Now that his desire had been slaked, there was a subtle difference in his embrace, a rich, more leisurely eroticism. She responded hungrily. All of her adult life, she had been suppressing her natural appetites. Finally she could set them free with the man she loved.

His caressing hand moved ever lower over the curve of her abdomen. Heat smoldered through her when his fingertips trailed through the dark silky curls and touched the secret flesh below. She caught her breath with surprise.

He murmured, "Should I stop?"

"No, it feels . . . nice."

His lips found hers again. She trembled with guilty delight as his fingers probed deeper. The tender folds were slickly moist to his touch. Distantly she wondered if something was wrong, for that had never happened before.

His deft touch found hidden places that blazed with sensation. Her head fell back and she dragged gulps of air into her lungs. Delicately he slid a finger into the place where once there had been only pain. This time there was excitement, and a queer aching emptiness. Her lips pumped against his caressing hand, no longer under her control. She felt urgent. Demanding. She gasped, "Merciful heaven . . ."

His thumb rubbed across a tiny nub of terrifying sensitivity. Heat spasmed through her with shocking suddenness. Writhing helplessly, she locked her arms around him. The fire swiftly burned out, leaving her limp. "Oh, my," she breathed. "Is that what you meant?"

"Exactly so." He kissed her forehead. "Did you find it distressing?"

She gave a choke of laughter. "It is rather upsetting to have one's body out of control, but I don't regret it. Now I understand why people bother." She also understood as never before Colin's selfishness in their marriage bed. With such urges driving him, no wonder he had seemed callous. It would be easy to lose oneself in lust.

As she had lost herself in fear. "I'm horribly sorry that I lied to you," she blurted out. "I hated doing it, but I felt I had no choice. I didn't think I would ever be able to speak of what was wrong with me."

"Forgiven and forgotten." Michael lay on his side and held her close with one arm. His velvet robe was soft on her hypersensitive skin. "Less and less do I believe you're abnormal. Apart from being abnormally wonderful, that is."

"You make me feel so *good.*" She rubbed her face against him like a cat. "Where did you learn such compassion?"

He sighed, some of his happiness dimming. "By making truly abominable mistakes."

"You said once that you loved—or were obsessed by—a married woman," she said hesitantly. "Was that one of them?"

"The worst." He hated speaking of his criminal folly, but it was only fair when he had forced Catherine to reveal her deepest shame. "She was the wife of a close friend. Devastatingly beautiful and utterly unscrupulous, though I didn't learn that until years later. She betrayed every man who loved her. From sheer malice, she did her best to poison the friendship between her husband and me, and very nearly succeeded."

His throat closed as he remembered the years of hell, and of the child Caro had been carrying when she died—the child that was probably his. The memory haunted him. "She said she feared her husband would kill her, and that I must avenge her if she died suddenly. Thinking she was exaggerating, I agreed. Then she died in a suspicious accident, and I was left with the choices of killing my friend, or breaking a vow made to the woman I loved."

"How ghastly." She propped herself on her elbow, her face reflecting his own anguish. "But you didn't do it, did you?"

"That was more from weakness than wisdom," he said painfully. "I ran away to war, half hoping I would be killed and never have to fulfill the vow I'd made. But eventually I had to come home. In my madness, I came within a hair's breadth of killing my friend. If it hadn't been for the generous spirit of the man I had betrayed, I would have ended by destroying both of us, and damning myself for eternity."

"But you didn't." She gave him a kiss of aching sweetness, the silken fall of her hair gliding across his throat. "For that I will be eternally grateful. No one else could do for me what you have done, Michael. Thank you from the bottom of my soul."

By giving Catherine the kindness and patience she had

not received as a bride, he was being rewarded a thousandfold. What had he done to deserve such luck? He swore that she would never regret trusting him. "I still haven't finished that massage. Would you like more, or would you prefer to sleep?"

She rolled onto her back and stretched with innocent provocation. "Finish the massage. I want to learn how, so I can give one to you."

He was surprised to feel a stirring of arousal. His long years of celibacy, combined with his passionate attraction to Catherine, had guaranteed that he would recover swiftly.

He retrieved the bottle of lotion and warmed some between his hands. Then he resumed what was a task of pure pleasure. In the firelight, her body was warm cream, her hair a dark glossy cloud around her face. His hands glided over her shoulders and arms, then down her torso and waist. Her eyes were closed, but she smiled dreamily when his fingertips traced the contours of her ribs. He took his time, repeating each stroke over and over, paying special attention to her magnificent breasts.

She was no longer wary when he touched her below the waist. A good thing he was still wearing his robe so she did not realize that he had ceased to be as harmless as a chick.

He sat by her feet and used a gentle, wringing motion on her legs. She made a muted, purring sound. Drawing her left leg up so that it bent at the knee, he circled her thigh with his hands. His lotioned hands slid effortlessly over her sleek skin.

She laughed a little when he did the right leg. "I feel like a lamb being basted so it can be baked for dinner."

"Not a bad idea. I think I'll taste you a little now."

He bent forward and licked the tender skin of her abdomen, drawing teasing circles around her navel with his tongue. Jarred from languor into vivid awareness, she exclaimed, "How can I be feeling like this again so soon?"

"Some women have the ability to reach fulfillment several times in rapid succession. Perhaps it's nature's compensation for the fact that it takes females longer to get there in the first place." He exhaled his warm breath into the soft mat of hair between her thighs.

Her fingers curled. "That feels very wicked."

"It isn't," he said peaceably, "but I'll stop if you like."

Her hand clenched on the folded blanket beneath her hips. "I . . . I think I'd rather be depraved. Sometimes I *hated* being Saint Catherine."

He kissed the inside of her thigh, triggering ripples of reaction in the acutely sensitive places he had found earlier. His firm lips moved higher, higher, until his heated mouth touched her most secret places. She gasped with shock.

His tongue stroked into the delicate feminine folds. The pleasure was indescribable, intense beyond any sensation she had ever known except pain. She whimpered, a long, drawn-out, racking sound. Dizzily she knew that after this night, she would never be the same. Sober Saint Catherine was gone forever, consumed by the flames of ecstasy. Yet even as she hovered on the edge of dissolution, she felt a queer hunger, a sense of incompleteness.

His hand replaced his mouth, his fingers inflaming, teasing, sliding inside her. She gave an inchoate murmur of protest when he stopped. A moment later, he caressed her again, pressing inward with a new, blunt kind of pressure.

It was another searing shock to realize what he was doing. Her eyes flew open and she stared at him. He had braced himself over her, a tremor in his broad shoulders and arms. Their gazes locked. There was a question in the depths of his eyes as he paused on the brink of full possession.

Suppressing her memory of those other, horrible times, she gave a faint, fearful nod. Her breasts rose and fell frantically as she waited for agony.

But when he pressed into her, there was no pain. Only a not-unpleasant stretching and a luscious, sliding friction as he advanced, a fraction of an inch at a time. When he had buried himself inside her, he panted, "Are you all right?"

"Yes." Her eyes were wide and startled. *"Yes."*

Her hips lifted against him gingerly. The sensation of him moving inside her brought stunning delight. *This* was what she had craved to fill her emptiness—this joining of two bodies to make them briefly one.

Her face blazed with joy as she wrapped her arms around him, bringing the length of his body against hers. "Yes, yes, yes!"

Her hips moved again, this time swift and hard so that

he was driven more deeply. He locked his arms around her with a harsh groan and began thrusting uncontrollably. This time she was no prisoner, but his partner in madness. Heat was building, building, threatening to consume her soul. She clung to him as the one source of safety in a world gone mad.

Fire blazed through her in glorious wildness, searing her with shattering force. He spilled himself inside her as she twisted against him, shuddering. This was true fulfillment, as far surpassing the simple physical release he had shown her as the sun surpassed a candle.

She was his, he was hers. Her man, her love, her mate.

After the turbulence of their lovemaking, they both dozed. Michael woke when the fire burned out and coaxed a drowsy Catherine into bed. She came willingly, and promptly twined herself around him, trying to get as close as humanly possible.

He smiled and stroked her head. "That was worth waiting six years for."

She blinked at him sleepily. "Six years?"

"That's how long it's been since I've lain with a woman."

She came awake, her eyes wide with surprise. "You've been celibate since that horrible affair with the married woman?"

He nodded. "At first, I was an emotional shambles—far too crazed to be a fit bedmate for anyone. Celibacy was aided by the fact that I seem to have spent half the time since recovering from wounds, or fever, or being in the wilds of Spain, or some damned thing." He kissed her on the tip of the nose. "Also, I hadn't met anyone like you."

"I'm glad it's been so long for you," she said softly. "That means that perhaps tonight has been a little special for you. I hope so, because it was miraculous for me."

"Tonight was equally special for me," he murmured. More so than he had words for. He continued petting her until she fell asleep again. It was amazing how completely she had been transformed. This was the passionate, loving woman Catherine was meant to be. He wanted to stay awake to savor the sweetness of it, but he was too tired.

He drifted off, only to jolt awake, covered with sweat. *She was not for him.* Such joy was too good to last. Always in the past, his happiness had been crushed by some unexpected blow.

Fiercely he told himself that such thoughts were mere superstition. What could come between him and Catherine now?

But it was a long time before he slept again.

Chapter 28

Pearly morning light shafted through the window when Catherine woke to find her head resting on Michael's shoulder, and her arm draped over his chest. He was also awake. His eyes held a certain wariness, as if wondering what she would feel about the events of the previous night.

She gave a slow smile. "That wasn't a dream, was it?"

He relaxed and smiled back. "The realest experience of my life. No regrets?"

"Nary a one." She made a face. "Except that I wish I'd realized sooner that I wasn't hopelessly flawed. It isn't going to be easy untangling the mess I've made by my deception."

"It doesn't have to be done instantly. Wait a bit. One of us might have a burst of inspiration if we think about it for a few days," he suggested. "Speaking of messes, Kenneth wrote that Colin's death left you with a number of problems."

"An understatement. When we married, we both had a little family money, but it's long gone now. I didn't know how bad things were until he died. Most of his creditors in the regiment were willing to overlook his gaming debts, but there were trademen's bills that had to paid before leaving France." She sighed. "Worst of all, he'd gotten one of his current mistresses, a housemaid, with child."

Michael winced. "How wretched for everyone involved."

Wretched did not begin to describe how she had felt when she had learned the news. She rolled onto her back and stared at the ceiling. "Marie was a country girl with no idea what to do. I told her to go home to her parents and say she was newly widowed after a brief marriage. An inheritance would make her story more believable, so I sold my mother's pearls and gave her half the proceeds. With that as a dowry, she should be able to marry and raise the child properly."

His brows rose. "You'll never get rid of the name Saint Catherine if you keep doing things like that."

"I could hardly let the girl and her baby starve, could I? It was the least I could do for Colin's sake." A shadow of old guilt fell across her. "God knows I wasn't a good wife to him."

"You must stop tormenting yourself, Catherine," Michael said quietly. "Now that I know the full story, I have great respect for the dignity you and Colin showed in a difficult situation. And though you were badly mismatched, your marriage produced Amy. Surely neither of you regretted that."

He had found the perfect way to allay her self-reproach. "You're right. Colin truly loved Amy. She may have been the only person he did love." She gave Michael a slanting glance. "I promise I won't be boringly guilty again."

He grinned. "You're never boring, even if you are a saint."

An uneasy thought struck her. "One reason I didn't want to tell you about Colin's death was that I saw you driving a lovely young girl in the park. It was assumed that you were seeking a wife, and something about the way you two looked at each other made me think you had found one."

"I took a variety of young ladies for drives, but I don't remember making calf's eyes at any. What did she look like?"

"Tall and slender, with soft brown hair. Pretty and very intelligent-looking, though she seemed a little shy."

"Kit," he said immediately. "My friend Lucien's wife. She and I are exceedingly fond of each other, in a strictly nonromantic way. You'll like her, too."

She felt a warm glow at the way he was assuming she would be part of his life in the future. Even more, she felt relief. That pretty girl was Michael's friend, not his beloved. She drew her hand over his shoulder, enjoying the feel of hard muscles beneath smooth skin. "She looked very likable."

His smile faded. "There's something I must tell you."

Concerned by the note in his voice, she said, "You don't have to tell me anything you don't want to. Whatever it is won't make any difference to me."

"Not even the fact that I'm a bastard?" he said ironically.

It took a moment for her to understand. "So the Duke of Ashburton wasn't your real father. From what you say about him, I'm not sorry. He sounded dreadful."

After an astonished moment, he fell back on the pillow, laughing. "That's all you have to say about the great scandal of my existence? Don't you want to know if my father was a footman or a lusty stable boy?"

Hearing the brittleness in his amusement, she said quietly, "I don't care who or what your father was. I do care how the situation affected you. Did the Duke of Ashburton know?"

Every trace of humor vanished from Michael's face. "He knew, all right. I was the result of an affair between the duchess and Ashburton's younger brother. For the sake of pride, the duke exiled his brother and let the world think I was his own son. He didn't tell me the truth until he was on his deathbed."

"Lord, that was just before we came down here! No wonder you looked so strained when we went through Great Ashburton." Catherine laid her hand on his forearm. "So you were the innocent victim of the sort of ghastly situation that tears families apart. It explains why the duke treated you so coldly."

"It was upsetting to learn the truth, but in a strange way, liberating. I don't need the duke's family."

She leaned forward and kissed him with all the love in her heart. Then she smiled wickedly. "It's too early for breakfast. Care to use the time making up for those six years of celibacy?"

He drew her into his arms. "We both have a lot to make up for. I'm looking forward to it immensely."

So was she. Saints in heaven, so was she.

The next two days were paradise. As she dressed on the third morning, Catherine wondered if anyone had noticed the change in her relationship with Michael. Oh, the two of them didn't touch each other in public, or sneak off to their bedroom in the middle of the day—though they had been tempted. But she had a permanent cat-in-the-cream-pot smile, and it was impossible to control what was in their eyes when they exchanged glances.

They had not talked of the future; Michael had not said

that he loved her, nor made a formal offer of marriage. As she had suspected, under his intensely capable surface there was a great deal of vulnerability, the result of never having received enough love. That must be why she had seen an uncertain, this-is-too-good-to-be-true expression in his eyes. Well, she felt the same way. In fact, she hadn't gotten around to saying how much she loved him, either. No words were strong enough.

Eventually they must be more practical, but she expected no problems. Though Amy might be startled to acquire a stepfather so soon, she had always liked Michael. Everything would be fine.

She smiled into the mirror as she brushed her hair. The biggest question in her mind was whether she and Michael should marry right away, or wait until a full year after Colin's death. The latter would be more proper, but she didn't want to delay. Also, if the natural consequence of passionate lovemaking occurred, they might have to marry in haste. She wouldn't mind.

Michael's image appeared in the mirror next to hers as he bent and pressed a kiss to the sensitive spot below her ear. Sighing with delight, she leaned back against him. "Do we have to watch people gather seaweed to fertilize the fields, or one of Davin's other jolly amusements? I'd rather spend the day here ravishing you. Tearing off your clothing. Pinning you ruthlessly to the floor and devouring you with kisses."

"Sounds wonderful." He gently rubbed her chin with his knuckles. "You grow less saintly by the day. But not so much that you will shirk your duty."

Alas, he was right. Catherine got to her feet. "Very well, I'll ravish you tonight. You can spend the day worrying about the violence I shall wreak on your helpless body."

He studied her with a scorching thoroughness that made her toes curl. "I'll spend the day thinking about it, though I can't promise that I'll be worrying."

He took her arm, and they went down to the breakfast parlor. When they walked in, her grandfather looked up from his plate testily. "For a pair that have been married a dozen years, you certainly are smelling of April and May."

She kissed his cheek. Though he still used the wheelchair, he was noticeably more vigorous than when they had arrived. "It's the marvelous sea air, Grandfather." She gave

Michael a private smile. "It makes us feel that we're just wed."

The laird spread butter on a slice of toast. "Clive's back from London. I want to speak with the two of you this morning."

Michael asked, "Am I specifically excluded?"

"Yes. You'll find out what I have to say soon enough."

Catherine stared at her coddled eggs. Surely the meeting was about the laird's choice of heir. The practical questions she had been avoiding would have to be answered, and soon.

Davin Penrose entered the breakfast parlor and greeted everyone, then helped himself to a cup of tea. Michael asked him, "What is on today's schedule?"

"That depends." The constable took a chair. "Do you know much about cannons, Captain Melbourne?"

"I've had some experience with horse artillery, but I'm no expert."

"You're bound to know more than anyone on Skoal. The island militia is quite efficient—the laird is the colonel, and I'm the captain. Besides muskets, we have two six-pound cannon that were sent to repel Napoleon if he should choose to invade us." Amusement gleamed in his eyes. "A good thing the emperor had other goals in mind, because the government didn't see fit to tell us how to use the blasted things."

Michael laughed. "That's His Majesty's army for you. I take it you want to fire them and need some lessons."

"Aye. Rocks are crumbling from an overhanging cliff in the harbor and endangering the boats moored below. I thought a few rounds of cannon shot might bring the weak bits down without hurting anyone. It would be much appreciated if you could show us how to shoot without killing ourselves."

"I know enough for that." Michael turned to Catherine. "Since you'll be busy, I'll go with Davin. It will take most of the day to condition the guns and train men to use them safely."

"Perhaps I'll come and watch later," she said. "One of the nice things about this island is that you can't go too far away."

He gave her an intimate smile, then left with Davin.

"Come to my study in an hour," the laird ordered. "Clive

will be here then." Briskly he wheeled his chair from the room.

Alone in the breakfast parlor, Catherine frowned as she thought about the upcoming meeting. She had not yet decided what to do about Skoal. She no longer needed the inheritance; in fact, the responsibilities that went with the legacy would be burdensome after she and Michael married. Yet she had grown fond of the island and its inhabitants, and she wanted to see them well governed. Her cousin Haldoran seemed too self-absorbed and capricious to be a good laird.

She shrugged her shoulders philosophically. The choice was her grandfather's. If he had already decided in Clive's favor, the matter was out of her hands. But if he had chosen her, she would have to do some hard thinking.

When Catherine went to the laird's study, her grandfather was behind his desk talking to Haldoran. The men broke off speaking when she arrived. She gave her cousin a courteous smile. "Hello, Clive. I hope your journey to London went well."

He rose politely. His expression changed when he saw her, something hard and angry showing in his eyes. It was gone in an instant, replaced by practiced charm. "An excellent trip. I achieved exactly what I wished."

The laird said, "Sit down, both of you."

Catherine complied. "Grandfather, are you ever polite?"

He gave a bark of laughter. "Can't see the point. There's always a thousand things to do. Why waste time with words?" His humor vanished, replaced by steely command. "You both know why you're here. Clive, I've decided to make Catherine my heir. You're capable and you've known the island longer, but your interests lie elsewhere. I think Catherine and her husband will do better by Skoal."

A few days earlier, she would have been limp with relief to hear that. Now her feelings were more complex. She felt honored, and a little trapped. She gave a sidelong glance at her cousin. Haldoran's face was rigid, rather like the time Michael had proved himself to be a better shot. However, his voice was smooth when he said, "You're quite sure this is what you wish?"

"When have you known me to be indecisive? Yesterday my solicitor came from the mainland to change my will in

Catherine's favor." The laird tapped a sheaf of papers. "I have a copy here. I want you both to read it so there will be no surprises when I'm gone."

"Your desire for clarity is admirable, Uncle. What a pity that your granddaughter doesn't share it."

His mocking tone made Catherine stiffen with foreboding. The laird snapped, "What the devil is that supposed to mean?"

"I am second to no one in admiration for my beautiful cousin." Haldoran's contemptuous gaze went to Catherine. "However, it is my sad duty to inform you that your only granddaughter is a liar and a whore, and she's been making a fool of you ever since she set foot on the island."

As Catherine froze with horror, her grandfather growled, "Damn you, Clive, you always were a filthy loser. That's one reason I don't want you to have Skoal. Don't think you can change my mind with a parcel of lies."

"It's true I don't like losing, but the lies are all Catherine's," Haldoran said icily. "The real Colin Melbourne died in France in April. Because your greedy little granddaughter feared losing her chance for a fortune, she talked one of her lovers into masquerading as her husband. While you've been debating her worthiness, she's been fornicating and laughing behind your back. Go ahead, ask her to deny it."

The laird's head swung toward Catherine, his face an alarming shade of red. "Is there any truth to what Clive says?"

Her shock and humiliation were tempered with relief that she would not have to lie anymore. Unevenly she said, "It's true that Colin is dead, killed by a Bonapartist. However, I don't have hordes of lovers." Stretching a point, she went on, "Michael is my fiancé. Soon, he *will* be my husband. I'm truly sorry for deceiving you, Grandfather. It seemed necessary at the time, but every day I've regretted it more."

"You sly little trollop!" Ignoring the latter part of her statement, her grandfather pushed himself to his feet, bracing his trembling hands on the desktop. His eyes burned with rage, and the pain of betrayal. "To think I was ready to trust Skoal to you! Well, you can think again, missy. You're no granddaughter of mine." He pressed one hand to his temple. "G . . . going to ch . . . change . . ."

Alarmed by his intemperance, she exclaimed, "Grandfather, please, calm down! If you want me to go away and never bother you again, fine, but don't make yourself ill over this."

Oblivious to her, he said thickly, "Ch—change my will . . ." He collapsed, falling forward onto his desk, then crashing heavily to the floor in a cascade of papers and quill pens.

"Dear God!" Catherine raced around the desk and dropped to her knees beside him. He was unconscious, and the left side of his face had gone flaccid. "He's having an apoplectic fit."

"Congratulations, cousin," Haldoran drawled. "Not only did you deceive him, but you've apparently killed him as well."

She shot him a look of furious dislike. "You're equally responsible, *cousin.* I was going to tell him the truth, but I would have chosen a less inflammatory way of doing it." Her probing fingers found a thready pulse in his throat. "Thank God he's still alive. Ring for a servant to go for help."

Haldoran did not move from the chair where he was lounging. "Why bother? There's no doctor on Skoal. It would take at least half a day to bring one from the mainland, and even then, it's doubtful that a physician could help him."

He was right, blast him. She must do what she could herself. Most of her nursing experience was with men who were wounded or diseased, but several times she had seen apoplectic patients in the field hospitals. She sat back on her heels and tried to remember what kind of treatment they had received. Ian Kinlock had said that bloodletting often helped apoplexy. And if it were done, it should be as soon as possible.

She stood and rummaged in the desk for a penknife. "I'm going to bleed him. Is there some kind of basin here?"

Looking martyred, Haldoran got to his feet and lifted a bowl of roses from a side table. After tossing the flowers into the fireplace, he brought her the bowl. "Here you are, but you're wasting your time. He had a similar attack last year. He came through that one, but I believe a second is usually fatal."

"Not necessarily." Praying that she was doing the right thing, she knelt by the laird again and rolled his sleeve above the elbow. Then she made a careful nick in the vein.

Her grandfather's blood splashed into the bowl as forcefully as if it were coming from an artery.

Clive opened a box on the desk and took out a cigar. "Do you mind if I smoke, cousin?"

"I don't care if you *burn*! How can you be so callous?"

He found a tinder box in the desk and lit the cigar. "There's nothing I can do, so why flap about like a guillotined chicken? Speaking of chickens, don't count yours before they're hatched. You think you've won because he's already changed his will." He drew on the cigar, then slowly released a mouthful of smoke. "You're wrong. I want the island, I want you, and I intend to have them both."

"You're talking utter rubbish," she said impatiently, her gaze on her grandfather and the slowing stream of blood. "Neither Skoal nor I are trophies to be won."

"Ah, but you are," he said calmly. "When Lord Michael returns, you will tell him to leave the island because you've decided to accept my most flattering offer of marriage. You and I will rule Skoal together, the last feudal monarchs in the British Isles."

She looked up from her grandfather, incredulous. "Send Michael away? You're mad."

"Not at all," he said with the same eerie calm. "You're going to do exactly what I tell you."

His assurance was beginning to unnerve her. "Why the devil should I pay any attention to your ridiculous orders?"

He gave a smile of mocking triumph. "Because I have your sweet little daughter, Amy."

Chapter 29

Catherine stared at her cousin, feeling as if he had struck her a physical blow. "I don't believe you."

"If you want the proof, we can go to Ragnarok. She is comfortably ensconced in one of my best guest rooms with a splendid view of the sea. She quite likes Skoal."

"You're lying," she said through stiff lips. "Amy is safe with friends."

"Not safe enough." Clive sat down and crossed one elegantly booted leg over the other. "Anne Mowbry was reluctant to let me take her without word from you, but the girl was keen to come, and of course I'm the gallant gentleman who conveyed the whole pack of brats to Antwerp last year. How could Anne doubt such a hero?" He pulled a cherry-colored ribbon from his pocket and tossed it at Catherine. It twisted in the air and fell to the carpet to lie like a trail of blood.

She had bought the ribbon for Amy's birthday. The bright shade was so vivid against her daughter's soft, dark hair . . . Her hands tightened on her grandfather's limp arm. "If you've hurt her, you're a dead man."

"Maternal devotion is such a touching sight." He tapped ash from the end of his cigar. "Don't worry, Amy is quite safe, and doesn't realize yet that she's a prisoner. She thinks I'm going to bring you to Ragnarok so you can be surprised."

She tried to make sense of what was happening. "You knew from the first that the man with me wasn't Colin."

"How could you think I wouldn't recognize someone as prominent as Lord Michael Kenyon merely because we were never introduced? I made it my business to learn about your friends, escorts, and dance partners." His eyes narrowed to slits. "The two of you weren't lovers when you came to the island, but you are now. I knew it the instant you came in that door."

That more than anything else made her realize what a formidable adversary Haldoran was. Like a spider, he had been spinning his web for a long time, watching and waiting. "Why didn't you expose my deception immediately?"

"It was a surprise to find you blandly presenting Lord Michael as your husband, but I was charmed at how well you carried it off. You and I are much alike, cousin. What were our privateer ancestors but legal pirates? Blood will tell."

She would rather be related to a scorpion. "If you want the island, I'll sign it over to you if the laird dies. That's only justice, since he doesn't want me to have it anyhow."

"The island is only half," he said gently. "I must have you as well. By marrying you, I will obtain both of my goals."

Clamping down on her fear, she forced herself to organize her thoughts. First, she must care for her grandfather. There was a pint or so of blood in the bowl and the flow had slowed to a normal rate, so she had better end the bleeding.

She used the penknife to cut strips from her petticoat and bandaged the laird's arm. His pulse seemed a bit steadier, but beyond that she had no idea of his condition. She got to her feet and retrieved the blanket that had fallen from the wheelchair, then spread it over her grandfather. Knowing that even a doctor could probably do no more for him, she stood and gave her cousin her full attention. "Michael will never allow you to get away with whatever mad scheme you've devised."

"Your lover is a capable man, but no match for me. Come over here. I've something to show you."

Wondering what new blow he had in store, she joined him at the window. He gestured at a carriage waiting in the courtyard. Two villainous-looking servants sat nearby, idly dicing. "I recruit my best employees from Newgate Prison, so they are even more dangerous than they appear. I have two more of similar stamp at Ragnarok. They've all committed murder, and will happily do so again if I wish. Four armed men, plus myself, are a rather small army, but it's large enough to rule Skoal. Your dashing former officer would have no chance."

Horror increased to nightmare proportions. "Are you saying you'll kill Michael if I don't send him away?"

"I've waited a long time for you, cousin. I don't intend to wait any longer." He cocked his head. "Did you really persuade Kenyon to marry you, or did you say that to mollify the laird?"

"No persuasion was required," she said stiffly.

"Quite a coup for someone whose birth and fortune are so inferior to his. A fine example of the power of beauty." He exhaled, the smoke wreathing diabolically around his head. "If you have any fondness for Kenyon, send him away. Having killed your husband, I will certainly not hesitate to kill your lover."

Stunned, Catherine swayed against the wall, on the verge of fainting. "It was you who murdered Colin?"

"Yes, though as a hunter I didn't take much pride in the kill. The average fox is harder to catch. He was too drunk to care when I shot him in the back." Haldoran smiled sardonically. "Surely you aren't going to claim you loved that fornicating oaf. You're a good liar, but not that good."

The horror was almost unbearable. Dear God, Colin, with his courage and brash good nature, was dead because of her. He had survived a decade of war only to be murdered by a madman. Haldoran was evil, *evil.*

And he held the lives of her loved ones in his hands. A lifetime spent with soldiers made her understand how five armed and ruthless men could terrorize a whole community, and she knew in her bones that if Haldoran and his killers began to run amok, they would not want to stop. Brutality bred further brutality.

She thought of the horrors she had seen in Spain, and closed her eyes, nauseated. For the sake of Michael and Amy and the islanders, she must go along with Haldoran, at least for now.

In the distance, a cannon blasted. Michael's artillery project. A second shot boomed across the island. The familiar battlefield sound made her thoughts go cold and clear. Haldoran had said that beauty was power. That gave her one frail weapon against him. That and her wits, which most men overlooked because they were dazzled by her face and form.

She opened her eyes, sweeping her lashes upward with provocative deliberation. "I underestimated you, Clive. I had thought you a bit of a dandy, all style with no substance. You are stronger and bolder than I thought."

For all his boasted cleverness, he was not immune to flattery. "You are coming to terms with the new order very quickly," he said, preening slightly. "Women are such practical creatures. In time, you'll be grateful for my taking charge of your life. I am richer and far more interesting than Kenyon."

"I'm already beginning to see the advantages," she agreed. "My grandfather keeps a brandy decanter here, doesn't he? Pour me some. It's time for plain speaking."

He bowed with ironic respect, then turned to obey. She took advantage of the brief respite to sit down and order her near-hysterical thoughts. She must learn Clive's intentions; she must protect Amy and Michael; most of all, she must buy time. That meant she must become the liar Haldoran thought her. She had convinced the world she was an adoring wife for more than a decade, and she had successfully hidden her love from Michael. Her skill in dissimulation must be called on again.

Haldoran returned and gave her one of the two glasses he carried. She waved him to a seat. "You say you want both Skoal and me. Why? The island is remote and not rich, and while I am beautiful, there are other women of equal beauty."

"I am a collector of objects that are rare and matchless. Granted, Skoal is not valuable compared to the rest of my holdings, but its feudal nature is unique. On Skoal, the laird has more authority than King George himself. The prospect of holding such power is irresistible. As for you . . ." His gaze traveled over her, dark and covetous. "You underestimate your looks as much as you underestimate my cleverness. There is not a man in the world who will not envy me for possessing you. It was revolting to see you wasted on a boor like Melbourne."

She shrugged, and started the most cold-blooded lying of her life. "At the time my parents died, Colin was the best choice. I suppose I could have left him to become a rich man's mistress, but such positions are precarious. Marriage and reputation are a woman's best protections." She sipped her brandy, and prayed that he would accept her next condition. "Which is why I will not allow you into my bed until after we are wed."

His eyes darkened. "You slept with Kenyon."

"Not until he had offered for me." She pursed her lips. "Perhaps I should have waited, but I wanted to attach him more securely. He's the honorable sort, which means that he would never have broken a betrothal after promising marriage and lying with me. I wouldn't have done it if I had realized the extent of your interest, cousin. You should have spoken sooner."

A slow smile curved Haldoran's lips. "I always knew that under your saintly facade beats a heart of pure brass. We shall deal very well together"—he scanned her face with dangerous shrewdness—"as long as you don't think you can deceive me with the pretense of cooperation. Here on the island, my little army makes me invincible. If you betray me, it will be simple to dispose of you and make it look like an accident on the cliffs. I will do it in an instant if you make it necessary."

"I believe you. I'd be a fool not to."

He swirled his brandy in slow circles. "Your daughter is very like you, and she is on the verge of womanhood. Did you know that on Skoal, girls can be married at the age of twelve?"

The threat was unmistakable, and more horrifying than everything that had come before. Choking back a desire to physically assault him, she said, "You will find a woman far more satisfying than a child." She made herself give a seductive smile. "As you observed, women are practical creatures. We are attracted to the most powerful males. If you deal fairly with me, I shall return the courtesy."

He laughed out loud. "Catherine, you are wonderful. I should have done this months ago."

"Why didn't you?"

"I was busy." His gaze went over her again, lingering on her breasts. "I wanted to be able to give you my full attention when the time came."

She tried not to think of what it would be like to be bedded by a man she loathed. It would make her marriage to Colin seem like paradise. "That's all well and good, but before anything else, we must see how my grandfather fares."

"True. We can hardly allow him to expire on the floor. People would talk. I assume you intend to nurse him, so I'll leave one of my men to help. I will also move into the castle myself, to be on hand should my support be required." He tapped the edge of the brandy glass against his teeth thoughtfully. "Since you'll be busy, I think it best for Amy to stay at Ragnarok until the laird dies. That won't be long. You needn't worry about Amy—someone will be with her at all times."

In other words, she and Amy would be constantly guarded. But for the time being, safe. Now to ensure Michael's life. "I'll order Lord Michael's things to be packed. Will you arrange for a boat to take him to the mainland?"

Haldoran nodded. "The sooner Kenyon is gone, the better. When he returns from his artillery shoot, speak to him in the laird's sitting room. I shall be listening from the bedchamber." His expression became feral. "And if you feel a sudden temptation to tell him how I persuaded you to accept me—resist it." He let his coat fall away to expose the butt of a pocket pistol. The message was blindingly clear.

"Do you take me for a fool, cousin? There is no advantage for me in trouble." She stood. "Now that we have settled the essentials, ring for the servants. We must put my grandfather to bed and send for a physician, even though nothing can be done."

He rose and went to the bell pull while Catherine knelt beside the laird. His breathing was shallow but steady, and his eyelids flickered a little when she whispered, "Please don't die on me, Grandfather. I need you alive." But he did not wake.

As she tucked the blanket closer around the old man, she thought about what she should say to Michael. He would never believe such an abrupt change of mind if she simply told him to go. What could she do to make him leave without asking awkward questions that would get him killed?

The answer came, quick and ugly. She must be like the bitch who had betrayed him. She must trigger his hidden core of doubts by using her knowledge of him to weave a web of lies so potent that he would believe she was a selfish, callous slut.

The prospect was agonizing. He had forgiven her first set of lies and shown her the greatest kindness she had ever known. Now she must pervert the honesty and trust that had grown between them to send him away. In the process she would wound him horribly. Given his past, she might forever destroy his ability to trust another woman. But if she did not persuade him to leave, he would be murdered out of hand.

The cannon boomed again, the sound of war echoing in a place of peace. She drew a shaking breath. Amazing how the threat of death hardened one's resolve.

Michael returned to the castle in midafternoon feeling vastly content. Artillery practice involved fire, filthy smudges of black powder, and ear-numbing amounts of racket. In other words, it satisfied all the guilty pleasures of boyhood. The islanders he had trained had been apt pupils. By the end of the afternoon they had blasted away the most dangerous overhangs in the harbor. A pity Catherine hadn't joined them, but she was probably not fond of the noise. Most women weren't.

He knew something was wrong as soon as he rode into the stableyard and saw the head groom's face. "What has happened?"

"The laird had a fit of apoplexy," the groom said tersely. "They've sent for a doctor, but it . . . it don't look good."

"Damnation!" Michael swung from his horse. "Is my wife with him?"

"They say she's nursing him with her own hands."

"If anyone can save the laird, Catherine can."

He entered the castle and went up to the laird's rooms two steps at a time. He slowed when he entered the sitting room. One of Haldoran's burly servants—Doyle?—was gazing out a window and looking bored. However, when Michael entered, Doyle moved quickly across the room to block the bedroom door. "The lady says no one is to go in," he said gruffly.

Suppressing his irritation with the man's officiousness, Michael said, "Tell my wife I'm here."

Doyle went into the sickroom. A minute later Catherine came out, her face pale. Michael went to embrace her, but she stopped him with an upheld hand.

Bracing himself for bad news, Michael said, "I heard the laird had a stroke. How bad is it?"

"He's in a coma. I don't expect him to survive."

So she was going to lose her grandfather so soon after finding him. "I'm sorry," he said quietly. "What can I do?"

She bent her head and pressed her hands to her temples for a moment. Then she looked up, her expression hard. "There's no easy way to say this. It's time for you to go, Michael. Yesterday my grandfather changed his will in my favor, so I have achieved my goal. Thank you for your help. It was essential."

"I don't want to leave you even for a little while." He moved to take her into his arms. "I've been wounded so often that I know my way around a sickroom. I won't get in the way."

She pulled away before he could touch her. "I didn't make myself clear. You must leave permanently. Our affair is over."

He stared, sure he had not heard correctly. "Affair? I had assumed we would marry."

Her brows arched. "Oh? You talked vaguely about the possibility, but you never got around to proposing."

Remembering how much strain she was under, he reined in his temper. "Perhaps I should have been more explicit, but the situation was clear. You're not the sort of woman who has affairs, nor am I a man who seduces respectable women for sport."

Her eyes narrowed. "You don't really know me very well, Michael. Most of my life has been governed by expedience. For the first time I have choices, and they don't include marriage."

He felt blood beating in his temples. "I thought that I might have changed your mind," he said carefully. "Or if I hadn't yet, I soon would."

She shook her head. "Accept that it's over, Michael. I'm fond of you, but I don't want you for a husband."

" 'Fond,' " he repeated numbly. "Is that what you feel?"

She shrugged. "I never said I loved you."

It was true: she hadn't. He had assumed it from her actions, just as he had assumed that of course they would marry. "Forgive me if I'm having trouble understanding," he said tightly. "You seem to have become another woman in the hours since I left this morning."

"Keep your voice down—the laird needs quiet." She glanced anxiously at the bedroom door.

Concern for her grandfather must have scrambled her wits. Desperate to bring this nightmare to an end, he crossed the room in three swift steps and pulled her into his embrace. Passion had healed her fears before, and it could again.

She was warm and familiar, and for an instant she was the woman he knew. Then she jerked away, her expression savage. "Damn you, Michael, you don't own me! I saved your life, and by coming to Skoal, you've paid your debt. The scales are even. Now leave me alone and *go*!"

Before he could respond, the bedroom door swung open and Haldoran stepped out, his expression menacing. "If you don't stop harassing my fiancée, Kenyon, I shall be forced to take steps to improve your manners."

Stunned, Michael looked from Haldoran to Catherine. "You're going to marry him?"

"Yes." She edged toward her cousin. "Clive is of island blood, he has known Skoal all his life. He is also discreet. He recognized you immediately, but kept the knowledge to himself. Today he and I have discovered how much we have in common."

Haldoran smiled with gloating satisfaction. "And in the process, she realized that I am the better man."

"Rubbish." Michael was about to add that she didn't even like her cousin.

Catherine cut him off, her aqua eyes ruthless. "I tried to let you down gently, but since you're forcing me to be blunt, I'll spell it out—Clive is wealthier, he's a peer, not a younger son, and he's far more worldly. He and I have agreed that marriage need not restrict either of us unduly. After I've given him an heir, I'll be free to sample some of the choices that I mentioned earlier. When I was desperate I was willing to overlook your deficiencies of birth and fortune, but not now. Nor do I want to tie myself to a possessive man who would want me to spend the rest of my life in one bed."

Her words were sledgehammer blows. He stared at her, his lungs so constricted he could scarcely breathe. He didn't know Catherine any more than he had known Caroline. Again he had made an utter fool of himself over a woman. Christ, would he never learn? "You're right—I have some rather old-fashioned notions about monogamy. I have no desire to marry a trollop."

Her face paled. "I never belonged on that pedestal you built for me, Michael. I wish we could part friends, but I suppose that's impossible."

"Friends," he said incredulously. "Not bloody likely, Catherine."

Her eyes narrowed to feline slits. "Since I didn't think you would want to linger, I had your belongings packed and loaded in a cart. A boat is waiting to take you to Penward."

If he didn't leave this room instantly, he would do something he would regret. Not sure whether it would be tears or murder, Michael spun on his heel and left.

Halfway down the stairs, he had to catch at the banister while he fought for breath. Slowly in and out. Think only of the air moving into his lungs.

When he could breathe again, he let go of the banister and continued down to the courtyard. He had survived Caroline and Waterloo, and he supposed he would survive this.

But he wished to God Catherine had let him die in Belgium.

Knees shaking, Catherine folded into a chair as soon as the door closed.

"Well done, my darling, but I didn't like what you said about wanting to spread your legs for the multitudes," Haldoran drawled. "My wife must be mine alone. You will be very sorry if you forget that."

She swallowed. "I said what I did to give Lord Michael a disgust of me. You needn't worry about my fidelity when we are wed. Monogamy with you will suit me very well."

Haldoran smiled complacently as he crossed the room to the door. "I'll go make sure that Kenyon really leaves."

"He will. He won't ever want to see me again." After her cousin left, Catherine leaned back in the chair, her heart hammering so violently that she wondered if she was on the verge of an apoplexy like her grandfather's.

If she lived to be a hundred, she would never forget the expression on Michael's face when he left.

She closed her eyes. Twice on the Peninsula she had killed men who were dying in such excruciating pain that they had begged her for the coup de grace. It had been hard, terribly hard, to go against her healing instincts, but she had done it.

She drew a shuddering breath. Someday, when the opportunity came, she would kill Haldoran. And that would not be hard at all.

Chapter 30

Instinct and a violent need to escape took over after the taciturn boatman set Michael down in Penward. At the small inn, he bought the best horse available, along with saddle, bridle, and saddlebags. Since he couldn't carry all his baggage on horseback, he arranged for most of it to be shipped to London.

His small portmanteau held a few basic necessities, so he dumped the contents into his saddlebags. As the items fell, he saw the silver gleam of the kaleidoscope Lucien had sent after Waterloo. Obviously it wasn't as lucky as the first one had been. He shoved a shirt on top of it. Then he loaded the horse, swung into the saddle, and set off. It would have been more civilized to hire a chaise, but he craved the physical exertion of riding. Perhaps it would tire him to numbness.

He rode through the rest of the day and into the night, thinking compulsively about how he had made such a disastrous misjudgment. After learning the truth about Caro, he had been able to look back and recognize the signs of dishonesty and malice that had always been visible under her beauty and sparkling charm. He had simply been too in love—and too obsessed by her avid sexuality—to pay attention.

It was equally possible to identify signs of Catherine's selfishness and deceit. In London, when he had questioned her ability to carry off an elaborate deception, she had smiled and called him Colin with chilling authenticity. She had been masterly in her charade on the island. When Kenneth's letter exposed her lies, she had explained her actions with touching earnestness. It had been easy to believe she had acted from desperation, and to forgive.

Easy, and profoundly rewarding. He remembered how she had looked in his arms when she had discovered passion. Or had that been a lie also? Had she really been terrified by sex, or had it been a brilliant act designed to make him feel splendid and manly? He had no idea. Perhaps she had always been a wanton, and she had acted that elaborate scene of tears and fears because it gave her perverse amusement to deceive him. Yet even now, after all she had said, she was like a fever in his blood.

Blood again. Ah, God, Catherine . . .

No matter what else she had done, she had surely saved his life. From generosity? Or had she thought it would be useful to have the son of a duke indebted to her? The so-called son of a duke. Though she had claimed otherwise, perhaps the revelation of his bastardy had mattered to her. Her final speech had hinted as much. All of his life he had struggled to be the best he could be, and it wasn't enough.

It would never be enough.

In the dark hours after midnight, he made the bitter discovery that he was not really surprised at what had happened. Shocked, yes, and hurt beyond words, but not surprised. He had known Catherine was too good to be true. The drumming of his horse's hooves matched the words pounding in his brain. *She is not for you. Love will never be for you.*

Saint Michael, trying to slay all the wrong dragons.

He traveled all through the moonlit night. Though he automatically put his mount through the changes of pace that kept it moving steadily, by dawn the exhausted beast was foundering. He stopped at a coaching inn and traded the horse and a handful of gold for another mount, then set out again. But no matter how hard he pushed himself, he could not outrun the pain, or the anguished self-reproach for his own stupidity.

His belief that he was part of a family, albeit an unpleasant one, had been false. The great love affairs of his life were worse than lies—they were pathetic travesties. The only genuine, enduring relationships of his life were his friendships. In the future, he would confine himself to friendship and forget all hope of love.

In the late afternoon, after twenty-four hours of virtually nonstop riding, he realized the scenery was familiar. He was nearing the town of Great Ashburton. The Kenyon family seat was less than three miles away.

He wondered what would happen if he stopped at the

Abbey. Had the servants been told to bar his entrance, or would he be permitted to stay, a beneficiary once more of the family passion for maintaining appearances? It didn't matter, because he would burn in hell before he would ask for shelter under a Kenyon roof.

He was already burning in hell.

It was time to decide whether to swing north and return to his home in Wales, or continue east to London. The effort of choosing a destination was beyond him. A glance at his lathered mount showed that it was also time to get a new horse. The current one was on the verge of collapse.

For that matter, so was he. He would have to stop for the night. Even though the town was an oppressive reminder of his bastardy, at the same time there was a strange comfort in its familiarity. He stopped at the Red Lion, the best coaching inn. After leaving his horse with an ostler who glared at him for abusing the beast, he went inside with his saddlebags.

Most inns would have condemned such a filthy, unshaven traveler to the attic rooms, but Barlow, the landlord of the Red Lion, recognized him. "Lord Michael, what an honor. Are you on your way to the Abbey?"

"No," he said tersely. "I want a room for tonight."

Barlow surveyed him curiously, but said only, "Very good, my lord. Do you want a bath or a private parlor?"

"Just a bed."

The landlord took him up to the inn's best bedchamber, urging him to ring if there was anything he wanted. As soon as Barlow was gone, Michael dropped his saddlebags, turned the key in the lock, and drank a glass of water from the pitcher on the washstand. Then he sprawled facedown on the bed without removing his boots or clothing.

Unconsciousness came with merciful swiftness.

Thunder. Guns. Instinct dragged Michael up from the depths of sleep. He blinked groggily, not recognizing the darkened room.

The racket continued. Not guns or storm, but pounding at the door.

"Michael, it's Stephen," a voice barked. "Let me in."

Christ, the new Duke of Ashburton. The man whom he had called brother. "Go away," he called brusquely. "I'm trying to sleep."

The pounding stopped. He rolled onto his back. The last of the long summer twilight showed in the sky outside, so he had slept only a couple of hours. Every muscle ached from the long ride. He was also thirsty, but getting up was too much effort. He closed his eyes and hoped he would be able to sleep again.

A key grated in the lock. Then the door swung open and a tall man entered with a branch of candles. Michael closed his eyes and threw his arm across his face to block the sudden light.

Ashburton's clipped voice said, "Michael, are you ill?"

The last thing he wanted was an ugly scene with his brother, but apparently it couldn't be avoided. Dryly he said, "I should have known that in the Duke of Ashburton's own town, there is no such thing as privacy."

"Barlow sent a message to the Abbey saying you had arrived here looking like death and behaving strangely," his brother said with equal dryness. "Of course I was concerned."

"Why?" Michael smiled mirthlessly. "I always behave strangely. The old duke pointed that out often."

Ashburton muttered an exasperated curse under his breath. "Why the devil can't we have a civil conversation for a change? I've written you several times, and you've never replied."

Michael drew a deep breath. Ashburton was right; he was behaving abominably. "My apologies," he said in a more moderate tone. "Frankly, I burned your letters without reading them because I didn't think we had anything to say to one another. But I suppose there must be legal matters relating to the old duke's death. If you have papers that need signing, bring them now or send them to me in Wales. I'll take care of them."

A chair creaked, and a wisp of cigar smoke drifted across the room. "I'm not interested in any blasted legal papers. I merely wanted to talk to you. Will you sit up and look at me?"

Michael would be damned if he would go to that much effort for an interloper, but he did lower his arm and open his eyes. Ashburton was sitting on the far side of the chamber and staring broodingly at the glowing tip of his cigar.

Michael studied the other man's face. Though he preferred the family he had adopted at Eton, there was no denying the bond of blood. The Kenyon lineage showed in the hard planes of Ashburton's face, in the mahogany tones in his brown hair, in the shape of his long hands. Anyone would know they were kin.

Ashburton looked up, his eyes narrowing as he got a clear view of his younger brother. "Christ, man, you look ill. Do you have a fever?" He stood and came to the bed to lay a palm on Michael's forehead.

Michael knocked the hand away, irritated equally by the other man's presumption and the suffocating spirals of smoke. "I'm fine. Only filthy, unshaven, and tired from a long ride."

"Liar." His brother gazed down, his brow furrowed. "I've seen corpses that look better than you."

Michael coughed as smoke from Ashburton's cigar twisted into his face. He opened his mouth to tell his brother to put the damned thing out, and inhaled a choking mouthful of acrid smoke.

With shattering suddenness, his lungs spasmed in a full-fledged asthma attack. He couldn't talk, couldn't breathe, couldn't think. He doubled up convulsively as heat and suffocation enveloped him. His chest was being crushed, his lungs cramping as they struggled desperately for air.

He tried to sit up so his lungs could expand more easily, but failed. He floundered, his fingers clawing the counterpane, as consciousness faded away. Somewhere beyond the bonds of itchy fire was the ability to breathe, but he couldn't find it. Frantic fear, and fierce irony that after surviving years of war he was going to die in bed in the town where he had been born. There was a special horror to the fact that he was dying prostrate in front of the brother who had never been his friend.

Then strong hands raised his helpless body and supported him in a sitting position on the edge of the bed. Accompanied by a murmur of soothing words, a soaking cloth washed over his face and throat again and again. The blessedly cool water damped the fire and dissolved the choking smoke.

Panic receded, and with it the strangling constriction. A trickle of air seeped into his lungs. The fierce red pressure faded. He braced his palms on his knees and exhaled slowly. Inhaled. Exhaled. Again, more deeply. The darkness began to ebb, and he realized with dull wonder that he would survive.

It was the first asthma attack he'd had since Caroline died. The worst since the one that had almost killed him when he learned of his mother's death. With grim humor, he reflected that women had a lethal effect on him.

Catherine. The mere thought of her caused his lungs to clench again. But this time he was able to control his reaction and stave off another attack.

When he had regained the rhythm of breathing, he opened his eyes. Most of his anger had been scoured away, leaving him limp as a rag but relatively sane.

The window was open, letting in the fresh night air, and the cigar was gone. His brother sat on the edge of the bed beside him, his face pale with strain. "Drink this," he ordered, placing a glass of water in Michael's hand.

Michael obeyed, swallowing thirstily. The cool water washed away the bitter, vegetal aftertaste of cigar smoke. After he emptied the glass, he said in a rasping voice, "Thank you. But why did you bother? Letting me choke would have been a simple way of removing the blot on the family escutcheon."

"If you don't drop the Shakespearean melodrama, I'm going to pour the rest of this pitcher of water on your head." The duke got to his feet and built the pillows up against the headboard so that Michael could rest against them, then stepped back. "When was the last time you ate?"

Michael thought. "Yesterday morning."

The duke tugged the bell pull. Within seconds, Barlow's voice called through the door, "Yes, your grace?"

"Send up a tray of food, a pot of coffee, and a bottle of burgundy." Turning back to his brother, Ashburton said, "I thought you would have outgrown the asthma, like I did."

"Mostly I have. That's only the second attack I've had in over fifteen years." Michael's brows drew together. "You had asthma, too? I don't think I knew that."

"Not surprising, when you spent so little time at home. My asthma wasn't as bad as yours, but it was bad enough." His brother looked away, his expression rigid. "I'm sorry about the cigar. I wouldn't have smoked if I'd known it might kill you."

Michael made a deprecatory gesture. He occasionally

smoked himself, largely because it was a minor triumph to be able to do so. "You weren't to know. That attack was totally unexpected."

Moving restlessly across the bedchamber, Ashburton said, "Was it? My asthma usually struck when I was badly upset. Given Father's wonderful deathbed performance, you have every right to be distressed."

After all that had happened, it was a mild surprise to realize that the old duke had died only a fortnight before. "I accepted that reasonably well. This is different. Woman trouble." Such an easy, man-to-man answer. Much better than explaining that his heart had been neatly sliced out of his breast, taking with it most of his faith in himself.

"I see," his brother said quietly. "I'm sorry."

Wanting a change of topic, Michael said, "If you haven't any legal issues, why have you been writing me? As I said in London, I won't trouble you or the rest of the family. I'm no more keen on airing the Kenyon dirty linen than you are."

"You know that Father's revelation was as much a surprise to me as to you?"

"I guessed that from your reaction."

The duke stared at the burning candles. "That day, I suddenly recognized what had happened," he said haltingly. "Because Father and his brother hated each other, he ensured that you and I would do the same."

"You weren't alone in that. Claudia has no use for me, either." Michael's mouth twisted. "From what I know of family history, it's traditional for Kenyons to hate each other."

"It's a tradition I don't like one damned bit. When I looked back, I saw how badly Father treated you. Constant criticism, contempt for everything you did, frequent whippings. You were the family scapegoat." Ashburton grimaced. "Being monsters like most children, Claudia and I sensed we could torment you with impunity. And we did."

"That's an accurate analysis of my childhood, but what about it? The duke's revelation of my parentage explains his behavior." Michael's jaws clenched as he thought of the vicious beatings he had endured. "I'm lucky he didn't kill me in a rage. He might have, if I'd been at the Abbey more." It had been the unspoken terror of his childhood.

Instead of looking shocked, Ashburton said somberly, "It

could have happened. I can't believe he would have deliberately tried to murder you, but he had a wicked temper."

"Another trait that runs in the family."

"Too true." Ashburton leaned against the mantel and folded his arms. "It wasn't until Father blamed you for your superior abilities that I realized how much resentment I felt. I was the heir and raised to have a high opinion of myself, yet my younger brother was as intelligent as I, a better rider, a better shot, a better athlete." A gleam of humor showed in his eyes. "I rather resented God for not arranging matters more suitably."

Michael shrugged. "I don't know if my natural abilities were greater than yours, but I tried harder. I guess I thought that if I achieved enough, the duke would approve of me. I didn't know the cause was hopeless."

"You certainly proved you had more than your share of Kenyon damn-your-eyes arrogance. No one could pierce your armor." Ashburton smiled faintly. "I also resented the way you disappeared for years at a time, spending holidays with your Eton friends instead of coming home. It was one thing for us to reject you, quite another for you to reject us. Besides, I suspected that you were having more fun than I."

"You're wrong about my armor," Michael said with wary honesty. "It was pierced regularly and bloodily. That's why I avoided the Abbey as if it were a plague site. But what's the point of rehashing the past? I've done my best to forget it."

"Because the past is part of what we are now and will be in the future," Ashburton replied gravely. "And because Father cheated me out of having a brother."

"Bastard half-brother."

"We don't know that."

That startled a laugh from Michael. "You think the old duke made up his story? I doubt it. He had all the warm charm of a flint wall, but he didn't lie. It would have been beneath him."

Ashburton made an impatient gesture. "Oh, I don't doubt there was an affair. That doesn't necessarily mean that Roderick was your father."

Michael pointed out, "The duke said Mother admitted I was Roderick's child."

"She might have said that out of sheer contrariness. She

was probably sleeping with both of them and wasn't sure who had fathered you," Ashburton said with iron detachment.

Both fascinated and repelled by the conversations, Michael asked, "What makes you say that?"

His brother smiled cynically. "Father couldn't resist her. Even when they were fighting in public, they still slept together. That's why he resented her so much. He hated anyone having such power over him."

"But the old duke said I have Roderick's green eyes."

"That means nothing," Ashburton retorted. "Claudia's daughter has the same green eyes even though Claudia doesn't. There is no way to be sure who your father was, nor does it really matter. If you're not my full brother, you're my half-brother and first cousin. Either way, we have the same four grandparents, and you are my heir. No one else can ever fully understand what it was like to grow up in that house." He stopped, a muscle jerking in his cheek. "Though it may be too late for us to become real friends, at least we can stop being enemies."

There was a knock at the door, which was fortunate because Michael didn't have the remotest idea what to say. Ashburton admitted Barlow and two servants bearing savory-scented trays.

As they laid out the food, Michael realized to his surprise that he was hungry, though he was still so debilitated that it took all his strength to rise and walk to the table. The Red Lion's best sliced beef, ham, and trimmings, washed down by good red wine, went a long way toward restoring him. Ashburton ate little, preferring to drink coffee.

When Michael finished eating, he pushed back his chair and regarded his brother quizzically. "I really don't know you at all. Were you always reasonable?"

"I don't know what I am myself," Ashburton said slowly. "Since Father's death, I've felt like a plant that's been put in the sun after a lifetime of trying to grow under a basket. I don't want to be like him, bullying everyone in sight simply because I'm a duke. It may sound sanctimonious, but I want to live a just life. That includes making amends for having treated you unfairly."

Michael glanced away, moved but too accustomed to concealing his feelings around his family to reveal it. "It occurs to me that one reason we fought so much as boys was because we're alike in many ways. I hadn't realized how alike."

"True. But we didn't always fight. Remember the time we slipped away from our tutor and went to the Ashburton fair?"

"I remember." Michael smiled at the memory. They had played games with the villagers, eaten too much, and been children together rather than the Duke of Ashburton's antagonistic sons. They'd been flogged together when they went home, too.

There had been other happy times as well. By turning his back on his childhood, Michael had buried the good as well as the bad. Stephen was right: the past was part of the present, and it was time to reclaim those lost years. The true source of poison had been the old duke. His uncle? His father? No matter; the man was dead. But his brother and sister were still alive. They had not been his friends, but neither had they been the enemy.

He gazed into his wineglass. Most of his friends were quite different from himself. It might be pleasant to have a friend with a more similar temperament. He and Stephen should be old enough to control the infamous Kenyon temper. And if his brother had the courage to try to build a bridge between them, Michael could do no less. Softly he said, "Several weeks ago, I met a charming young American lady in London. She described an Indian custom that involved the chiefs of warring tribes burying their stone hatchets as a treaty of peace. Shall we do the same?"

"I trust you mean that figuratively." Ashburton gave a wry smile. "As a soldier, you've probably acquired all sorts of weapons, but I only have my Manton pistols. I'd hate to bury those."

"Figuratively will do very well." Hesitantly Michael extended his hand. "I've had enough of fighting, Stephen."

His brother took his hand in a warm, hard clasp, the long Kenyon fingers a mirror of Michael's own. Though the handshake ended quickly, it gave Michael a sense of peace. In one of the blackest nights of his life, a flower of hope had bloomed.

"It's a long way off, but consider spending Christmas at the Abbey," Stephen said, sounding almost shy. "I'd like to have you. And since you're the heir, it would be good if you made an appearance now and then."

"Thank you for asking. I'll think about it—I'm not sure I could face the entire clan at once." Michael shrugged. "As for being heir, that's only until you have a son."

His brother sighed. "That may never happen. Louisa and I have been married eight years, and there's no sign of offspring yet. Which makes it all the more important that you marry. You mentioned woman trouble. Nothing too serious, I hope?"

Michael's temporary calm vanished. "Not serious—catastrophic. Becoming obsessed by destructive women may be another family trait. I had thought the lady in question and I were going to marry, but I . . . I misunderstood her intentions."

"Care to talk about it?"

"It's a long story."

"I have as much time as you need," Stephen said softly.

Michael realized that he had a powerful desire to tell somebody what had happened. And—strange thought—his brother was the right person to tell.

He poured more burgundy, then sprawled on the bed, piling pillows to prop himself against the headboard. Not looking at his brother, he said, "I didn't really meet Catherine until Brussels, but I had first seen her in Spain, in a field hospital . . ."

Chapter 31

After describing how Catherine had held a dying youth through the night, Michael moved to Belgium. The universal esteem in which she was held; the frustrations of honorable behavior when living under the same roof; how she had saved his life. Though he didn't speak of his feelings, it was impossible to keep emotion from his voice. More than once he had to stop, covering his weakness by sipping wine. His brother listened intently, without interruptions.

Then he explained how Catherine had asked him to impersonate her husband, and his shock at discovering her deceit. He sketched in everything, in fact, except her fear of sexual intimacy and the brief, passionate interlude when it had seemed that everything was going to be all right. That he could not speak of. He ended by saying expressionlessly, "I thought we had an understanding, but obviously I misjudged her feelings. I should have stuck with war. Much simpler and less painful than women."

After a long moment of silence, Stephen said, "Perhaps."

Hearing the reservation in his brother's voice, Michael asked, "What are you thinking?"

"I probably shouldn't comment. I don't want you to dig up that war hatchet and bury it between my shoulder blades."

"Comment away." Michael ran restless fingers through his hair. "I still don't understand how I could have been so wrong."

"Actually, that's what struck me," his brother said slowly. "Being heir to a dukedom makes one a good judge of character, since so many people flatter to gain favor. One thing I learned is that basic character doesn't change. I have trouble believing that a woman who was so giving could become a greedy harpy in a matter of hours. Either the warmth was false, or the greed."

"Not the warmth. There were too many instances over too much time for it to be pretense." A haunting voice filled his mind—Catherine singing lullabies to a dying boy, or perhaps to himself. He swallowed hard. "Unfortunately, the talent for deceit was also quite genuine, as was the greed."

"Perhaps some other factor came into play, one you're unaware of." Stephen rubbed his chin as he thought. "For example, perhaps the illness of Lord Skoal triggered an attack of conscience and Catherine confessed that she'd lied about her husband. I've met the laird, and he's a crusty old devil. He might have said he'd forgive her if she would marry her cousin, and she agreed from guilt."

"Would a woman marry a man she disliked because of guilt?" Michael said doubtfully. And would she say so many vile things?

"As I said, that was only an example. There could be a thousand reasons. I've usually found that if behavior seems inexplicable, it's because I don't understand the other person's motives." Stephen sighed. "Or maybe she really is a harpy. I shouldn't have spoken. Never having met the woman, I'm in no position to have an opinion." He got to his feet. "Time to go. Do you want to come back to the Abbey? I'd like to have you."

"Not tonight. I'm too tired. Perhaps tomorrow." Michael rubbed his aching eyes. "Ask Barlow to send up some hot water. I'll sleep better if I wash off the travel dirt."

"A good idea. If I were a French soldier who saw you in your present state, I'd surrender on the spot."

"A number of them did." After they both laughed, Michael added quietly, "Thank you for making the effort to bury the hatchet. I never would have thought to try."

"I know. That's why I had to." Stephen's hand dropped briefly on his younger brother's shoulder. Then he left.

Michael lay unmoving on the bed, his mind a jumble of confused thoughts, until the hot water was delivered. Washing and shaving were an effort, but did make him feel more human. He was returning his razor to his saddlebags when he came across the kaleidoscope. He lifted the silver tube to one eye. A crystalline star sparkled inside. Shattered rainbows. Splintered hopes. Broken dreams. He turned the tube and the colored glass shifted with a soft rattle to form a new design.

His first kaleidoscope had provided comfort at earlier times in his life. After Caro's death, he had gazed into it for hours, trying to lose himself in the shifting, hypnotic shapes as he sought order in the chaos of his life.

Unlike Stephen, he was not a good judge of character. He could not stop wanting Catherine even though she had deceived him again and again, then coldly rejected him for a better offer.

He turned the kaleidoscope. The original figure dissolved into a shimmering, multicolored snowflake.

Until tonight, he would have said he and his brother were doomed to a lifetime of barely veiled hostility. He had been wrong. If he could be so wrong about Stephen, could he also be wrong about Catherine?

Basic character doesn't change.

Another twist, and the rainbow fragments formed into flatter angles. He stared at the shape, unseeing, as new patterns formed in his mind, analyzing them with the same cold detachment he would have used on a problem of military tactics.

Even when he had been most hopelessly besotted by Caroline, he had been aware of her character flaws. Though he did not discover the depths of her malice and deceit until years later, he had recognized her vanity and her petty deceptions, her selfishness and her need to always have the upper hand.

Catherine was different. Though she had lied often and well, it had always been from necessity. She had been honest otherwise. And she had never, ever been cruel. Stephen was right: to an objective observer, her behavior at their horrendous last meeting had been strange to the point of being unbelievable.

He had blindly accepted the premise that Catherine didn't really want him. Caro had made it easy for him to believe he was a fool where women were concerned. But perhaps he had accepted dismissal too quickly.

Forget what Catherine had said; bury her brutal words and the pain that went with them. Think about her actions instead. What unknown factor would have convinced her to send him away?

Not greed; a greedy woman would not sell her mother's pearls to provide for her faithless husband's bastard.

A desire to placate the dying laird? Perhaps, but she had

only known her grandfather a few days. Her loyalty to the laird should not be stronger than her loyalty to himself.

Had she feared that being disowned by the laird would deprive Amy of the girl's rightful heritage? That was a real possibility. Michael would have provided for the girl's future as if she were his own daughter, but Catherine might not have realized that. Also, she had no idea of the extent of his wealth. If she had thought he had only the usual portion of a younger son, she might believe maternal duty demanded that she do whatever was necessary to secure Skoal for her daughter.

Yet while such a motive made sense, it was still not enough to explain the cruelty of her behavior.

He turned the kaleidoscope again. Could Catherine have been struck by mad lust for Haldoran? Highly unlikely. Her cousin's nature was essentially cold. He was no partner for a woman reveling in newfound sensuality, particularly one who already had a satisfactory bedmate.

Michael sorted through possibilities until he arrived at the most likely cause for Catherine's inexplicable behavior: fear. But what would she be afraid of?

He tilted the kaleidoscope and a spiky, fragile star formed, bringing a sharp new awareness.

Haldoran was his enemy.

According to Catherine, her cousin had recognized Michael immediately. An honest man would have exposed them then. Concealing the knowledge marked Haldoran as a man with hidden motives. He was ruthless, and his hatred of losing might extend to Skoal. What better way to keep it than to force his beautiful cousin, the chosen heir, into marriage?

Such a goal might be hard to achieve elsewhere, but in the small, feudal world of the island, it was possible. Haldoran had been listening when Catherine had told Michel to go. By the end of their interview, she had been almost frantic to drive Michael away. If Haldoran was holding a gun on her, it would explain everything.

He lowered the kaleidoscope. Perhaps he was creating a mystery where none existed, perhaps not. The only way to be sure was to return to the island and speak to Catherine when Haldoran was not within earshot.

If he was wrong, the worst she could do was slash his emotions to ribbons, reduce him to suicidal depression, or trigger another life-threatening asthma attack. His mouth twisted. He'd survived that once, and was willing to risk it again. Because if his deductions were correct, Catherine's life might be in grave danger.

He wanted to leave immediately, but that would be madness in his present state of exhaustion. He must wait until morning.

Mind racing, he dowsed the candles and settled back into bed. Rather than ride back to Cornwall, he would hire a chaise. It would be faster and less tiring, getting him to Penward by tomorrow evening. No, not Penward; the village was too closely connected to Skoal. It would be impossible to make a covert journey to the island from there. He must look for transport in one of the neighboring villages.

Then he would go to the island. And this time, he would not be so easily dismissed.

The Duke of Ashburton frowned over the note from his younger brother. How typical of Michael to do something exhausting like bolt back to Skoal at the crack of dawn. It would have been pleasant to spend a little time together. Explore the dimensions of their new relationship.

His frown deepened when he thought of what his brother might find in Skoal. No doubt the situation was harmless and Catherine Melbourne was merely a heartless slut. But there might be more dangerous game afoot. Stephen had met Lord Haldoran several times and had found the man disturbing. Dangerous, even. Perhaps he should go to Skoal himself. Michael was the expert at violence, but as a duke, Stephen knew quite a bit about throwing his weight around. Perhaps that would be useful.

Decision made, he rang for his valet.

The crescent moon that faintly illuminated the beach made the shadows seem even blacker when Michael stepped ashore at Dane's Cove. He reached under the dark fisherman's jersey he wore and brought out a letter he'd written to Lucien, asking for an investigation if Michael disappeared. Though it wouldn't save his life, it might save Catherine, and it would ensure that Haldoran was punished. To his boatman, Caradoc, he said quietly, "If I don't return by dawn, go back without me, and send this letter to London right away."

Caradoc nodded and tucked the letter away. A former Royal Navy boatswain, he not only knew the waters around Skoal, but he had unquestionably accepted Michael's request for secrecy.

Michael had set off by chaise early that morning. He'd found Caradoc in the village of Trenwyth, a few miles east of Penward. The boatman's mother, a famous local knitter, had also provided the wool jersey. The warm, flexible garment was better suited to a clandestine mission than the garb of a gentleman.

Dressed in dark clothing and with lampblack smeared on his face, he silently went up the precarious cliff path. Fortunately he'd always had a feline ability to make his way through the night. Other, harder-to-describe senses informed him that the fair weather was about to change. There would be a major storm within the next day or so.

It didn't take long to reach the castle. Since it was past midnight, the building was entirely dark.

Deciding to try the direct approach, he went up the front steps and tried the doorknob. Locked. Interesting on an island where theft, criminals, and locked doors were unknown.

A shadow among shadows, he circled the castle. Though he hadn't done any housebreaking since that amusing little episode with Lucien, he didn't think the castle would be difficult to enter. The real question was where to find Catherine. She could be in their old room, or—stomach-turning thought—she might be sharing a bed with Haldoran in Ragnarok. But if her grandfather was still critically ill, she was probably with the old man.

Michael reached the back wall of the castle and studied the windows of the laird's rooms. A light glowed in the bedchamber. Hoping Catherine was there, he decided to enter by the sitting room so he could approach her without warning.

A cherry tree grew near the balcony. The upper limbs would put him within jumping distance. He leaped and caught the lowest limb, the bark rough against his palms. Then he began to climb.

Chapter 32

Catherine always slept lightly when she was staying with a patient. A faint sound brought her awake quickly. She glanced toward her grandfather. The light of the night candle showed that he was making feeble, restless movements, so she rose from her pallet and went to his bedside.

A physician had come from the mainland, examined the laird, and agreed that the problem seemed to be apoplexy. Impressed with Catherine's nursing experience, he had bled the patient again and returned to the mainland, leaving the sickroom in her charge. She had been grateful, both for the chance to care for her grandfather and because the task separated her from Haldoran.

She checked her patient's pulse. A little faster than it had been. "I have the feeling that you're very close to waking, Grandfather," she murmured. "Can you hear me?"

His fingers twitched, then went still. She found it encouraging that both sides of his body seemed to be working. That meant that the apoplexy might not have caused massive damage. She uttered a brief prayer that he would wake soon, and in reasonable control of his faculties.

A barely audible creaking, like a floorboard, came from the sitting room. Her stomach knotted. Perhaps Clive was coming to check on her; he had moved into a room across the hall. Or maybe it was one of his horrible men. Day and night, one of them waited outside the laird's door. Since the laird's valet was ancient and infirm, Haldoran was in theory lending his servants to help in the sickroom. In practice, she was as much a prisoner as if she were locked in a dungeon.

Another faint sound. She composed her features, glad she had lain down fully dressed instead of donning a nightgown.

She opened the door to the sitting room. At first glance

all was normal. Then a dark figure emerged from the shadows. Tall and powerful, it moved toward her with the supernatural silence of death. And most frightening of all, the creature had no face. She gave a soft, involuntary cry.

A hard hand clamped over her mouth, cutting off her voice. She shoved wildly at her assailant, feeling the solid weight of reality, not the chill of a phantom.

With one lithe movement, he pinned her against the wall, immobilizing her with his weight. "Quiet!"

She recognized the feel of his body even before she saw the green eyes blazing in the blackened face. Michael had returned.

"I'll take my hand away if you promise not to scream," he whispered. "Nod if you agree."

She nodded. He wore his menacing warrior's face, and she was not sure whether she was more afraid *of* him or *for* him. Nonetheless, her heart surged with involuntary pleasure in his presence.

"Given your record, I'm a fool to take your word," he said in an iron voice as he released her. "Remember that I can silence you quickly enough if necessary."

Wondering whether she dared tell him the truth or if she should try to send him away for his own safety, she asked warily, "Why are you here?"

His icy gaze bored into hers. "To learn what's really going on. When I thought things through, I realized your behavior didn't make much sense. Was Haldoran threatening you?"

If he had deduced that much, she would never be able to deceive him again. "Worse," she said with searing relief. "He has Amy."

"Damnation!" He closed his eyes for an instant, his expression rigid. "How?"

"On his trip to London, he called on the Mowbrys and told Anne I'd sent him to bring Amy to Skoal. Since he'd escorted them in Belgium, she saw no reason to doubt him." The defenses that had sustained her crumbled, leaving desolation. "Michael, I'm sorry, so sorry for what I did. I had no choice."

Desperate for his support, she reached out to him. After a moment of hesitation, he took her into his arms. She was shaking all over. His wool jersey was warm and softly scratchy against her cheek, as comforting as he was. Yet even in the midst of her grief, she recognized that he was different, more guarded than he had been before. That was not surprising. Though his mind might accept that she had acted under coercion, his emotions had taken a battering that would not easily heal. But for a few moments, she basked in the illusion of safety.

When she regained a measure of control, she said starkly, "It was Haldoran who killed Colin, not the Bonapartists."

"The *bastard*." Michael released her, his expression deadly. "So he's been planning this for some time."

"He said that if I didn't obey, he would kill you. And . . . and he made a point of saying that the island's legal marriage age is twelve, and Amy will be twelve next year."

Michael swore again. "Killing is too good for him. We must get Amy away immediately. Is she in the castle?"

"She's at Ragnarok. We haven't been able to talk, but Haldoran took me there yesterday and let me watch her walk in the garden. She's guarded whenever she leaves her room."

"Is she unharmed?"

"Yes. She doesn't know anything is wrong yet. He told her I was too busy nursing the laird to see her, and that she must be a good soldier and follow orders. But soon she'll start to become suspicious." Catherine swallowed. "I'm terrified that when she realizes she's a captive, she might do something reckless. She's like her father—utterly without fear."

"We'll have her before that happens," Michael promised.

Catherine rubbed her forehead, trying to think amid the tempest of her emotions. "Haldoran is sleeping in a room across the hall. He has four convicts working for him. I think two are here in the castle, one just outside the door. Thank heaven he didn't hear me cry out."

Michael glanced at the bed. "How is the laird?"

"A little better, I think, but still unconscious."

"No help there." He frowned. "If you leave him, will he be in any danger from Haldoran?"

It had occurred to Catherine how easily her grandfather could be smothered with a pillow. "I don't think so," she said, her voice troubled. "There's no advantage to killing him while I'm alive and the heir—but I don't know what Clive will do. I think he's half mad."

"Not mad. Evil." Michael ushered her toward the balcony. "It's time we were away."

The hall door opened and Haldoran swaggered into the room with a wolfish smile. Behind him were Doyle and another convict, both carrying shotguns. "Neither of you is going anywhere," Haldoran said curtly. "You shouldn't have given that charming little squeal of surprise when your lover arrived, Catherine, and the two of you shouldn't have wasted time talking."

Before Haldoran could say more, Michael sprang into action, hurling himself toward the intruders. At the same time, he shoved Catherine to one side so that she fell behind the sofa.

She was knocked breathless. For an instant she lay gasping, braced for the blast of a gun. It didn't come. Instead, there were sounds of smashing furniture.

Guessing that Haldoran didn't want to shoot for fear of waking the sleeping servants, she peered around the end of the sofa. Michael's swift assault had been effective, and Haldoran and Doyle lay stunned on the floor. Michael was now engaged in a ferocious struggle with the other convict. As she watched, he wrested the gun away and swung the stock in an arc. It smashed into the man's jaw with an ugly sound of breaking bone.

Haldoran leaped up and grabbed the poker from the fireplace. Catherine bolted from behind the sofa, crying, "Look out!"

Michael was pivoting and raising the shotgun when Haldoran cracked the poker against his skull. He crumpled to the floor, the gun falling beside him.

Catherine was gathering herself for a desperate assault when Haldoran snatched the shotgun and wheeled on her. A vicious bruise was forming on his jaw where he had been struck. "Don't try it, cousin. I'll blow you to pieces and tell the servants that your jealous husband shot you before we killed him. And if they don't believe me, I'll kill them, too."

She halted, knowing it would take very little to trigger lethal violence. In the tense silence, Michael groaned and shifted, on the verge of consciousness.

Haldoran snapped to Doyle, "Tie him up. It would be too messy to kill him here, so we'll have to take him to the cliffs. A rock on the skull and a few weeks in the water will take care of him nicely." His gaze raked Catherine.

"Shall I kill you with your lover, or gamble that you'll behave when he is dead?"

Though her face was expressionless, her mind was raging. If she hadn't cried out when she first saw Michael . . . if they had left immediately instead of talking . . . if she had warned him about Haldoran an instant sooner . . .

She cut off the useless regrets. Michael was doomed, and probably her with him. As for Amy . . .

It was the blackest moment of her life. Yet she could not give up and leave her daughter to Haldoran's evil. Trying desperately to sound persuasive, she said, "I always take the best opportunity available. Once again, that is you."

Haldoran scowled at her, clearly unconvinced, while Doyle searched Michael's limp body with rough efficiency. The convict removed a concealed pistol and boot knife, then lashed Michael's wrists together.

By the time Doyle was finished, Michael was conscious again. Blood oozed crimson from his scalp when he sat up, but the dark force that was so much a part of him was blazing like hell's own fire. "Congratulations, Haldoran," he said contemptuously. "You managed to bring me down with the help of only two other men. You must be terribly proud of yourself."

Haldoran glared at him. "I could have beaten you alone."

"Oh?" The lift of Michael's brows was eloquent with scorn. "I can outshoot you, outfight you, and I let you draw blood when we fenced because I was bored with your company and wanted to leave. You're an amateur, Haldoran. You fancy yourself a great sportsman, but you've never had the courage to face a real test."

Catherine's heart clenched as her glowering cousin took a step forward. "Rubbish. I'm the best rider to hounds in Britain, and I've defeated Jackson in his own boxing salon."

"Jackson is a clever fellow," Michael said with a mocking smile. "It's good business to let his vainer customers win now and then. I repeat: you're an amateur. Instead of joining the army and competing in the greatest game of all, you chased foxes in England and smirked about what a fine fellow you are. So much easier than actually risking your life."

Michael came very near death in that instant. Catherine

made an anguished sound as Haldoran whipped the shotgun to his shoulder and prepared to fire.

Checking his fury, Haldoran contented himself with kicking Michael in the stomach, sending him sprawling again. "It's easy for you to taunt, but notice who's in control here."

"With professional help," Michael gasped when he had regained his breath. "I commanded a number of convicts like your men, and I have a certain respect for them. It takes strength and cunning to survive prison. For you, Haldoran, I have nothing but contempt. You're a bully who preys on women and children. You don't dare face a man who might be your match."

"Bastard!" Haldoran snarled. "I could defeat you in any fair contest, but you're not worth the effort."

"Poor devil." Michael shook his head with exaggerated sorrow. "Not only a bully and a braggart, but a coward. I'm surprised you can face yourself in the mirror."

Haldoran kicked him again, this time in the ribs. Michael rolled across the floor and into the sofa. Catherine shuddered, unable to understand why he was inviting such brutality.

Again it took Michael several moments to recover his breath, but he did not back down. "Everything you do confirms that I'm right," he panted. "If you weren't such a coward, I'd give you a challenge that would truly test you. But you would never accept it. You're afraid of me, and well you should be."

Eye glittering, Haldoran snapped, "What kind of challenge?"

"A hunt, since you're such a great huntsman." Michael's eyes narrowed, becoming feral. "You and me on the Isle of Bone. Give me five minutes' head start and you'll never catch me. Give me a day and you're a dead man, even if you're armed and I'm not."

Catherine caught her breath, understanding. He was trying to buy time, and a chance of survival.

Haldoran hesitated, his gaze going to Catherine.

"There's a kind of medieval grandeur to thc idea," Michael continued. "You and I meet in single combat, and the winner gets the lady. Catherine won't give you any trouble if you manage to kill me. She didn't want me here.

When I came in, she told me to leave, that I would ruin everything."

Haldoran's anger flared again. "Liar. She was ready to go out the window with you."

His lips whitened as he looked from Michael to Catherine and back. Then they curved in a cruel, triumphant smile. "I don't have to prove anything to you, Kenyon. Single combat belongs to the Middle Ages. I prefer the pleasures of the chase. We'll go to Bone, but it will be me and Doyle tracking you and my deceitful cousin with only the sheep and gulls to see."

Michael's face paled, revealing underlying pain.

"That worries you, doesn't it?" Haldoran said, his voice almost crooning. "Alone, you might be able to elude me for some time, but not with Catherine to slow you down. You'll have to choose between abandoning her to preserve your own skin a few hours longer, or staying and dying together. Either way, you'll die, and I'll have the pleasure of hunting the ultimate game."

"You're a fool to kill a woman as beautiful as Catherine," Michael retorted. "A wife like her is the ultimate trophy. You'll be the envy of every man you meet if you marry her."

Haldoran gave a smile that didn't reach his eyes. "True, but I can't help suspecting her good faith. She's the sort who could go meekly for years while she waits for the right moment to slip a stiletto between my ribs. Her daughter will be more malleable."

Voice lanced with anguish, Catherine said, "I'll swear any oath of obedience you want if you promise not to touch Amy."

"But I want to touch her. The thought of molding a virgin to my will is rather appealing." Haldoran smiled again, and this time it came from the depths of his black soul. "The knowledge that my saintly cousin Catherine died cursing me will add spice."

She glanced at Michael. His green eyes were fierce. She could almost hear him saying not to give up hope.

A measure of calm came to her. Michael had almost defeated three men single-handedly, and she was less helpless than her cousin thought. Certainly she would not go tamely to the slaughter. "A pity you didn't join the army,

Clive. An officer like my father or Michael might have made a man of you."

Virulent dislike on his face, he waved his gun toward the door. "Move, both of you. We must leave Skoal before dawn. Don't try to call for help. My men and I can easily handle a parcel of unarmed servants, but I'd rather not have to kill them. My little kingdom needs all of its subjects."

Wincing, Michael got to his feet. "I realize that fairness isn't part of your nature, but you really should allow Catherine to change her clothing. It's going to be a damp, cold hunt."

Haldoran shrugged. "She can wear breeches if she likes. In fact, I'd rather enjoy seeing her in them. But I'll only allow her ten minutes in her room to change. If she isn't ready, she'll have to run in her shift."

Catherine's mind raced as her cousin escorted her to her room. In fact, she had brought to Skoal the breeches she had worn on the Peninsula when conditions were particularly harsh. They would make it easier for her to run for her life. With luck, she would also be able to conceal a few small items about her person.

What a pity that her room did not contain a gun.

Chapter 33

It was a beautiful dawn for sailing, with indigo clouds edged in crimson and salmon pink. But the swirling currents and lethal rocks lived up to the channel's perilous reputation. Catherine would have found the trip alarming if greater danger weren't imminent.

Haldoran's island background had made him a good sailor. As the sun inched above the horizon, he steered his boat capably between the reefs and barked orders at Doyle and another of his men, a ferret-faced fellow called Spiner. The convict with the broken jaw was nursing his injury at Ragnarok.

Catherine felt very alone and afraid. Haldoran had made a point of tethering her and Michael in positions where they could not see each other. She was within her cousin's view, though. She schooled her face to impassivity whenever his avid gaze went over her breeches-clad legs. If he caught her alive, he would surely rape her before she died.

But her masculine attire would be useful later. Besides riding boots and tan breeches, she had followed Michael's lead and donned a knitted jersey that had been the gift of an elderly island woman. The garment was made from undyed wool in colors ranging from cream to dark brown, which should help her blend into the landscape.

All too soon they reached Bone. The boat glided into a small bay surrounded by steep hills. It was a desolate place, the only sound the splash of waves on the shingle beach and the harsh cries of gulls. Haldoran docked the boat neatly at a crude jetty. Then Doyle cut the prisoners' bonds and roughly shoved them from the boat. Spiner stayed inside, under orders to guard the vessel while his master hunted.

Catherine's position in the boat had been cramped, and her strained muscles caused her to stumble as she climbed onto the jetty. Michael caught her before she could fall, then wrapped an arm around her waist and led her to the shingle beach. "Get your body flexible so you can run when the time comes," he ordered.

Blood had dried in his hair and his face was dark with soot and bruises, but he looked magnificent and dangerous, like an ancient warrior king. His shrewd gaze was scanning the hills, assessing conditions. The sight of him gave Catherine a glimmer of hope. She began bending and stretching her limbs.

After Haldoran collected his expensive sporting rifle and ammunition pouch, he followed them to the shingle beach. "You said you could escape me with a five-minute start, but I'll be generous and give you ten minutes. It will take at least that long for you to get out of sight."

Michael regarded him coolly. "Since you know the island and we don't, there's a chance you might win. But you'll find no satisfaction in it. For the rest of your life, you'll have to live with the knowledge that I was the better man. The only way you could defeat me was by stacking the deck in your favor."

"It sounds like you've resigned yourself to losing and are preparing your excuses," Haldoran said scornfully. "Try to give me a good run, Kenyon. It's been damned boring on the island lately." He pulled a watch from his pocket. "You have ten minutes starting *now*."

So soon? Catherine stared at him. Despite her cousin's stated intentions, she had not truly grasped the brutal fact that in the space of a heartbeat she could be transformed from an ordinary, civilized woman to prey.

More experienced with savagery, Michael had no such problem. "Time to be off, my dear." He caught her hand and tugged her forward. "We'll take that path to the left."

Her paralysis broken, she set off beside Michael at a fast jog, the best pace possible on the rounded stones of the beach. Once they reached the surrounding grassland, her speed increased. Michael loped beside her, matching her pace effortlessly.

It took about two minutes to reach the foot of the animal track that zigzagged up the steep, clifflike hill. She quailed at the sight of the narrow path. She would never be able to reach the top in the time allotted.

"You first," Michael said. "Don't set a pace so fast that you'll exhaust yourself halfway up."

She balked. "You go ahead. I'll slow you down."

"We stand or fall together, Catherine." He gave her a slap on the backside, as if she were a nervous pony. "*Move.*"

She began to climb. Years of campaign life had hardened her physically, and in peacetime she had stayed active with walking and riding. Yet though she was strong for a woman, she could never keep up with a man like Michael. Haldoran had been right—if Michael stayed with her, it might well cost him his life. Yet for honor's sake, he would never abandon her. Knowing his survival depended on her performance increased her determination.

The grass was damp and several times she slipped. She kept her eyes on the path. A twisted ankle would be a death sentence.

By the time they reached the midway point, her breath was coming in hoarse pants and her legs were shaking with strain. The spot between her shoulder blades began to feel itchy. How many minutes had passed? Six? Seven? As long as they were on the hill, they were in deadly peril.

Haldoran's voice boomed out, echoing menacingly across the bay. "Eight minutes gone, and you're still easy targets."

"Don't waste time worrying," Michael snapped. "When he shoots, he'll aim at me first, and at this distance he'll probably miss."

In spite of the admonition not to worry, a clock began ticking in her mind, counting off the seconds. *Eleven, twelve* ... She gasped and doubled over when she was struck by an agonizing stitch in her side. Straightening, she forced herself to ignore the pain and keep going. *Thirty-five, thirty-six* ...

How much farther? *Fifty, fifty-one* ... She glanced up and saw despairingly that there wasn't enough time. *Sixty-two, sixty-three* . . . She was staggering and on the verge of collapse.

Michael said sharply, "Think of Amy."

Energy from some unknown reserve renewed her. The brink of the hill was tantalizingly near. *A hundred one, two, three* ... The pitch steepened. She caught at the tough clumps of grass and used them to drag herself upward. Her lungs were burning with a desperate need for air. *Fifteen, sixteen . . .*

The clock in her mind reached two minutes. Only a few more yards and they would be out of danger, but Haldoran could start shooting at any moment.

The pitch flattened and the path became wider. Michael drew even and hooked his arm around her waist, virtually carrying her the last stretch. As soon as they crested the hill, he dragged her to the ground. The harrowing blast of the rifle rang out even before they hit the grassy turf. Almost simultaneously, a spurt of earth marked the spot where the ball struck a few feet behind them.

"That's a good rifle and he's a good shot," Michael panted. "But we've won the first round. We should go a few feet farther. Then we can rest for a minute."

She nodded mutely and crawled across the grass on her hands and knees until they were well beyond the edge. Then she rolled onto her back, her lungs pumping frantically. Michael was treating her exactly as if she had been a particularly feeble soldier under his command. No doubt he was wise to avoid the personal issues between them. Nonetheless, she would have been humiliatingly grateful for any word or touch that showed that they had been lovers.

Michael was also breathing hard, but he kept his head up, studying their surroundings with cold concentration. "One thing that might cheer you a little. I gave a letter to the boatman who brought me to Skoal. He was to post it to London if I didn't meet him at dawn. Since I missed the rendezvous, the letter is on its way to my friend Lucien. I explained my suspicions and asked him to investigate if I disappeared. He spent years as the government's chief spymaster, so he will be able to discover what happened and take appropriate measures against Haldoran."

She raised her head, desperate with hope. "Will he be able to free Amy?"

"I guarantee it. It may take a little time, but she will not be left in Haldoran's hands."

"Thank God." Though it was a tremendous relief to know that her daughter would not be a victim for long, the thought of what might happen first was sickening. Catherine lay still for another dozen heartbeats, then pushed herself to a sitting position and surveyed the island.

Bone was a wild, barren place that reminded her of the

Yorkshire moors. There were only a handful of stunted trees, not enough to break the force of the ceaseless sea winds. The right end of the island rose to rugged hills. However, most of the landscape was a plateau of rocks and vividly green grass that was cropped short by grazing animals.

The fuzzy gray shapes of several hundred sheep were scattered across the plateau with a sizable flock a few hundred yards to the left. There were also occasional cows, stocky russet beasts with long horns and shaggy coats. "There aren't many places to hide. Should we head into the hills?"

"Haldoran will probably assume we'll go that way. Better to go to the left, through the flock of sheep. The ground is more irregular than it appears, so there are plenty of places for concealment. We're also fortunate that this grass is so springy. If we're careful, we'll be almost impossible to track."

Wearily she got to her feet. "Lead on, Colonel. You're in charge of strategy and tactics."

Michael walked quickly until they neared the flock. Then he slowed to keep from frightening the sheep, which might alert their pursuers. The leisurely pace made Catherine's skin crawl. How long until the hunters reached the plateau?

Once through the flock, they went faster. Michael was right about the roughness of the ground. Gentle rises and depressions offered more cover than she had expected.

When the cliff edge was no longer visible, he cut left and circled until they were behind a small ridge crowned with squat shrubs. "Wait here," he said quietly. "If I've judged rightly, we should be able to see without being seen."

He went up the rise at a crouch, crawling on his belly when he reached the shrubs. A minute later, he whispered, "Success. If you want to see, come forward carefully."

She dropped down and crept up beside him. Their ridge offered a clear view of the spot where they had come onto the plateau. The small figures of Haldoran and Doyle were visible there now, catching their breath from the climb. Both carried rifles. Her cousin slowly scanned the plateau, then gestured toward the hills. The two men set off briskly, moving away from their quarry.

She gave a long sigh of relief. They had won a second round, and it gave them some respite. Keeping her voice low even though the hunters could not possibly hear at this distance, she asked, "Do you have a plan?"

"To avoid getting caught," Michael said dryly. "I don't have plans, merely contingencies. There's a bad storm coming, probably tonight. That will work in our favor. The island will not be a pleasant place when the storm hits. Haldoran and his men will probably return to Skoal to avoid being caught in it."

"I suppose it's too much to hope that they would drown on the trip back. Is there any chance that the shot Clive fired will attract attention on Skoal?"

"Not with the wind blowing from the east. Even if a fisherman heard and investigated, it wouldn't help us. Your cousin would give some plausible lie for being here. If that didn't work, I don't think he would hesitate to kill."

She should have known that Michael had already thought out the possibilities. "What do you think of our chances of surviving? The truth, please."

"It's hard to say." His expression was troubled. "I think it's possible to hide and live off the land indefinitely, but Haldoran's patience won't last for more than a day or two. My fear is that he'll bring dogs to track us."

The idea sent a chill through her. Hounds baying at their heels . . . "Is there any way to turn the tables on him?"

"Perhaps. I want to study the lay of the land. There might be a spot for an ambush, though it won't be easy to bring down two armed men." He gazed toward the sea, his eyes narrowed. "As a last resort, it might be possible to swim to Skoal."

She stared at him. "Are you serious? The channel between the islands is notoriously dangerous. I can swim a little, but I'd never make it that far in rough seas."

"I might be able to do it. If I succeed, I could send help back to you." He frowned. "But I'd rather not leave you alone."

The idea appalled her. Not only would Michael be braving cold water, rocks, and vicious currents, but he would probably have to attempt the crossing at night to avoid being seen. The odds of him surviving were not good. "Swimming is definitely a last resort."

He shrugged. "Drowning while trying to escape would be better than being shot like a deer."

Stealthily he withdrew from the shrubbery. Catherine followed him down the slope. At the bottom was a tiny brook. He pressed his palms into the muddy bank, then wiped smudges on her tan breeches with impersonal hands. "You'll be harder to see if dark patches break up the lightness. Wipe some on your face, too. If we find any light-colored clay, I'll use it to splotch up this dark outfit of mine."

"You seem to know a great deal about being hunted."

He grimaced. "Once as a very new officer in Spain, I became separated from my men during a scouting patrol. Not my finest hour. The French learned a British officer was lost behind their lines and organized a manhunt. Though I eluded them for three days, eventually I was captured. I managed to escape, but the other officers in my company teased me unmercifully for being so inept. It was a very chastening experience."

She smiled a little, though her mood was somber. She had brought so much trouble on Michael, as she had on everyone close to her. Colin had died because of her, Michael might die as well, and Amy was a prisoner who faced an unspeakable future. Rationally Catherine knew she was not responsible for Haldoran's wickedness—yet even so, crushing guilt weighed on her.

She studied Michael, who was washing the mud from his hands. He would do his best to get her out of this alive. For honor's sake, he would probably sacrifice his life if it might save hers. But he would not want her in his life after all that had happened. She had placed her darts well when she sent him away, and the fragile trust that had been growing in him had been crushed, probably beyond repair.

But one thing must be done while there was still time. "I'm sorry for all of the horrible things I said when I asked you to leave Skoal. Perhaps there might have been another way, but I couldn't think of it." She shivered as the anguish of that scene returned vividly to her mind. "Colin died because of me," she said starkly. "I could not have endured being the cause of your death as well."

He gestured her to start walking. "Don't blame yourself for Colin's death. It was Haldoran who pulled the trigger."

Her mouth twisted as she fell in beside Michael. Though intellectually she knew he was right, it didn't make her feel any better. "The fact remains that if Colin had not been married to me, he would not be dead."

"No?" Michael held back a branch of shrubbery so she could pass. "He said himself that he and Charles would have died at Waterloo if I hadn't lent him my horse. The loan was a direct result of the fact that you generously allowed me to share your billet. For that reason, I didn't want to see your husband do something fatally stupid. Because of you, Charles is alive, and Colin gained almost a year of extra life."

Her brows knit together. "I'm not sure that makes sense."

He shrugged. "It makes as much sense as crucifying yourself for what you could not have changed. I didn't know Colin well, but I don't think he would have wanted you to spend the rest of your life crippled by guilt."

Michael was right; Colin did not have that kind of pettiness. She gave her companion a slanting glance. "Thank you for everything," she said softly. "For being clever enough to see trouble, and brave enough to face the dragon."

"Let's hope my dragonslaying skills are good enough," Michael said sardonically.

From his expression, she guessed that she had said the wrong thing. Waiting to erase the bleakness in his eyes, she said, "I managed to bring along a tinderbox and a pocketknife." She reached under the neck of her heavy jersey and removed the small pouch that she had made from a scarf and suspended between her breasts. "I'm sorry I didn't have a better weapon available."

Michael stopped walking, his bleakness replaced by interest. "The odds for our survival have just improved. I had a knife and a pistol, but Haldoran's men found them when they searched me in Skoal." He opened the pocketknife and tested the blades. "Later I'll find a stone and do some sharpening, but this will do well enough to slit a man's throat."

"I'm glad you approve. I'm sure you know more about slitting throats than I do."

He folded the knife and slipped it into his pocket. "One other bit of luck—I wasn't sure what I would find when I came to the island, so I tried to come prepared. Doyle found my pistol and knife, but not the rope I have wrapped around my waist. I brought it because I thought it might be useful for scaling a cliff or breaking into the castle." He gave a faint smile. "Though I didn't need the rope for that, at least it gave me some protection from Haldoran's kicks."

He did look heavier than could be accounted for by the thickness of his jersey. Feeling for weapons, Doyle had missed the layers of rope. "Good. You've taken enough punishment."

"There will be more before this is over," he said dryly. "It's time to explore. According to the guidebook I read on the way to Skoal, Bone has some features that could prove useful."

"What are they?"

"Sea caves. I don't want to get trapped in a place with only one entrance, but we'll need shelter if the storm is as bad as I think it will be. A cave might be our only choice."

Catherine's brows drew together. "My grandfather once mentioned a cave at the west end of Bone. It's the largest in the islands and can only be reached at low tide. He said we must be sure to visit before we went back to the mainland. But my cousin must know it, so it wouldn't be safe."

"True, but there should be others. There may also be buildings left from the days when Bone was inhabited. The more we know about the island, the better." He pocketed the tinderbox. "Shall we see what we can find?"

They set off in the opposite direction from that which the hunters had taken. Michael was a master at moving unobtrusively cross-country, taking advantage of whatever cover the terrain provided. Though his long strides were relaxed, his sharp eyes never stopped scanning for danger. He had been telling the truth when he had baited Haldoran on Skoal: Michael was a professional who had learned his skills in the most dangerous game of all. Surely Haldoran was no match for him.

Haldoran frowned at the surrounding hills, his hunter's instinct nagging at him. He asked his companion, "If you were trying to hide on this island, where would you go?"

Doyle blinked, his scarred face puzzled. "These hills. The rest of this bloody rock is too exposed."

Haldoran uttered a mental oath; any answer that Doyle could come up with was too obvious to be right. "Kenyon went the other way. I should have guessed that."

"The west end of the island is dead bare," Doyle said doubtfully. "Didn't see hide nor hair of 'em that way."

"There are places for a clever man to take cover," Haldoran snapped, furious with himself for not having tried sooner to get into his quarry's mind. He whirled and began striding back the other way. "Come on. We've lost precious time."

Chapter 34

Several hours of exploration confirmed Bone's barrenness. Catherine and Michael cut across the island and followed part of the coastline, but apart from several long-ruined farmsteads, they found no traces of humankind. The soil was thin, supporting mostly tough grasses and occasional patches of wildflowers. The only dense vegetation was in small hollows protected from the wind.

The prettiest of the hollows contained a delightful "fairy wood," with gnarled trees and a stunning carpet of bluebells. As Catherine gazed at the flowers, she could not help thinking that it would be a splendid place to picnic and make love. But they had no food, and they were no longer lovers. It had been such a brief spell of happiness, over almost before it began.

Michael gave her a quick glance. "Sit down for a while. You must be exhausted."

Gratefully she lay down among the bluebells. "Not exhausted, precisely, but certainly tired."

Instead of sprawling like Catherine, Michael sat against a tree trunk, every sense alert. Again she thought of medieval knights and slaying dragons, though she was too old and bedraggled to be a proper damsel.

After fifteen silent minutes, he rose and offered his hand to help her to her feet. She felt as tired as when she had sat down. "Would this be a good place to stay?"

He shook his head. "The trees offer a false sense of security, and the place is too distinctive. There's a good chance Haldoran will look for us here."

"But we can't walk forever. What would be the ideal place for us to go to ground?"

"One where we can see in all directions without being seen," he said without hesitation. "There would also be several lines of retreat, so we could withdraw safely if necessary. Plus, a good fire and a nice dinner of roast beef and Yorkshire pudding."

She groaned, though his wry humor heartened her. "Did you have to put that last in? I was too worried to eat much the last few days, and I've had nothing since yesterday noon."

"Sorry. If the storm drives Haldoran off the island, we'll have time to find food."

They were nearing the edge of the hollow. He crouched and signaled for her to wait while he moved stealthily forward. After scanning in all directions, he beckoned her to join him.

"We'll need to be more careful," he said quietly. "Haldoran may have realized by now that we're not in the hills. He could be at this end of the island already. We're safe as long as we avoid notice, but if he once catches sight of us, it will be very hard to shake him again."

Anxiety returned with a vengeance. "At least that storm you predicted is well on its way."

"That's to our advantage. Storms favor the hunted." He glanced up at the sky, where dark clouds were thickening. In the time they had spent in the fairy wood, the wind had picked up. A few dead leaves from the previous autumn blew past. "Let's hope your cousin decides to return to Skoal before the storm hits."

And after the storm, Haldoran might return with dogs to track them. She shrugged the thought off. They must survive today before tomorrow could become a problem.

They continued their zigzag survey of the island. Catherine suspected that Michael was now on a first-name basis with every tree, every boulder, and every irregularity in the surface of the area they had covered. They came to a ridge and circled around the flank; Michael was adamant about never becoming silhouetted against the horizon.

On the other side of the hill they discovered a small valley with a ruined village on its floor. "Civilization," Catherine said ironically.

"As civilized as it gets on Bone. There are other, older signs of habitation here as well." Michael gestured toward the left end of the valley. On top of the ridge was an ancient Druid circle, the irregular stones looming dramatically against the clouded sky. More prosaically, a small herd of the shaggy cows were grazing among the standing stones and on the hill below.

More interested in practical matters, Catherine said, "Though it's been a long time since the village was abandoned, there could be vegetables that have gone wild in the old gardens. Also, that looks like an orchard over there. There might be early apples in a protected spot like this."

He studied the circle of hills warily. "It's worth a try, but let's not linger. It would be easy to be trapped down here."

They walked down the slope to the village. Several dozen houses were scattered along the single street. All were plain stone ovals roofed with turf. The roofs had long since collapsed, and many of the walls as well. Weeds and flowers grew within the confines of what were once homes. Catherine tried to imagine what it would have been like to live here. "The houses are very primitive-looking."

"They're similar to the blackhouses in the Scottish Hebrides. I visited one once. A peat fire was built in the center of the house, with the smoke wandering out a hole in the middle of the roof. A layer of smoke that would choke a horse hung three or four feet above the floor." He made a face. "Not a good place for an asthmatic."

Something moved on the right. Michael spun to confront it, the open pocketknife appearing in his hand as if by magic.

A sheep trotted out from between two collapsed houses, its jaw moving placidly. Michael relaxed and put the knife away. "That beast is lucky we haven't time to build a fire. Roast mutton would taste very good now."

"Will you settle for apples? The orchard is in good shape. The Skoalans who tend the sheep must also prune the apple trees."

"Mutton roasted with apples," Michael murmured. "Rabbit stewed with apples. Fish baked with apples."

Ignoring his whimsy, she led the way to the orchard. Even a humble apple would taste like ambrosia now.

Fuming inwardly, Haldoran made his way westward across Bone. Doyle walked stolidly on a parallel course two hundred yards away. The convict was city-bred, not a real hunter, but he was fast at reloading his master's guns, and he was a good shot if by some chance a second gun would be needed.

Haldoran's gaze roved back and forth across the island. Though intuition confirmed that he had been right to abandon the hill region, he had yet to find signs of his prey. He should have brought hounds. He would later, if necessary.

Though he didn't doubt the ultimate result, the island was large enough that the hunt could take a long time. The damned resilient grass made it almost impossible to follow tracks. And on top of that, it looked as if a storm was coming.

His temper was not improved by the knowledge that he'd been a fool to let himself be baited into agreeing to this hunt. With the laird critically ill and Catherine vanished, it wouldn't do for the laird's closest male relative to be gone from Skoal for too long. He had left a note at the castle saying that his cousin had disappeared and he'd gone to search for her, but that excuse wouldn't hold up indefinitely.

Yet even though this hunt was unwise, he couldn't really regret doing it. He had always wanted a chance to track human game, and Kenyon was a wily quarry. As for Catherine—she would have to die, of course, but with luck he would have time to enjoy her lavish charms first. Doyle would also appreciate the chance to ravish a lady after his master was finished. The thought was almost as appealing as the prospect of killing Kenyon.

He found the first clear traces of the fugitives in the fairy wood. Crushed bluebells showed that two people had halted for a time. Knowing that they couldn't be far away, he pressed forward eagerly.

The old village was ahead. If they were there, it would be easy to corner them in the little valley. Anyone attempting to flee would be exposed on the bare, grassy flanks of the hills. And with a specially designed rifle like his, the entire valley was within effective shooting range.

He motioned for Doyle to join him. Together they breasted the hill. He made no attempt to hide their approach; he liked the idea of his quarry running in terror.

He paused at the top and studied the valley floor. Then he gave a sigh of voluptuous pleasure. "Eureka."

Barely visible among the orchard trees, the fugitives were eating apples. Fools. He could kill them both from where he stood. But that would be too easy. Too quick.

Raising his rifle, he cocked the hammer and took aim. "Let's watch them run before I finish them off."

Smiling, he squeezed the trigger.

The apples were good. Even better was watching Catherine's unabashed enjoyment as she finished her second apple. Michael felt an ache of protective tenderness when she licked a drop of apple juice from her lips. She was the gamest woman he had ever known, doing what had to be done without complaint and never reproaching him for having precipitated this disaster by returning to Skoal.

She swallowed her last bite. "Since it might not be wise to come back here, let's take some apples with us."

"A good idea." He stepped away from Catherine. As he stretched up for more fruit, a shot rang out. The rifle ball slammed into the tree trunk between them.

"Damnation!" Cursing himself viciously for watching Catherine instead of the hills, he grabbed her hand and pulled her into the middle of the orchard. The foliage would shield them from the view of anyone above. "They'll probably come down after us, so we'll have to retreat through the village."

There was fear in her eyes, but her voice was steady when she asked, "Won't they see us if we try to leave the valley? The hills offer no cover at all."

"You're right. Though it's risky, I think the best plan is to hide in one of the collapsed houses. I noticed a likely spot earlier. With luck they'll think we managed to get out of the valley without them seeing."

Moving like shadows, they slipped through the orchard toward the village. When they reached the edge of the trees, Michael motioned for Catherine to stay while he moved forward and scanned the hillside from which the shot had come. If the hunters had separated and one waited above with a rifle, Michael would be an easy target. But both men were descending into the valley. He caught a quick glimpse just before they disappeared behind the trees. The fugitives had at most four or five minutes before the hunters finished searching the orchard and came after them.

He beckoned for Catherine to follow him. The building he had noted earlier was in the middle of the village. One wall had collapsed, leaving the other ends of the rafters supported by the back wall. Vines grew profusely over the beams to create a natural curtain.

Catherine regarded the tentlike shape doubtfully, clearly thinking that it was an obvious hiding place. He indicated the opposite side of the wall. There was a mat of vines there also, but it was so close to the ground that there didn't appear to be space to hide below. Earlier, however, he had noticed that the earth under the vines was depressed, perhaps from the collapse of an old root cellar. There should be enough room for them.

He raised the vines to reveal the little hollow below. Catherine crouched and started to crawl into the hole backward. A small creature exploded from the hole and raced away, scaring the devil out of both of them. She clamped a hand over her mouth to stifle a gasp. Then she continued backing into the space and flattened down on her stomach. He did the same, arranging the grass and vines to look undisturbed.

The hollow was damp and earth-scented, and tendrils snagged his clothing and hair, but there was, barely, enough space for two people to lie side by side. He settled against Catherine and put an arm over her shoulders. Not only did that save space, but he welcomed the opportunity to hold her. Though the earth was chilly against his belly, she was warm. Tiny gaps in the vines allowed them to see out a little. By this time they were both so earth-colored that they should be invisible from outside.

After ten interminable minutes, the hunters came down the street. The first the fugitives knew was when Doyle growled, "Where could the bastards have gone?"

"They haven't left the valley or we would have seen," Haldoran said coolly. "And they aren't in the orchard, because we just searched there. Ergo, they must be hiding here in the old village." He raised his voice. "I know you can hear me, Catherine. Come out now and I'll spare you and release Amy."

Catherine's shoulders tensed under Michael's arm. For an instant, he thought she was going to stand up and accept her cousin's offer. He couldn't blame her if she did; if Haldoran could be trusted, she would be better off surrendering than staying in this wicked hunt.

If Haldoran could be trusted. Michael would put more faith in a rabid dog.

But Catherine did not try to rise. He turned his head a fraction and saw that her face was rigid with fury. If she had a gun, Haldoran would be a dead man.

The hunters approached with soft, rustling steps. Through the gaps in the vines, Michael glimpsed boots coming to a halt. "You just don't learn, do you, darling cousin?" Haldoran drawled. "Doyle, shoot in there. It's one of the few places large enough to hide two people."

A rifle discharged and the ball smashed into the other side of the stone wall, mere inches away. Debris spattered down on the fugitives.

If both hunters had fired, Michael would have risked an assault in the hope that he could bring them both down in the moments before they could reload. But Haldoran was too canny. Only one gun was discharged, and from the sounds, it was immediately reloaded. Then a rifle barrel prodded the vines on the other side of the wall, the metal scraping against the stone.

Within the circle of his arm, Catherine was trembling. He tightened his hold. Moving with absolute silence, she turned her head a little and rested her forehead against his jaw. He felt the quick beat of her pulse under cool, smooth skin. He closed his eyes, aching for what they had so briefly shared, and for what might have been. It was hard to imagine a future.

They stayed immobile as the hunters searched the village. Twice more there were gunshots, and once an indignant sheep fled, bawling furiously. Eventually the hunters came back along the street. Doyle grumbled, "They must have escaped from the valley when we were searching the orchard, my lord."

"I suppose you're right, though it's hard to believe they could run that fast," Haldoran replied testily. "Let's climb the ridge. The terrain is flat around the valley, so we should be able to see them. If not, we'll come back and search more thoroughly."

The sound of footsteps faded. Michael released his breath, almost light-headed with relief. Catherine said in the faintest of voices, "What next? If they come back, we might not be so lucky again."

"Yes, but if we leave the valley, they'll see us instantly. We're caught between the proverbial rock and hard place."

"I have an idea," she said hesitantly. "Do you think we

might be able to conceal ourselves among the cattle that were grazing around the standing stones? The ones we encountered earlier were placid beasts that didn't mind when we came close."

His heart jumped with hope. "That's brilliant! We'll give Haldoran a little longer to get away, then try the cattle."

It was a tense wait. Too long and Haldoran might be back, too short and the fugitives might be spotted from above. Since there was no way of knowing the best time to move, he relied on soldier's instinct.

When the time felt right, he crawled from under the vines, looking in all directions as he went. Nothing.

He motioned to Catherine. They moved down the street warily, darting from the shelter of one house to the next. There was no sign of the hunters in the village or on the hills.

About a dozen russet cows were grazing on the hillside below the Druid circle, with more at the top. After a last scan for danger, Michael gave the signal to advance. Keeping low, they sprinted up the hill, slowing only when they neared the cows. One edged away skittishly, but the others merely gave a glance of mild bovine curiosity before returning to their grass.

These cattle were as docile as the ones they'd seen earlier, for which Michael was grateful. Even so, he kept a wary distance from the long horns. The shaggy beasts were similar to the cattle of the Scottish Highlands, which were famous for their ability to thrive in difficult conditions.

They made it safely to the top of the hill, where several dozen cattle browsed around raised stones that were higher than a tall man's head. They were about to enter the densest section of the herd when a shot rang out, quickly followed by another. Chips flew from the nearest Druid monolith. Michael yelled, "Get behind a stone!"

They dived in opposite directions and took refuge behind adjacent monoliths. Keeping low, Michael peered around the edge.

The hunters were racing around the rim of the valley toward the stone circle, their forms silhouetted starkly against the sky. They paused long enough for the taller figure of Haldoran to fire his rifle. Then he traded weapons with Doyle and fired again as his servant reloaded. After trading guns again, they resumed the chase, Doyle reloading the second rifle on the run.

One of the bullets grazed a cow. After it bellowed with indignation, the nervous herd started moving away from the hunters. The next bullets would start a full-fledged stampede.

Michael glanced across to Catherine. "If I helped you onto the back of a cow, could you stay there as it ran?"

She blinked before saying succinctly, "Yes."

"Then let's go with the herd and see if we can catch some mounts." Keeping low and using the standing stones as a shield, the two of them darted among the cattle, keeping a wary eye on the horns. The animals were moving faster. Soon they would be impossible to catch.

Michael gestured at the cow nearest Catherine. "That one?"

She nodded and moved closer to the animal, running flat out to keep up. Michael stayed with her, a step away. When she leaped upward, he caught her waist and boosted her as smoothly as if they had rehearsed. She landed on the beast's back and threw one leg over. Then she leaned forward and locked her hands on the horns.

Bellowing with surprise, her mount threw its head up, trying to shake its burden. Catherine clung to its back like a limpet. The animal took off at full gallop, easily outpacing Michael, who watched admiringly for a moment longer. Who would have guessed that a woman who looked so delicately beautiful in a ball gown could also be so strong and so brave?

Then it was time to find a mount of his own. Most of the herd had passed, but a leggy young steer was overtaking him. He fell in beside the beast, barely able to match its speed. Then he sprang onto its back and flattened along its spine, grasping the horns as Catherine had done.

This steer was more temperamental than the other, and it twisted and bucked as furiously as a horse. Michael clung tenaciously, knowing that failure would probably be fatal. After a brief, violent battle, the steer decided it was more important to stay with the herd than to dislodge its unwanted burden. It settled down and charged after its fellows.

So far, so good. But now that they had been seen, it would be very hard to shake their pursuers. As he kicked his mount to greater speed, Michael wondered what the devil to do next.

Dumbfounded, Doyle said, "They're riding the bloody cows!"

"Ingenious." Haldoran glared after the stampeding herd. Already his quarry was beyond effective rifle range. Within a matter of moments it became impossible to see which beasts had riders. "Kenyon is the most challenging game I've ever pursued, and Cousin Catherine has unexpected tenacity. But the cattle will soon come to the cliffs. When they do, they'll swerve, probably to the west, since that will be a wider angle. If we cut straight across to the end of the island, we'll be waiting there when the animals tire."

Smiling wolfishly, he began jogging toward the sea. The end of the hunt was at hand. He would not have missed this for anything.

Chapter 35

Catherine found that she could control her mount a little by pulling on its horns. She tugged the head back so that the animal's jaw lifted. It bellowed and slowed down, falling farther back in the herd. Dragging at the left horn caused the cow to angle left, moving her within shouting distance of Michael. She called over the sound of pounding hooves, "We're going to reach the coast soon. Should we stay with them when they turn, or dismount?"

"We should get off," he yelled back. "We walked this section of shore earlier. The bluffs aren't too steep and there are a series of beaches below. We can climb down to the water level. With luck, Haldoran will follow the herd and not know where we got off."

She nodded, then returned her concentration to the rough ride. The cow's thick, shaggy coat provided some cushion, but its bony spine was still miserably uncomfortable. Her arms and legs were strained from the effort of staying on. If years of campaigning hadn't made her an expert rider, she wouldn't have lasted for five seconds.

The coast was approaching rapidly, the sound of the surf audible over the drumming of hooves. The leading cattle sheared off to the left, running parallel to the bluffs. They were tiring fast. Some had already slowed to trotting speed.

She and Michael worked their mounts over to the right, the side nearest the bluff. When she was in position, she pulled the cow's head back as hard as she could. The beast complained, but slowed enough for Catherine to slide off its back. She lost her footing when she landed and fell into a patch of brilliant yellow gorse. Luckily the ground was soft and none of the cattle were directly behind her, so she was unhurt.

A moment later Michael joined her. As he helped her up, he said, "We have to go over the edge immediately.

Haldoran and Doyle are cutting across to the shore. They're not more than a couple of hundred yards away."

She nodded and dashed the dozen steps to the edge of the bluff, wanting to be out of sight before they lost the screen of cattle. Then she saw the steepness of the incline. Her blood congealed with fear. "I can't go down that!"

"You can, and you *will*!" Michael snapped. "It's not much worse than the hill we climbed when we got here. Turn and go down with your face to the bluff. There are plenty of foot- and handholds. I'll go first, so if you slip I can catch you."

She stared at Michael. His chestnut hair was disheveled and his face smudged, but he had never looked more like an officer. And like the best officers, he made her feel she could do the impossible. Or perhaps it was that she would rather risk a fall than his wrath. She swallowed and nodded.

He turned and lowered himself over the edge. "Come along," he ordered. "It won't be as bad as you think."

She took a deep breath, then followed. Looking straight into the bluff rather than at the long drop did make it easier. Small bushes and tough clumps of grass offered adequate support.

They were halfway down when a foothold disintegrated under her. The grass clump she was holding tore out and she began sliding out of control. For a horrified instant she thought she would strike Michael and knock them both to their deaths.

Instead, Michael braced himself and caught her. An arm locked around her waist, stopping her descent. She grabbed for new holds, shaking convulsively.

They stayed like that for a moment, plastered to the bluff like flies, Michael's arm around her. Then he murmured in her ear, "To think I was afraid life would be dull after the army."

She almost laughed, though she was closer to hysteria than amusement. "I wouldn't mind a little tedium just now."

"With luck, it will be nicely dull on the beach below us. That overhang to the right should protect us from being seen. Are you ready to go on?"

She took a deep breath. "I'll make it."

He released her and resumed his descent, and she followed a moment later. Explore with one foot to find a hold.

Transfer weight gradually. Don't release the other holds until you know the new one is secure. Then again. And again. And *again*.

Finally one extended foot struck the rounded stones of the shingle beach. Intensely relieved to be on firm ground again, she followed Michael under the overhang. Once there, she sank down and leaned against the bluff, her limbs trembling with strain. "Did I ever mention that I'm not very fond of heights?"

"No, but I guessed." He rested his hand on her shoulder for a moment. "Well done."

She glanced up, absurdly pleased at his approval. His hard eyes radiated confidence. He was in his element now, using his physical mastery to defeat impossible odds. A warrior. While she was merely a cowardly female who brought disaster on everyone around her. "How long do you think it will take for them to deduce that we came down here?"

"Half an hour at most, perhaps less. We'll need to move on in a few minutes." He squatted beside her, his gaze sweeping the bluffs above. "That cave the laird told you about—did he say if it was entirely underwater at high tide? Or is some of it above the water line?"

Catherine tried to remember her grandfather's words. "He warned against getting trapped inside, so part of it must be above water."

"The next question is, where is the cave, and can we get there from here?" He frowned at the darkening sky. "We're going to need a refuge from the storm tonight."

Catherine agreed. Even though it was almost summer, the sea air was chilly. A night of exposure to a storm would be hard on both of them, especially her. Michael, she suspected, had the resilience of old leather.

They sat for a few minutes, gathering strength, as Michael continued his vigil. Suddenly he muttered an oath. "Damnation, he figured it out already. They're starting down the cliff, not far from where we came down. We'll have to get out of here fast and hope they're too busy climbing to see us."

Lips a thin line, she got to her feet. It was midafternoon, and she felt as if they had been running forever. With the hunters approaching on the right, she turned to the left, keeping to the cliff face and moving as fast as possible on the rounded stones. Michael followed, again taking the position of greatest danger. Gallantry was so much a part of his nature that he would not understand if she thanked him for it.

The beach curved to a stony headland that thrust out into the sea. It was possible to scramble over the slanted surface, but the rocks were slippery with seaweed and waves smashed menacingly only a few feet below. With all her concentration on her footing, the roar of a rifle almost sent her skidding into the water. Again Michael steadied her with a hard hand on her back. The man had the balance of a mountain goat.

She resumed her precarious trek, not wasting time to look back. Another bullet, this one striking so close to her hand that stone chips struck her fingers. Frantically she slithered around the corner out of range. After wedging herself securely behind a boulder, she glanced back, inhaling sharply when she saw a bloody hole in the upper arm of Michael's jersey.

"Strictly a scratch," he said in answer to her unspoken alarm. "I was hit by the ricochet, I think. No harm done."

She hoped to heaven he was right, because little could be done if the wound was serious. Breathing ragged, she continued around the headland.

She turned the final corner, then halted, stunned by the shrieks of thousands of gulls. They had found a seabird colony. Every ledge in the cliff seemed to hold a nest and the sky above was full of wheeling, screaming birds. Swallow-tailed terns and crested shags and dagger-billed gannets nested in the rock, and comical puffins in the grassier slope on the far side, along with half a dozen other species she couldn't name.

Behind her, Michael said pragmatically, "Thank heaven there's a sliver of beach here, though it won't last much longer the way the tide is coming in."

He dropped to the coarse sand, then reached up to help her down. The beach was smooth enough for them to run, but slimy white droppings were everywhere and the stench was unbelievable.

They were three-quarters of the way around the cove when another blast of the rifle announced Haldoran's arrival.

"He'll regret that," Michael panted.

The roar of the gun drove the bird colony berserk. Whirling wings were everywhere and the shrieks numbed the ears. Catherine gave a quick glance back and saw that seabirds were darting about so thickly that the hunters were invisible. Hoping the pursuers got their eyes pecked out, she continued on, one arm raised above her face to protect her from possible attack.

The headland at the far end of the cove plunged straight into the water, utterly impassable. However, centuries of pounding waves had scoured an irregular hole through the stone. Since light was visible, she scrambled up to the opening and crawled through the short tunnel, bruising her knees unmercifully.

She halted at the other end to survey the next stretch of shore. This bay was larger than the last and surrounded by sheer, impassable cliffs. A narrow sandy beach was littered with boulders. On the opposite side the dark mouth of an opening showed in the cliff face. When Michael joined her, she said, "I think that might be our cave."

Michael frowned at the turbulent incoming waves. "We'll have to run to get there before the tide cuts it off. Soon this beach will be entirely underwater."

They climbed down to the beach and started for the cave. For Catherine, it was a nightmare journey. The tide was advancing with unbelievable speed. Waves splashed around their ankles and fell back, then returned to strike with greater force. With no exit at the far end of the bay, they would be drowned or smashed to pieces against the rocks if they didn't reach the cave in time.

A triumphant shout sounded behind them. As the first shot blasted, Michael snapped, "Weave back and forth! You'll be a more difficult target."

Wearily she commanded her exhausted body to comply. Bullets buzzed by as she zigzagged back and forth, dodging behind boulders when she could. Her cousin must be shooting from the vantage of the stone passage through the headland. With time to aim and a skilled reloader, his shots were increasingly accurate, and most of them seemed aimed at Michael.

Her path took her deeper into the water and a wave knocked her from her feet. She went headfirst into the sea, the swirling current sucking her under. She swallowed a mouthful of cold salty water and gagged helplessly.

Michael caught her arm and yanked her to her feet. "Only a little farther! You can do it."

With his powerful arm supporting her, she staggered toward the cave. The lower half of the entrance was already submerged with waves crashing into the stone archway. If this was the wrong cave, with no high ground inside, they were doomed. The water was thigh-high, and the currents so powerful she could not have kept her feet without Michael's aid.

A bullet ricocheted off the stone arch and splashed beside her just before she entered the cave. With her last strength, she ducked and stumbled into the stone tunnel, Michael right behind her. At least they would be safe from bullets. Numbly she wondered if they would drown instead. She almost didn't care.

Haldoran swore furiously as his quarries vanished into the mouth of the cave. "Bloody hell! We won't be able to get at them until the tide has crested and fallen again. It will be after midnight by then."

Doyle said nervously, "If we don't get away, my lord, we'll be trapped here ourselves."

"No danger of that. The slope at this end of the seabird colony can be climbed." Which meant crawling through those filthy puffins, he thought sourly. "If we return to the boat now, we can sail back to Skoal before the storm strikes. That will give me a chance to explain sorrowfully how I couldn't find hide nor hair of dear Cousin Catherine. Frantic with worry about her dear grandfather, she must have wandered off and fallen from a cliff. A tragedy."

Uninterested in his master's alibi, Doyle jerked a thumb toward the cave. "What about them?"

"We'll come back and continue the hunt when the storm blows over." Haldoran gave a last, smoldering glance at the place where his quarry had vanished. "I'll bring dogs. Even if they leave the cave at low tide, they won't get far."

Chapter 36

The laird had been drifting in murky currents for so long that it was hard to believe he had finally returned to the surface. He blinked several times to clear his vision, then decided that the continuing grayness was more outside than in. Dusk, maybe, or an oncoming storm.

He did not try to move. It was enough to savor the knowledge that he was still among the living. Not that he feared death, for then he would join his wife and the others he had lost. But he wasn't ready for that yet. Not when there was so much to be done. He had learned a great deal while lying in bed like a log. People had assumed he couldn't hear, but he could, at least some of the time. He had learned important things that affected the future of the island. Treachery. Betrayal. If only he could put the pieces together . . . He shook his head in frustration.

A quavering voice said, "Are you awake, my lord?"

It was Fitzwilliam, his old valet. "Yes, and about time." The laird found that his mouth worked clumsily and the right side of his face was a little numb, but the words were clear enough. "Is my granddaughter here?"

Fitzwilliam's eyes shifted. "Not at the moment, my lord. She was nursing you most devotedly, but she . . . she needed a rest."

"Liar." The laird wanted to say waspishly that after fifty-seven years of close association, Fitzwilliam should know better than to try to deceive his master, but it was too much effort. He must save his strength for more important matters. "Clive?"

"Lord Haldoran has stayed at the castle since your illness began, but he . . . he went out this morning. We haven't seen him all day. Shall I send to Ragnarok? He might be there."

"No! Get Davin." The boy would know what to do. He always did. And Davin, at least, could be trusted.

Cursing himself for his weakness, the laird drifted into sleep again.

The cave was no more than a narrow tunnel for the first dozen feet. Then it opened up. Cautiously Catherine straightened. There was very little light, but the echo of the waves implied that the chamber was very large. The ceiling vaulted at least twenty feet above her head, and the back of the cave disappeared into darkness. As her eyes adjusted to the dimness, she saw that the pool in which they stood was surrounded by higher ground. The incoming tide would not drown them.

Since she was shaking violently from cold and exhaustion, Michael towed her from the pool with an arm around her waist. She stumbled against him as she climbed the embankment, sand crunching beneath her sopping boots, then sagged to her knees.

He crouched beside her. "Are you all right, Catherine?"

"N-nothing seriously wrong." She took advantage of his closeness to lean against him for a moment. His soaked jersey had the sharp, not unpleasant scent of wet wool.

To her regret, he soon stood, saying, "We won another round. We'll be safe here until the tide falls again."

"Safe," she repeated. "Such a beautiful word."

He glanced at the high, shadowy walls. "There's a draft, so there must be a source of fresh air somewhere. That means we can build a fire from the driftwood."

Though she wanted to help him gather wood, when she tried to stand, her body flatly refused to cooperate. Feeling as weak as a fever patient, she watched as he selected wood and laid a fire. A good thing she had been able to bring the tinderbox and that it was a water-resistant design.

She rubbed her arms in a vain attempt to warm herself. Fishermen wore heavy jerseys like hers because wool could hold heat even when wet, but her body was too chilled to generate any warmth for the wool to hold.

Michael struck a spark, then blew it into flame. Catherine was trying to summon the energy to walk to the fire when he came and scooped her up in his arms. She asked, "Don't you ever tire?"

"Yes, but usually not until everything vital has been

done." He set her on the coarse sand by the fire and added more wood. "Then I sleep for a day or two."

Flames blazed up, and the lower walls of the cave began to shimmer with subtle rainbow colors. She gasped and closed her eyes, thinking she must be hallucinating. But when she opened her eyes again, the colors were still there.

Michael glanced up and gave a low whistle of surprise. Lithely he rose and went down for a closer look. "The walls are covered with tiny sea creatures that are almost transparent. They shine like little rainbows when the light strikes them."

"I hope that's a good omen." No longer able to suppress her greatest fear, she asked tightly, "Do you think Haldoran will harm Amy if he goes back to Skoal tonight?"

"No." Michael came back to the fire. "Even if he's serious about marrying her when she turns twelve, he would be a fool to molest her now. If you die, Amy is heir to Skoal, and he's seen enough of her to know she's a strong-minded young lady. If he wants to gain her cooperation and her inheritance, he'll have to win her trust. My guess is that he'll treat her like a princess. Lucien will have her safe well before her twelfth birthday."

It sounded plausible. She prayed he was right. Not wanting to consider the alternative, she looked around, squinting into the darkness. "The laird said there is a natural hot spring in this cave."

"Really?" Michael sat back on his heels. "That would be welcome. I'll see what I can find." He pulled a burning piece of driftwood from the fire and raised it above his head, swinging it in small circles to intensify the flame as he walked away. "I've always liked the stillness of being underground. That's one reason why mining interests me. The water-carved walls and rainbow reflections make this cave downright otherworldly."

"The realm of Hades, I suppose," Catherine said, less enthusiastic about the location. "Look behind you. There seems to be steam rising over there, about halfway to the wall."

Michael went to investigate. "There's a sizable pool here." He knelt and tested the water. "Ahh, lovely. This is the temperature of a pleasantly hot bath." He touched his tongue to his fingers. "And it's fresh water, not salt."

Catherine rose and went to kneel beside him. The pool

was roughly oval, about a dozen feet long and seven or eight feet wide. She scooped up a handful of water. The warm fluid spilled sensuously through her fingers. "Would you think me terribly vulgar if I took off my clothing and climbed in?"

"I think that sounds very sensible." Michael stood. "While you get warm, I'll see if I can tickle a fish for our dinner."

Though it was clear that he preferred to keep his distance, she laid a hesitant hand on his wrist. "Later. You must be almost as cold and tired as I. It wouldn't do for you to come down with lung fever, so warm yourself first."

His muscles tensed under her palm, then relaxed. "Very well, but we should set our clothing to dry first. I'll improvise some racks. Just leave your things here on the edge."

As she stripped off her jersey, he turned abruptly and moved away. For a moment he was silhouetted against the firelight, his broad shoulders and lean muscular frame a dark symbol of masculine power and grace. The sight mesmerized her. She wanted him, physically and emotionally, with a yearning that was almost unbearable. Perhaps passion would melt Michael's iron reserve and narrow the breach between them.

Slowly she removed the rest of her clothing. Her gaze stayed on Michael as he collected fantastically twisted pieces of driftwood and shoved them into the sand by the fire. She wondered if she would have the courage to make an advance. Probably not, since rejection was likely to be his response. Nor was a subtler approach likely to work; she was too new to passion to be skilled at seduction.

With a sigh, she released her hair and slid naked into the pool. The bottom was formed of water-smoothed stone, with an average depth of about four feet. At first the temperature was almost painful, but as her body warmed, the water became a silken caress. She drifted across the pool. Heated water flowed intimately around her breasts and between her legs, bringing her flesh to life with profound sensuality.

Though her desire did not go away, her tension faded to a manageable level. She exhaled with pleasure and propelled herself across the pool with a couple of lazy kicks. There was so much unsaid between her and Michael. Perhaps later they might resolve their differences. For now, she would simply accept the distance he had put between them.

Michael did his best not to stare at Catherine when he came to collect her wet clothing, but his best wasn't very good. As she floated across the shadowed pool, she was as lovely as a sea nymph, her hair flowing around her shoulders in a gossamer cloud.

She reached the far end of the pool and twisted lithely to change direction. His gaze slid over her supple curves, from the graceful arc of her spine, over her rounded hips, and down the shapely lengths of her legs. Once more he thought of the Siren Kenneth had drawn in Brussels, beckoning a man to ruin.

Throat tight, he scooped up her boots and other garments. After wringing out the excess water, he draped them across the driftwood by the fire. Steam began to rise gently.

He smiled without humor, thinking that steam should be rising from him as well. They had barely escaped with their lives, and the danger was far from over. Yet all he could think of was Catherine. He craved her more intensely than food or drink or warmth. But everything was so damned tangled that it was impossible to simply take her into his arms and make love.

If he had any sense, he would go fishing.

However, Catherine had been right that he needed to get warm. That meant controlling himself. He had done so before, he could again now. Lips compressed, he stripped and hung his clothing on the improvised racks, then unwound the rope that had been chafing against his torso.

He crossed the cave to the pool. Catherine was on the opposite side, lounging back against an angled stone with her eyes closed and water to her chin. The faint golden wash of firelight illuminated the planes of her face and the pale contours of her upper body. He stared, entranced, at a glossy strand of hair that coiled sinuously over her shoulder and between her magnificent breasts. They were buoyant, as round and ripe as forbidden fruit. Below, her torso tapered into the shadowy water, which revealed only faint hints of narrow waist, womanly hips, and the dark triangle between her legs.

Near paralysis, he forced himself to look away. When his

breathing was steady, he slipped into the pool. The warm water was as sweet as sin.

Sin seemed to be all he could think about.

He settled onto a rock that allowed him to submerge all of his body except his head. The heated water was wonderful, soothing the bruises he had received earlier.

Catherine's eyes opened lazily, the thick dark lashes sweeping upward like a raven's wing. "A good thing we must leave with the next tide, or I'd be tempted to spend the rest of my life soaking here."

"It's like the hot springs in Bath," he agreed. "Fit for a Roman emperor."

She uncoiled from her lounging position, her hair swirling and clinging to her slim neck. Then she bent forward and glided across the pool with a kick, settling beside him as lightly as a bird. "I want to look at that wound on your arm."

"Really, it's nothing." Acutely aware of her nearness, he tried to edge away.

Firmly she grasped his forearm and turned him so that his upper arm was illuminated. After gently examining the raw flesh, she said, "You're right, it's not much more than a graze. It won't even scar." Her fingers skimmed down his arm to the ragged mark left by one of his Waterloo wounds. "It's impressive that you've survived so much without becoming permanently crippled."

She traced the thin hard line where his ribs had been sliced by a saber. The scar arced downward toward his groin, and her touch triggered a fierce jolt of arousal. Hoping his state was concealed in the shadowy water, he tried to move away again.

Her hands came to rest on his waist so that he could not detach himself without using force. "You certainly got bruised fighting Haldoran and his men," she observed as her experienced gaze went over him. "It's amazing that you were able to move so quickly when we were haring around the island."

He felt sweat on his brow, and knew it was not from the heated pool. When her palm began to skim down over the saturated hair of his chest, he caught her right wrist. "Catherine, don't. Being merely a man and not at all a saint, I can't help but respond when you touch me."

The tendons in her wrist went rigid and the atmosphere

changed, going from camaraderie to vivid physical awareness. She raised her gaze to his, her eyes smoky with desire. "I don't feel very saintly myself. Since we might not have a tomorrow, let us use well what time we have."

Her left hand dipped beneath the surface, flattening against his groin as it glided slowly downward. Then her palm curled around his heated flesh and fire seared through him. His control shattered. Catching her around the waist, he lifted her from her feet and swept her across the pool. The water buoyed them both, giving every movement the weightless grace of dancing.

He laid her along the angled stone and followed her down, covering her mouth with his. Her lips were damp and hotly welcoming. She made a rough, needy sound and her hands curled around his neck. The kiss deepened, became devouring as the terror of the day transmuted into pure sexual fire.

Finally he broke away, panting. His gaze went over her entrancing Siren's body, more hinted at than seen in the dim light. Her moist throat shimmered faintly, betraying the frantic tempo of her heart. He kissed the pulse point, then licked downward over smooth, flawless skin. Her back arched and rosy nipples broke the surface. He captured one with his mouth, the tender flesh hardening instantly under his tongue.

Her knees separated and he moved between them, cradling her buttocks while he suckled her. With her lower body supported by the water, she began moving her legs up and down restlessly, caressing his hips with her inner thighs. The heated water lent a liquid sensuality to every touch. He breathed, "You are more beautiful than I ever dreamed a woman could be." He moved his mouth to her other breast and tugged at the nipple with his lips.

She moaned, "Oh, Michael." Her legs locked around his waist, drawing him closer until his taut male flesh pressed against her with stark intimacy. She twisted her pelvis, trying to take him within her.

"Jesus! Not yet." Chest heaving with the effort of trying to restrain himself, he pulled away a little and braced his hands on the stone beside her shoulders. Then he hung above her and rocked his hips so that his engorged shaft rubbed up and down against exquisitely sensitive female folds. Rapturous, maddening. Heaven and hell merged into erotic torture. She writhed under the voluptuously carnal strokes, breathing in desperate sobs. Her hands moved convulsively up and down his arms, slipping frictionless over his water-slicked muscles.

When her whole body shivered on the verge of explosion, he drew back a little, touching her to guide himself. Under the feathery curls she was all hot, pliant yearning.

He entered her with one slow, possessive stroke. Silken heat enfolded him, the pleasure almost beyond bearing. She moaned and rolled her hips, triggering a fierce exchange of thrust and counterthrust. Water surged around their churning bodies. Then she cried out and her nails dug deep into his back.

Her chaotic contractions triggered his own release. He gasped, feeling as if his whole self was pouring helplessly into her. The culmination was searing, desperate with savage uncertainties.

Passion ebbed swiftly, but instead of repletion, he felt aching sorrow. Even now, when he was deep in her body, he could not escape the haunted echo in his mind. *She is not for you.*

Chapter 37

Though Michael's body pinned Catherine to the slanting stone, most of his weight was supported by the water that surrounded them. She savored his closeness and the blessed peace of fulfillment. She could have fallen asleep holding him, but all too soon he withdrew, leaving her empty.

"I don't know if that was wise," he said huskily, "but it was certainly good. For a few moments, the rest of the world didn't exist."

Though he brushed a kiss on her temple, she sensed that emotionally he was far away. She wanted to cling to him, to tell him how much she loved him, but she did not dare. Having grown up in the army, she recognized that Michael's formidable skills were focused on survival. Passion had been a pleasing diversion, but distracting him with agonizing personal issues would endanger them both. Forcing her voice to matter-of-factness, she said, "I'm ravenous. I wish we'd been able to bring a few of those apples."

"I wasn't joking about catching a fish. There must be some in the main pool, since it connects to the sea. I'll see what I can find for supper." He straightened and ran his hand over his face, wiping away droplets of moisture. "If you'll wait here, I'll get my shirt for you to wear. It was fairly dry."

She obeyed, content to drift in the warm water and watch him. He climbed from the pool and went to the fire. There he toweled himself briskly with the singlet he had worn under his shirt. His bare, beautifully proportioned body was godlike in its lithe power. Considering the scars, she supposed the god in question would be Mars. It still amazed her that a man who was supremely gifted in the violent arts of war could be so gentle.

After he pulled on his drawers, he returned to the pool with his shirt. She took his proffered hand and reluctantly emerged from the water. Now that she had been so thoroughly warmed, both outside and in, the air no longer seemed cold.

She used the singlet to sponge off most of the water before pulling his shirt over her head. The garment fell to her knees. When her head emerged from the voluminous linen folds, she saw that Michael was watching her with a dark, hooded gaze. Uneasily she wondered if he wished he had not succumbed to her brazen advance. Perhaps they should have talked rather than . . . doing what they did. Yet she could not be sorry. "How can you catch a fish without a hook or a line?"

"It's time to use the tickling technique I learned from my Gypsy friend Nicholas. All you have to do is let your hand trail in the water, moving your fingers a little. When a fish comes to investigate, you grab him."

She had to smile. "I'm sure that's harder than it sounds."

"It takes patience and speed," he admitted. "But I've done it before, and hunger is a wonderful incentive."

He went down to the tidal pool and lay down on a rock, then slid his arm into the water. She offered a fervent mental wish for his success as she went in search of fresh water. Soon she found a small spring that trickled down the cave wall and pooled in a stony basin before disappearing into the sand.

She drank thirstily, then returned to the fire. She was sitting by the flames, plaiting her wet hair into a single braid, when Michael gave a crow of triumph. He leaped up and came toward her, a fine fat fish still thrashing in his hands. "I'll clean this if you'll figure out a way to cook it."

She considered a moment. There weren't really many choices. "How about if I wrap it in seaweed and bake it in the coals?"

"Sounds excellent."

The cleaned fillets baked quickly, with delicious results. The fish could not have been fresher, and salt from the seaweed had steamed through the delicate flesh. Of course, Catherine was hungry enough to enjoy a rock-hard chunk of army biscuit.

After the meal, she leaned back and linked her arms around her drawn-up knees. Taking advantage of the relaxed atmosphere, she asked, "What made you decide to return to Skoal?"

He stared at the fire, the flickering flames casting a harsh light over his chiseled features. "My brother, mostly."

She raised her brows. "The new duke? I thought you were barely on speaking terms."

"We weren't." Not raising his gaze from the fire, Michael described a long, exhausting ride, and how his brother had come to the inn at Great Ashburton to bridge a lifetime of conflict. The terse words said perhaps more than he had intended about his despairing state of mind when he had left the island.

He finished by saying, "Stephen seems to think I was as likely fathered by the old duke as by brother Roderick, so that the whole issue of my legitimacy should be ignored. After all, we'll never know for sure, and it makes no real difference."

"Your brother sounds like a wise man," she said quietly. "And a generous one. I'm so glad."

"It was like meeting a stranger whom I had known all my life." Michael shook his head, then got to his feet. "I want to explore the cave further. When I was fishing, I noticed a branch cave over there. The way the light falls makes it almost invisible unless it's seen from the right angle."

"Sounds interesting. I'll go with you."

Both of them carrying crude torches, they went to investigate. The tide was at its crest, almost filling the narrow branch with water. However, by bending almost double they could wade along the shallow edge instead of having to swim.

When the tunnel enlarged, Michael straightened and raised his torch. The chamber was much smaller than the main cave. He looked around. "Good God, we've found a smuggler's storehouse."

Catherine's eyes widened when she came forward to stand beside him. Dozens of small kegs were stacked on the higher ground. "Grandfather mentioned that the islands were a hotbed of smuggling during the war, but I'm surprised that these kegs were left in a cave which is a local landmark."

"This section would be easy to overlook. Besides, it's doubtful if any islanders who discovered this would tell the authorities. Most communities protect their free traders." Michael examined the nearest kegs. "Usually smuggled goods would be transferred fairly quickly, but these appear to have been here for months, even years. Perhaps the smugglers' boat went down and this cargo has been waiting unclaimed."

"I suppose it's French brandy?"

"A small fortune's worth." He scanned the rest of the chamber, then caught his breath. "Look. Here's something far more valuable."

Hearing the excitement in his voice, Catherine turned to see. Her heart jumped. Pulled up on the sand and half-hidden in the shadows was a medium-sized rowboat. "Merciful heaven! Do you suppose this could take us to Skoal?"

"I certainly hope so." He circled the tidal pool for a closer look, Catherine right behind him. "The oars are here, there's a tin bucket for bailing, and the hull seems sound. Help me haul it down to the tidal pool."

She shoved the end of her torch into the sand, then dragged on the gunwale opposite from Michael. The boat slid into the water with a splash.

He waded in beside it. "There don't seem to be any major leaks. We've just found our way to escape."

Wanting to believe but doubtful, she asked, "Can a little boat like this manage the rocks and currents?"

"In some ways, it will be easier than in a larger vessel. Certainly our chances will be better than if we tried to swim." He studied the entrance tunnel. "The storm will have passed by the time the tide drops enough to get this out of the cave. It will be dark then. Even if Haldoran is waiting in the bay, which I doubt, we'll have a good chance to evade him."

Hoping he was right, she asked, "When do you think the storm will hit?"

"It already has. It's raging outside now."

She stared at him. "How do you know that?"

He shrugged. "It's only a feeling. A kind of inner restlessness, for lack of a better word. The storm struck about an hour ago. Though it's very intense, it will pass quickly."

She still didn't understand, but was willing to take his word on it. "What's underneath the oar on your side?"

He moved the oar, then inhaled sharply. "A sword." Reverently he lifted it from the bottom of the skiff. Light from the torch flashed along the blade. "It was greased to protect it from damp." He made an experimental cut. As weapon met warrior, the sword came alive with glittering, lethal life.

Once more thinking of gods of war and the archangel who led the hosts of heaven, Catherine uttered a fervent mental thanks. The voyage between the two islands would be dangerous, but now they had a chance. If anyone could turn a chance into a victory, it was Michael.

Amy had gone to the library to read, but when the storm hit she curled up in the window seat to watch. Ferocious wind and rain rattled the windowpanes. Far below her, waves smashed into the cliff, the spray flying upward to mingle with the raindrops.

Though it would be more ladylike to fear the storm, she found a certain satisfaction in the violence. For days she had been chafing in the ridiculously named Ragnarok. Lord Haldoran kept saying Mama was too busy nursing the laird to see her daughter, but Amy was increasingly impatient. She had been helping her mother in the sickroom for years. She would be a help, not a hindrance.

The next time she saw Lord Haldoran, she would insist on being taken to her mother. Or maybe she wouldn't wait. He wasn't home much; she hadn't seen him since early the day before. Tomorrow morning, after the storm had passed, she would slip out on her own. The island wasn't very large. Surely she could find her way to the laird's residence.

Not long after she made her resolution, the door to the library opened and Lord Haldoran entered. She swung her feet to the floor and went to him. "Good day, my lord." She bobbed a curtsy. "Can I go visit my mother now? If she is working so hard, she'll be glad to have my help."

He shook his head, his expression grave. "I'm afraid I have bad news for you, Amy. Please sit down." He ushered her toward the sofa. "You're going to have to be brave, my dear."

She jerked her elbow from his grasp and stared at him, paralyzed with fear. Those were almost the same words the colonel of the regiment had used when he came to break the news of Papa's death. "No," she whispered. *"No."*

Pity in his voice, he said, "We don't know for sure, but probably last night your mother decided she needed a break from the sickroom. She must have gone for a walk on the cliffs, and . . . she didn't come back. We've searched the island, but she isn't here. None of the boatmen took her to the mainland. There were marks on the cliff top as if someone fell and tried to catch a hold to stop from going over the edge. This was found washed up in the bay below." He handed a sodden shawl to Amy.

She gave a whimper of anguish. Her mother had bought the shawl in Brussels. The prices had been so reasonable there, though Mama had to be persuaded to buy something for herself. . . . "Mama can't be dead! She followed the drum her whole life. How could she fall off a silly cliff?"

"It was misty and she was very tired," Haldoran said gently. "A slip on damp grass, a gust of wind . . . the island can be very dangerous to newcomers." He laid a hand on her shoulder.

Amy froze. There was something wrong with the way he touched her. His hand was heavy, possessive. And in spite of what he said, she couldn't believe her mother could be so stupid as to fall off a cliff. She looked up at Lord Haldoran, wanting to protest further, then bit back the words. If there was something wrong, his lordship was part of it.

"There, there, my dear." He tried to put his arms around her. "You mustn't worry, Amy. You're family. I promise that you will always be provided for."

She shoved him away. "I'm going to my room. I . . . I need to be alone." She allowed her agonized tears to spill out.

"Of course," he said in that same soft, solicitous, *false* voice. "Such a tragedy. Your mother was a wonderful woman. Just remember that I'll always take care of you."

She bolted from the room, deliberately acting more like seven than eleven, and didn't stop until she reached her room two floors above. As she ran, she noticed one of his lordship's men following her. There were several of them, all tough and sullen and so similar that she called them the trolls. Unlike the common soldiers she'd known in the army, the trolls were silent and unfriendly. For the first time, she realized that one was always nearby. Guarding her?

She slammed the door to the room and turned the key, locking out the world. Then she threw herself onto the bed and buried her face in her hands as she tried to stifle her sobs. After she succeeded, she rolled onto her back and stared at the ceiling.

She had never questioned Lord Haldoran's honesty. After all, he was a friend and cousin of her mother's. But he hadn't really been that close a friend, not like Colonel Kenyon or Captain Wilding. What if his lordship had lied about being sent by Mama? Aunt Anne had almost refused to let her go because his lordship didn't have a note.

But why would Lord Haldoran bother to kidnap her? He didn't even like children.

She thought hard. Maybe he wanted to force Mama into marriage, like in a Gothic romance. Real life wasn't supposed to be like that, but Mama was the most beautiful woman in the world. Men often became strange around her.

Whatever the reason, one thing was clear. She must get away from that man and this house, and she must do it soon.

Amy rose and went to the window. Gusts of wind and rain were rattling the panes, and it was a long way to the ground. However, she could make a rope from her bedsheets. Luckily, the house was built in a style that included lots of ledges where she could rest if necessary. She would escape when the storm died down. Then she would find her way to the laird's house. Maybe her mother would be there.

She closed her eyes, trying to block fresh tears. *Please, Mama, be alive.*

Chapter 38

They left the cave as soon as the tide dropped enough to get the boat through the entrance tunnel. Catherine and Michael lay flat in the boat while he pushed at the irregular roof to propel the vessel forward. They scraped against stone with every swell of water, but eventually they emerged into the pitch-black night.

The back of her neck prickled as she sat up. She felt like a mouse emerging from a hole that was being watched by a hungry cat. But there were no shouts or shots; Haldoran and his men had either returned to Skoal or taken shelter for the night.

As Michael had predicted, the storm had passed, but before he could set the oars in the locks, a wave struck them broadside. Inches of water splashed into the boat, saturating their recently dried clothing. Michael hastily began rowing. As the boat stabilized and moved away from the shore, he said, "Keep a good lookout. This bay is full of rocks."

Catherine nodded and knelt in the bow to watch for low-lying hazards. With his back to the bow, Michael could not see what lay ahead, but she was acutely aware that she lacked his superior night vision. Scudding clouds covered most of the sky and she could see very little. She squinted. There was a paleness just ahead to the left, an irregularity that looked like foam. "Pull right. I think there's a reef on the left."

"Right," he repeated. The boat angled to the side and a half dozen oar strokes took them by a partially submerged rock.

The water ahead appeared clear, so Catherine spared a moment to turn and bail. Thank God the smugglers had left the bucket.

As soon as they left the bay for the open ocean, conditions worsened. The storm had left huge waves in its wake, and they pushed ferociously at the small boat. She wondered grimly if Michael would be able to hold a course among the waves and currents. The chase on Bone had shown that he had a phenomenal sense of direction and a feeling for terrain, but this was water, a channel he had crossed only once, and that in the daylight. They might easily miss Skoal and become lost on the open sea.

She cut off her thoughts. All she could do was watch and bail, and by God, she would do that well.

Amy dozed a little, leaving the window of her room partially open so she could monitor the weather. The stillness after the storm awakened her. She had left a candle burning, and the mantel clock showed that it was almost two in the morning. Perfect. She padded to the window and looked out. There was still a brisk wind, but the rain had stopped. There was no sign of movement anywhere around Ragnarok.

She peeled off her nightgown and donned the boy's clothing she had worn for long rides on the Peninsula. She'd brought the garments in case she went climbing on the cliffs in Skoal. The breeches were a little tight; she'd grown. But they would do.

When she was dressed, she cautiously opened the door and peered into the corridor. As she expected, one of the trolls was dozing in the corridor a dozen feet away. To leave, she would have to step right over him. It would have to be the window.

She relocked the door and retrieved the rope she had made from sheets. After tying one end around a bedpost, she threw the other end out the window. It just reached the ground.

She climbed out the window and started down. The clawing wind made her swing from side to side across the cold granite facade. She'd never been afraid of riding, or of French troops, but she didn't like heights one bit. Determinedly she stared at the wall as she lowered herself. As long as she didn't look down, she would be all right.

Then the sheet began to rip. As she felt the vibration in her hands, her heart spasmed. A fall from this height would kill her. She looked down. One of the ledges was several feet below.

The last fibers of the sheet separated with a horrid rasping sound. Using all her tomboy strength, she jumped toward the narrow ledge, praying that she would be able to keep her footing when she landed.

The journey across the channel was a nightmare without end. Catherine's arms ached from bailing, and her eyes burned from the strain of her vigil. Luckily, a stiff wind was breaking up the clouds. The quarter moon appeared, the cool light revealing a small islet to the right. It was too far away to be a danger, but her gaze sharpened. Islets were often surrounded by vicious little companions. From the corner of her eye, she saw a boiling of water. "Hard left *now*!"

Michael obeyed, but not fast enough to save them from scraping the jagged reef. The rowboat shuddered and tilted to the left. A wave crashed in, soaking them both. Catherine blinked the water from her eyes. "Now *right*."

A few minutes of rowing brought them through the danger zone. Then Catherine bailed until most of the water had been removed. When she was finished, she asked, "Do you have any idea how close we are to Skoal?"

Michael paused, letting the oars drift. In the moments before clouds veiled the moon again, she saw his broad shoulders slump with fatigue. He answered, "Not far, I think. Listen."

She strained her ears. There was a heavy, throbbing undernote to the sounds of the night. "Breakers ahead."

"Good." He began rowing again. "If I've judged rightly, we'll land on Little Skoal, not far from Haldoran's house."

She turned to the bow again, frowning into the darkness. "How on earth can you tell?"

"Homing pigeon blood. A useful talent for a soldier."

She hesitated. "My heart wants to go after Amy right away, but my head says we should go to the castle for help."

"Perhaps. But it might take time to persuade anyone that Haldoran is a villain." His voice became grim. "Also, she'll be safer if we can take her out in a quiet raid rather than a pitched battle."

He was right; Catherine would not put it past her loathsome cousin to hurt Amy from sheer spite if he thought he was going to be defeated. She swallowed hard. "Onward to Ragnarok."

* * *

The laird came awake more easily this time. It was still dark, but there was a hint of dawn in the sky. He turned his head. Davin Penrose sat by the bed, his face drawn with concern.

The laird whispered, "H-how long since I sent for you?"

A smile of relief crossed Davin's face. "I got the message last evening, about eight hours ago."

Good. The laird had feared that days might have passed while he slept. "Catherine?"

"She disappeared," the constable said gravely. "We've searched the island, but there's no trace of her. She had been nursing you day and night. It seems likely that she went for a late walk the night before last and fell from a cliff."

"No!" Knowing his strength was limited, the laird chose his words carefully. "Clive kidnapped her daughter and blackmailed Catherine into sending away that so-called husband of hers."

Davin's brows rose. "So-called?"

"Her real husband's dead. This one is a friend or lover or something," the laird said impatiently. "The fellow came back to see Catherine. Clive found them together and captured 'em. He was planning to take them to Bone and hunt them down like rats."

"Good God!" Davin's face paled. "Once or twice yesterday, I thought I heard shots coming from Bone."

The laird closed his eyes, trying to control the unexpected rush of emotion. It might be too late. Catherine had deceived him, but . . . he'd grown fond of her.

"How did you learn all this?" the constable asked.

"Everyone talked in front of me as if I were already dead." The laird took a deep breath, struggling to organize what must be said. "Clive has Catherine's daughter at Ragnorak. Take some of the militamen and get her out. I don't know if Clive is there, but go armed. He's mad and dangerous. After you have the child, cross over to Bone and see if . . . Catherine and that fellow are alive. If she isn't . . ." His voice faded away.

Accepting the outrageous story without question, Davin got to his feet. "I'll be on my way as soon as I can collect half a dozen men. First Ragnarok, then Bone."

"Don't trust Clive."

"I never did." The constable turned and was gone.

The laird closed his eyes and tried not to weep. He was an old man. He should be used to loss by now.

There wasn't a single light visible on Skoal, though that wasn't surprising at this hour of the night. As they approached the island, Catherine sharpened her vigil, knowing that this last stretch was the most hazardous.

The currents worsened, whipping the boat back and forth. Michael was panting with exertion as he fought to keep them steady. The boom of the surf intensified, vibrating in her bones. The silhouette of an islet appeared ahead. She warned Michael and he managed to pull away, but a ferocious current grabbed the boat, sweeping it toward a jagged rock. She shouted another warning. The stony pinnacle loomed above her, almost close enough to touch. In the nick of time, Michael pulled them beyond the lethal obstacle.

The moon came out again, illuminating what lay ahead. "We're only a couple of hundred yards out," she reported. "From the sound of the breakers, it's a beach, but I can see boulders."

"Good," he said breathlessly. "That's what the shore is like on the south side of Little Skoal."

The surf caught the boat, hurling it toward land. They were close enough to see the pale, undulating lines of breaking waves. Catherine clamped her hands on the gunwales, frightened by the speed with which they were flying toward shore. One small part of her mind said that they would never survive this wild ride, while another said that Michael could do *anything*. The rest of her mind, and all of her body, was focused on watching what lay ahead.

Too late, she saw the rock lurking just below the surface. "Look out, to the right!"

As Michael tried to pull away, one oar crashed into the stone and shattered. He yelled, "Brace yourself!"

Out of control, the boat spun sideways and slammed into another rock. Catherine was almost pitched out by the impact. Water gushed in through the crushed planks.

But they were moving too quickly to sink. An immense surge of water swept them into the air with a wrench that turned her stomach. The boat seemed to hang endlessly. Then the wave smashed them onto the beach. The boat capsized and Catherine was thrown out. A vicious undertow dragged her back toward the sea, rolling her over and over along the seabed. She was drowning, helpless to break free . . .

Then Michael seized her and dragged her to her feet. "Get up! We're almost there!"

The waves fought to pull them under, but he kept her upright, his grip the one sure thing in a tumultuous world. The last stretch was interminable, a treacherous slope of stone and seaweed and crushing waves. Then suddenly they were beyond the reach of the water. They staggered a dozen steps farther before sinking to the ground, clinging to each other. Catherine felt as if her heaving lungs would burst through her chest.

Michael gasped, "Are you all right?"

She took stock of her aches and pains. "Some bruises, and a passionate desire never to board a boat again."

He gave a breathless chuckle. "Intrepid Catherine."

"No," she said firmly. "Cowardly, exhausted Catherine."

"We only have to keep going a little longer."

She left his embrace with reluctance. His touch made everything seem possible.

As they stood, she saw that Michael had managed to retain the smuggler's sword and the coiled rope. Amazing. "Do you recognize where we are?"

"I think that Ragnarok is less than half a mile away." He pulled off his jersey and wrung the excess water from it, then squeezed what moisture he could from his other garments. "It won't take us long to climb this hill and reach there."

"Then what?" Catherine asked as she wrung out her own jersey.

He smiled, his teeth a white, wolfish flash in the dark. "Then, my dear, we'll brave the dragon in his own den."

It took time for Davin to rouse a handful of the island's best militiamen. They gathered at the castle stables, where he handed out rifles and tersely explained the situation. His words were received with matter-of-fact nods. No one appeared to have trouble believing that Haldoran was a villain. On the other hand, Catherine and her husband—or whoever he was—had made a good impression on the islanders.

The men were harnessing horses to a flat wagon when a well-dressed stranger strolled into the stableyard. Davin raised his torch and stared at the man. "Who the devil are you?"

The newcomer's brows rose. "And a very pleasant good morning to you, too." The fellow was tall and brown-haired, with a voice as elegant as his clothing.

"Sorry, I didn't mean to be rude," Davin said, "but we're about to leave. There's some trouble."

The stranger sighed. "If there is trouble, my little brother is probably right in the middle of it. What's wrong?"

Brother? Davin studied the newcomer and realized that there was a distinct resemblance to the man who had been known as Catherine Melbourne's husband. Countering with another question, he said, "Who are you, and what are you doing here at this hour?"

"My name's Ashburton, and I came to the island last night. I believe my brother is visiting here. Since I'm acquainted with the laird, I decided to pay a call," the gentleman said rather vaguely. "Because of the storm, we arrived so late that the boatman who brought me over suggested I stay at his house. I woke early and decided to go for a stroll."

"If you say so," Davin said dryly.

Ashburton's gaze went over the wagon. "Do you need any help on this expedition of yours? I happen to have my traveling pistol with me."

Ashburton seemed sound, and if he was the brother of Catherine's alleged husband, he had a right to come along. "Climb aboard. I'll explain what little I know on the way to Ragnarok."

"The twilight of the gods?" Ashburton said, startled.

"I sincerely hope not." As the small band rattled toward Little Skoal at full speed, Davin hoped the name would not prove to be prophetic.

In spite of Catherine's fatigue, she was almost running when they approached Ragnorak. The sun rose early at this season, and the sky was lightening in the east.

More cautious, Michael held her back and made sure that they used what cover was available. As they neared the house, he said quietly, "Did Haldoran indicate where Amy is being held?"

Catherine thought back. "He said she was in one of the best guest rooms with a fine view of the sea."

"Then we'll go to the ocean side and see if we can deduce where she might be."

Stealthily they circled the house. Though the sky was brighter, the shadows were still dense. Catherine scanned the windows, wondering if maternal instinct could do what vision couldn't. Something long and pale was fluttering across the wall of the house. "Can you make out what that light-colored thing is?"

Michael looked where she pointed, then sucked in his breath. "It looks like a rope made of sheets. And below—Christ, I think that dark blob is Amy huddling on a ledge."

Catherine gasped and broke away from Michael to run to the house. At the foot of the wall, she called in a trembling voice, "Amy, is that you?"

"Mama!" The dark shape wavered. For a horrified instant Catherine thought her daughter was about to fall. Then the girl leaned back against the wall. "I . . . I'm stuck here."

Michael came to Catherine's side. "Keep your voices down!" Softly he went on, "It's Colonel Kenyon, Amy. Are you uninjured?"

"Yes, sir." There was a muffled sniff. "I was trying to escape."

"Brave girl. Stay where you are and I'll come get you."

"How can you do that?" Catherine asked, her throat tight.

Michael unlashed the rope. "I'll go up that tree on the corner. From there, I can throw a loop of rope over that stone thing under the roof and swing to Amy's ledge. Then I'll bring us down." He undid the sword and laid it on the ground.

She stared upward, barely able to see Amy, much less the "stone thing." There was a special horror in having Amy so close, yet in such danger. She said tightly, "Be careful."

He touched her shoulder for a moment. "I always am." Then he went to the tree and began climbing.

Catherine watched her daughter, so frightened she could scarcely breathe. Though Michael had made the rescue sound easy, she knew how perilous it would be. The rope might break, the stone thing might fail, someone might see them.

The two people she loved most were at risk, and all she could do was pray.

A strange cry brought Haldoran from his sleep. Not a gull, or any other form of local wildlife. He rose and went to his window. It was dawn. Time to get up, breakfast, and return to Bone. He looked forward to the day's hunt.

He saw a movement from the corner of his eye and turned to look more closely. What the devil?

A dark shape swooped recklessly across the wall, halting about halfway to the ground. *Kenyon!* And that was Catherine on the ground, the pale oval of her face tilted upward. Damnation. Not only had the pair of them somehow escaped Bone, but they had the audacity to come to Ragnarok.

The slowly increasing light enabled him to see that there was a second, small figure beside Kenyon. Amy. It looked like the brat had been trying to escape. She was as untrustworthy as her mother. Now he'd have to dispose of her as well.

Swiftly he turned and pulled his bell. He was already half dressed when Doyle appeared sleepily. "Get the other men up and dressed, and have them bring their weapons to the front hall *now*," he barked. "It's time to move in for the kill."

As Michael landed on the ledge by Amy, he said in a conversational tone, "What happened?"

"I made a rope of sheets and it broke." She wiped her smudged face with the back of her hand. "I managed to jump to this ledge, but I couldn't go either up or down."

"Have you been here long?"

"Forever!" Her voice quivered. "Last night Lord Haldoran told me Mama was dead, so I decided I must escape to find out if he was telling the truth."

The *bastard*. Michael muttered an oath that he should not have used in the presence of a child. Haldoran must be in the house, which made their situation even more perilous. Concealing his concern, he said calmly, "As you can see, he was lying."

"I could kill him for what he said!" There was nothing childlike in her voice.

"I'll do my best to kill him for you."

As he tested the line, she asked, "Why are you with Mama?"

Michael thought quickly to come up with an edited form of the truth. "Your mother was nervous about visiting Skoal. Since we're friends, she asked me to come with her."

Amy accepted that without comment.

He continued, "The fastest way down is for you to ride piggyback. It will be scary. Can you do it?"

She nodded vigorously. "Whatever it takes to get down!"

With a smile, he turned and crouched so she could mount. Though her slim body was icy cold, she wrapped her arms and legs around him tightly. "Ready?" he asked.

"Yes, sir."

He stepped from the ledge, Amy clinging like a monkey. The wind whipped at them, making the rope sway, and Amy's weight drastically unbalanced him. The slow descent became a test of pure strength, a resource that was in perilously short supply after days of virtually nonstop exertion. One hand at a time. Then another. Keep it smooth so Amy won't be jarred off. By the time his feet touched the ground, his palms were raw and his arms shaking with strain.

"Mama!" Amy jumped free and hurled herself into her weeping mother's arms.

Michael leaned against the wall and drew deep, shuddering breaths as he watched their reunion. What would it be like to experience such tender mutual love? He hoped Amy realized how lucky she was. It looked as if she did.

He turned and picked up his sword. "Time to be going. Haldoran is here, so we must get away without being seen."

"Yes, *sir*, Colonel." A wide grin on her face, Amy turned to him, her hand in her mother's. Catherine's face was glowing.

Even Michael allowed himself to feel hopeful as he led his charges away from the house. In a few more minutes, they would be safe. Only a few more minutes. . . .

Chapter 39

Though the sun was rising and objects were clearly visible, Michael didn't try to keep his small party behind cover. Speed was more important than stealth. After they crossed the Neck to Great Skoal, they would be able to disappear into the scrubby bushes, but until then they were vulnerable. He carried the sword in his hand, hoping it wouldn't be needed.

When the sound of crashing waves indicated that they were close to the Neck, he said, "Amy, did you come this way when Haldoran brought you to his house?"

She made a face. "The Neck. It's narrow and scary. I'm glad it's light enough to see the way across."

"Then you know to be careful."

"I will." She tightened her clasp on her mother's hand. "I don't like heights."

Catherine chuckled. "I'm afraid I don't, either, my love."

"Then it's fortunate you won't be crossing," a lazy voice drawled. There was sudden movement in the bushes on both sides of the track. Five men stepped onto the road, swaggering with the confidence of well-armed bullies. Haldoran and Doyle were on the left while the other three convicts stood directly in front of the fugitives, blocking the way to the Neck.

Knowing he had only an instant to act, Michael leaped at the convicts in front of him. His first sword stroke slashed the trigger hand of the man whose jaw he'd broken in their earlier encounter. Without pausing, he spun and stabbed the second convict in the shoulder. As the fellow reeled backward, Michael jerked his blade free and swung on the third convict, chopping deeply into the fellow's thigh. As his victim crumpled to the ground with a howl, Michael yelled, "Run!"

Catherine and Amy bolted through the gap Michael had

created and raced onto the Neck. Not wasting a glance after them, he turned to face his opponents.

The first three men hadn't yet recovered, but Doyle was aiming his rifle, murder in his eyes. As the gun blasted, Haldoran struck the flat of his sword on the barrel, sending the ball harmlessly into the earth. "Don't kill him!" he barked. "I want to do that myself."

He stalked forward, his blade raised and ready. The early morning light gleamed on the superb Saracen weapon he had wielded against Michael once before. "That point goes to you, Kenyon. You attacked as quickly as when I caught you and Catherine in the laird's bedroom. I should have remembered the tactic."

"If you weren't an amateur, you would have." Michael backed onto the Neck, watching the other man like a hawk. The eyes would signal the moment and direction of an attack.

Haldoran scowled. "I wish I could take my time, but I'll have to kill you quickly so we can catch Catherine and her brat."

"You'll have to come through me to get them," Michael said flatly. "That may be harder than you think."

"Oh?" Light-footed and eyes gleaming, Haldoran stepped onto the Neck. "I defeated you before and you weren't exhausted then. I know damned well you were goading me when you claimed later you'd let me win. This time, there will be no question of my victory." He lunged with lightning swiftness.

Warned by the flicker of his opponent's eyes, Michael parried. Fatigue had dulled his reflexes, and he barely managed to block the blow in time.

Haldoran responded with a series of brutally powerful thrusts. The blade glittered blood red in the rising sun as he slashed forward, nearly breaking through his opponent's guard. As Michael retreated, Haldoran sneered, "That isn't much of a sword. Where did you find it?"

"In a smuggler's cave. It's a standard-issue naval weapon," Michael panted. "A real soldier doesn't need elaborate weapons."

Haldoran struck again. When Michael warded off the blow, he was aided by the gusty wind, which kept his opponent off balance for a moment. Michael took advantage of the brief respite to glance over his shoulder. Catherine and

Amy had vanished. Profoundly relieved, he returned his attention to his enemy.

Exhaustion had dulled his wits, his speed, even his desire to survive. The only thing left was the steely core of skill forged in the hardest of schools. Endless drill and more skirmishes and battles than he could remember had taught him to strike, to parry, to lunge, even when his sword seemed too heavy to lift and his muscles trembled with strain.

They fought in grim silence, the ring of their weapons piercing the dark roar of the waves and the occasional cries of gulls. They were both sweating now. Though Haldoran was always on the verge of making a fatal thrust, he never quite succeeded. Somehow Michael's tired arm and leaden feet always managed to parry and withdraw before the other man could strike.

Michael found bleak satisfaction in his modest successes. He would not win this fight. Even if by some miracle he defeated Haldoran, he'd be shot by the waiting convicts. But every moment he endured gave Catherine and Amy more time to escape.

When he fell back another step, Haldoran snarled, "Stand, damn you! Fight like a gentleman, if you know how."

It was an enormous effort to answer, "All I can do is fight like a soldier—to win."

Enraged, Haldoran charged forward. The razor-sharp tip of the Saracen blade grazed Michael's forearm, slicing through the bulky jersey and probing for a vital spot. Hastily Michael retreated—and his right heel landed on open air. The Neck had tightened to its narrowest width, and completing the step would be fatal.

He twisted to the left like an acrobat. The movement saved him from going over the cliff, but he ended sprawling on the edge of the precipice.

Haldoran smiled with vicious satisfaction. "Say your prayers, Kenyon." He stabbed down toward Michael's throat.

Barely in time, Michael raised his sword to block his opponent's blow. The Saracen blade struck the naval sword with a ringing shriek and splintered the inferior metal. Most of the blade spun away, leaving him with a hilt and a ragged steel stub.

His mind accepted that the end had come, but his trained body was incapable of surrender. He grabbed a fistful of pebbles with his left hand and hurled them into his enemy's face. Haldoran swore and fell back, clawing at his eyes. As he did, Michael made a sweeping motion with his left leg. His ankle smashed into the other man's legs.

Haldoran fell sideways. Michael raised himself to his knees and struck his opponent's sword hand with the viciously edged stub of his own weapon, severing the tendons. Haldoran cried out as the sword fell from his grasp. For the first time, his face showed fear. Growling like an animal, he kicked the broken sword from Michael's grasp. Then he dived forward and locked his good hand on Michael's throat.

They began wrestling feverishly, rolling back and forth on the brink of the precipice. But the balance of power had shifted. Berserker wildness surged through Michael, carrying him beyond fatigue and fear to a place where action was all. Relentlessly he forced Haldoran back toward the cliff.

As their locked bodies teetered on the edge, Michael stared into his enemy's eyes, seeing the fear grow. He spat out, "*Amateur.*" Then he broke Haldoran's hold with a violent thrust that propelled the other man toward the edge.

Haldoran grabbed at Michael, for support or to take them both to their deaths, but Michael chopped the other man's wrist with the edge of his hand. Fingers still scrabbling desperately, Haldoran pitched into space. He screamed all the way down, his terror reverberating from the cliffs and hills, until the sound ended with horrifying finality.

It was victory, of a sort. But as Michael lifted his head and saw the gun barrels aimed at him, he knew that the end had finally arrived.

At least he was dying for a reason. *Live long, Catherine, and live well.*

Catherine and her daughter took cover in the shrubbery when they reached the far end of the Neck. As they fell to their knees, gulping for breath, Catherine cautiously parted the branches so they could see what was happening. There had been no more gunshots. Was that a good sign, or did it mean that Michael had fallen?

She caught her breath as she saw Haldoran lunge at Michael with a sword. As Michael threw off the blow, Amy whispered, "Will Colonel Kenyon win?"

"I don't know. He's a wonderful fighter, but he's been performing superhuman feats for days. He's exhausted while Haldoran is fresh." Catherine flinched as her cousin's blade swept toward Michael's belly. Michael evaded the slash by a hair's breadth and fell back again. The duelists were halfway across the Neck, and two of Haldoran's men were advancing a safe distance behind, their guns ready.

Tears running unnoticed down her face, Catherine said painfully, "We must leave now. When the fight ends, Haldoran's men will come after us no matter who wins."

"I call them the trolls. They're awful." Amy made a face of disgust. "We can't abandon Colonel Kenyon, Mama."

"We have to, love, or his sacrifice will be wasted."

"I won't go," Amy said flatly. "You know how good I am at throwing things. I think I can hit the trolls from here."

Catherine stared at her daughter's face. There was a warrior light in Amy's eyes. She had never looked more like her father. And it was certainly true that her tomboy daughter had demonstrated a fine throwing arm when playing cricket.

As a mother, Catherine would do anything to preserve her child. Yet honor and loyalty mattered, too. A fatalistic calm descended on her. If they left without doing whatever they could for Michael, neither of them would be able to forgive herself. "Then let's gather some stones."

There was no shortage of rocks on Skoal. They collected a pile, then watched tensely as the duel continued. Catherine laid a warning hand on her daughter's arm. "If Michael is . . . is killed, we must run to the right, down this hill. There are enough bushes to cover us. With luck, Haldoran will think we followed the road."

Amy hefted one of the stones in her hand. "But if the colonel wins, we're ready for the trolls."

Catherine gave an anguished cry when Michael fell and his sword shattered. As the two men wrestled, there was a horrifying moment when it looked as if both would go over the edge. Then suddenly Haldoran was hurtling downward, tumbling through the air until he crashed into the pitiless, wave-tossed rocks below.

There was a moment of absolute stillness, in which the only sound was the eternal wind and the crying gulls. Then Amy wound up and threw. Her stone flew swift and true to slam into the cheek of Doyle, who was on the verge of shooting. The man bellowed and his rifle jerked, the ball kicking up dirt a yard away from Michael.

Catherine hurled her own stone. It bounced once, then hit the knee of another troll who was leveling his gun at Michael. Though the impact wasn't great, it was enough to spoil the fellow's aim. Michael crouched and began a laborious retreat toward Great Skoal, staying low to keep out of the path of the missiles.

The thundering wheels of a fast-moving vehicle sounded behind Catherine. Who on earth would be coming to Little Skoal at this hour, and at such a speed? She glanced over her shoulder and saw a wagon with half a dozen men careening toward the Neck. Then she looked back to see if Michael had reached safety.

The barrage of rocks had baffled and confused the three wounded men to the point where they were no longer a threat. Tougher and more determined, Doyle had dropped to the ground behind a large rock. The only thing visible from Catherine's position was his rifle barrel, which was swinging toward Michael. Dear God, after surviving so much, Michael couldn't be killed now, he *couldn't*.

The wagon stopped and a shot rang out, the report rolling across the hills. Doyle's rifle jerked. Then his body rolled out from behind the boulder, blood pouring from his skull.

A deep voice shouted, "If you others want to live to see another dawn, throw down your weapons!"

Almost beyond shock, Catherine looked up to see Davin Penrose standing in the wagon. A curl of smoke rose from the rifle in his hands. She had not realized how commanding the constable could be. How much like their mutual grandfather.

"Thank God," she whispered. "Oh, thank God." Shakily she stood and walked from the shrubbery, Amy beside her. "Michael?"

He lurched to his feet and walked the last steps from the Neck to Great Skoal. In spite of being damp, rumpled, and unshaven, he was the most beautiful sight imaginable. She embraced him, tears of relief in her eyes. He was alive. *Alive.*

"We did it." He hugged her back for a moment, then released her. "We took on the Napoleon of Skoal and won."

"Not *we.* You." She tilted her head back. There was so much she wanted to say that she didn't know where to begin.

The moment to speak ended when their rescuers approached. Most of the Skoalans went to collect Haldoran's remaining men, but Davin and another man came to the battered band of fugitives. The second fellow, a tall, fashionably dressed stranger, said, "What happened to your arm, Michael?"

Bemused, Michael looked down at a crimson-drenched sleeve. "Haldoran cut deeper than I thought when he slashed my jersey. His blade was so sharp I didn't notice." His brows came together. "What the devil are you doing here, Stephen?"

Stephen. Catherine studied him with interest. With that name and face, he had to be Michael's brother.

The duke said, "Your rather cryptic note made me decide to see what was happening here." He regarded the bloody sleeve uneasily. "Shouldn't you do something about that?"

"If you'll contribute your cravat, I'll bandage it," Catherine said to the duke.

Wordlessly he unwound the snowy length of linen and gave it to her. For what seemed like the thousandth time, she started to bandage Michael.

He gave a tired smile. "Stephen, allow me to introduce Catherine and Amy Melbourne. Nurse extraordinaire and champion hurler, respectively. That's an amazing arm you have, Amy. Your father would be proud of you."

The girl smiled with pleasure.

Catherine tied off the bandage. "I've never been so happy to see anyone in my life, Davin. How did you know to come here at such a fortunate time?"

"The laird overheard a good deal when he was semiconscious," the constable explained. "Early this morning, he woke up enough to tell me what he thought was going on."

"He's that much better? Thank heaven." Catherine draped an arm around Amy's shoulders.

Davin gave Michael a cool glance. "The laird said you're not Colin Melbourne. If this fellow is your brother, I assume your name is Ashburton."

"I'm Michael Kenyon. Ashburton is Stephen's title."

Davin's expression blanked. "As in the Duke of Ashburton?"

"Yes," the duke admitted. "But you needn't look like that. I scarcely ever bite."

Michael sighed and ran a hand through his rumpled hair. "I'm sorry about the deception, Davin. For what it's worth, the military experience is real. Catherine and I are friends from the army, which is why she asked me to accompany her to Skoal."

Before Catherine could say more, the duke said, "Instead of standing about talking, we should drive these exhausted folk back to the castle before it starts to rain again. The laird will be anxious to know what happened."

"An excellent notion," Michael muttered. He was weaving on his feet. Catherine wanted to go to him, but it was Stephen's hand that steadied his brother and helped him into the wagon.

On the ride back to the castle, Michael lay flat on the planks, his face gray and his eyes closed. Almost equally tired, Catherine sat against the side of the wagon, hugging Amy close. Quietly she told her daughter everything that had happened, including the fact that Haldoran had murdered Colin.

Amy took the news stony-faced. Her only comment was, "I wish I'd killed Lord Haldoran myself." Then she cuddled against her mother for the rest of the trip.

Catherine settled back with a sigh. Against all the odds, they had been spared. Yet underneath her relief was a rueful wish that she didn't have to face her grandfather.

Chapter 40

The laird was propped up against the pillows, looking much like his old self, when the rescued party was ushered in. "So you were in time, Davin. Well done." His gaze went to the duke. "What the devil are you doing here, Ashburton?"

"Just passing by," the duke murmured, amusement in his eyes. "Pretend I'm a fly on the wall."

Taking the duke at his word, the laird listened intently as Kevin gave a terse description of events. When the constable finished, Catherine said hesitantly, "I don't know if I'm welcome here, Grandfather, but I'm glad you're so much improved." She drew Amy forward. "This is your great-granddaughter, Amy."

The laird scowled at the girl. "Wearing breeches like your disgraceful mother. You look like her, too. Are you equally pigheaded?"

Amy raised her chin. "Worse."

"Then I expect we'll get along. Come here, both of you."

Overwhelmed with relief, Catherine went to her grandfather's bedside and kissed him. "I'm truly sorry for deceiving you."

The laird patted her hand awkwardly, then studied Amy's face. After giving a nod of approval, his gaze went to Michael, who was leaning wearily against the wall. "Since you're not Colin Melbourne, who the hell are you?"

"Michael Kenyon, formerly of the 95th Rifles."

"He's also *Colonel* Kenyon of the 105th," Amy added, wanting to be sure the importance of that wasn't missed.

"And my only brother," the duke volunteered.

The laird's shaggy brows rose before he retorted, "I don't care if he's a bloody major-general. Lord Michael has compromised my granddaughter."

Michael's gaze flicked to Catherine and away. "Yes."

She hated to think that all of the kindness they had

shared could be reduced to the damning word "compromised." Coolly she said, "I'm a twenty-eight-year-old widow, not a girl from the schoolroom, Grandfather. Any fault is entirely mine. Mr. Harwell said you wouldn't leave Skoal to a single woman. Since Colin was recently dead, I asked Michael to masquerade as my husband. He was extremely reluctant to enter into such a deception, but I begged him to help. His behavior has always been honorable."

"I was less reluctant than Catherine implies," Michael said dispassionately. "When she saved my life after Waterloo, I gave her carte blanche to ask anything of me."

There was nothing remotely loverlike in the statement. She wondered what was in his mind.

The laird sighed. "Harwell was right—I didn't want to leave Skoal to a single woman. However, now that I've met you, I know you'll take good care of the island." He smiled sourly. "Besides, I've no other choice, now that Clive is dead. I was never comfortable with the idea of him as laird. I should have listened to my instincts." He looked at Amy. "Someday you might be the Lady of Skoal, if your mother doesn't have a son. You'll need that stubbornness then."

Catherine gasped, stunned that her grandfather was willing to make her his heir in spite of all that had happened. Even if Michael didn't want her, she and Amy would have independence, a comfortable income, an honorable position in the world.

She looked out the window at the wild, windswept beauty of the island. *Lady of Skoal.* She had lied and deceived to achieve this goal, yet her victory tasted like ashes. It was time to make amends. Other widows managed to care for their children without inheriting an island, and she could do the same.

She looked at her grandfather again. "Haldoran told me that Davin is Harald's son. That's true, isn't it?"

Dead silence dropped over the room and Davin's face went rigid. The laird took a deep breath. "Yes, it's true. It's an open secret on the island."

"Then you do have another choice." She moistened her dry lips. "Davin should be the next laird. He knows and loves every inch of the island. It is he who is the true heir to the ancient traditions of Skoal. It would be wrong for me to take that away from him." She looked at her daughter. "I think Amy would agree with me." Amy gave a silent nod.

Her grandfather's fists clenched on the counterpane. "I considered him, but dammit, Davin is a bastard."

"You take great pride in the island's Viking past, Lord Skoal," Michael said unexpectedly. "The customs of the Northmen were different from those of Southern Europe. William the Conqueror was of Nordic stock. His parents weren't married, which is why he was also called William the Bastard. Yet he was a great warrior and king." His eyes narrowed. "Why should the twenty-seventh Laird of Skoal refrain from doing what he knows is right because of petty English customs?"

Catherine silently applauded. Michael was living proof that dubious parentage was no measure of a man's worth.

The duke added, "It might even be possible to arrange for Mr. Penrose to receive the title. The Prince Regent owes me a favor or two."

The laird drummed his fingers on the bed as the silence stretched. Finally he gave a rasping chuckle. "Maybe you're right. Very well, Davin it is. He's already bred sons to follow him, and I won't have to worry about whether he'll decide to move to some more fashionable place."

Davin gasped. His face was ashen, and in his eyes was the expression of a man being offered what he had never dared hope for. "I've never asked or expected anything of you, my lord, not even acknowledgment of my blood."

"I know. That's one reason I have such respect for you," the laird said gruffly. "You've served me and the island faithfully, with never a word of complaint or self-pity. When the time comes, you'll make a good laird, but you need to work on your temper. It won't do to be too reasonable."

Catherine gave a choke of laughter. "I'm sure you've never had to worry about that, Grandfather."

He glared at her. "I'll have no impertinence from you, miss. You've behaved disgracefully, and the only way to right things is to marry Kenyon."

Her levity vanished and her gaze went to Michael. His face showed no reaction to the laird's outrageous statement. "It's been only three months since Colin's death," she said uncertainly. "It would be most improper to consider remarriage."

"Marrying too soon is less scandalous than what you've been doing," her grandfather snapped. "Kenyon?"

"Naturally I am willing to do my duty," Michael said expressionlessly. "However, I don't know if Catherine or her daughter would accept such an arrangement."

"She'll consent—she's a good example of why a woman needs a husband to keep her in line. If you can command a regiment, I suppose you can manage her, at least most of the time. Catherine, are you going to balk like a mule or behave as a decent woman ought?"

She bit her lip. This was all wrong—yet it was also what she desperately wanted. Perhaps it would be best to agree to a betrothal now. It could always be ended. She glanced at her daughter. "Are you willing to have Michael as your stepfather?"

"If you don't marry someone, beasts like Lord Haldoran will keep trying to abduct you." Amy studied Michael critically, then grinned. "I'd choose you over anyone except Uncle Charles, and of course he's married to Aunt Anne. You'll do."

"I'm very flattered," Michael said gravely.

Her throat dry, Catherine said, "Then . . . I'm willing if you are."

"That's settled," the laird said. "Both of you come over here and I'll perform the ceremony. Davin, Ashburton, you can stand witness."

Catherine's jaw dropped. "We can't get married without banns or a special license or a vicar!"

Her grandfather gave a wicked smile. "The Laird of Skoal has the power to perform weddings, and considering the mischief you've gotten into, the sooner you two are riveted, the better."

It's too soon! But Michael was leaving his position by the wall to stand by the laird's bed. In a daze, Catherine joined him. In a last effort to stop this madness, she said feebly, "We don't have a ring."

The duke promptly pulled a ring off his little finger and gave it to Michael. "That's easily remedied."

The laird grasped Catherine's icy left hand and Michael's right and began the ceremony. At the end, he joined their hands together. "I now pronounce you man and wife, and may you bear strong sons together."

Amy said under her breath, "That's a silly ceremony. What about daughters?"

Ignoring her, the laird said, "You can kiss the bride now, Kenyon. I don't imagine it's for the first time."

There was a pause that seemed to stretch forever. Then Michael's lips touched Catherine's, cool and passionless. Releasing her hand, he said, "Now that the pressing business is out of the way, I'd like to be excused so I can sleep twelve or fourteen hours."

"Me, too," Catherine said in an unsteady voice.

The laird sighed and leaned back against the pillows. "I need rest also. It's been quite a day. Davin, see that rooms are made up for Amy and Ashburton."

After shaking his brother's hand and offering hearty congratulations, Ashburton embraced Catherine. "Welcome to the family." There was far more warmth in his voice than there had been in Michael's. Turning to Amy, he said, "It looks like we may be the only ones awake soon. Since I'm now an uncle of sorts, shall we further our acquaintance? Perhaps the constable can find someone to give us a tour of Skoal."

"I'd like that," Amy said. "Can we also get my things from Lord Haldoran's house?"

Davin said, "The head groom will be glad to oblige. I'd do it myself, but . . . but I must tell Glynis what has happened." He swallowed hard. "Thank you, Catherine. I'm still stunned that anyone could be so generous."

"Not generous. Just." She stood on her toes and brushed a light kiss on his cheek. "I hope you'll let us visit. I've grown very fond of the island."

He smiled with a warmth that touched his aqua island eyes. "You will always be welcome on Skoal, and in my home."

Everyone left the laird's chamber in a group. After hugging Amy, Catherine turned and accompanied a silent Michael upstairs to the chamber they had shared. He seemed farther away than when she had been on Skoal and he was on the mainland.

As soon as they entered the room, they separated, Michael going to the window to look out at the soft gray rain and Catherine glancing in the mirror. Lord, she was a wreck, with circles under her eyes and hair rioting from her single braid. No one would think her beautiful now.

Nervously she untied her braid and combed her fingers through the tangled locks. Needing to break the killing silence, she said, "That's all you have to wear, isn't it? You and your brother are about the same size. Do you think he would lend you some clothing?"

"Probably." He opened the window to let in the cool rain-scented air. "I'll have to send a message to Lucien to tell him that everything is all right. Otherwise he'll be down here taking Skoal apart in a few days."

As conversation it wasn't much, but at least he was talking. She looked at her oversized wedding ring. It was a gold signet bearing what must be the Kenyon arms. The duke's seal of approval on the marriage. But what about Michael's? Voice low, she said, "So much has happened in the last few days. It's hard to believe we're actually husband and wife."

Michael's breathing changed to a harsh wheeze that made her blood freeze. She whirled around and found him bent over, one hand clinging to the bedpost and the other pressed to his chest. "Dear God, Michael," she exclaimed. "What's wrong?"

"Mild . . . asthma attack," he panted. "Just need. Fresh air." He managed the two steps to a window and threw open the casements so he could draw the cool sea air into his lungs.

Catherine poured a glass of water from the pitcher on the washstand and took it to him. "Would you like a drink?"

He emptied the glass in two swallows. After handing it back, he turned and slid to the floor, supported against the wall. His face was gray with strain and the pulse at the base of his throat was beating like a trip-hammer. "I'm fine. Really. But, Christ, the second asthma attack in a week. I'm falling apart."

Catherine knelt beside him, watching his face like a nurse as well as a wife. "The second?"

"I had a much worse one when Stephen found me in Great Ashburton." The skin tightened over his cheekbones. "That one was as bad as when my mother died."

Painfully aware that this attack must have been triggered by her remark about them being husband and wife, Catherine said carefully, "Is this one a result of general exhaustion and stress, or is it because you don't wish to be married to me?"

He gazed at her with bleak honesty, too tired to conceal anything. "I've never wanted anything more in my life than for you to be my wife."

Her heart began to beat in triple time. "You've *wanted* to marry me? You weren't acting from duty?"

"In this case, duty and inclination went together."

Wanting desperately to understand, she asked, "Then why do you look as if you've just been sentenced to be hanged?"

His lips curved in a travesty of a smile. "I'm rather good at mayhem, but I don't know much about being happy."

She realized that he was telling her the exact truth. Though Michael had a great capacity to love and be loved, he had never had the chance to truly express it. If she could reach him now, begin to heal his wounded spirit, he would be hers forever.

Praying for the right words, she said slowly, "When I was full of fear, a wise man told me that my fears weren't created in an hour, and they wouldn't be healed in an hour. The same is true for damaged hearts."

She leaned forward and kissed him with aching tenderness. "Because you were wise and kind, you cured me of my fear. Let me do the same for you, Michael. Your heart was not damaged in a day, and it won't be healed in a day. But let me love you, and I promise that in time you will come to like it."

Michael made a raw sound in his throat and pulled her into his arms, holding her with rib-bruising force. "All my life, no matter how hard I tried, I was never good enough," he whispered. "It's easy to believe that will always be true. I sacrificed honor and decency for a false love. After that kind of criminal folly, does one get a second chance?"

Catherine raised her head so she could look into his eyes. "You said that the friend who betrayed you gave you a second chance at friendship," she said softly. "Your brother has given you a second chance at family. Why can't you have a second chance at love? If anyone has ever deserved it, it's you. I've never known another man with such strength and character and kindness. I fell in love with you in Brussels, even though it would have been wrong to say the words aloud."

He drew her into his arms again, feeling an intensity of emotion so great that he did not know if it was pleasure or pain. "When I first met you in Brussels, I felt as if a mountain had fallen on me," he said haltingly. "You filled my thoughts and mind from the beginning, even though I hated myself for becoming obsessed by a married woman. I took secret comfort in knowing that your blood flowed in my veins—when I yearned for you the most, I could tell myself that you were with me."

"I was," she said quietly. "In spirit, if not in body."

Closing his eyes, he simply held her for a long time. Catherine was warm and giving and offering her love. The only thing that stood between them was his inability to accept it. He opened his eyes and released her from his embrace. "Let's go to bed, Catherine. After I've slept, I might be more sane."

He stood and helped her to her feet. Then he halted, his gaze going past her to the sky outside. The rain had stopped and arcing through the heavens was a rainbow, as transcendently beautiful as Catherine herself.

He stared at it, and in a single instant the alienated fragments of his spirit fell into place. In a world that contained rainbows and kittens and friends like Nicholas, why was it so hard to believe that with Catherine he could find love? At the very core of his being, he felt a slowly blossoming peace unlike anything he had ever known.

He put his hands on Catherine's shoulders as she studied him with searching aqua eyes. "I always thought of my kaleidoscope as holding shattered rainbows and broken dreams," he said quietly. "Looking inside it was a way of seeking order out of chaos. But I don't need that anymore. Look."

She followed his glance out the window. The rainbow still shimmered, heaven's promise to the earth. He continued, "It's you who brings order into my life, Catherine. Order, and love."

"Then it appears that we love each other. How simple, and how right." Her eyes filled with joy, she raised her face and kissed him. It was not an embrace of raging lust or desperation. Instead, it simply *was*, an interval of peace and gentle communion such as they had not had a chance to experience in the turbulence of the past days.

With peace came exhaustion. He released her, saying, "Now, my dear, let's go to bed and sleep for a day or two."

Her smile turned mischievous. "And we're finally sleeping together legally."

"A pity I'm too tired to behave like a bridegroom."

"There will be time enough for that later." She covered a yawn, then began stripping off her clothing.

He did the same, moving by rote because he was unable to take his eyes from her. She had always been lovely beyond belief, but now she was his wife. His *wife*. She raised her arm to push back her hair, exposing the faint transfusion scar on the inside of her elbow. He felt a wave of tenderness that began in his heart and swiftly expanded to suffuse through his whole body. For as long as he lived, the gift of life she had given would be part of him.

She slid under the bedcovers, giving him a quizzical glance to see why he was delaying. He smiled wryly. "Do you know, I may not be quite as tired as I thought."

She reached out one hand, her smile rainbow-radiant. "Then come to bed, my love, and we'll find out."

Epilogue

Isle of Skoal
Spring 1817

The christening had gone off with considerable decorum. Louis the Lazy attended, but he was a very well behaved dog. Even the guest of honor had given only one small, startled squawk when cold water was dripped on his head. The party that followed, however, was best described as a roaring good time.

Since the day was warm, Catherine sat in the shade with several of the other women. The newly christened Nicholas Stephen Torquil Kenyon was passed from lap to lap, reveling in the attention. On the far side of the garden, a casual game of cricket was being played on the smooth emerald lawn. Nearer to hand, a baby corral had been set up for the smaller children.

Clare shaded her eyes with one hand. "Catherine, that daughter of yours is dangerous with a ball in her hand. If Oxford took women, they'd recruit her for their cricket team."

Catherine laughed. "Amy's game isn't hurt by the fact that the umpire is her great-grandfather and he looks ready to whack his cane over anyone who fails to appreciate her." It was amazing how well the laird had recovered. The wheelchair was a thing of the past, and he got around beautifully with only a slight limp. Publicly acknowledging Davin as his grandson and heir had given the laird a new lease on life.

Catherine continued, "I've never seen a cricket match with so many peers and peeresses playing."

Clare chuckled and patted her rounded stomach. "I'm glad I've got a good excuse not to play. Kit and Margot are both far more athletic than I."

The next batsman was Kit Fairchild, the slender brunette whom Catherine had once seen in the park with Michael. She stepped up to the wicket and swung her bat menacingly. The bowler was her husband, Lucien. With a gentlemanly desire to avoid damaging his wife, he gave the ball a soft toss. For his pains he was forced to duck swiftly when Kit blasted the ball to the far end of the garden. Four runs were scored before Davin Penrose managed to catch the ball and hurl it back.

Lady Elinor Fairchild, two years old and blond as a sunbeam, gave a crow of delight and headed for her mother with impressive speed. As dark as she was blond, Kenrick Davies, Viscount Tregar, set out after her. At two and a half, he was in the throes of his first love affair, with Elinor the object of his adoration.

Scenting excitement, Louis the Lazy lurched to his feet and went galumphing after the children. The ball flew over his head. To the shock of everyone present, he uncharacteristically leaped into the air, ears flying, and caught the speeding cricket ball. Amid general laughter, it was agreed that it was time to take a break and sample the refreshments that were being laid out on tables. As Rafe pointed out, it would give the ball time to dry out.

Clare rose and went to collect her husband and son, who were rolling around in the grass together. There couldn't be another earl in England as easygoing as Nicholas. Catherine was delighted to have her son named after him. Living across the valley from Clare and Nicholas was one of the loveliest benefits of her marriage.

Michael abandoned his fielding position and went against the hungry crowd to join Catherine, who had stayed lazily in her chair, her baby in her lap. She watched her husband approach with pure pleasure. Even after a year of marriage, she was not tired of admiring his face, or the powerful body that she knew so well. The thought made her face warm.

Michael grinned. "Having unsaintly thoughts, my dear?"

She glanced around. Luckily no one else was within earshot. "You know me too well."

"Never that." He dropped a kiss on her forehead, then on their son's, before settling on the grass beside her chair. "Your suggestion of having the christening here was brilliant. Skoal is a perfect place for a spring holiday."

"A pity that Kenneth couldn't come, but it's lovely that

so many of your other friends are here." Catherine's gaze went to dark Rafe and golden Margot, who were retrieving their nine-month-old son. The infant marquess, as dark as his father, waved his hands and gurgled cheerfully when his mother scooped him up.

"You Fallen Angels have a very handsome lot of babies," she observed. "I wonder if the children will be as good friends as their fathers are."

Michael smiled at the sight of Kenrick and Elinor, who were stickily sharing an ice under the indulgent supervision of their mothers. "I'm sure the next generation will be friends, but they won't need each other as much as their fathers did."

She stroked her hand through her husband's hair. Thank God for the Fallen Angels, and for the friendship that had helped them become the remarkable men they were. Most of all, thank God for Michael, who gave her more love and tenderness than she had known existed. "Do you remember our first evening on Skoal, when you woke me up to go down to dinner?"

He gave her a wicked glance. "How could I forget? It was all I could do to prevent myself from making a meal of you."

Her cheeks burned again. "You woke me out of the most wonderful dream."

Michael made an encouraging noise.

"I dreamed that I was normal, that you were my husband, and that we were expecting our first child." She bent forward and kissed Michael with the love that grew greater with every day they spent together. "Who says that dreams can't come true?"

Historical Note

Experiments in blood transfusion date from the seventeenth century. Many involved transfusion from animals to humans, on the theory that since men ate roast beef, they could perfectly well accept the blood of calves. It didn't work, of course. Subsequent human-to-human experiments had results that were erratic, to say the least. Practical transfusion had to wait until Karl Landsteiner's discovery of blood groups in 1901.

Nonetheless, in 1873 a study was done of 243 transfusions from the previous half century. According to the data, forty percent resulted in complete recovery. Obviously there was a high degree of blind luck involved (I described the techniques used to a hematologist and a vascular surgeon, both of whom were horrified), but in at least some cases transfusions probably did save lives. (Michael is AB positive, a universal recipient, for those of you who were wondering.)

Michael's 105th Regiment was fictional. However, the remarkable courage of the men who held their ground and died at Waterloo was not.

The island of Skoal is also fictional, but many of its characteristics are modeled on the Channel Island of Sark, which claims to be the last feudal enclave in the world.

Louis the Lazy was real. Who could possibly dream up such a basset hound?

Also Coming in February

"So, the day of reckoning has finally arrived." A wicked glint brightened Lady Sophia Tremayne's sharp old eyes. "You have danced to your own tune for thirty years, my lad, but the time has come to pay the piper."

Jared Neville Tremayne, eighth Duke of Montford, Marquess of Brynhaven, and various other titles too numerous to mention, raised his quizzing glass and stared down his elegant nose at the crusty old woman. Lady Sophia was both his aunt and his godmother, and one of the few people in all of England rash enough to address him with such a lack of deference.

"If there is a point to that obscure statement, Lady Sophia, please make it and be done with it," he said stiffly. In truth, he knew all too well what her point was; it was the very reason he had given up his morning to this duty call on the two old tabbies who inhabited this stuffy, overfurnished town house in Grosvenor Square. More to the point, it was what had afforded him countless sleepless nights during the past month and soured his outlook on every aspect of his formerly pleasant existence.

Lady Sophia matched her godson's haughty stare with one of her own, and the temperature in the small salon chilled at least ten degrees. "My point is, Your Grace, I remember a promise you made your dying grandfather some ten years ago, and I feel it my duty to inquire how and when you intend to honor it." She raised a questioning eyebrow. "You do remember the promise of which I speak?"

"Of course he does, Sophie. The dear boy has a memory every bit as retentive as your own. I'm the only one in the family so dreadfully forgetful." Lady Cloris Tremayne, lace cap askew and ribbons flying, fluttered through the open doorway like a small, bright-colored moth to perch on the rose velvet settee next to her austerely gowned sister. "What is it he is supposed to remember?"

"That today is his thirtieth birthday, of course, and—"

"Thirty years! I simply cannot credit it. Why, it seems only yesterday I was listening to him recite his sums." She fixed her nephew with her usual vague, sweet smile. "I suppose, my dear, I must try to remember to address you as 'Your Grace' from now on."

"And," Lady Sophia continued, scowling at her chatty sister, "he promised the old duke he would make a suitable marriage in his thirtieth year, if he had not already done so, and produce an heir."

"A family wedding! How delightful!" Lady Cloris's faded blue eyes took on a new sparkle. "And what a stroke of fortune that my friend Lady Hargrave taught me to knit last spring while we were chaperoning dear little Lady Lucinda's dance classes. I shall have no trouble at all keeping Jared's children in caps and mittens." She smiled shyly at her nephew. "Is she exceedingly lovely and good-natured?"

The duke frowned. "Who, my lady aunt?"

"Why, the girl you have in mind to marry."

"I have no one in mind," he said tersely. "No one at all. In fact, considering the disastrous marital history of the previous dukes of Montford, I am more inclined to remain a bachelor forever." He raised his hand to forestall the objection he could see forming on Lady Sophia's tightly pursed lips. "Be assured, you need not remind me of my obligation to secure the title, my lady. I am fully aware of my responsibilities, and if nothing else, the thought that that blithering fool, cousin Percival, is next in line to inherit would compel me to set up my nursery."

Crossing one impeccable buckskin-clad leg over the other, the duke surveyed his two elderly relatives through narrowed eyes. He had learned one sad fact during the soul-searching month he had just endured—an awareness of his obligations to the title did not make the idea of taking on a set of leg shackles one whit easier.

He was an intensely private man; the last thing he needed was some silly female cluttering up his life. Not that he lacked appreciation for the gentler sex—he'd had a series of very engaging mistresses in the ten years since he had reached his majority and had thoroughly enjoyed every one of them . . . for a brief time. But a mistress didn't live in a man's house and share this table; nor did she have the right to expect him to spend the season in London when he would much rather be at one of his country estates—and when a man's passion for a mistress abated, he had only to present her with a suitably expensive bauble and send her on her way. It was not so easy to dispose of a wife!

He sighed deeply. But as the Duke of Montford, he was obliged to produce a legitimate heir and to accomplish that, he must take a wife. At times like this he found himself wondering if the obligations of nobility didn't sometimes outweigh the privileges.

But, to the business at hand. His two aunts were already eyeing him speculatively, and he schooled himself to hide his seething frustration behind the mask of aristocratic indifference he had inherited along with the ancient title.

"I am aware the time has come when I must marry," he said as dispassionately as if he were discussing changing the method of tying his cravat. "But since I have no inclination to expend a great deal of effort on the tedious business, I was hoping I could count on the two of you to take care of the preliminaries for me. It is the sort of thing I feel would best be handled by a woman, but somehow I cannot picture any of my bird-witted female cousins rising to the task."

"What preliminaries?" both ladies asked simultaneously.

"A list, if you will, of whom you consider the five most eligible young women to come out this season. Nothing less than an earl's daughter, of course, but spare me those two horse-faced creatures spawned by the Duke of Ashford. The ladies' bloodlines may be unexceptionable, but I should not care to risk producing progeny with features so closely resembling one of my prize stallions."

The duke momentarily toyed with his quizzing glass, then thrust it impatiently into the pocket of his fawn-colored satin vest. "I am leaving this afternoon for the races at Newmarket," he said, brushing an offending speck of lint from the sleeve of his beautifully tailored coat of forest green superfine, "but I shall plan to inspect the candidates when I return and consequently make my choice."

"And just where do you propose to 'inspect' these candidates, Your Grace?" Lady Sophia asked acidly. "At Almack's? You have not entered the halls of that hallowed establishment in years. If you should do so now unannounced, the hostesses would undoubtedly all be taken with apoplexy."

Montford's stern mouth curved in what, in a less imposing man, might have been thought humor. "Never fear, my lady. I am not *that* anxious to conclude the business at hand."

He crossed to the window and stood for a moment looking at the small formal garden at the rear of the town house. "Arrange a house party, in my name, at Brynhaven and invite all five of them, with their parents, for a fortnight's stay beginning Friday next. That is where I shall expect my"—he nearly strangled on the word—"wife to live until she produces the necessary heir, so it will be well to observe them in that venue."

"Let me see if I have the straight of this," Lady Sophia said. "You refuse to shop for your bride at the season's social functions like the rest of the eligible bachelors of the *ton,* but propose to hold a private marriage mart of your own at Brynhaven starting Friday next."

"Precisely," the duke declared with an impatient scowl.

"Surely you jest. Not even *you* could be that autocratic, Your Grace. You cannot expect people of consequence to leave London at the height of the season with less than ten days' notice. They will already have accepted other social obligations for that weekend."

"Which they will cancel, I am sure, once they sniff out the reason for the invitation. From what I have seen of the rapacious matrons of the *ton,* they will harness themselves to the family carriages and trot to Brynhaven before they'll miss the chance of obtaining the title of Duchess of Montford for their vacuous little daughters."

Lady Sophia's smile was a bit thin around the edges. "You may be right at that. Ah, well, if nothing else, such a blatant disregard for convention will certainly enhance your already legendary reputation."

"As well as accomplish my aim with the least possible inconvenience to myself," the duke said dryly. With that, he strode across the room, yanked the gold-tasseled pull cord, and retrieved his stylish brushed beaver and gray kid gloves from his aunts' ancient butler. "I leave you to your list-making, dear ladies, certain that the commission will be well and truly accomplished."

Lady Sophia raised a deterring hand to halt his exit. "I

cannot say I entirely approve of your unconventional behavior, Your Grace, but I commend your good sense in allowing responsible female relatives to separate the wheat from the chaff in the matrimonial mill. Men are notoriously bad judges of women; witness the deplorable mistakes your predecessors have made by relying on their own judgment."

The duke nodded. "My thoughts exactly, my lady."

"But," Lady Sophia continued, "for the sake of propriety, I feel we must also invite a suitable number of young gentlemen as well. There will, after all, be four very disappointed young ladies who will not come out the winner in this high-handed lottery of yours. We should consider their tender feelings."

"You are right of course, as usual, godmother." Montford sighed deeply. "Very well. Invite whomever you wish. I, for one, intend to mention it to Brummell when I see him at Newmarket. The Beau is always amusing, and I suspect I shall have sore need of a diversion before the infernal fortnight is over."

With a last perfunctory bow, the Duke of Montford took his leave of the two ladies, secure in the knowledge that with two such *arbitri elegantis* in charge, this blasted business of arranging a socially correct marriage would soon be a fait accompli.

For the first time in all her twenty-four years of hand-to-mouth, catch-as-catch-can existence, Miss Emily Louise Haliburton found herself deeply grateful she was the plain-faced daughter of a penniless third son.

Listening in horror as her aunt, the Countess of Hargrave, read aloud her note from Lady Cloris Tremayne, Emily even counted herself fortunate that she had inherited her mama's mousy brown hair and pudding bag figure. At least *she* would never have to worry about being caught in the kind of insidious trap she could see closing around her beautiful young cousin, Lucinda.

The note had arrived at an unseemly hour, as if of too much import to wait until fashionable London was officially astir. Lady Cloris's elegantly liveried footmen had hand-carried it to the Earl of Hargrave's equally elegant footman, who in turn had handed it to the earl's austere butler, who had delivered it on a small silver tray to the countess while the ladies of the house were still at breakfast.

"My stars and garters, I cannot take this in with just one reading. I must read it again," the countess said, and promptly proceeded to do so.

Dearest Hortense:
Enclosed you will find an invitation addressed to the earl, yourself, and Lady Lucinda to spend a fortnight at Brynhaven, one of the country homes of my nephew, Jared Tremayne, Duke of Montford. The duke has decided the time has come when he must consider taking a wife and setting up his nursery, and has requested my sister and me to recommend five eligible young ladies from whom he might choose his duchess. Naturally, because of the warm friendship we share, I insisted Lady Lucinda's name head the list. I do not know the names of the other four, who, with their parents, will join you at Brynhaven, as they will be my sister's recommendations, but I am certain your dear little daughter will outshine them all.

With most heartfelt regards,
Cloris Tremayne

Emily could scarcely believe her ears. What kind of cold fish was this Duke of Montford to blithely relegate the choosing of his wife to two elderly spinsters? Lady Hargrave's cook gave more personal attention to choosing the mutton for Sunday dinner than this peer of the realm did to choosing the future mother of his children.

In the two months since she had joined the earl's household as her cousin Lucinda's companion, Emily had observed that most of the high-sticklers of London society were a shallow, jaded lot. But this top lofty duke must surely be the most outrageous of them all.

She shuddered. A cruel twist of fate had landed her amongst these philistines, and here she must stay for the next four months until she could receive the modest portion her grandmother had willed her. But then, God willing, she would leave the dirt and decadence of London behind forever and return to her beloved Cotswolds.

Warily, she looked to her aunt to gauge her reaction to this amazing missive just received. As she might have expected, a smile as bright as the sun flooding the window of the cheerful morning room lighted Lady Hargrave's plump face. Laying the note aside, she reached across the table to clasp her daughter's hands. "Never say your mama has not looked out for your welfare, my darling. Now do you wonder why I spent all those tedious hours teaching Lady Cloris to knit? Just think of it. My little girl is a duchess!"

Lady Lucinda's already pale skin blanched a shade whiter. She was a timid little thing who, at the slightest provocation, swooned gracefully away. Emily normally found such missish behavior very off-putting, but in this case she could scarcely blame her cousin for feeling faint.

"But, Mama," Lucinda gasped, clutching the edge of the table as if it were a lifeline, "I do not think I would like to be married to the Duke of Montford. He is so . . . so stiff and so grand."

"Of course he is, you silly goose. He's Montford. The first Tremayne crossed the Channel during the reign of Charlemagne, and they have been rich as Croesus ever since. Why, even the regent and the royals compete for the honor of entertaining the Duke of Montford." Lady Hargrave breathed an ecstatic sigh. "Just imagine, you may soon be visiting Carlton House on the arm of your husband, the duke!"

Tears welled in Lucinda's china blue eyes. "I should be absolutely terrified," she declared, "but at least the regent is rather fat and jolly-looking, and when I was presented to him at Lady Halpern's musicale last Tuesday, he tweaked my chin and said I was 'a rare little beauty.' The duke just walked right past me without a single look."

"Well, he won't ignore you at Brynhaven, my pet."

Lucinda gulped back a sob. "But what shall I do if he expects me to talk to him? I am not at all clever like cousin Emily."

"He won't," Lady Hargrave said with absolute certainty. "The last thing a man like the duke is looking for in a wife is clever conversation. Just curtsy and smile prettily and make certain you never step on his toes when he dances with you."

"I shall be required to dance with him?" Lucinda shrieked. "Oh, Mama, never say you expect me to do such a thing. I would simply die if he touched me. He does not look at all kind."

Lady Hargrave shrugged. "Dukes rarely do. I am sure it has something to do with being catered to from the moment one is born. But"—the corners of her mouth lifted in a sly smile—"I know this is not a topic for innocent young ears, and I only mention it so you will understand what is at stake here."

Her voice lowered to a discreet whisper, and, fascinated, Emily leaned across the table to hear her aunt's latest *on-dit*. "Montford is rumored to be excessively generous to his paramours. That emerald necklace of Lady Crawley's which you admired at the opera Sunday last was a gift from the duke—and she is merely his mistress and unattractively plump at that. Think, my precious darling, how generous such a man would be to a beautiful young wife who presented him with his heir!"

Lucinda's finely arched brows drew together in a puzzled frown, and she looked at Emily as if for guidance. "I would very much like an emerald necklace like Lady Crowley's," she admitted.

"And furs and jewels and elegant dresses and a carriage of your own with the duke's lozenge on the door," Lady Hargrave prompted.

"Of course, Mama. Who would not? But I still would not like to marry the Duke of Montford. My abigail said that any man who marries me will expect to share my bed. I most certainly would not want to share my bed with *him*! I am quite certain I should die of mortification if he ever saw me in my night rail."

Two angry red blotches stained Lady Hargrave's cheeks. "That insufferable chatterbox will be given her walking papers today and without one word of reference," she declared vehemently.

Emily turned away, afraid the disgust she felt for her aunt must surely be stamped on her face. It was difficult to believe this crass schemer could be dear Mama's only sister. Aunt Hortense had the sensitivity of a turnip; without the slightest compunction, she was tossing Lucinda to this wolf, who was currently prowling London's fashionable marriage mart, without explaining any of the more intimate aspects of marriage to the poor innocent.

While Emily had no actual experience in the ways of men and women, she had, like most country girls, a working knowledge of the breeding of sheep and horses and dogs. The correlation with human procreation seemed fairly obvious. She was very much afraid her pretty little cousin would find there was much more to the marriage bed than being viewed in one's night rail.

She saw the fear in Lucinda's eyes, and her heart ached for the girl. She found herself wondering just how sensitive to such fears a jaded aristocrat like the duke would be.

Lady Hargrave had maintained a long moment of ominous silence while she gathered her forces. Now she resumed her attack on Lucinda's objections to the duke's bizarre invitation with a vengeance. Emily listened as words poured off the countess's tongue like rain off a clogged gutter spout, one tripping over the other in their eagerness to be said. "I will hear no more of this foolishness," she screeched. "The die is cast. We have been invited to Brynhaven, and to Brynhaven we will go. I cannot believe you are such a featherhead as to think we would dare refuse the hospitality of the Duke of Montford even if we should want to. We would be social outcasts, my girl. Pariahs. Every door in London would be closed to us. Is that what you want?"

"No, Mama."

"I should think not! And if you care not a whit for me, at least give a thought to your poor father. With all the financial reverses the man has suffered this past year, he was forced to cash in his precious consols to give you your season. 'But never fear, my lord, your daughter will not fail you,' I assured him. 'With her pretty face and winning ways, she is bound to attract a rich *parti* who will keep you out of dun territory.' "

She pressed her hand to her ample bosom and sighed dramatically. "But Montford! Oh, my stars and garters, never in my most blissful dreams did I hope to reach that high. Wait until I tell the earl.

"But first things first," she declared, ignoring the fact that her daughter was still sobbing quietly into her soggy handkerchief. "Emily, alert John Coachman that we shall need the carriage in a half hour. I want to be away from here before that insufferable gaggle of fribbles who moon over Lucinda descend upon us."

Emily smiled to herself. Just yesterday that "insufferable gaggle of fribbles" had been delightful young men who, as potential suiters for Lucinda's hand, were welcomed with open arms by the countess.

"We must hurry to Madame Fanchon's salon and engage

her services before someone else thinks of it," Lady Hargrave explained. "As it is, she will have to put on extra seamstresses to finish everything we need in time."

"But, Mama, have you forgotten how unpleasant Madame Fanchon was the last time we visited her. I am certain she meant it when she said we could run up no more credit."

"Nonsense. Watch that French needle pusher change her tune when she learns she is dressing the future Duchess of Montford—which reminds me, one thing you absolutely must have is a new riding habit. The duke is famous for his brilliant horsemanship. He will most certainly expect his duchess to ride to the hounds."

"But, Mama," Lucinda cried, reaching for Emily's hand beneath the table, "I am not at all good with horses. They frighten me to death."

"You will simply have to get over it. Mind over matter, my girl."

"But, Mama—"

"But me no more buts, young lady. You have been blessed with the opportunity to make the most brilliant marriage of this or any other season. I expect you to make the most of it."

Lady Hargrave turned to Emily. "And I expect you to talk some sense into this foolish child. You know all too well what it is to be poor and without prospects. Tell her how humiliating it is to have to wear your cousin's ill-fitting, cast-off dresses and hire out as a paid companion to keep body and soul together." She shuddered. "Ask her what she thinks her life—indeed, all our lives—will be like if her father is sent to debtors prison . . . and all because she failed to bring the duke up to scratch."

With a last admonishing glance at Emily, the countess swept from the room clutching Lady Cloris's precious missile to her breast and demanding, at the top of her voice, that someone find the earl.

She had scarcely closed the door behind her when Lucinda flung herself into Emily's arms. "I cannot bear it," she sobbed. "I'd rather die than marry the Duke of Montford. He is a horrible man . . . and he must be a thousand years old."

"You are exaggerating as usual," Emily said, giving her cousin's heaving shoulders a comforting pat. "I was at Lady

Halpern's musicale too, you know. I remember the duke well. He was neither old nor horrible. A bit stiff-necked and proud, I admit, but quite amazingly handsome . . . in a chilly sort of way."

In truth, she knew exactly why Lucinda found Montford forbidding; she'd developed a few shivers of her own in the brief instant she'd come under his frosty regard. She had even found herself thinking of him at odd moments ever since, and each time she thought of his dark, brooding countenance, those same shivers traveled her spine.

She racked her brain for something to say which would comfort the frightened girl. "Think of all the lovely new gowns you will have to wear."

"What good will they be if I die of fright?" Lucinda wailed, dropping in a crumpled heap onto a nearby chair.

"Isn't it early days to be turning this into a Cheltenham tragedy? After all, there is only a one-in-five chance the duke will choose you."

Lucinda's eyes widened in astonishment. "How could he not choose me? I am this season's Incomparable. Everyone who is anyone says I am the most beautiful girl to make her come-out in years." She sniffed. "I cannot even imagine who the other four might be."

Emily grudgingly acknowledged that while not exactly humble, her cousin's statement was probably true. Even now, when such a fit of weeping would have left any other woman with puffy eyes and a mottled complexion, Lucinda's perfect golden beauty remained undiminished.

"Brynhaven is known to be one of the grandest country homes in all of England," Emily said, deciding to try a practical approach to the problem. "I sincerely envy you the chance to see it. And since you really have no choice in the matter, why not make the best of it and enjoy your fortnight?" She paused. "And pray for a miracle."

Lucinda raised her head—her lovely eyes wide and frightened. "What do you mean, you envy me the chance to see Brynhaven? Never tell me you mean to let me face this terrible ordeal alone!"

"The invitation was addressed to you and your parents," Emily reminded her gently. "I do not remember any mention of other relatives."

"But surely it includes maids and valets and footmen and such. Everyone takes one's own staff to such affairs."

Emily gritted her teeth. She had grown very fond of her pretty, flutter-brained cousin in the short time she had spent with her, but there were times when the girl's tongue ran ahead of her wits. "Much as it may sometimes seem so, Lucinda," she said crossly, "I am not a servant. Just a 'poor relation,' as my aunt so aptly put it. I am afraid you will have to do without my services in this instance."

"I shall do no such thing! If I *must* spend a fortnight at Brynhaven with the dreadful duke, I shall need you beside me every minute to tell me what to do. You know very well thinking gives me a headache."

Lucinda's perfect, heart-shaped face assumed a mulish mien Emily had never before seen. "I'll tell Mama and Papa I will not go to Brynhaven unless I can take you as my companion. Not even if they lock me in my bedchamber with nothing but bread and water for the rest of my life."

She tossed her silky, burnished curls defiantly. "So you might as well begin packing your portmanteau, dear Emily. Mama will simply have to make the proper arrangements when she pens her answer to Lady Cloris."

From *The Duke's Dilemma* by Nadine Miller

WE NEED YOUR HELP

To continue to bring you quality romance that meets your personal expectations, we at TOPAZ books want to hear from you.
Help us by filling out this questionnaire, and in exchange we will give you a **free gift** as a token of our gratitude.

- Is this the first TOPAZ book you've purchased? (circle one)

  YES NO

  The title and author of this book is: ____________________

- If this was not the first TOPAZ book you've purchased, how many have you bought in the past year?

  a: 0 - 5 b 6 - 10 c: more than 10 d: more than 20

- How many romances in total did you buy in the past year?

  a: 0 - 5 b: 6 - 10 c: more than 10 d: more than 20 ____

- How would you rate your overall satisfaction with this book?

  a: Excellent b: Good c: Fair d: Poor

- What was the main reason you bought this book?

  a: It is a TOPAZ novel, and I know that TOPAZ stands for quality romance fiction
  b: I liked the cover
  c: The story-line intrigued me
  d: I love this author
  e: I really liked the setting
  f: I love the cover models
  g: Other: ____________________

- Where did you buy this TOPAZ novel?

  a: Bookstore b: Airport c: Warehouse Club
  d: Department Store e: Supermarket f: Drugstore
  g: Other: ____________________

- Did you pay the full cover price for this TOPAZ novel? (circle one)

  YES NO

  If you did not, what price did you pay? ____________________

- Who are your favorite TOPAZ authors? (Please list)

- How did you first hear about TOPAZ books?

  a: I saw the books in a bookstore
  b: I saw the TOPAZ Man on TV or at a signing
  c: A friend told me about TOPAZ
  d: I saw an advertisement in ____________________ magazine
  e: Other: ____________________

- What type of romance do you generally prefer?

  a: Historical b: Contemporary
  c: Romantic Suspense d: Paranormal (time travel, futuristic, vampires, ghosts, warlocks, etc.)
  d: Regency e: Other: ____________________

- What historical settings do you prefer?

  a: England b: Regency England c: Scotland
  e: Ireland f: America g: Western Americana
  h: American Indian i: Other: ____________________

- What type of story do you prefer?

  a: Very sexy　　b: Sweet, less explicit
  c: Light and humorous　　d: More emotionally intense
  e: Dealing with darker issues　　f: Other

- What kind of covers do you prefer?

  a: Illustrating both hero and heroine　　b: Hero alone
  c: No people (art only)　　d: Other___________

- What other genres do you like to read (circle all that apply)

  Mystery　　Medical Thrillers　　Science Fiction
  Suspense　　Fantasy　　Self-help
  Classics　　General Fiction　　Legal Thrillers
  Historical Fiction

- Who is your favorite author, and why?_______________________

  ____

- What magazines do you like to read? (circle all that apply)

  a: *People*　　b: *Time/Newsweek*
  c: *Entertainment Weekly*　　d: *Romantic Times*
  e: *Star*　　f: *National Enquirer*
  g: *Cosmopolitan*　　h: *Woman's Day*
  i: *Ladies' Home Journal*　　j: *Redbook*
  k: Other:_______________________________

- In which region of the United States do you reside?

  a: Northeast　　b: Midatlantic　　c: South
  d: Midwest　　e: Mountain　　f: Southwest
  g: Pacific Coast

- What is your age group/sex?　　a: Female　　b: Male

  a: under 18　　b: 19-25　　c: 26-30　　d: 31-35　　e: 56-60
  f: 41-45　　g: 46-50　　h: 51-55　　i: 56-60　　j: Over 60

- What is your marital status?

  a: Married　　b: Single　　c: No longer married

- What is your current level of education?

  a: High school　　b: College Degree
  c: Graduate Degree　　d: Other: ____________

- Do you receive the TOPAZ *Romantic Liaisons* newsletter, a quarterly newsletter with the latest information on Topaz books and authors?

  YES　　NO

  If not, would you like to?　　YES　　NO

Fill in the address where you would like your free gift to be sent:

Name:_______________________________

Address:_____________________________

City:_______________________Zip Code:__________

You should receive your free gift in 6 to 8 weeks.
Please send the completed survey to:

Penguin USA•Mass Market
Dept. TS
375 Hudson St.
New York, NY 10014